A SLICE OF MURDER

I started to think about what my sister was proposing and I wondered if I had what it took to dig
into people's lives. I wasn't nosy by nature, and I was
more than a little reluctant to start prying where I
didn't belong. Then I looked around the shop and
realized that with my pizzeria gone, I would have
one less tie with Joe. This had been more his dream
than mine, but I'd grown to love the Slice as much
as he had. Maddy was right about one thing: if the
killer wasn't unmasked, and fairly soon, I would
lose the restaurant, and that was something I just
couldn't take.

"Okay, I'm in," I said.

"Are you sure?"

"No, but do we really have any other choice? Let's
make a game plan and figure out what we're going
to do."

"Hang on a second. I was just talking off the top
of my head."

"This time I agree with you. You don't have to
help, but I'm going to track down a killer."

"You're serious, aren't you?"

"I've never been more serious in my life . . ."

Books by Chris Cavender

A SLICE OF MURDER

PEPPERONI PIZZA CAN BE MURDER

Published by Kensington Publishing Corporation

A Slice of Murder

Chris Cavender

KENSINGTON BOOKS
www.kensingtonbooks.com

KENSINGTON BOOKS are published by

Kensington Publishing Corp.
119 West 40th Street
New York, NY 10018

All Kensington titles, imprints, and distributed lines are
available at special quantity discounts for bulk pur-
chases for sales promotion, premiums, fund-raising, and
educational, or institutional use.

Special book excerpts or customized printings can also
be created to fit specific needs. For details, write or phone
the office of the Kensington Special Sales Manager: Attn.
Special Sales Department. Kensington Publishing Corp.,
119 West 40th Street, New York, NY 10018. Phone: 1-800-
221-2647.

Kensington and the K logo Reg. U.S. Pat. & TM Off.

ISBN-13: 978-0-7582-2949-6
ISBN-10: 0-7582-2949-6

First hardcover printing: August 2009
First mass market printing: July 2010
10 9 8 7 6 5 4 3 2 1

Printed in the United States of America

To Harry James "Jim" Pickering and Robert Dale "Slick" Hickman, the two best friends a kid could wish for growing up!

We live in an age when pizza gets to your home before the police.
Jeff Arder

Chapter 1

"911? I need to report a murder," I said, clutching my cell phone in my left hand as I steadied the warm pizza box in my right. I should have put the pizza on the porch before I called the police. Instead, I was holding on to it as though it were the last life preserver on the *Titanic*. At least the heat radiating from the box felt good. We were two weeks past New Year's, and though only dustings of snow had found their way to our part of the North Carolina mountains this winter so far, I knew it wouldn't be long before it would make its first full-blown appearance.

My voice was calmer than I expected it to be as I spoke; I was startled to discover that I didn't really know how I would react to finding a body until it happened to me.

From the threshold, I glanced back in through the house's doorway and saw the long black handle of a kitchen knife sticking out of Richard Olsen's chest. There was a pool of dark liquid spread out on the floor around him that I guessed had to be blood, though I was in no hurry to confirm my suspicions. From the instant I'd arrived, it had been pretty clear that there was no need to check for a pulse.

"Did you have anything to do with the homicide?" the voice from the police hotline asked. I immediately recognized it as Helen Murphy. That was one of the advantages of owning a pizzeria in a small town: there weren't many folks in Timber Ridge, North Carolina, I didn't know. I'd gone through school with Helen's niece, Amy, and growing up, I'd had dinner with the extended family on more than one lazy Sunday afternoon cooking out by the Dunbar River.

"Helen, this is Eleanor Swift, though I suspect you already know that. What kind of question is that to be asking someone? I brought Richard Olsen the pizza he ordered, and when I got here, I found him dead."

There was a slight pause, and then Helen said, "It's my job to ask these questions, Eleanor. Is there anyone else there with you?"

I hadn't even thought of that possibility. Could the murderer be hiding just behind the doorway, lurking in the shadows while he was waiting to make his escape? I looked intently from my vantage point on the front porch, but I couldn't see anyone inside.

That didn't mean no one was there, though.

"I don't think anyone else is around." *But thanks a lot for putting that thought into my head, Helen. I owe you one.*

Again, there was a slight pause. Then Helen said, "Don't touch anything, Eleanor, and don't go anywhere until one of our officers gets to the scene. Do you understand?"

"Yes, ma'am. I'll be waiting right here."

I thought about the dismal prospect of standing alone on the porch near the body, but it was dark, I was cold, and there wasn't anything I could do for Richard, so I carried the pizza box back to my car and waited for the police.

I never should have been the one who found Richard Olsen's body in the first place, but Greg Hatcher—A Slice of Delight's number-one teenage delivery guy—had called in sick that night and left me shorthanded, though I suspected it had more to do with his girlfriend, Katy Johnson, than the flu he claimed to be experiencing. I'd thought about turning the late-night order down since I'd been hustling all evening trying to keep up with things at the restaurant, but my dearly departed husband, Joe, had taught me that every dollar counts, and I'd kept his credo strong long after he'd died and left me with a small business on my hands and a heart full of broken dreams. I probably shouldn't complain. Having the restaurant to run after Joe's car accident had kept me sane and focused when I had every right in the world to find the nearest hole and crawl into it.

I'd shoved the pizza—one of my specials decked out with pepperoni, sausage, ham, bacon, hamburger, and little bits of sliced sirloin—into one of the bright red boxes I use and headed for the address I'd been given on the phone. I hadn't recognized the house number right away, but then again,

I didn't know where everyone in Timber Ridge lived, despite what my sister, Madeline, thought. Maddy helped me out at the restaurant, but she'd never made a delivery in her life. She claimed she was above schlepping pizzas all over our small town, but she wasn't too good to run a rag over a table or carry a pie ten yards to a likely-looking bachelor. Maddy came to work with me after Joe's death—coinciding with her most recent divorce—and despite a few relapses where we reenacted some of our childhood squabbles, it was good having her there with me.

A police siren brought me out of my reverie, and I looked up as it skidded to a stop less than a foot from my rear bumper. As I got out of my car to meet our chief of police, Kevin Hurley shot out of his cruiser like he was jet-propelled. Kevin and I had a history, one that wasn't all roses and wine, but at the moment it was great seeing his familiar face. I hadn't realized how tense I'd been while waiting for someone—anyone—to show up until he got there.

"Ellie, are you all right?" he asked, and I could see the concern clearly in his face as we stood under the street lamp. Kevin was still tall and lean, a kid who'd been one class behind me all through school, and was now a nice-looking man. A year didn't seem like all that much these days, but it seemed like a lot when I'd been eighteen and he'd just turned seventeen. Kevin had pursued me all one summer, and I'd finally let him catch me, but then one night by Miller's pond I'd caught him parking with Marybeth Matheeny, and that had been the end of that.

I gestured to the house and said, "I'm not the one you should be asking about. Somebody put a knife in Richard Olsen's heart." It sounded callous, the way I'd blurted it out, but there was no other way to phrase it, at least not while my shaky nerves were starting to kick in.

"Stay right here," Kevin said.

"Don't worry. You don't have to tell me twice."

I leaned against my car and watched him enter the house as he drew his firearm. That long-ago summer Kevin had begged for my forgiveness, but I'd been young and hurt, and I hadn't been willing to listen to him. Two months after I'd left for college, he'd married Marybeth in a hastily arranged wedding, and seven months after that his son had been born. Josh was seventeen now, and he worked for me at the pizzeria three nights a week after school. Though Kevin and Marybeth had separated off and on at least three times in the past dozen years, she still bought her pizzas in Edgeview, even though it was fifteen miles from Timber Ridge. I didn't mind. I'd never been all that big a fan of Marybeth's in the first place.

An ambulance arrived a scant thirty seconds after Kevin disappeared into the house, and I nodded to the attendants, two of my regular customers. They rushed inside; then after spending two minutes there, they calmly walked back out.

"He's gone," Hannah Grail said as she approached. "There was nothing we could do for him."

Her partner, Dave Thornton, shrugged. "And now we wait." He added with a grumble, "We're not going to eat until morning." I suddenly remembered the pizza box sitting on the passenger seat of my car.

"I've got an all-meat special that's going to waste, and it should still be warm. You're welcome to it, on the house."

Dave looked like he wanted to kiss me, but Hannah said, "Thanks for the offer, Eleanor, but we can't interfere with evidence."

"Of what, the fact that I was delivering a pizza to Richard's house? It's not like it was a murder weapon or anything. Nobody poisoned him, least of all me. Go on."

Dave said to his partner, "She's right. You don't want her to have to throw it away, do you?"

Hannah shrugged. "I guess not."

I grabbed the box and handed it to them, and after thanking me, they went into the back of their ambulance to eat.

Kevin came out a minute later and looked around for the AWOL EMS techs. "Where'd they run off to?"

"They're eating. You know how I hate for anything to go to waste, so I gave them the pizza I was delivering to Richard."

The chief of police frowned in their direction and said, "They shouldn't be doing that."

"Come on, Kevin. That pizza never made it into the house. It's got nothing to do with what happened to Richard, and neither do I. Now, can I go home? It's late, I'm freezing, and my feet are killing me."

He shook his head curtly. "I know what time it is, but I need to ask you a few questions first."

"How long is it going to take?"

Kevin smiled at me, and for a second I forgot he was our chief of police and thought of him as that teenage boy with a grin that could melt my heart back when I'd been pretty innocent myself. "Less time if you quit complaining about it, I can promise you that."

He flipped open a small notebook, then commanded, "Tell me what happened tonight."

"Richard called in his order. I made it and delivered it. That's when I found him like that."

He shook his head. "Come on, Ellie, I need more than that."

"Sorry, it's all I've got. And it's Eleanor, remember?"

He shook his head as he said, "You never used to mind when I called you Ellie."

"That was a lifetime ago, Kevin, and you know it."

His only answer was a shrug. Then he asked, "Isn't it a little unusual for the owner to deliver pizzas herself? I thought that was Greg Hatcher's job."

"Greg came down with a bad case of the lovesick blues. He said he was sick, but I suspect he was out with Katy tonight. It wasn't a big deal. I cover for all of my employees now and then."

Kevin stared at me for a few seconds, then asked softly, "And there's no other reason you were visiting Richard Olsen's house alone at night?"

What was he trying to imply? Then it hit me. "You think I was making some kind of booty call? You've been a cop too long, Kevin. You'd suspect your own grandmother, wouldn't you?"

"If she had the motive, means, and opportunity, I might," he said, not rising to my bait. Nanna Hurley was a sweet old lady who thought a slice of apple pie would cure whatever ailed you. In other words, she was my kind of people.

The severity of Kevin's tone finally struck home. "You can't be serious. Do you honestly believe I had something to do with what happened in there?" I could barely bring myself to look at the house now. The shock of what I'd found was finally sinking in.

He put the pad away and started ticking off fingers. "Look at it from my point of view. You had the opportunity; you're the one who found the body. The knife was from his kitchen; I saw the empty slot on the block of knives on his kitchen counter. That's two parts of the murder triangle."

"I had no reason to kill him," I said.

He raised one eyebrow as he asked, "Are you forgetting the Harvest Festival?"

I couldn't believe he was bringing that up. "Richard was drunk, and he wouldn't take no for an answer. A good slap sobered him up long enough for him to realize what he'd tried to do, and after that, we were fine." Richard Olsen had tried to kiss me by the beer tent, even after I'd protested that I wasn't interested. I blamed Luke Winslow for not cutting him off sooner when he saw the man was clearly drunk, but to Luke's credit, he'd been the one to step in after I'd landed an open, stinging slap on Richard's cheek. My handprint had still been etched there ten minutes later, and I was pretty sure everyone in Timber Ridge had seen my brand on his cheek.

Kevin didn't let up. "Are you sure it wasn't some kind of lovers' quarrel? Maybe tonight you two finished whatever you'd been arguing about at the festival."

I wasn't about to stand there and listen to his wild accusation. "Kevin, I'm going home."

He put a hand on my car door, stopping me from getting in. "I'm just saying, you have to admit that this looks bad."

"I'm serious—you're going to have to lock me up, or let me go."

He reluctantly moved his hand, and I got into my Subaru and drove home without a glance back.

I sat in my driveway ten minutes before I realized I didn't want to be alone tonight. My sister, Maddy, had a spare room at her apartment, and I figured she owed me a couple dozen favors, so it was time to cash in on one of them.

If it had been me, I would have been sound asleep at nearly eleven P.M., but Maddy looked lively and alert when she answered her doorbell.

"Hey, what are you doing here?" Maddy was tall and thin, while I was quite a bit shorter and had more curves than a backwoods mountain road. Growing up, we'd both been brunettes, but sometime around her ninth-grade year, Maddy had decided that she was truly a blonde deep down inside, and she'd dyed her hair and never looked back. Though my sister was two years younger than me, most days she acted half my age.

"I need a place to stay tonight," I said.

She moved aside. "Well, come on in, then. I was just about to make some popcorn. Would you like some? *Casablanca* is coming on in ten minutes."

I walked into her apartment, a lively swirl of oranges, golds, and greens, and plopped down on her sofa. "Don't you even want to know why I'm here?"

She shrugged. "We don't need an excuse for a sleepover."

"Richard Olsen is dead."

Maddy didn't even look all that upset as she shook her head. "That's too bad. What happened? Was it a car wreck?"

"Why would you ask me that?" Even the sound of the two words linked together still gave me nightmares about losing my husband.

Maddy frowned. "I was on my way home tonight, and he nearly ran me off the road in that beefed-up truck of his. He looked like he was running from the devil himself."

"You need to tell Kevin Hurley that," I said as I grabbed my cell phone.

"Why on earth would I want to do that?"

"Because there must have been some reason Richard was racing around town, and frankly, at this point, anything that diverts suspicion away from me is pretty welcome."

That got Maddy's attention. "Why on earth would he think you had anything to do with Richard's car wreck?"

"Because it wasn't a wreck that killed him. Someone shoved a knife into his chest, and I found the body when I delivered his pizza."

"That's terrible." Maddy frowned, then added, "Wait a second. I didn't take any orders for Richard Olsen tonight."

"That's true, he called right after you left. Since Greg wasn't there, I decided to deliver it myself on the way home."

"What are you going to do? Oh, no, I bet Kevin said something about what happened at the Harvest Festival, didn't he?"

"He did, but it doesn't matter. It was a clumsy pass, and I blocked it. End of story," I said.

"You know that, and I know that, but the rest of Timber Ridge saw the imprint of your hand on Richard's face. You almost took his head off."

"He was drunk. I had to get his attention."

Maddy grinned. "I'd say you accomplished your goal, then. Give me that phone. I'll call Kevin right now and tell him what I saw."

After a brief conversation with our chief of police, Maddy handed my cell phone back to me.

"What did he say?" I asked.

Maddy just shook her head. "He told me that he understood why I'd lie to protect you, but that it wasn't going to do anybody any good if I muddied the waters with rumors and lies about Richard Olsen."

It was starting to sink in that I was in deeper trouble than I'd realized. "This is bad, isn't it?"

Maddy nodded. "It's starting to look that way. But there's nothing we can do about it tonight. Let's make that popcorn and get lost in Bogart's eyes."

I stifled a yawn. "If you don't mind, I'm going to go straight to bed. I'm beat."

She nodded. "Absolutely; I understand completely. Let me move a few things and you'll be all set."

We walked into her spare bedroom, and I saw four dozen little quilted squares lying on her spread.

"When did you start quilting?" I asked. It was entirely out of character for the freewheeling woman she liked to portray to the rest of the world.

"It's something I started doing when I'm not at work, and I really enjoy it," Maddy admitted. "I've been reading Earlene Fowler's quilting mysteries, and it seemed like fun, so I decided to give it a try."

That was more like it. My sister was crazy about mysteries, and she read every chance she got. As she devoured mysteries on candle making, card making, soap making, and more, she had to try her hand at each of the hobbies as well, sometimes with mixed results. For instance, her soap would barely raise a lather. At the other end of the spectrum, I had several of her exquisite handmade candles decorating my home.

As Maddy gathered up the quilting squares, she said, "Don't worry; this will just take a second."

"I don't want to put you out," I said.

"Are you crazy? I love having you here." She stacked the small squares and put them on the dresser. "There you go." She looked me over, then said, "Hold on, I'll be right back."

My sister returned a minute later and handed me a checkered flannel nightgown. "No promises, but it might fit."

Since it belonged to her, I doubted it. "I'll try it on."

"One of my husbands thought it would be hilarious to get me a nightgown six sizes too big."

"And was it funny to you?" I asked as I held it up. It just might fit, and I wasn't exactly in a position to be overly choosy.

"I'm not married to him anymore, am I?" she asked me with a smile, then added, "I put a disposable toothbrush and a travel-size toothpaste on the vanity. There are fresh towels in the bathroom, and I changed the sheets yesterday, so you're all set."

Sometimes I forgot how much I loved my sister. It amazed me how truly neat a woman she'd grown up to be.

I laid the gown on the bed and hugged her.

"What's that for?" Maddy asked.

"For being here for me."

She smiled. "What's family for? Now, if you'll excuse me, I'm going to go hide all my knives, just in case you're not through with your little rampage tonight."

I frowned at her. "That's not funny, not even a little."

Maddy grew serious. "I'm sorry. You know I try to diffuse tense situations with humor. If you need me, all you have to do is shout, and I'll be here."

"Thanks."

After I squirmed into the nightgown, prepped for bed, and turned off the light, it took me some time to get to sleep. Maddy had been joking—I was familiar enough with her skewed sense of humor to get that—but would the rest of Timber Ridge think I was capable of murder, no matter what the circumstances? How was I going to deal with whispers behind my back? Would folks stop coming to A Slice of Delight? Would I lose the restaurant my husband and I had worked so hard to establish?

Eleanor, get hold of yourself. Kevin's a good cop, and he's going to find the real killer soon enough, I told myself as I finally drifted off to sleep. There was no sense in borrowing trouble, but I had a feeling that it had found me nonetheless, and if my ex-boyfriend didn't have any luck discovering who had killed Richard Olsen, I was going to have to step in and do it myself.

I woke up the next morning at the crack of nine, breathing in the aroma of waffles and bacon, which isn't a bad way to start the day. After a quick trip to the bathroom, I walked out and found Maddy just pulling a golden, homemade waffle out of the iron.

"Wow, did you do all this for me?" I asked as I took a seat at her bar.

"No, I make waffles every morning," she said with a smile and a raised eyebrow. "Of course it's for you. I figure you had a rough night. Did you sleep much?"

I took a sip of orange juice, then said, "As a matter of fact, I did. It's kind of odd, given what happened, isn't it?"

She split a waffle in half, putting one section on my plate and taking the other for herself. Maddy had even gone to the trouble of heating the syrup, just like our mom had done when we'd been growing up. I took a bite and realized that this comfort food was exactly what I needed.

As we ate, we chatted about this and that, carefully avoiding the subject of Richard Olsen's murder. I almost forgot what had happened when there was a knock on Maddy's front door.

"I'm not dressed for company," I said as I headed back into the guest bedroom. I didn't mind if Maddy saw me in one of her old nightgowns, but I wasn't about to go on parade in one of them for the world.

I could peek out and see Maddy as she opened the front door.

It was Kevin Hurley, our esteemed chief of police, decked out in his crisply ironed khaki uniform, and from the frown on his face, it was pretty clear he wasn't there for waffles.

Without preamble, he said, "Where is she?"

"The queen? I believe she's still in England."

He frowned at her as he said, "Don't mess with me, Maddy. We aren't in high school anymore. Where's your sister?"

My sis shook her head. "Sorry, but I can't hear you. It's the oddest thing, but I go deaf when people are rude to me. Now if you'll excuse me, I've got a waffle in the iron. I'd offer you one, but there's not enough."

That was an obvious lie, since there was a bowl on the counter still sporting a hefty amount of batter.

"I ate breakfast hours ago," Kevin said. "If you don't tell me where Eleanor is, I'm going to arrest you for obstruction of a police investigation."

"I'd love to see you try," Maddy said with a grin. Even I didn't know if she was bluffing.

That was all I could take. Kevin didn't call me Eleanor often, so I figured I'd better come out. I grabbed my coat and put it on over the nightgown, then stepped out into the living room. "Were you looking for me?"

"Where have you been?" Kevin asked. He tried to step past Maddy, but she wouldn't budge.

"It's okay," I said. "Let him in."

Maddy shot him a wicked look, then went back to the waffle iron.

"I asked you a question," Kevin said as he stared

at me. "Are you going someplace? You weren't trying to get away, were you?"

I flashed him a bit of my nightgown. "You caught
me. I always run away whenever there are waffles
in the room. They scare the daylights out of me."

"You weren't at your house last night." He made
it sound more like an accusation than a question.

"I've been here all night. Now, would you mind
telling me what this is about?"

Kevin studied my outfit, then said, "You need to
get dressed. I have more questions for you, and I'm
not going to ask them while you're wearing that."

Maddy called out from the kitchenette, "She
hasn't had breakfast yet. Come back in an hour."

Our chief of police said, "You can nuke them
for her later. I need her now."

Before Maddy could protest, I said, "I don't mind.
Hold on to the rest of the batter. This won't take
long."

"I wouldn't be so sure of that," Kevin said.

Maddy unplugged the waffle iron, then reached
for the phone.

"Who are you calling?" Kevin asked.

Her only answer was a smile.

He started to ask me a question despite Maddy's
phone call, but I held up one hand, curious about
my sister's phone call myself.

After a few seconds, she asked, "Is he in? I just
need one second. Tell him it's Maddy."

A moment later, she said, "The chief of police is
in my apartment, and he wants to ask my sister
some questions about last night. Yeah, that's right,
about Richard Olsen's murder." Maddy listened a
second, then grinned. "I'll tell her. Thanks."

"Who was that?" I asked as she hung up the phone.

"I thought we needed some backup, so I called Bob Lemon. He said not to say a word until he gets here, and he can't make it until at least ten."

"Calling a lawyer just makes you look guilty, Ellie," Kevin said.

"It's a good thing I didn't call one then, isn't it?" I looked over at my sister and saw her grin, which I tried to ignore. Turning back to Kevin, I said, "I don't mind talking about what I saw last night. I don't need to be represented by counsel."

Maddy's smile suddenly disappeared. "If you say one more word to him before Bob gets here, I'm quitting my job at the pizzeria and moving to California. Look at me. I'm serious, Eleanor."

Her threat of quitting was one she'd never used before, no matter how bad our arguments got.

Kevin shot her a look full of acid, then shook his head as he turned to me. "You're not going along with this, are you?"

I shrugged, locked my lips with an invisible key, then threw it over my shoulder. I couldn't run A Slice of Delight without Maddy, and I wasn't about to call her bluff, if she was indeed bluffing. With her, even I didn't know all the time whether she was kidding or not.

Kevin threw his hands up in the air, then started for the door. "When Lemon gets here, you two can meet me downtown in my office."

"I've got to get dressed first, and I'm not about to wear what I had on last night again," I said.

Maddy added her own protest. "She still has to

eat breakfast, too." That was a bald-faced lie, since I had already stuffed myself with waffles and bacon.

Kevin glanced at his watch, then said, "Be there by eleven, or I'm sending a squad car after you."

After he was gone, Maddy asked, "I wonder what that was about? Is there something we don't know?"

"We would have already found out if you hadn't called your boyfriend."

Maddy shook her head. "He's not my boyfriend, and you know it. We're just friends; that's it."

"Does he know that?"

Maddy frowned. "I can't be held responsible for any delusions that man might have." She bit her lip, then added, "I just didn't like the tone Kevin was taking with you."

"To be honest with you, I didn't care for it, either," I said as I hugged my little sister. "Thanks for looking out for me."

"Hey, it's what I do." We both knew it was always the other way around ever since we were kids, and our laughter cut the tension of the moment.

After we quit chuckling, I looked at her and said, "Would you have really quit your job if I had defied you?"

She shrugged. "Let's not find out, okay? Now sit down and I'll plug in the iron for another waffle. I know you've got room. I have to call Bob and get him over here."

My jaw dropped. "You didn't just talk to him on the phone?"

"All I found out was that the temperature is thirty-nine degrees, and the time is nine-nineteen," she said with a grin. "Like I said, I wasn't going to

let him push you around like that without somebody watching your back."

"I think somebody already is," I said. My sister
wasn't always the best worker, and sometimes her
skewed sense of humor was totally inappropriate,
but I knew I could count on her when it came
right down to it, and that was what really mattered.

I just wondered what Kevin wanted to talk to me
about. I'd already told him all I knew about what
I'd seen the night before.

Was there something else that tied me to the
crime, something I didn't even know about? Suddenly, I was glad Maddy was calling an attorney to
keep me from getting into this mess any deeper.

Chapter 2

"It doesn't look good," Bob Lemon said as he finished another waffle. I'd changed back into the clothes I'd worn the night before, finishing just before he arrived. I didn't know what kind of hold Maddy had over him to get him out of his office on such short notice, but for once, I was glad she had some pull with the best local attorney we had.

"But I didn't do it," I protested.

Bob shook his head. "Eleanor, guilt or innocence rarely comes into play in the legal profession." In his early fifties, Bob's hair was still dark and thick, though gray was touching each temple. He kept fit by walking, making paths in and around Timber Ridge until he knew every square inch of the place. I often saw him walking past the pizzeria, but he rarely saw me. He had eyes only for my sister, no matter how much she protested the fact. The only evidence I needed to back up my point was that he was sitting in her kitchen eating waffles, allowing himself to be summoned with no more information than my sister asked him to be there.

"That's a pretty cynical point of view," Maddy said to him.

"You don't approve?"

"Honestly?" she said. "I do. I just never realized you felt that way."

Bob pushed his plate away. "If you'd agree to go out with me, you might discover there are more facets to me than you realize."

"I hate to interrupt," I said, "but can we get back to me for a second?"

"Of course," Bob said, pulling his gaze away from Maddy. "Let's go to the station so we can satisfy the chief. Then you and I are going to have a long talk."

"I need a shower and fresh clothing first," I said. "I'm not about to face him in the same clothes I was wearing last night."

I could see that Bob was ready to protest, and then he caught Maddy's frown. "That's fine. I'll follow you home and stay outside in the car while you get ready. It will give me a chance to make a few telephone calls while I'm waiting," he said.

Maddy unplugged the waffle iron, then said, "Good, it's settled then. Let's go."

"You shouldn't go," I said.

"Just try to keep me away," Maddy replied.

To the surprise of both of us, Bob said, "I'm afraid Eleanor is right. You can't come, Maddy."

"That's not the way to get on my good side," my sister said, playing her trump card.

"I'm afraid I'm just going to have to take that chance," Bob said. "If you're with us, the attorney-client privilege doesn't exist."

Maddy didn't like it; that much was clear.

I put a hand on hers. "I appreciate all you've done, but you called Bob for advice. Let's do what he asks."

She nodded, though I could see how grudging it was. "Call me the second you finish with Kevin."

"I promise," I said.

As Bob followed me outside to my Subaru, I said, "I can't believe you just risked the wrath of Madeline for me."

He laughed. "You're my client, I have to do what's best for you." He held my car door open for me, then said, "Before we go any further, I need a dollar."

I dug into my wallet and got him a crumpled single. "Okay, but I don't think we should be borrowing money from each other, given our new professional relationship."

He pulled out a pad and started scribbling in it as he said, "It's a retainer." After he finished writing, he tore off the top sheet and handed it to me. "Here's your receipt."

"I'm not going to let you give me any special breaks just because you like my sister," I said, refusing it.

"Don't worry, I won't. This is just a formality until we can work up a real agreement. We'll talk to the chief, and then we can discuss my fees."

I started to realize that although I had a bit of a cushion in my savings account, it could quickly vanish with his billable hours. "Maybe we'd better discuss it now."

He shook his head. "Don't worry, I'm very reasonable. Hey, I might even take it out in trade. How about a free pizza a week until your bill's settled?"

"I don't know," I said.

"Sorry, but I'm pretty firm on getting at least that."

"I meant that it wouldn't be enough," I said.

"If I'm satisfied with the payment arrangement, why shouldn't you be?" He glanced at his watch, then said, "We can stand here and keep arguing about it, but you're just costing yourself more pizza."

"Okay, I'm sold," I said. "Thanks, Bob."

"Don't thank me yet. I haven't done anything."

"Don't kid yourself. Just being with me means a lot."

"Then you're welcome."

I drove off toward home, with Bob following me in his Mercedes. If I had to make him pizzas for the rest of his natural life, it would be worth it. Given the way things were starting to look, my freedom was more important to me than him having the world's largest tab at A Slice of Delight.

I showered and changed, then walked back outside and found Bob in his car on his cell phone in a deep conversation with someone.

After he hung up, he said, "Sorry about that. A client and I had a disagreement as to how much of my time he was entitled to."

"I didn't mean to wreck your schedule today," I said as I got in his car.

"Please. Some folks need a reminder that they aren't my employer, no matter how much they're giving me on retainer," he said as he started the car and pulled out.

"I'm guessing it's more than a dollar in most cases," I said as he drove to Kevin's office, which was in the basement of the courthouse.

"Just a little," he said with a smile. I couldn't understand why Maddy wouldn't go out with him. Sure, he was a little older than most of the men she dated—or even married—but he was nice looking, had excellent manners, and seemed to really care for her. Maybe I'd give her a little nudge after all of this was over.

We got to the courthouse too quickly for my taste, and as Bob pulled around to the police department in back, he said, "Let me do the talking, no matter what the chief says. He's going to try to get you to admit to little things at first, then lure you into a false sense of security. Once he's got you agreeing with him, you're a step away from confessing. Trust me, he's good at his job."

"Won't it make me look guilty if I refuse to answer his questions?"

He shook his head. "No, it will make you look smart, listening to your attorney. I mean it, Eleanor. If he asks you if the sky is blue, you turn to me and make sure it's all right that you answer. Do you understand?"

"Got it," I said. "But it's not going to be easy keeping my mouth shut."

He smiled. "If it were, you wouldn't need me, would you?" He looked into my eyes, then asked, "Are you ready?"

"I guess so. I didn't do it, so why am I so nervous?"

He shrugged. "It's the way things work."

* * *

We walked into the police station, and I saw four officers—three men and a woman—at their desks doing paperwork or talking on the telephone. Every last one of them had been in my pizza place in the past month, but none made eye contact with me when we walked in. Helen Murphy was at the front desk, where she met with the public and dispatched officers around town wherever they were needed.

"Hi, Helen," I said. "We're here to see Kevin."

She tried to smile at me, but it died on her lips when Bob pulled me aside by the arm. "What are you doing?" he asked me.

"Saying hello to an old friend," I said, startled by the intensity of his glare.

"You're not here on a social call, remember? The chief of police is getting ready to question you about the murder of a man you had a public confrontation with. This isn't going to work if you act like it's a family reunion. No talking, remember?"

"Can I at least shrug every now and then?"

"I'd prefer it if you didn't," he said. "Eleanor, this is serious, and I expect you to treat it as such. Do we understand each other?"

"I'm sorry. I won't let it happen again."

"Make certain of it," he said. "Now listen carefully. When you see me nod, answer his questions, but not until then. When you speak, give him as brief a reply as possible. If you limit your answers to yes or no, I'll be a happy man."

"What if I have to explain something?"

"Don't," he said. "That's where you'll get yourself in trouble."

His lecture was a dose of reality, one I clearly needed to hear. He was right. Bob was my attorney, there to protect me and my rights, but he couldn't very well do that if I didn't listen to him.

We approached Helen again, and Bob said, "We're here to see the chief of police, at his request."

"Take a seat. He'll be right with you," she said curtly. I had a feeling there was no love lost between the two of them.

Since the station was empty of other visitors, we took seats by the door and waited. I wanted to ask Bob how long we were going to wait when he pulled out his cell phone and started making more whispered telephone calls. I found a current copy of *Timber Talk,* our local newspaper, on the table beside us and started looking through it. No surprise, Richard Olsen's photograph was on the front page, and most of the rest of the space was taken up with the story of how a local deliverywoman had discovered the body. They didn't mention me by name, but they might as well have used an eight-by-ten photograph from the way they described me. I wondered what kind of impact the story would have on my business and then realized I should be more concerned about tainting the jury pool. Still, without my business, I might as well be in jail. Since Joe died, it had become my life.

After waiting twenty minutes, I'd read the thin paper front to back twice and was ready to interrupt one of Bob's telephone calls when Kevin walked out of his office. He scowled in our general direction, and Bob held one hand up as he finished his call. It was clear Kevin was not pleased with my attorney's presence, and just as clear that Bob couldn't care less.

For a second I thought Kevin was going to go back to his office, but Bob finished his call and said, "You wanted to speak with my client, Chief?"

"How long ago did she hire you? One hour or two?"

"Is that really relevant?" Bob asked.

"Come on. Back in my office," he said, and my attorney and I followed the chief to a small workspace that offered a little privacy, at least more than anyone else had in the department.

I sat in one of the visitors' chairs and immediately felt something wasn't right. It took me a few seconds to realize that we were below Kevin's eye level when we were all seated. It gave me the distinct impression that I was a bad student in the principal's office waiting to be disciplined. I knew in an instant that the arrangement was anything but random. If it bothered Bob, he didn't show it, so I decided to act as though it didn't bother me either.

Kevin shuffled some papers on his desk, then said, "Let's get started. Ellie, what time exactly did you find the body?"

I was about to answer when I felt Bob's fingertips press my arm, so I remained mute. My attorney said, "You've got the 911 call, Chief. I'm sure you have a record of the exact time the telephone call was made."

Kevin leaned back, crossed his fingers over his uniformed chest, then said, "What I'm trying to determine is how long she waited to call us after she found the body."

Bob nodded to me, and I answered, "Almost immediately."

"Why the delay?" Kevin asked.

"She answered your question," Bob said.

"I had to get my telephone out of my purse," I said abruptly.

One glare from Bob was enough to shut me up.

"Did you go inside when you saw the body?"

I looked over at Bob, who nodded again.

"No," I said, remembering to keep my answers brief, as he'd instructed.

"Why not? Why didn't you try to save him?"

I started to answer when Bob shook his head. "My client has already given a statement that she ascertained the victim was dead when she got there."

"She has a medical degree, does she?"

I started to answer when Bob rose from his chair, instructing me to follow. "My client came here of her own free will, and I won't allow her to be bullied."

"Sit down, counselor," Kevin snapped. My one-time boyfriend was gone, replaced by the chief of police he'd become. I'd never had any reason to see him in his official role, and I wasn't enjoying it very much now.

"You'll be civil?" Bob asked.

"Sure. Fine. Whatever."

"And please address my client as Mrs. Swift from now on," Bob instructed him.

There was a slight eye roll before Kevin nodded, and we all sat down again.

"Now, Mrs. Swift," he said with more than a touch of sarcasm in his voice, "tell me about the events on the night of December twenty-seventh of last year."

Before I could answer, Bob asked, "What does that have to do with her discovery of the body?"

"It was the night of the Harvest Festival," Kevin said. "Your client and the murder victim had a pretty heated confrontation in public, and two weeks later he's dead. It's a legitimate line of questioning."

"It may be, but my client and I haven't had time to confer about the night in question. I'd appreciate it if you'd limit your line of queries to last night's events."

"Yeah, well, I'd appreciate a straight answer," Kevin said. "You're not making this any easier on yourself; Eleanor, you know that, don't you?"

"That's it," Bob said. "We're leaving."

Kevin shook his head in obvious disgust, but he didn't make any moves to stop us. I held in my shaking until we got outside.

"That was pretty unpleasant," I said.

Bob laughed. "That? It was nothing. Just a little cat and mouse. We're just getting started."

"Oh, boy," I said. "I can hardly wait. What do we do now?"

Bob looked surprised by the question. "There's nothing we can do. Don't talk to anyone about anything involving this case—especially the chief—without me by your side. Understand?"

"I guess so. Is that it, then? We just wait?"

"Despite the impression your former boyfriend might have just given, he's a decent police officer. I have every confidence he'll get to the bottom of this."

"And in the meantime, am I just supposed to sit around and wait?"

As Bob opened the door for me, he said, "I can't tell you how to act, but in my opinion, that's exactly what you *should* do."

Bob dropped me off at my house, pleading an impending court date that he hadn't been able to postpone. I went inside, changed from the dress I was wearing back into my more familiar blue jeans and T-shirt, and tried to decide what to do. As I walked around downstairs, I marveled again at how much the house had changed since Joe and I had first bought it as newlyweds. Over the years before we found it, most of the Arts and Crafts style in the bungalow had been buried under layers of paint and outdated carpets until it was nearly unrecognizable. I thought my new husband had lost his mind when he insisted that there was beauty under all that mess, but I was young, in love, and willing to walk through fire for him, so I gladly signed the mortgage papers right alongside him. It had taken us seven years of hard work and a great deal of imagination, but the results were indeed spectacular. Lustrous quarter-sawn oak was everywhere, ecstatic to be freed from its painted bonds. Rich, mellow wood with fine, black-lined grain filled the place, from the built-in bookcases to the floors to the ceiling beams. It was cozy, a home worth coming back to every day, but it lacked one thing that I sorely needed: my husband.

I picked up a framed picture of the two of us standing in front of a fireplace. We were smiling and laughing in the foreground, with the cabin interior of the place we loved to rent at Hungry Mother State Park in the background. It was autumn, and the leaves had just begun to burst into dazzling arrays of red and gold. I could feel my gut wrench as I remembered that day, and how happy we'd been, not knowing that we had less than two weeks left to be together. I'd forgotten all about the photograph, but Maddy had found it in my camera months later, and had used a picture frame Joe had made out of some oak that had been in too bad shape to use for anything else.

My cell phone rang, dragging me back to the present, and my new set of troubles.

"You were supposed to call me, Sis."

"I'm sorry; I guess I just lost track of time."

Maddy asked, "What happened?"

"Nothing much," I said. "Bob took over, and there wasn't anything left for me to do. I probably didn't answer half the questions Kevin asked me, and before I knew what was going on, we were leaving."

She couldn't keep the crowing out of her voice. "Bob is good. I knew he'd be able to get you off."

"Don't kid yourself," I said. "I'm nowhere near in the clear. It feels like Kevin's determined to pin this on me, and I'm not sure I'm going to be able to stop him. As much as I hate to admit it, he's got a point. There's an awful lot of evidence that leads right to me."

"But we know something he doesn't, don't we?"

"What's that?"

She paused, then said, "We both know you didn't do it."

"There's that," I said.

Maddy took a deep breath, then asked softly, "You're not going to just give up, are you?"

"Of course not," I said. "I'm just feeling a little overwhelmed today. Why don't we close the pizzeria today? I'm not really in the mood to face anybody."

Maddy paused, then said, "That's exactly the wrong thing to do. We need to be open for business today with smiles plastered on our faces."

"I don't think I could smile if I had a gun pointed to my head."

She laughed, and I felt a little of my energy coming back. As much grief as Maddy gave me at times, she could pick me up when no one else on earth could. "I could arrange that, but I didn't say the smile had to be sincere. Be like Andy: fake it till you make it."

I laughed despite the dire shape I was in. We'd gone to school with a boy named Andy Grant, who'd been mediocre at just about everything but kissing up to the teachers. The funny thing was, though, he believed he could bluster his way through any situation, which led to some comical results. The time he'd borrowed Kyle Monroe's stick-shift Mustang without a clue how to drive it was a legend around Timber Ridge. Andy had worked most of one summer to earn enough money to replace the wrecked clutch.

"Got it," I said. "Do you want to pick me up, or meet me over there?"

"What are you talking about? I got to the pizzeria about the time you were visiting the police chief. I've done all the prep work, even the dough." She paused, then added, "If you get your tail down here, you can be the one to unlock the door for our first customer of the day."

"I'm on my way," I said. "And, Maddy? Thanks."

"Hey, it's what I do," she said.

I felt better as I drove to A Slice of Delight. Working there had gotten me through some tough times in the past. Maybe it would help again. But could I face the folks who lived in Timber Ridge? Would they support me, or accuse me of killing Richard Olsen? What would I say to them? If Bob had his way, I'd meet the questions with silence, but even he realized I couldn't do that. Still, I had to do the best I could not to say anything that could be misinterpreted.

I drove the Subaru behind the pizzeria and pulled into my spot, beside Maddy's car. We took deliveries in the back, and it was usually how we came and went, choosing a much shabbier facade than our fancy front entrance. I tried my key in the lock to the back door, but the huge, red metal door wouldn't budge. What was going on? I pounded on the door, but Maddy didn't respond. Now I was getting worried. Had something happened to my sister since I'd spoken to her? I could have gotten back into the car and driven around the abutted cluster of buildings, and it's what I should have done if I'd been thinking straight. Instead, I hit the remote lock on my car and ran toward the walkway that separated the long line of facades, a set of spaces twelve feet wide that ran the entire ninety feet of the buildings' depths. The town had really done a wonderful job decorating the square in an attempt to bring folks back to our downtown area for shopping. A huge mural in the walkway, filled with scenes of Timber Ridge a hundred years ago, nearly covered one wall, and the shortcut featured a brick, two-tiered footpath with benches, quaint electric lights, and individual plantings interspersed along the way.

I barely noticed it this time through, though. As I came out onto the plaza, I rushed past the dress shop; the pharmacy; the candle shop; and the Shady Lady, a store that somehow managed to stay afloat selling only lamps, shades, and accessories. There was an empty space beside mine, one that had last featured a yarn shop that had barely lasted three months. Finally, I was at my door.

I started going through my keys as I reached A Slice of Delight—searching for the right ones—as I peered inside. There was a light on in back, but I couldn't see Maddy. If anything had happened to her, I'd never be able to forgive myself. What was that noise coming from inside? It sounded like someone was pounding in an odd, rhythmic order.

I finally managed to get the door open and was hit by a wave of music that nearly deafened me. I rushed through the front dining area, where we had several booths and tables for our customers, then went past the front register, through the kitchen, and into the back prep area. Maddy looked up from her chopping station, waving a knife in the air and singing to the odorous tune slamming out.

"Hey, I didn't hear you come in," she said as I lunged for the radio and killed the music.

I looked at her with disbelief. "Really? It's not

like I haven't been pounding on the back door or anything."

She winked at me. "That's a good thing. I put the old barricade up, so you wouldn't have been able to get in even if you'd tried."

The fire marshal had questioned the wisdom of an old-fashioned timber dropped between two metal brackets across the back door when he'd first inspected the place, but Joe had assured him that it would be taken down whenever anyone was in the store, and the fire marshal had let it pass. I wasn't positive money had changed hands, but I wouldn't have put it past my husband. He and I had different ideas about security. I didn't think there was that much worth stealing in the shop, but he acted as though we were guarding Fort Knox and all its gold. Maddy and I had gotten out of the habit of blockading the door, but it appeared that she was beginning to reacquire it.

"Since when did you start blocking the back door?" I asked as I removed the timber. It was cumbersome and heavy, one of the reasons I'd stopped moving it back and forth.

"I feel better having it there when I'm here alone."

I raised an eyebrow. "Are you here alone much?"

"Not these days, but there was a time. . . ."

I knew what she was talking about. After Joe's accident, I'd been absent quite a bit, and honestly, if my sister hadn't stepped in, I probably would have lost my restaurant along with my husband, a double blow that I doubt I would have ever recovered from.

"I understand," I said as I surveyed her work, try-

ing to change a subject neither one of us wanted
to discuss. "Everything looks good," I added.

She pointed a knife at the mushrooms. "I have a
few more to cut. Then we should be ready for business."

We normally opened at noon, but the call-in orders usually started around eleven. At least on normal days.

"No orders yet?"

She shrugged. "It's still early."

"It's not that early." I picked up the telephone,
found a dial tone, then put it back into its cradle.
"I was afraid of this."

"Of what?" she asked.

"Timber Ridge is a small town. It doesn't take
much to kill a business here; the hint of scandal
and murder is probably enough to do it."

Maddy frowned. "Don't be such a drama queen.
You don't know that's what's happening."

"Do you honestly think the entire town got tired
of our pizza all at once? There's got to be a reason,
and I know what it is."

"Then we'll just give them a few days to forget
what happened," Maddy said. "In the meantime,
we'll be here if anyone comes to their senses."

"They'd better not take too long," I said. I had
enough in savings to cover six weeks of expenses
before I had to shut the place down. Joe and I had
planned to use the surplus on a honeymoon we'd
never taken, but with A Slice of Delight requiring
so much of our time and attention, we'd never gotten around to it.

"You worry too much. Can I make you something to eat? You can have any pizza or sandwich on the menu, and you don't have to lift a finger."

"Thanks, but I can make my own lunch," I said.

"You still don't trust me? I told you, that wasn't my fault. How was I supposed to know that those canned tomatoes had gone bad? Besides, you act like it killed you or something. You bounced right back."

"I was seventeen, I missed my prom, and I was sick in bed for the first three weeks of summer vacation. I hardly call that bouncing back."

Maddy shrugged. "Water under the dam and all that. Come on, live a little. Let me make you something."

"Why not. I'll have a pepperoni sub." At least she shouldn't be able to mess that up.

"Give me something challenging," she said.

"If it's too far beneath your culinary skills, move out of the way and I'll make it myself."

"No, I'll do it," she said as she waved her knife in the air.

"Hang on a second. I don't want any special little extras, you understand? No fancy hot peppers, no secret sauce, no outlandish toppings. Just our pizza sauce, some pepperoni, and a handful of cheese in a hoagie bun. Agreed?"

"You're no fun," she said.

"Agreed?" I repeated.

"Fine, have your boring old sandwich. I'm making something special for me, though, and you can't have any."

"That's the best thing I've heard all day," I said.

"You're just a commoner at heart, aren't you?"

she said, laughing as she put my sandwich together. As Maddy slid it onto a wire grid and put it on the pizza oven's conveyor, I glanced at her sandwich to see what she was making for herself. I wasn't sure why anyone would want banana peppers, pickles, anchovies, and onions on a sandwich, but at least I didn't have to eat it.

After she slid hers onto the conveyor, Maddy said, "We should look at this as an opportunity. We could always paint the dining area again."

"I thought our job was to present a solid front to the world. It took us three months to agree on the last paint color, remember?"

"That's because you were just being stubborn."

"Maddy, I still think black walls send the wrong message to our customers."

"We would have lightened the place up with candles," she protested.

"That's fine, if you like eating in a cave," I said. "How are those sandwiches coming along?"

She glanced at the conveyor. "They've got a few more minutes, and you know it. You're just trying to distract me, aren't you?"

I grinned at her. "You caught me. How am I doing?"

"Miserably," she said.

A few minutes later, my sandwich was the first one to appear on the other side, the bread neatly toasted and the cheese melted into a golden sheen. As she plated both sandwiches, she asked, "Where should we eat? Here, in back?"

"Tell you what. Why don't we take a table by the front window? At least if anyone happens to be passing by, they'll see us here and know we're open."

"Sounds good to me," she said. "I'll grab the sandwiches, and you get the glasses. Do you want chips with yours?"

"I'd better not. I don't want soda, either. I'll have water to drink."

"Watching your calories, Eleanor? I don't know how you do it," she said as she grabbed two bags of chips.

"Hey, I just said I didn't want any chips," I protested.

"Who said either one of these was for you?"

I didn't have the slightest idea how my sister could eat whatever she wanted with no apparent consequences, whereas if I just walked past a cake I somehow managed to gain three pounds. It just wasn't fair.

As we started to eat, I looked out over the plaza, too conscious of the people going out of their way not to pass by the pizzeria. A family with four small children was playing beside the captured German howitzer from World War I that stood on one edge of the square, balanced two hundred yards away by a twenty-five-foot obelisk that honored three doctors who had saved scores of townsfolk during a flu epidemic in the 1800s, and who had died themselves from their efforts to save others.

There was a wide expanse of brick and stone pavers that made up the walkways in front of the twenty shops that lined the way like soldiers standing arm to arm, with no gaps between nearly all of the buildings. The only available parking was away from the plaza, fifty feet from the nearest storefront. The walkway itself was dotted with shrubbery and tree plantings, benches of wood and wrought iron, and a pair of copper-covered display areas where residents could post news about lost dogs, yoga classes, and garage band concerts. There were quite a few people milling about despite the cold, but none came within a hundred yards of A Slice of Delight.

Maddy must have caught drift of my thoughts. "Don't worry, it'll be all right."

I stared at most of the uneaten sandwich on my plate. "I don't see how." I'd suddenly lost my appetite.

"You know what? You're right. It's not going to get any better all by itself."

That caught my attention. "What are you talking about?"

"If we wait for the police chief to figure out what happened to Richard Olsen, you're going to lose this business, and we can't let that happen."

"I can't afford to hire a private detective, and even if I could, I wouldn't have a clue how to go about finding one."

Maddy said, "That's why we're going to solve this murder ourselves."

I had to look at her to see if she was kidding, but her face was dead serious. "You've been eating too many anchovies. They've pickled your brain."

"Think about it," Maddy said, gaining steam with her new idea. "Who knows this town better than we do? We've got more contacts in Timber Ridge than the police department, and while people won't be willing to come clean with Kevin, I'm willing to bet they'll talk to us."

"I don't see why they should answer our questions if they won't tell the police what they know."

Maddy stood. "That's because we won't be asking questions, at least not as openly as they'll be. We can do this. We have to."

"Why are you so stoked about this idea?"

She laughed. "Who else am I going to find who'll hire me, given my spotty work history? If this business goes under, I'm out of a job, remember?"

I started to think about what my sister was proposing, and I wondered if I had what it took to dig into people's lives. I wasn't nosy by nature, and I was more than a little reluctant to start prying where I didn't belong. Then I looked around the shop and realized that with my pizzeria gone, I would have one less tie with Joe. This had been more his dream than mine, but I'd grown to love the Slice as much as he had. Maddy was right about one thing: if the killer wasn't unmasked, and fairly soon, I would lose the restaurant, and that was something I just couldn't take.

"Okay, I'm in," I said.

It was Maddy's turn to study me. "Are you sure?"

"No, but do we really have any other choice? Let's make a game plan and figure out what we're going to do."

It was Maddy's turn to pull back. "Hang on a second, Sis. I was just talking off the top of my head. I do that; you should know me well enough by now to realize that."

"This time I agree with you. You don't have to help, but I'm going to track down a killer."

She looked at me as though we'd never met. "You're serious, aren't you?"

"I've never been more serious in my life."

Chapter 3

"Let's make a list," I said as I grabbed the white board where we usually wrote our daily specials. "We can't just go off and start investigating the murder without some kind of plan."

Maddy nodded. "Okay, I agree with that, but where do we start? How well did you know Richard Olsen?"

"Not as well as he would have liked," I said. "It's going to take a little work to fill in the gaps of who might want him dead, but I know where to start. If we can figure out a motive, it should be a little easier to match it with the murderer."

"Fine," Maddy said as she continued staring at the blank board. "So, why would someone want him dead?"

"We have to go beyond that, at least for now," I said. "Why does anyone kill anybody else? That's the first question we need to ask."

"Greed," Maddy said, and I wrote that down.

"Love," I said, adding it to the list.

"Lust has to be there, too," she said.

"Isn't that the same thing?"

Maddy laughed. "Not in my world, and I'm willing to bet not in Richard Olsen's, either."

After I wrote down "lust," I said, "You could kill to protect someone."

"Or something," Maddy added. "Or you could commit murder to hide something."

"Okay, I'll buy that. What else?"

"Isn't that enough? I think we've covered the basics. Most of the motives for murder are there."

I studied the board, then nodded. "Then let's make them more specific," I said as I drew a line under our motive list and started adding columns. "Greed comes first. How can we apply that to Richard?"

"He could have been stealing from someone," Maddy offered.

"Or someone could inherit his money when he died," I added.

"Do you honestly think Richard Olsen had that much?"

"Maddy, how much does it take? Even if he didn't have a lot of assets, he could have had life insurance."

"That's a point. What about lust?"

"Or love," I said. "Did Richard have a steady girlfriend, despite his drunken behavior toward me? Was there anyone he broke up with recently?"

Maddy shrugged. "I'd still rather think about lust. Was he fooling around with someone else's wife and got caught doing it?"

I stared hard at my sister. "Do you honestly think anyone in Timber Ridge could have an affair without the entire town knowing about it?"

"It's a possibility we have to consider. That's all I'm saying." Maddy tapped the board, then said, "Let's skip down to the next category."

"We've still got 'to hide something, or to protect someone,' " I said.

"I can't imagine Richard protecting anyone but himself," Maddy said.

"But he could have had something to hide," I said. "Most folks do."

"Even you?"

Maddy was watching me closely, waiting for an answer.

"Sorry, I hate to disappoint you, but there aren't any secrets in my life." I studied the list, then added, "We need to get to know Richard Olsen better."

"We can't exactly ask him out for drinks, Eleanor, unless you're suggesting we hold a séance, which could be fun, now that I think about it."

"There are other options," I said. "I'm going to talk to—"

I was interrupted as the front door slammed open so hard it almost shattered the glass.

A wiry-haired woman with fiery eyes stormed into the pizzeria, stopped in front of me, and screamed, "You killed him!"

"I did not," I said, trying to keep my voice at a calm level, though I was screaming right back at her on the inside. "Don't believe everything you hear," I added.

"Trust me, I've heard enough to know it's true."

Maddy said calmly, "Sit down. Why don't I get you something to drink, and we can discuss this calmly."

"I don't want to be calm!" she shouted at us. I

could see her chest rising and falling under her sweater as she panted for breath, and it was clear she was on the edge of a breakdown. "Why did you have to kill him?"

Before I could answer, she collapsed on the floor in front of us.

I pushed a chair aside and knelt down beside the woman as Maddy said, "It's not safe being around you, is it?"

"She's not dead," I said as I found a pulse at her neck. "Call nine-one-one."

"I've got a better idea," Maddy said. Before I could stop her, she grabbed my water and poured it on the woman's head.

I was about to chew her out when the woman sputtered a few times, then opened her eyes and looked at me blearily. "You didn't call the paramedics, did you?"

"No, we haven't had a chance, but we'll phone them right now," I said, trying my best to reassure her.

"Don't do that," she ordered. "I faint sometimes. It's nothing serious."

"It looked serious to me," I said.

The woman ignored my comment and started to pull herself upright, but she slumped back down to the floor before she made it.

"Should you be getting up?" I asked.

"I'm fine, I tell you. This just tends to happen when I get overly excited."

"Then maybe you should calm down," Maddy said. "Unless you like being helpless on the floor like that."

That got the woman's attention. "I won't scream

again," she said, lowering her voice. I tried to help
her up, but she refused my aid and finally managed to stand as she held on to the back of a chair.

In a calmer voice than she'd used since she'd arrived, the woman repeated her question. "Why did
you kill him?"

"I didn't," I replied, for what felt like the hun-
dredth time since she'd come in.

Maddy looked at her, then said, "You know, you
look familiar, but I can't place you. I'm Eleanor's
sister. Have we met?"

"No, but it's pretty clear you knew my brother.
I'm Sheila Olsen."

"I'm sorry for your loss," I said automatically.
Then I added, "But I didn't cause it. I found your
brother on the floor like that. I didn't kill him."

"Everybody I've talked to thinks otherwise."

Maddy butted in again. "Who exactly have you
been talking to?"

"Since I got in from Charlotte, I haven't been
able to shut people up."

"Can you be more specific than that?" I asked.

Sheila said, "You want a list? Okay, here goes. The
man at the newspaper, one of your shop's neighbors, just about anyone you'd care to ask."

"Was the man at the newspaper in his forties, a
little portly, and almost completely bald?" I asked.

"Yes, that was him," she admitted. Her eyes narrowed. "How did you know that? Have you been
following me?"

"Lady, you're the one who just burst in on us, remember?" Maddy snapped.

"I mean before I got here," she explained.

"No, but I'm not surprised by anything he might have told you about me. He'd rather print a lie than the truth if it gave him a chance to smear me," I said.

"Why would he do that?" Sheila asked.

"There's been bad blood between his family and ours for generations," I said. "His grandfather started that newspaper so he could attack our family in print, though he's never come out and said anything we could sue over, though just barely."

"I don't believe you," she said as her gaze took in the board Maddy and I had been writing on. "What's that?"

My sister tried to hide what we'd written, but I said, "Let her see it. She has a right to know."

"She does not," Maddy insisted.

"Know what?" Sheila asked.

"We were sitting here when you stormed in trying to figure out who really killed your brother."

She looked at me as though she knew I was lying, but as she studied the board, her face began to soften. "It's true, isn't it? You didn't just do this to ease my suspicion, did you?"

"How could we have done that?" Maddy asked. "We didn't even know you existed until you stormed in here a few minutes ago. If we had, I'm sure you would have made it onto the board, too."

I was about to scold my sister when Sheila nodded her agreement. "Okay, I'm convinced. But I've got one question: if you didn't kill him, who did?"

"That's what we're trying to find out," Maddy

said, her patience with this woman obviously worn thin.

"Then I might just help," Sheila said as she took off her jacket and threw it onto a chair at our table. When she spotted my barely touched sandwich, she asked, "Is anyone going to eat that?"

"No, help yourself," I said before Maddy could stop me. "Would you like something to drink?"

"A Coke would be great," she said.

"I'll get it for you," I replied.

"I'll help you," Maddy added.

I was about to tell Maddy that I didn't need any assistance when she motioned me to the back of the dining room with her glance.

"We'll be right back," I said, though I doubted Sheila heard me. She was too busy devouring my sandwich to even notice we were leaving.

"What are you doing?" Maddy hissed at me at the drink fountain.

"I'm getting her a Coke, unless you want to do it yourself," I said.

"I'm talking about inviting her to join us on our hunt."

"I didn't ask; she volunteered," I said.

"Eleanor, do we really want a narcoleptic hothead helping us?"

I let the foam settle, then added more Coke to the glass. "Are you kidding me? She's perfect. We didn't have an excuse to start digging into Richard Olsen's life before, and when one comes stumbling in through our door, you want to throw her out. She's our ticket to finding out what really happened, Maddy."

My sister paused to think about it, then nodded

slowly. "You know what? I'm beginning to think you're smarter than you look."

"I'm sure there's a compliment buried in that somewhere."

"Quit fishing. It's the best you're going to get from me, and you know it." My sister looked back at Sheila, who'd finished half the sandwich and had started working on the other half. "How do we go about using her?"

"With her blessing, of course," I said as I picked up the Coke and started back to the table. "We're going to ask her."

Maddy grabbed my arm. "Hang on a second," she whispered. "We can't be so blatant about it. This calls for some stealth and subterfuge."

I peeled her hand off me. "I love you dearly, but sometimes I think you've read too many mysteries."

"How can anyone possibly read too many books?" she asked.

"When you start acting like Inspector Clouseau," I answered, "maybe it's time to take a break."

"Get your references right, Eleanor. He was in the movies. For novels, I'd like to think I'm more like Kinsey Millhone," she said.

"I'd say Miss Marple," I said.

"I adore Agatha Christie," she said with a smile. "I'll take that as a compliment."

"Even though it wasn't meant as one?" I asked.

"These days, I take them where I can get them."

Our conversation was interrupted by a summons from the dining room. "Are you two going to stand there chatting all day, or am I getting that Coke?"

"Coming right up," I said as I turned to Maddy. "Will you be joining us?"

"Try to stop me," she said as she followed close on my heels.

I gave Sheila the drink, which she downed in a few gulps. "Refill?"

Maddy rolled her eyes, but I reached for the glass. "I'll be right back."

Thirty seconds later I was back with the topped-off Coke and found Maddy and Sheila in earnest conversation.

"I wasn't gone that long," I said. "What are you two talking about?"

"I was just saying it's a shame we don't know more about Richard's life. It's going to be hard knowing where to start looking if we're going to have any chance of solving his murder," Maddy replied.

I couldn't tell if Maddy was trying to be clever or not, but as long as we were recruiting Sheila to our cause, whatever she was doing was all right with me.

"I want you to know how much I appreciate you changing your mind about me so quickly," I told Sheila.

Maddy shot a warning glare at me, which I'd grown skilled at ignoring.

"When I'm wrong, I'm the first to admit it," Sheila said as she let out an indelicate belch. "Sorry, I haven't been able to force myself to eat since I got the news."

"When did you find out?" I asked.

"The police chief came around this morning."

I glanced at the clock on the wall and saw that it was barely past one. At least she'd missed breakfast on account of the bad news.

Maddy cut me off from saying anything else by stepping into the void with a rather direct question. "Should we go look at Richard's house now?"

"We're still open for business here, remember?" I asked.

"I don't think Timber Ridge is going to miss us for a few hours, do you? Rita didn't even bother showing up."

In my foggy state, I'd forgotten that one of my other employees had failed to make even a token appearance. "You didn't talk to her, did you?"

She shook her head. "Did you check the answering machine in your office?"

"When have I had time?" I asked. "I'll be right back." Before I could duck into my small office in the kitchen, I said, "Don't you two go anywhere."

"I'd be more inclined to stay if I had some dessert," Sheila confessed.

"Sorry, we're out of brownies, and the cheesecake hasn't been delivered yet," I said.

"That's a shame," Sheila said as she started to stand.

Maddy frowned, then said, "I suppose I could pop over to Paul's and get you something."

Sheila shook her head. "I don't expect you to ask a friend to feed me."

I said, "Paul isn't a friend. Well, he is, but he runs Paul's Pastries. It's just down that way," I said as I pointed toward the obelisk. "And Maddy wouldn't mind going at all, would you?"

She made a face at me as she said, "I'd be delighted."

"I'll keep Sheila company while you're gone," I said.

"I don't mean to be a burden," Sheila said.

"Good," Maddy said at the same time I said, "Nonsense. No trouble at all."

Maddy left, albeit reluctantly, and I settled back into my chair.

Sheila said, "I won't steal anything. You can go check your messages, it's all right."

"Are you sure? It'll just take a second."

"Go on. I'll wait."

I hurried back to my office, a small space I'd carved out of a former closet, and saw that there were several messages on the machine. I punched PLAY and heard my employee calling to check in. Rita said that she'd come by before opening time and had failed to get into the pizzeria, much as I had myself, since Maddy and I had the only two keys. She had assumed we were closed, given the circumstances, and I could hardly blame her. Maddy's theory that we should stay open had been a good one to show the community that I wasn't afraid to show my face, but unfortunately, it appeared that Rita was afraid to show hers. The last part of her message was that it was all for the best anyway. She was quitting, and she told me that I could send her last check to her dad's house.

The messages were still playing when Maddy came back, clutching a bag from Paul's.

"Where'd she go?"

"She's not out there anymore?" I asked as I hit the pause button on the answering machine.

"No, she's gone," Maddy said. "All you had to do was keep her company, and yet she managed to walk right out of the pizzeria."

"I couldn't keep her here against her will," I said. "She promised me she'd stay."

"What do we do now?"

"There are a couple of options. We could try to find her, or we could keep the pizzeria open and look for her later," I said.

"I vote you stay here and work while I go out looking for her," Maddy said.

"I'm sorry, were you under the impression that you got a vote? This is a benevolent dictatorship, not a democracy."

"Okay, great leader, then what do we do?"

"I'm not sure. Rita just quit," I said as I pointed to the answering machine.

Maddy shook her head. "We're better off without her, if she's too afraid to show up for work."

I decided not to tell my sister that she'd tried, or had at least claimed to have made the effort.

I heard the front door chime and said, "I need to see if we have a customer, or if Sheila's decided to come back."

"Wait for me," Maddy said as she followed me back out front.

I'd been hoping Sheila had changed her mind about bolting and had returned. Second best would have been an actual customer, willing to cross the unseen boundary and actually come into the shop and eat. Instead, it was my last choice, our very own chief of police.

"What do you want, Kevin?"

"Is that how you greet everyone who walks in here?" He looked around the empty room, then added, "If it is, I'm guessing that might be one of the reasons the place is deserted."

"Sorry, I'm a little on edge right now. But honestly, unless you're going to place an order, you might as well turn around and go. My attorney has instructed me not to talk to you unless he's right beside me."

Kevin looked around. "Funny, I don't see him here now."

"You know what? You're absolutely right." I turned to my sister and said, "You take care of him. I've got work to do."

I headed back toward my office when Kevin said, "I'm not here on official business. Eleanor, could I talk to you a second as a father and not as the chief of police?"

I turned back to look at him, and there was a somber expression on his face. This wasn't going to be pleasant. Kevin's son, Josh, worked for me three nights a week, and it had been a bone of contention between us from the start.

"Don't tell me," I said. "I think I already know. You're not going to let your son work here anymore."

His frown deepened, but instead of letting him answer, I lit into him. "Kevin Hurley, you've known me over twenty years. Do you honestly think I'd do anything to hurt your son? I'm a big fan of Josh's, though I can't say the same thing about his dad at the moment."

"How you feel about me doesn't matter," he said. "Eleanor, be reasonable. He's all my wife and I have in this world that means anything to us, and I'm not going to let him be painted with the same brush folks around town are using on you. I've told him he has to quit."

"What did he say to that?"

Kevin shrugged. "That doesn't concern you. I'm just saying, if he shows up anyway, I want you to send him home."

"Shouldn't Josh be the one deciding this?"

Kevin looked like he was ready to explode, but he managed to rein in his temper. After a few seconds, he said, "You don't have kids. No matter what you think of me, consider him. That's all I'm asking."

"I need to think about it. Is that it?"

"For now," he said.

"Then consider your message delivered."

I heard Maddy gasp slightly, but I didn't dare look at her. My gaze was locked on Kevin. After ten seconds, he nodded, then left the shop without another word.

"Have you lost your mind?" Maddy asked. "I thought for a minute there he was going to shoot you."

"No, Kevin would never do that," I said, shaking from the confrontation. I was like that, calm in the actual battle, but full of nerves afterward. I guess it was the best order for things to happen, come to think of it.

Maddy asked, "What makes you so sure? I saw the fire in his eyes."

"Too much paperwork," I said as I gathered up Sheila's dirty dishes. "Where do you suppose she ran off to?"

"I have no idea, especially with a free dessert on its way."

I looked at the bag, then asked, "What did you get?"

"Paul had just finished icing freshly baked brownies when I walked in, so I got two of them."

"Perfect. I'll take mine now."

Maddy held the bag away from me. "Not so fast. I didn't think you could bring yourself to eat anything."

"What can I say? Sheila was a good influence on me. My appetite's suddenly returned."

"Okay," Maddy said reluctantly. "I guess I can share, but I get first pick."

"I can live with that," I said.

The brownie, just like everything else Paul made, was delicious. It was a huge square, and I doubted I'd be able to finish it, but much to my surprise, I managed just fine. I regretted the calories, but only for a split second. After all, there were times of stress that demanded I spoil myself a little, and if being openly regarded as a murderer wasn't one of them, I didn't want to come face-to-face with what might rank as worse.

"Now that you've gorged on sweets, what do we do?" Maddy asked.

"I can see you didn't have any trouble with yours, either," I said.

"That's beside the point," she said as she wadded up the wrapper of her own late, great brownie. "You know me—I have a high metabolism."

"And I've got a sweet tooth the size of the Smoky Mountains," I said. "It's great having an excuse to give in once in a while, isn't it?"

"Be that as it may," Maddy said, "we can't just sit here and wait for the killer to fall into our laps."

"You're right," I said as I looked around the empty pizzeria. "There's no sense staying open if no one comes in. Let's make a sign for the door. Then we can head into town and see what we can find out about Richard Olsen."

"Shouldn't we look for his sister first?" Maddy asked as she wiped down the table we'd been using.

"I wouldn't know where to start looking, would you?"

"We could try Richard's house," Maddy said.

I thought about it and quickly decided that it was as good a plan as any. "Okay, then that's what we should do."

Maddy smiled. "Do you mean the great and powerful Oz is actually taking one of my suggestions now?"

"When it makes sense, I do," I said as I scrawled out a note on the inside of a new pizza box. I couldn't think of what to write, so I just put, "Back later," and held it out for her inspection.

Maddy read it, and as I taped the cardboard to the glass, she said, "You've got the heart of a poet, Sis."

"Hey, it gets the point across, doesn't it? Now, are you going to stand there criticizing my signage skills, or are we going to do something a little more productive?"

"Let's go," she said.

I turned off the lights and locked the front door, something I hated doing during our usual working hours. But if I wanted to stay open on a long-term basis, I was going to have to forgo some cash flow temporarily, no matter what my late husband might have thought about it. I hoped he would have understood, but since he'd never been accused of murder himself, I couldn't be positive.

Sometimes my dear husband could have tunnel vision when it came to the bottom line. I'd seen it as my job to give him some perspective from time to time.

At the moment, I would have traded having his arms around me for ten seconds for everything I owned in the world.

I glanced back at the pizzeria as we walked out onto the wide swath of brick in front of it. We'd picked up the building's lease on the plaza after it had housed an unsuccessful clothier named The Blue Note. The owner, obsessed with the color blue, had gone so far as to paint most of the brick facade a shade darker than the deepest sky, though she'd adorned the architectural trim with a lovely off-white that somehow worked well. Joe and I had priced the job of having the paint removed, but the process was such a delicate one, given the age of the bricks, that we knew we'd never be able to afford to have it done. That had led to us playing with dozens of names for our business, from The Blue Pizza to A Pizza of an Entirely Different Color, but we finally decided to ignore the blue instead of incorporating it into our name. A Slice of Delight was our original name when we couldn't come up with anything we liked better, and somehow it just stuck.

As we walked down the steps between the buildings—the same steps that I'd raced up a couple of hours earlier—Maddy must have sensed my concern for shutting down. "Closing is the best thing we can do until we figure this out. You know that, don't you?"

"This isn't going to become a habit," I said. "We've got today to dig around, but tonight we re-open, even if it's just the two of us."

"I'm still not delivering any pizzas," she said defiantly. "Who knows what we'll find the next time we do it."

"Don't worry, I won't ask you to," I said. "If none of our staff shows up, I'll do it myself, if it comes to that."

"That's what you get for hiring high school and college kids," Maddy said.

"It's all I can afford," I said as I shrugged. "They're happy for the work and I'm thrilled I don't have to charge twenty-dollar-minimum orders. It's the only way we can afford to stay open."

"I know. It's just that sometimes working with these kids makes me feel so old."

It was a rare admission for my sister, so I said, "There's no way you're ever going to be old. You've got too much spirit. Sometimes I wish I had some of yours."

"Are you kidding me? You've got a lot more guts than I do."

I looked at her as we walked to the back parking lot, where our cars were waiting for us. "How do you figure that?"

"You married a man you barely knew, and on your wedding day you bought a run-down house that no one else in town saw any potential in. The two of you defied all odds and renovated it without even coming close to divorce, so what do you do after that? You open up a pizza parlor, of all things. I'd say those were all bold moves, and you still managed to stay in love all along the way."

I smiled at her. "When you put it that way, it sounds like I am pretty adventurous. It just seemed so normal the way Joe proposed it all. I had the confidence that he could do anything he set his mind to, and he never let me down."

"I won't, either," she said. "We'll find out what happened. Don't worry."

"Are you kidding me? Worry's about all I've got right now. If you take that away from me, I'd be lost."

She laughed. "Then we'll worry together. Now, who's going to drive, you or me?"

"Let's take my Subaru," I said. "I need gas anyway, so we might as well fill up the tank on the way to Richard's."

We stopped at the Ezee Fill, and as I was pumping my gas, a car pulled up behind me. There were two other pumps open. Why didn't they just pull around and take one of those, instead of lingering behind me?

I glanced back to point that fact out when I saw who was in the car.

As she got out, I tried my best not to throw the pump to the ground and drive away.

Instead, I bit my lower lip as she approached.

"I'm almost done, Joanna," I called out as I cut the pump off.

"Go on and fill it," Joanna Grant said. "I need to talk to you."

Joanna was a thin, older woman who darted around people like a hummingbird looking for nectar, and I tried to avoid her whenever I could. In her seventies, she could still manage to stir up more trouble than a marauding gang of monkeys armed with paintball guns.

"Sorry, we're running behind," I said as I secured the gas cap. Now all I had to do was print out the receipt, and we'd be gone. I hit the print button, only nothing came out. The blasted thing was out of paper, which meant that I had to go inside to retrieve a receipt. I thought about abandoning it, but the bookkeeper inside me wouldn't allow it. I had to have receipts for everything, from donuts to automobiles, a personality quirk that I would have given anything to abandon at the moment.

"I'll walk in with you," Joanna said. "So, you're closing the pizzeria. It's probably for the best. What are you going to do now?"

How in the world did she know we'd shut the doors? Had she followed us here after reading the sign? "Madeline and I are running a few errands," I said as I cursed the employee whose job it was to keep the receipt paper filled.

She waved a quick hand in the air. "I mean in the long term. I understand you've hired Bob Lemon. He's very good. Who knows? You might even get out while you're still a young woman." She studied me for a moment, then said, "Well, relatively young."

The impact of her words spun me around to face her. "Joanna, I didn't kill Richard Olsen. I'm not going to jail, and I'm not closing the pizzeria. I'm simply taking a few hours off to run a few errands."

She looked taken aback by my blast, then managed to say, "Of course you are. How brave of you. If you need a confidante, don't be afraid to call me, at any hour. I rarely sleep, you know."

Too busy prying into other people's lives, I thought, though didn't dare say. Joanna had no compunctions about embellishing every story she told, and no doubt she'd be telling all of Timber Ridge by dark that I'd made a full confession of the murder to her while standing in front of the Ezee Fill gas station.

I grabbed the receipt from the clerk, who must have seen me glaring at him through the window, turned back, and left Joanna in my wake.

"Call me!" she yelled out as I ducked back into the Subaru.

As I drove away, Maddy was nearly doubled over in her seat from laughter.

"What's so funny?" I asked. "You could have helped me deal with her, you know. Two against one and all that."

"Are you kidding? It was too much fun watching you go after her yourself."

"I wish I could share the joke with you, but this is serious. That woman is a character assassin, and it's pretty clear I'm the one in her sights right now."

"Don't let her get to you," Maddy said. "She's mean, but she's harmless."

"Don't kid yourself. I won't be able to get an unbiased jury in twelve counties once she's done with me."

Maddy said, "This will never go to trial. You have to believe that."

"Sorry I don't have your faith in our local law enforcement, and it's important to remember that if we don't find out what really happened to Richard Olsen, a trial is exactly where I'm heading. But even if it doesn't make it that far, the longer this hangs over my head, the more easily folks in town are going to start believing I actually did it."

"We won't let that happen," Maddy said.

"I'm counting on it."

We traced my route of the night before, and I felt my hands start to shake as they grasped the wheel of their own accord. The image of Richard lying there with a knife in his chest was one I doubted I'd ever be able to wipe completely away from my memory, certainly not this soon. I was beginning to wonder about the wisdom of revisiting the scene of the murder when suddenly and almost without warning, I had no other choice.

We were there.

I parked in front of the house and studied it in daylight. Richard had kept it up nicely, from the careful paint job to the well-tended lawn. I'd let mine go to weeds, hoping snow would cover the worst offenders at some point, but Richard's looked like it was ready to green up at the slightest encouragement.

Maddy looked over at me, then asked, "Are you ready to do this?"

"No."

"We don't have to, you know," she said softly.

"We both know that's not true, though, don't we? Let's go. Who knows? Maybe we'll get lucky and Sheila won't be home."

We walked up the steps, and as we neared the door, I saw that it was ajar.

"What should we do?" Maddy asked.

Instead of answering her, I called out, "Sheila, it's us. Are you there? Is everything all right?"

I saw that the carpet where Richard had lain was gone, and someone had cleaned up the blood that had spilled around it. Nothing else looked out of place.

"Hello?" I called out again.

There was no answer, so I took a step forward.

"What are you doing?" Maddy asked me. "We can't just walk in."

"We can be bold, or we can be gone. I don't see any other options," I said. "She could be in trouble. That's a two-car garage, so there's room for her car as well as her brother's inside. We don't know she's not in there, helpless or in trouble."

Taking a deep breath, I walked in. To my sister's credit, she didn't even hesitate.

As she stared down at the naked hardwood floor, Maddy asked, "Is this where it happened?"

"As far as I can tell. There wasn't a whole lot of light coming in, so I didn't get a clear look, but that seems to be right."

I knew I'd come in looking for clues, but I couldn't pull my gaze away from the freshly scrubbed floor. The image of Richard Olsen's body kept superimposing itself on the floor in flashes, no matter how much I willed it to disappear.

I don't know how long I stood staring at the spot, but Maddy gave me all the time I needed.

I was about to suggest that we start looking further into the house when a car drove up and stopped in the street.

It appeared that someone besides Joanna was keeping tabs on us.

Chief Hurley got out of his squad car, and from the expression on his face, I prepared myself for the worst.

Chapter 4

"Eleanor, have you completely lost your mind? Do you want me to lock you up?" Chief Hurley asked as he approached us.

"We're not doing anything wrong," I said, though I knew we hadn't had permission to cross the Olsen threshold. I just hoped he didn't know that.

"Breaking and entering is still a crime, in case you hadn't heard," he said.

"The door was open," Maddy explained.

"Then that makes it unlawful trespass," Kevin said. "I can't believe you'd be this foolish."

"Then you really don't know me all that well at all," I said. "I've done things a lot more foolish than this."

Maddy said, "It's true. Would you like a list?"

"Spare me your vaudeville act. Do I need to handcuff you both, or will you come with me quietly?"

I was about to say something I knew I'd regret when Sheila came out of the back of the house, obviously startled to see us all standing there.

"What's going on?" she asked, carefully avoiding our glares.

"Don't worry, ma'am. I caught these two trespassing. I'm handling it."

Sheila said, "How can they be trespassing if I invited them here, Sheriff?"

"It's Chief," Kevin explained automatically. "Are you trying to tell me you knew they were here? Don't lie; I saw the look on your face when you turned the corner."

"I admit I was startled to see you all standing there." She turned to me and said, "I wasn't expecting you two until tonight."

"We decided to close early today," I said. "Thanks for having us over."

"Why exactly did you invite them here?" Kevin asked, a perfectly legitimate question that Sheila clearly didn't have an answer for. "You were ready to kill Eleanor this morning."

"That's before I spoke with her," Sheila replied. "I've come to believe that you're focusing on the wrong suspect."

Kevin looked ready to explode, but he buried his temper as quickly as it had fought its way to the surface. "You're mistaken," he finally said.

"That's your opinion, not mine," Sheila snapped. "Now if you'll excuse me, we've got work to do."

"What work is that?" the chief asked.

"These ladies have kindly offered to help me go through the house. There's a great deal of work to be done, and I can't do it all by myself."

"This is still a crime scene," Kevin snapped.

"But you released it to me this morning, remember? Unless you're afraid there was something you missed the first time you went through it."

He had the choice of admitting that he'd been sloppy, or giving us what we wanted. I was certain neither option was all that attractive to him.

"Fine, we'll play it that way for now," he said, then left.

I turned back to Sheila once I was certain he was gone and said, "I don't know whether to hug you or scream. Why did you disappear like that?"

"I didn't disappear. I simply changed my mind about dessert."

I wasn't buying that, but there was really no way I could call her a liar, not after she'd stepped in and saved us.

"That's good, because it's all gone," Maddy said. "Now, where should we get started?"

"I'm not sure this is a good idea," Sheila said. "The police chief seemed pretty upset with you being here."

"You don't want to find out who really killed your brother? Is that what you're saying?"

My sister had that edge in her voice that I'd heard a million times before. She was going to bully Sheila into helping us, and I wasn't going to stand for that. "Madeline, back off. She's already helped us by keeping us out of jail."

"Whose side are you on?" my sister asked me.

"Sometimes I wonder myself." I turned to Sheila and said, "If you want us to leave, we'll go. Just say the word."

Sheila seemed to think about it, then said, "No, I meant what I told the chief. I do need help here, if you don't mind."

"On the condition that we're allowed to search for clues while we work," Maddy said.

Maddy glared at me, daring me to overrule her, but I wasn't about to. I wanted to dig for information myself.

"I suppose that would be all right," Sheila said.

"Good, then that's settled. Let's get to work," I said before she could change her mind.

I looked around the house and realized that Richard Olsen had two sides to him. The living room was neat, clean, and well organized. It wasn't until I looked inside the two bedrooms that I realized that deep down, he was a slob. Clothes were thrown everywhere; newspapers were bound with twine and stacked in the corners of the rooms, while boxes full of who-knew-what littered the rest of the floor space.

"How did he live like this?" I asked, forgetting for a second that we were there by his sister's goodwill. "I'm sorry. I didn't mean it to sound like that."

"You haven't been thinking anything I didn't say to him a thousand times while he was alive," Sheila said. "He's been like this since he was a boy." She turned to Maddy and added, "Why do you think I was so eager to let you help me?"

"I'm beginning to understand," my sister said.

They both sounded so defeated, I knew I had to brighten things up a little. "Come on, ladies, we can do this. Sheila, you start carrying bundles of newspapers outside so we can recycle them. Maddy, find some empty boxes and start gathering up clothes.

Are you going to keep them, Sheila, or are they being donated?"

"I have no use for them," Sheila said.

"Good, I know the Salvation Army will be able to use them."

"If we're doing all that, what are you going to be doing?" Maddy asked.

"I'm going to tackle the paperwork, if that's all right."

Sheila nodded. "That's fine with me. If you find a will, let me know. I have no idea what Richard wanted done with his things. Oh, and if there's a bank account, or an insurance policy, anything at all like that, I'd appreciate it if you'd let me know."

"Consider it done," I said.

As Sheila started carrying the first bundle outside, Maddy whispered, "How in the world did you get her to agree to that? You've got her schlepping old newspapers while you're going through his personal things."

"I'm not quite sure, but let's just take advantage of it before she changes her mind," I said.

Maddy laughed. "You're kidding, right? We could turn on rap music and start chanting along and she wouldn't say a word. Look around. Would you complain if you were getting free labor from us?"

"No, I guess you've got a point, but I still don't want to push it."

"Go on, then. I've got clothes to sort."

I heard the front door open, so I said quickly, "Search the pockets as you go. You might find something."

"That doesn't sound like much fun, riffling through a dead man's jackets and pants."

"Do you want to switch?" I asked.

I was talking to Maddy, but Sheila must have thought I was speaking to her. "No, thanks. Paperwork makes my head hurt. If it's not too much trouble, I'd really appreciate you sorting through that mess. It's much nicer just dealing with these newspapers."

"I just thought I should offer," I said as I shook my head in my sister's direction.

She rolled her eyes, then started sorting clothes. I moved into the other bedroom, where it was apparent Richard had set up a home office. Four file cabinets surrounded the desk, a structure that was nothing more than cinder blocks and an old door. He hadn't even removed the knob, but I didn't discover that until I got down to that level. There was a copier tucked into the corner, too.

This was going to take forever.

I ducked into the kitchen and found a new box of trash bags in the cupboard. I was probably going to need every last one of them. I returned to the bedroom, and as I began sorting through the stacks of papers on the desk, I found receipts for everything from Richard's brand-new Honda Accord to a donut he'd had for breakfast the week before. There were receipts from three days ago, when he hadn't had a clue he was about to die, and receipts from all the way back to when he'd first moved into the house. How was I going to make any sense of any of it, especially when I was surrounded by all the clutter? It was enough to make my head throb. I decided the only way to look through it all was at home, where I had room to spread out and form some kind of logical system. I stopped being so careful studying each receipt, shoving piles of them into bags. Once I had the desktop and file drawers empty, I wasn't certain I'd be able to fit it all into my car, even with the spacious back.

One of the file folders flipped open as I crammed it into a bag, and I was surprised to see some kind of key taped there. I pulled it out and saw that it was from Southern Wheat Bank and Trust, a business that had been in our part of North Carolina for over a hundred years. It was a miracle it hadn't been gobbled up by some corporate takeover, but it was probably too small for any of the big boys to care much about.

"I found something," I said to the others.

Maddy came rushing in, with Sheila right behind her.

"What is it?" my sister asked breathlessly.

"A safety-deposit box key from Southern Wheat," I said. "Sheila, the papers you need are probably in there."

"That would be wonderful," Sheila said. "But how do we go about getting into it?"

"Let's go by the bank and see if they'll let you open it," Maddy said.

"Not without a lot of red tape," I replied. Then I remembered retrieving our will from ours after Joe died. "Sheila, is there any chance you were listed on the account, too?"

"I don't know. I signed a few things for Richard over the years, but I can't remember what they were."

I nodded. "Then at least it's worth a shot. Why don't I drive us?"

"Someone needs to stay here and keep working," Sheila said as she looked at all the bags I'd generated. "Have you gone through everything?"

"No, I need to have space to sort things out, so I thought I'd take them home with me. I was going to ask you first, of course."

"I don't know," Sheila said, the doubt heavy in her voice. "I hate the thought of anything leaving the house until I have a clearer idea of where things stand."

Maddy spoke up. "Why don't I go to the bank with you, and Eleanor can stay here and keep sorting through those papers?"

I was about to protest when Sheila said, "That would be perfect. Thank you both so much. Just let me grab my purse."

As she ducked into the living room, I said, "Thanks for nothing. I wanted to go to the bank myself. After all, I found the key."

"Does it really matter which one of us goes with her, as long as one of us does? I didn't mean to throw you under the train tracks like that, but I was afraid she was getting ready to say she was going by herself, and then we might never know what was inside. Forgive me?"

"I guess so," I said as I looked at the bags of papers I'd so cavalierly thrown together. If they'd been separated by any type of system before, it was long gone. I was afraid I'd made myself even more work than I'd meant to.

Sheila was at the door again. "Are you coming, Maddy? If you'd rather stay here and work, I could always go by myself. I've got my broken-down old Mercedes parked in the garage."

"Nonsense," I said. "She'd love to go with you. Besides, you don't know anybody in town, so having Maddy with you might expedite things at the bank."

I knew full well they wouldn't, but I was counting on Sheila not knowing that personal contacts went only so far in our banking institutions.

After they were gone, I focused on the bags in front of me. I quickly developed a triage system to deal with the masses of paperwork. One area was for discards, while I put possibly useful information in one of the boxes I'd scavenged away from Maddy. Once the system was in place, I had a neat stack of papers in one box, and half a dozen trash bags on the front porch that were ready for the shredder or the landfill.

I looked over what I'd found and wondered when Maddy and Sheila would return. There were five bank envelopes, each containing two brand-new one-hundred-dollar bills. I'd nearly thrown them away, since they'd been buried in banded stacks of fifty envelopes from the same bank, the others all empty. After finding the first two bills by accident, I'd slowed my search until I was certain I'd found every bill in the stacks. It told me one thing besides the fact that Richard liked to have cash around the house: he liked to hide things in plain sight, something I was going to have to keep in mind as I kept searching. The bills weren't the most unusual of my finds, though. I'd also found six separate deposit slips for the same bank where Sheila and my sister now were—each for nine thousand nine hundred ninety dollars, dated the first of each month for the past six months.

Maybe I could catch Maddy while they were still there. I used my cell phone to call her. "Hey, it's me."

"Hi. I should have stayed there with you. This is taking forever."

"Then Sheila's name wasn't on the safety-deposit box account?"

Maddy snapped, "It was there, all right. The problem is, the only employee with the proper key to let us in is on her lunch break, and as of right now, she's seventeen minutes late."

"Sorry about that," I said. "While you're there, have them do a search of Richard's other bank accounts to see if Sheila's name is listed on them as well. I'm willing to bet if she was listed on the box, she'll be in the other accounts, too."

"Fine, it'll give us something to do while we're waiting. That's a good idea. What did you find, a checkbook or something?"

"Or something," I said. I told her about the deposit slips, and she whistled loudly over the phone. "Where did he get that kind of money? That's a lot of cash to keep in a checking account."

"All of them are just under ten grand," I said. "That means the bank doesn't need to report them to the Feds. Richard was hiding something."

"Maybe we should look a little harder as we search," Maddy said.

"I found a thousand dollars in cash already," I said. "Let me talk to Sheila and tell her. She's entitled to a little good news after the past couple of days."

"She's right here," Maddy said.

As Sheila answered, I said, "I've found a thousand dollars in cash here."

"That's so honest of you," Sheila said. "You could have kept it and I never would have known."

"My integrity's worth a lot more than that to me," I said. "It's not my money. It belongs to you now."

"Maybe," Sheila said. "If they ever get the safety-deposit box open, we might find out. You'd think they'd have more than one key for the thing, wouldn't you?"

"What can I say? Small towns have small-town ways sometimes. Consider it some of our local flavor."

"It's certainly not how we do things in Charlotte," she said. "Thanks for your honesty, Eleanor."

"It's my pleasure," I said.

"Hang on a second," Sheila said. "The teller's saying something."

I didn't have a chance to warn her about the large balance there might be in the checking account. I couldn't hear what the teller said, but I did hear a scream as Maddy's phone suddenly went dead.

Two minutes later my cell phone was ringing. I didn't recognize the number in the display, but I had a pretty good idea who was on the other end of the line.

"What happened, Maddy?"

"What, are you psychic now?"

"No, but who else would be calling me. Is Sheila all right?"

Maddy's voice lowered as she explained, "She's

fine. I caught her in time, so she didn't crack her head open on the marble floor. I can't say the same for my cell phone. It's in so many pieces, I doubt we'll ever find them all."

"She fainted when she heard about the money, right?" I asked.

"Your thousand bucks? Not even close."

"Maddy, I'm talking about the bank balance. Did you hear how much it was?"

"No, the teller wrote it down on a piece of paper, but Sheila told me as soon as she came to again. It's close to a hundred grand, and Sheila's not going to have to pay a penny of taxes on it."

"What do you mean?"

"She and her brother co-owned the account, so legally, it's not part of the estate. She gets it all without going through the hassle of a will."

"You know, I usually don't understand fainting spells, but I've got to give her that one. I'd probably pass out myself with that kind of news."

"Don't worry, I'm leaving you all my money, too. It's in a shoe box under my bed, in case something happens to me."

"Wouldn't it be safer in a bank?" I asked, touched that my sister had thought of me.

"No, I tried to open an account with it, but they said I needed more than nine dollars, so I'll have to wait till next payday."

"You're a riot," I said.

"Hang on a second. I'm going to have to call you back. The assistant manager just came back from lunch, so we should be able to get into the box now. I'll call you back later."

She hung up before I could say a word. If

Richard Olsen had close to a hundred grand in his checking account, how much must be in his safety-deposit box? I tried to imagine how it must feel to have that much money, but I had a hard time wrapping my mind around it. As I waited to hear back from Maddy, I tried to keep working, but in all honesty, I was more than a little distracted by the news, even though I'd seen some of the deposit slips myself. As I looked around the house, I had to wonder, if he had that much money, why didn't he live any better than he did? Sure, I knew Richard liked flashy clothes and had driven a nice new car, but the man had nothing to reflect the amount of money he had.

Why would he do that? Was he modest, or was it that he couldn't afford to let people know how much he had? And if he was hiding it, that begged the question, why? He was in sales for an industrial shredding service in Raleigh, based in Timber Ridge. I couldn't imagine him making anywhere near that kind of money, even given people's heightened levels of paranoia these days.

My cell phone rang again, and I saw that it was the same number Maddy had called me from earlier.

"What was it full of? Hundred-dollar bills?" I asked.

"No, there were two rolls of pennies there, and one roll of nickels."

"You're kidding," I said as I slumped down on the couch. "Are they supervaluable or something?"

"Not that we could tell. One of the tellers is a coin buff, so she offered to look at the rolls. The most valuable coins were a few wheat pennies, but he barely had enough value to cover the cost of the box for a month."

"And that's it? There was nothing else?"

"Just some scribbles on an old, torn envelope," Maddy said. "That's all there was inside."

"Could that be of value?" I was trying to come up with some reason Richard had so carefully guarded the safety-deposit box, given that its contents were so meager.

"I doubt it, but we'll bring it with us along with the coins. We're just getting ready to leave. I've got to say, Sheila wasn't all that upset about finding the coins. I think she's still in shock over the hundred grand. I know I would be."

"Forget it, I'm not worth anything near that amount, especially in cash."

"Yeah, but I have hope for you," she said.

"Hang on a second," I said. "I just had a thought. See when Richard was in his safety-deposit box last. It should be listed on the signature card."

My sister was many things, but stupid was nowhere near the list, though headstrong was somewhere near the top. "That makes sense. You want to see if he cleaned it out recently. I'll go check."

And then she hung up on me again. We were going to have to replace her cell phone, and quickly. It was driving me crazy that the number was being blocked and I wasn't able to contact her whenever I wanted. What had the age of technology done to me, making me so dependent on instant access to nearly everyone I knew?

Maddy called back, and without even saying hello, she said, "He came by three days ago, and one of the tellers said he was acting odd."

"How so?"

"Normally he was a friendly, open guy—you know that as well as anybody. Well, when he came in the last time, she said he looked rattled by something. From the way she tells it, he barely made eye contact with her. Anyway, he had a briefcase with him that looked like it had gained some real weight by the time he left. I looked at the signature on the card, but it was hard to tell he'd written it, his hand had been shaking so badly."

"But it was him and not someone else, right?" Could someone else have come in and cleaned out the contents, whatever they were?

"Oh, yes, she's certain, because he usually hit on her when she let him into his box, but this time, nothing. What do you think it means?"

"I'm not sure yet, but it's clearly another piece of the puzzle," I said. "Are you two coming straight back here?"

"No, we've got one more stop to make. Sheila's buying me a phone to replace the one she dropped." Maddy lowered her voice, then added, "Come on, it's not like she can't afford it. The woman's loaded now. She withdrew every dime in the account and opened a new one in only her name. The man's been dead less than a day and she's making sure nobody touches a cent of his money."

"Don't take advantage of her," I said, but I was talking to dead air.

As I waited for them to return, I decided that there was time for a little more digging. Who knew what else I might find while I had the house all to myself.

* * *

I was about to give up hope of finding anything else by the time they got back when a balled-up piece of paper caught my eye in the trash can by the desk. When I flattened the sheet, I saw that it was clearly a handwritten note, but done in block letters. Who writes in block letters anymore after the third grade? The words written there weren't done by a schoolkid, though. The note said, "PAY, OR RISK BEING EXPOSED," only "exposed" was spelled "expoced." That explained why Richard had started over, but why was he writing the note? It was pretty clear he was blackmailing someone, but whom? And where was the proof? Was that why he'd cleaned out his safety-deposit box? Or was the evidence still hidden somewhere in the house? If it was, I needed to redouble my efforts. It could quite possibly lead us to the real killer and get me off the hook. I folded the sheet into quarters, then stuffed it into my purse. I didn't want to be the one to tell Sheila that her late brother had also been a blackmailer, at least until I had more proof than the note. I kept digging through the trash, and buried in the bottom was an envelope that had been torn up by hand. I nearly missed it at first, but then I saw a corner had "P.O. BOX 10" on it, with a Timber Ridge zip code. Was that significant? Could it be how Richard had contacted his victim, or was it his mail drop? Either way, it bore looking into, so I slid it into my purse as well, just as I heard the front door open.

Maddy called out, "We're back."

I buried the latest evidence deeper into my purse, then left the room to greet them.

As I walked out into the living room, Sheila held out her hand.

"Let me have it," she demanded, and I wondered how she knew I'd found another clue.

Chapter 5

"I'm not sure I know what you're talking about," I said, trying to meet Sheila's gaze with a steady look of my own. If she'd seen me tuck something into my purse, I was dead. But how had she managed it, without Maddy warning me sooner?

"The money you mentioned. Surely you haven't forgotten it already," Sheila said.

I nearly let out a sigh of relief as I said, "It's on the desk. Let me get it for you."

"That's fine, you can stay right here. I'll get it myself," Sheila said as she brushed past me and moved into the office.

"What's going on?" I whispered to Maddy the second Sheila was out of range. "What happened on the way home?"

"I don't know," Maddy admitted. "We bought a replacement telephone, and then she clammed up on me."

"Did you spend too much of her money?"

"Give me some credit. We got the exact same phone I had, okay? They were even able to reprogram my old numbers into it. The outer casing was totally smashed, but they didn't have any trouble salvaging the data inside."

"So why her change of heart?"

Maddy didn't have time to answer as Sheila came back out, counting the bills in her hand.

"It's all there," I said, maybe just a little too defensively.

"Just checking," Sheila said as she stared at the money, then at me. "I appreciate your help, but I've decided this is too big a job for us to tackle. I'm hiring someone in the morning to do the work and boil the papers down to a manageable size."

"We don't mind helping," Maddy said.

"Honestly, we're glad to do it," I added.

"Thanks, but I've made up my mind." She grabbed two twenties from her wallet, then handed one to me and another to my sister. "That's for your help."

I wanted to tell her that if I'd been looking to make a little money, I could have just held on to the grand I'd found, but I doubted that would get me what I wanted, either. "You don't need to pay us. We were glad to do it."

"Okay, if that's the way you feel," Sheila said as she quickly withdrew the offer of even that paltry payment. "Now, if you two will excuse me, it's been a long day."

Actually, we hadn't been working very long, but the hint was obvious.

Sheila walked us outside, and I saw those stacks of newspapers on the porch. "What are you going to do with those?" I asked.

"Throw them in the garbage," she said.

"Let me at least recycle them for you," I said.

"If you feel you must," Sheila said. She stepped back inside, then clicked the dead bolt in place, clearly done with us.

Maddy grinned at me as she said, "Thanks, you just cost me twenty bucks."

"I'll pay you back when we leave," I said. "In the meantime, grab a few bundles of newspapers and put them in the back of my car."

"You and your green consciousness," she grumbled as she did what I'd asked. When we had the porch cleared, the back of my Subaru was noticeably weighed down.

"Where to now?" I asked as we got in.

"I'd like to go home and take a quick nap, but I know that's not happening. Sorry the safety-deposit box was a bust. I had high hopes for that trip. I should have let you go after all." She paused, then said, "There's something I need to show you, though."

"Me first," I said. "If you'd let me go to the bank, I wouldn't have found this." I pulled out the blackmail demand and handed it to her as I drove away from the curb.

She looked at the letter, then looked up. "Hey, my car's back at the pizzeria, remember?"

"I know, but why don't you come home with me while I shower? We can talk about what we found, then go back to the Slice and figure out what to do."

"Fine," she said as she put the note back in my purse. "I didn't get dirty at all." As I drove, she said, "So, it appears that Richard was digging himself into all kinds of trouble."

"That's what it looks like," I admitted.

"Hang on a second. Do you think that's what he was doing at the bank when he cleaned out his safety-deposit box? Was he getting ready to expose someone for not meeting his demands?"

"It might be," I said. Then I remembered the return address. "I found something else in the trash can. Look for an address in my purse."

She glanced inside my bag, then said, "You're kidding, right? I'm not going to risk whatever might be lurking in there."

"Don't be such a sissy. Okay, I'll tell you. There's an address, P.O. Box 10 in Timber Ridge, and I've got a feeling it's got something to do with this mess."

"Fine, we'll just ask the employee behind the post office counter to tell us who owns the box."

I shook my head. "That's a violation of federal law, Maddy. I doubt even you could bat your eyebrows enough to get that particular bit of information."

"Then how do we find out?"

"I've got an idea," I said. "Why don't we send the box number a bright orange envelope, then watch the post office to see who picks it up?"

Maddy asked, "What are we supposed to do, stand in the lobby waiting to see who goes to the box? We don't have that kind of manpower, Eleanor."

"Do you have any ideas yourself?"

She shrugged, then said, "Let me think about it."

By the time we got to my place, Maddy said, "I've got an idea, but it might be a little risky."

"What did you have in mind?"

She looked at me, then said, "We could always send a note asking the holder to contact us."

"Have you lost your mind? If we're right, whoever has that box could very well be a killer. Do you want to invite them into our lives? That's just nuts."

"We wouldn't be as open about it as that," Maddy said. "Let me think about how we could do it without giving ourselves away while we're at it."

"You do that," I said as I parked the car. "In the meantime, I'm going to unload these newspapers, then take a shower."

"Would you like me to help? I'll get dirty if you insist."

I laughed. "They're not that dirty. With both of us working, we'll be done in no time at all."

"And then what?"

"We keep digging," I said. "I don't know what choice we really have."

Twenty minutes later I was clean from my shower and wearing fresh clothes, but I'd come no closer to figuring out who had killed Richard Olsen. Maddy was waiting impatiently for me in the living room.

"That took forever."

I looked at my watch. "I'm ten minutes short of half an hour."

She smiled softly, and I knew she'd been holding out on me. "What else did you find out when we were investigating?" I asked.

"Me? What makes you think I found something?"

"Come on, Maddy, I know that look. Now come clean."

She nodded. "I found this in Richard's suit jacket pocket when I was going through his clothes."

I took the lavender envelope and immediately caught a whiff of perfume. I knew the fragrance but couldn't place it.

Maddy said, "It's Obsession. Remember when I went through that phase?"

"It's pretty hard to forget," I said. I opened the envelope and took out a sheet of matching lavender stationery. The handwriting was so florid it was hard to read at first, until I managed to decipher the wide loops and exaggerated swirls. It said,

> *My love,*
> *I can't wait to hold you in my arms again. Steve will be out of town next Monday, and I hope desperately that you'll find your way into my bed.*
> *With much anticipation,*
> *Faith*

Maddy was staring at me, and as I looked up at her again, she said, "The names are pretty unmistakable, aren't they? That's quite a bombshell."

"It's TNT," I said. "Why didn't you tell me about this before?"

"I just opened it ten minutes ago," she said. "Honestly, I nearly forgot about finding it until then."

I tapped the letter with one finger. "Why was Richard hitting on me when he was already seeing the mayor's wife on the side? Faith is always so prim and proper, I never would have believed she had it in her to step out on Steve Baron."

"The man owns a gun shop," Maddy said. "How dumb was Richard, anyway?"

"He was stabbed, remember?"

Maddy said, "Steve's not stupid. He probably knew if he shot Richard, he'd be arrested before morning."

"I'm not sure that's true," I said. "People acting in the heat of the moment don't always act rationally. I had no idea Richard and Faith were fooling around. Did you?"

"No," Maddy admitted. "But that letter's pretty hard to deny, isn't it?"

"Truthfully, I'm not quite sure how to handle this," I said as I slipped the letter back into its envelope. "We can't exactly walk up to the mayor's wife and ask her if she or her husband killed Richard Olsen, can we?"

"No, but we can't let it go, either. Do you think this is what the blackmail was about?"

I bit my lower lip, then said, "Do you think Richard seduced her, and then when he got tired of her, he started blackmailing the woman? That's dangerous business."

"Look what happened to him," Maddy said. "It fits."

"So do half a dozen other explanations," I said. "But that doesn't make any of them right."

"Then we keep digging," Maddy said.

We got into my car and headed back to the pizzeria.

Maddy said, "What should we do now?"

"I thought we might make a pizza and spend some time figuring this out."

"Sounds good," Maddy said. "You know me— I'm always interested in food."

I parked in back, more out of habit than anything else. There were probably a dozen spots in front of the pizzeria, but I could barely ever bring myself to park in one, even when we were open for business, just in case a customer needed one. I wondered if I'd ever have another customer, or if I'd served my last slice. I started to unlock the back door when I realized that I hadn't removed the barricaded bar.

"We've got to go around to the front," I said.

Maddy nodded, and as we walked through the shortcut, I saw that the parking area was jammed. At least someone was making money.

Then when we turned the corner, I realized that there was a cluster of people standing in front of the pizzeria.

"What's going on?" I asked Maddy.

"I don't have a clue," she said, "but it appears that we're going to have to put our investigation on hold."

As I walked through the dozen folks standing in line, I said, "Sorry about that. We're running late, but we'll be open in a few minutes."

There were some grumbles, but nobody left, which was a good thing.

As Maddy and I went inside to get ready to open the pizzeria, I wondered what had brought everyone there. Had they come for the food, or did they want to get a close-up look at a killer? Either way, I was going to do my best to feed them, and make a profit while I still could.

"Oh, no. We don't have any pizza dough," I said as I walked into the kitchen. I made fresh dough every morning, and we nearly always used it all by the end of the day. Once a week I discarded any dough I'd frozen during the week so I could start fresh again on Monday morning, but I knew for a fact that the freezer was empty at the moment.

Maddy grinned at me. "Remember, I made some this morning as soon as I got here. Check the fridge."

"How did you have time to do it before I got here?" I asked as I opened the refrigerator door.

"I might have rushed it a little," she said. "I used my recipe, not yours."

Under normal circumstances I would not have been pleased. Maddy's dough skipped a few steps, and I thought you could taste it in the finished product, though no one else seemed to be able to. But at the moment, I had two choices: use Maddy's, or send everyone home.

I hugged her briefly, something she was clearly not expecting.

"What was that for?"

"For saving us tonight," I said.

She was clearly uncomfortable with the show of affection.

"It was my turn," she said. "I'll get the ingredients, and you turn on the oven."

We had a conveyor oven, though Joe and I had lusted after a wood-fired one when we'd first opened the pizzeria. The wood oven wasn't as expensive, but neither my husband nor I had wanted to get into the firewood business. The conveyor oven would heat up in fifteen minutes—it was pretty much foolproof—and if we needed to, we could churn out a lot of pizzas in a hurry. The negatives were that it was expensive to repair, the fan was louder than I would have liked, and it had been a pretty substantial investment when we could ill afford it.

Still, normally it was a pretty good match to our business.

I preheated the oven, then started shaping crusts as Maddy worked on toppings. She'd prepared a nice mix earlier that morning, so we were in good shape.

"I'm going to go ahead and open up," I said.

Maddy wiped her hands on a dishrag and took off her apron. "I'll take care of it. You stay in the kitchen, and I'll handle the front. We can do this, but you have to turn down deliveries tonight. I know you don't want to, but we don't have much choice."

"To be honest with you, I don't know if I'll ever be able to deliver another pizza in my life." The memory of what had happened last night was still fresh in my mind, and I doubted it would ever go away.

"It'll be all right," Maddy said as she touched my shoulder lightly. "Now, let's make some pizza and pay the rent."

"Sounds great," I said, and I meant it. Creating pizzas had pulled me out of tailspins before, and that was what I needed now. Thank goodness all of my customers hadn't deserted me.

Maddy opened the doors, and I kept myself busy while I waited for the first order. I'd just gotten things ready when Josh Hurley—one of my few remaining employees—walked into the back.

"I'm ready to get to work," Josh said as he grabbed an apron.

I put my hand on his shoulder. "Sorry. I can't let you."

"What do you mean? What did I do?" Then his face clouded up. "You talked to Dad, didn't you?"

"He doesn't want you working here, Josh."

"He's not in control of my life," Josh snapped. I could see that he'd inherited his father's temper, though he hadn't yet learned to master it as well as his father had.

"Until you're out on your own, he is," I said. "I can't afford to give him another reason to come after me."

"I took your side!" Josh yelled. "I stood up for you, and now you're turning your back on me?"

"Josh, listen to me. This is for the best."

"Mom said you'd do this, but I didn't believe her." He threw the apron at my feet, then stormed out.

Maddy came rushing back. "What was that all about?"

"Josh and I had a difference of opinion."

"Is that what you're calling it?" she asked. "I half expected to find you crumpled up on the floor back here."

"Maddy, go take care of our customers. I'm fine."

"Okay," she said, though it was pretty clear she didn't believe me. "Here's what I've got so far."

She put the orders on magnetic clips and stuck them on the wall where we had a metal strip. I studied the orders so far and got to work on the pizzas. We offered fresh ingredients on our pies, and I made the sauce myself. After I spread it out evenly onto the four crusts I had waiting, I dealt the toppings out like they were playing cards, then drowned each pizza with the whole-milk mozzarella and white cheddar blend of cheese my customers preferred.

After I slid them onto the conveyor, one after the other, I started on the sandwiches, making two Turkey Clubs, a Garlic Chicken Sub, and a Raging Panini with every hot pepper I had in stock included. It kept me busy enough for a time that I nearly forgot about Richard Olsen, at least for the moment. The phone rang a few times, but I let the machine pick it up. Not only was I too busy to take orders over the phone, but I was in no mood to tell folks we weren't delivering. It was a fair part of our business income, but for tonight, we were going to have to do without it.

Maddy came back to pick up a pizza and said, "Someone wants to see you."

"I'm not in the mood to be on public display," I said.

"I think you'll want to make an exception."

"Why would I want to do that?" And why was she suddenly smiling? "Maddy, what are you up to?"

"Me? Nothing. I can't believe you'd accuse me of being up to something without any proof."

"I'm sorry," I said contritely. "It's just been one of those days."

"I accept your apology. Hang on a second."

Maddy vanished for a second, then came back with David Quinton.

"Hi, Eleanor. Sorry to bother you, but I just wanted to see how you were doing."

David and I had gone to high school together, and we had even dated a few times before I'd gotten involved with Kevin Hurley. There still was animosity between the two men all these years later, at least from what I'd seen, though I doubted it could possibly still be over me.

David had aged well, his boyish good looks transforming him into a handsome man, with a strong chin, a very fit body, and a pair of baby-blue eyes that had melted more hearts around town than just mine fifteen years ago. David had never married—devoting himself to his business instead— and eleven months after I'd lost Joe, he'd come calling on me, stating his wish to get reacquainted. I'd rebuffed him, the pain of losing my husband still fresh in my heart, but he'd been persistent, asking me out once a month every month since then. Why he didn't give up and move on was beyond me, but my refusals had done nothing to decrease his ardor. Maddy thought I was crazy for turning him down, but then again, she hadn't had Joe.

"Hi, David. It's sweet of you to check on me, but I'm fine, honestly, I am."

"Do you need help hiring a good lawyer? I'm happy to do anything I can; all you have to do is ask."

"Thanks, but Bob Lemon is representing me," I said.

"He's a good man," David said as he nodded. "Isn't there anything I can do?" He looked around the kitchen and saw that I was alone. "I'm handy with a knife and a cutting board, so I can help you back here."

"I've got it covered," I said, trying to keep the smile off my face. He was like a puppy in his earnestness, and I felt my heart finally start to soften toward him some. It was a slow thaw, but a thaw nonetheless.

He still wasn't going to give up. "Deliveries, then. I can surely do that for you."

I looked him steadily in the eye. "David, I appreciate the offer, honestly, I do, but I'm fine. Everything's under control."

His features softened for a moment. "Eleanor, you don't always have to be so strong and independent. There's something to be said for letting someone else see that you can be vulnerable, too."

"I know," I said. He was right, but I could no more change the way I'd become than I could transform myself into a tall blonde, like my sister had. I just wasn't built for it.

"Don't wait too long," he said.

"Why? If I do, are you finally going to take my advice and start asking other women out?"

"This isn't about me. It's about you. I'd hate to see you close yourself off to life after Joe. He wouldn't have wanted you to do that, and you know it."

"That's enough of that," I said, suddenly cold. He had no right to bring Joe into our conversation. "Now, if you'll excuse me, I've got work to do."

He looked so sad at my response that I almost apologized, but I couldn't bring myself to do it.

Instead, he left the kitchen looking as though he'd just lost his last friend.

Maddy came back thirty seconds later, a scowl plastered on her face. "What did you do to that man? He looked like he was getting ready to go look for the tallest building he could find so he could throw himself off it."

I waved a hand in the air. "I don't want to talk about it."

Maddy wasn't having any of that, though. "I don't care what you want, Eleanor. He's a good man, and he deserves better than the way you treat him."

"Do you like him? If you want him, he's all yours."

"Don't be thick," Maddy said, her voice rising with every word. "He wants you. What did you say to him to make him slink out of here like he did?"

"He brought up Joe," I said, trying to choke back my tears. I wasn't going to cry, I promised myself. I wasn't.

Maddy's voice softened. "Kiddo, nobody in the world loved your husband as much as you did, but I had to be next in line. He was a great guy, but he wasn't a saint."

"I know that," I said, fighting to keep the quiver out of my voice. "But he was mine."

Maddy took my hands in hers. "He's gone, Eleanor. You know as well as I do that he wouldn't want to see you like this. He wanted you to be happy."

"I'm happy," I said as I pulled a hand from hers and wiped a few tears from my cheeks. I hadn't even realized that I'd started crying.

"Yeah, you look overjoyed," she said.

I pulled my other hand away. "Listen, I appreciate your concern, but I'm fine." As I sniffled a little, I asked, "Don't you have customers to wait on?"

"You're as stubborn as Dad was, you know that, don't you?" Maddy asked.

"Well, you're as nosy as Mom," I said.

Maddy shook a finger at me. "There's no need to be mean. I'm going back to work."

"That's a good idea," I said.

After she was gone, there was a lull in the orders, giving me too much time on my hands, and too many thoughts swirling around in my head. How did everyone feel they had the right to tell me what Joe would have wanted? He was my husband, my best friend, and my one shot at happiness. Was that true, though? Could I love another man? Was there room in what was left of my shattered heart to let someone else in? I didn't honestly know the answer, and I wasn't certain I ever would.

It was all too hard, too much to deal with at the moment, and as I longed for enough new orders to distract me, Maddy came back. There was no sign of our previous conversation in her gaze, though I was sure mine was still displaying it like a billboard by the side of the road.

"I hope you've got more dough," she said.

I'd recounted the rounds we had left. "We've got enough for fourteen more crusts," I said. "Surely that's enough to see us through the rest of the night."

"Twelve will do just fine," she said. "Carrie Wilkes just came in and ordered twelve specials to go. I told her we could do it."

"Let me get started on it," I said as I began pulling out balls of dough. "Is she having a party or something?"

"Or something," Maddy said. "She's taking them

to Rick's dorm room over at the college. I'll go tell her you'll get started on them right now."

Carrie would never learn, but I wasn't about to say anything to her. She had been divorced for sixteen years, leaving her with a son to raise alone, and a stack of bills that continually grew. She'd started an office-cleaning business so she could work at night while her sister watched Rick, and she'd built up the company until she had branches spread out over Virginia, North Carolina, and Tennessee. Carrie had insisted that her son go to North Carolina Mountain University, a forty-minute drive from Timber Ridge. He'd agreed but had set some ground rules that Carrie continually broke. I wasn't sure how he'd feel about getting the pizzas, but I wasn't about to challenge her on it. Carrie had developed a hair trigger when it came to conversations about her son. Still, the more I thought about it, the more I realized that I couldn't do it to Rick. He'd worked for me during high school—over his mother's protests that he didn't need a job—and I had a great deal of affection for him. He'd given me his number at college, as many of my alums had given me theirs.

I called him up and heard party music in the background.

"Hey, Rick. It's Eleanor Swift."

"Eleanor, how's life?" There was a pause, and then he laughed. "You're calling about my mom, aren't you?"

"Did you know she just ordered a dozen pizzas?"

"Yeah, it was at my request. I'm inviting the whole floor to my room for pizza, and yours is the best anywhere."

"You're just a little prejudiced," I said. "I'll start on them now."

"Thanks," he said, "and thanks for checking with me. She's getting better, honestly. I've got her weaned down to one visit a week."

"That still sounds like a lot," I said. I remembered the sense of freedom I'd felt during my freshman year of college, and how much I'd cherished my privacy from my parents and from Maddy.

"Are you kidding? She wanted to go to class with me the first week I was here. I'd say we're making great progress."

If he knew about what had happened to Richard Olsen, he didn't mention it, which was fine with me. For once, it was nice talking to someone without having that shadow looming over me.

"Okay, they'll be on their way soon. You should have them in about an hour."

"Sounds great. Bye."

After he hung up, I got started on the pizzas. Then after I slid them onto the conveyor I began to clean up. It was close to ten, our regular closing time, and I was tired, though I'd put in quite a bit less than a full day. It was probably from the strain of trying to find a killer and run a business at the same time. Maddy and I were going to have to figure out a way to balance the two, or I'd be worn thin in no time at all. Still, it was good having customers back in A Slice of Delight. It had felt less than whole without the sounds of people enjoying themselves there. By the time we'd ushered the last customer out the door, I was ready to go home.

But we still had work to do. Maddy grabbed a dishrag and started wiping the tables down as I ran our register reports and balanced our cash in the drawer. We'd had a good night, but it had meant a great deal more to me than the money we'd made. I'd been back in my element, making pizzas and sandwiches and, for the most part, not worrying about anything else.

The totals matched, and Maddy and I managed to finish cleaning the place up in record time.

I was feeling pretty good about the world when we got to our cars in back. Hers was pristine, but my driver's-side window had been shattered by a cinder block that now lay on the front seat.

Someone had painted "KILLER" in red on the block, and I could feel my heart pounding in my chest. Some folks had been willing to give me the benefit of the doubt, but it appeared that some were still under the impression that I had something to do with Richard Olsen's death.

And there wasn't a thing I could do about it.

Chapter 6

I was reaching for my keys when Maddy grabbed my hand. "What do you think you're doing?"

"I'm going to get the cinder block out and drive home."

"We've got to call the police," she said.

"Why? I'm pretty sure you can't get fingerprints off a concrete block. What good will it do?"

"The chief needs to know that someone's threatening you." I'd never seen Maddy so eager to call Kevin Hurley in my life.

"He's just going to say it was a prank," I said. "It's an exercise in futility."

"Call him," Maddy said.

"Fine, if it will make you happy."

I dialed the police station and was told by Helen Murphy that the chief was off duty. Didn't they ever let the poor woman go home? "Okay, then I'll tell you. This is Eleanor Swift. Someone threw a concrete block through my car window, and they spray painted 'killer' on it before they chucked it.

Do you need to send someone out, or should I just forget about it?"

"Are you still at the Slice?" Helen asked.

"For the next two minutes. Then I'm going home."

"Don't do anything until we get someone over there."

She hung up on me, and I turned to Maddy. "I still don't think it's that big a deal. I'm guessing someone did it as a prank."

"It's not a good idea leaving," Maddy said. "We have to give them more than two minutes."

"We'll give them all the time they need," I said as I pounded my hands together. "Can we at least wait in your car? It's cold out here."

"I don't see what that could hurt," Maddy said. We got in her car, and she turned on the heater. After a few minutes, it began to blow out warm air, and I finally began to warm up.

"Who would do something like that?" Maddy asked as she stared at my shattered window.

"Somebody with too much time on their hands, and not enough sense," I said. "If I had to guess, I'd say alcohol was involved, too."

"You seem to be taking this pretty calmly," my sister said.

"What do you want me to do, go hide in a corner until it's safe to come out again? To be honest with you, I half expected something like this to happen."

"I don't understand you sometimes," Maddy said.

"Right back at you," I replied amicably.

We were still chatting when a police car flashed

its lights as it drove silently toward us. Maddy and I got out of the car, and I was surprised to see the chief of police himself get out of his cruiser.

"I thought you were off duty," I said.

"I am," he admitted. "Josh stormed off after he chewed me out for talking to you, and I was kind of hoping I'd find him so we could talk about it."

"He's a good kid, Kevin. He'll be all right once he calms down."

Kevin gave me a burst of his lopsided grin. "Like father, like son, I know. Don't think my old man doesn't laugh about it all the time." He dropped the conversation, then shined an industrial-sized black flashlight into my front seat. "Unbelievable."

"I know. I really feel the love."

Maddy stared at us both. "Have you two lost your minds? This is clearly a threat, and you both need to take it seriously."

"It's not a threat," Kevin and I said in almost perfect unison.

She shrugged, then said, "If you need me, I'll be in my car."

After she got back in, Kevin said, "I'll get the cinder block. Then we can patch your window with some cardboard until you can get it fixed. Sorry this had to happen, Eleanor."

"It didn't have to happen; someone did it on purpose," I said. "But thanks for the thought, anyway."

Kevin just shrugged, and after he put on gloves, he gingerly reached down and picked up the block, carried it to the trunk of his car, then returned with a piece of cardboard and some duct tape. As he taped it in place, he said, "Can Maddy take you home, or would you like a ride?"

"I have no desire to ride around town in a squad car, no matter what time of day or night it is," I said with a hint of laughter in my voice.

"Fine, I just thought I'd offer."

I could see he was in some real pain about his son's reaction to his banishment. "Don't worry, he'll be fine."

"I just wish I could believe that," Kevin said as he got into the squad car. Then he drove away.

I rejoined Maddy and said, "How about a ride home? I'll call Bob Pickering in the morning." Bob ran an auto repair service, but he was much more than that. His realm of problem solving went well beyond the normal service, diving into problems from where to hold a wedding to when to plant peas in the garden.

"Would you like to stay with me again this evening?" she asked. "We can make another night of it."

"No, thanks for the offer, but I need to go home. It's where I belong."

Maddy nodded, and as she drove to my place, she said, "You know, I could always stay with you."

"I'm fine, Maddy."

"Okay," she said. "But I'm going in with you when we get there to make sure everything's all right."

"What are we going to do if it's not?"

She laughed. "Are you kidding? The Spencer women can handle anything."

"Yeah, but I'm a Swift now," I said.

"You were a Spencer first, though," she said.

* * *

Fortunately, as Maddy and I went through the house, it was clear that the cinder-block thrower hadn't ventured to my home.

Once Maddy was gone—with my reassurances that I would call her at the first sight of trouble—I took another long shower and went to bed. With everything that had happened, it was amazing that I dropped off so quickly, but that was another testament to how the turmoil of the day had affected me.

I managed to sleep through the night and didn't wake up until my alarm clock shook me from a deep and dreamless sleep at seven the next morning. We didn't have to be at the pizza parlor until nine, so that gave us a little time to do more digging around town. With the clues we'd found at Richard Olsen's place, we certainly had enough places to start looking.

I'd just gotten out of the shower when I heard my doorbell. After donning my robe and wrapping my hair up in a towel, I peeked outside and saw Maddy standing there, holding two coffees and a bag of something.

"Hey, you're actually up?" I asked. My sister was notorious for her ability to sleep in if given the least bit of notice.

"I got up before you, it looks like," she said as she walked inside. "Have you had breakfast yet?"

"No, I just need a few minutes to get ready and we can go." I took the coffee from her, enjoyed that first sip, then gestured to the bag. "Is there something good in there for me, too?"

"Cinnamon buns, highly caloric and extremely

decadent. If you want to pass, you won't hurt my feelings."

"If I'm ever near death, wave one of Paul's cinnamon buns under my nose. If that doesn't rouse me, you have my blessing to go ahead and bury me."

I made a grab for the bag, but Maddy pulled it out of my reach. "I thought you were getting dressed first."

"That was before I knew what we were having for breakfast."

"Clothes first, and then we eat."

I broke my previous record for getting ready and met her in the kitchen nook as she was halfway through with her treat.

"Your hair has to be dry, too," she said with a mouthful of bun.

"You said get dressed, so I got dressed. Now, are you going to hand mine over, or are we going to start the day with trouble?"

She laughed as she tossed me the bag. "I know when I'm licked."

I took my first bite right out of the bag, before I grabbed a plate or even bothered to sit down. It was just as good as I remembered, the still-warm bread with hints of cinnamon, and the icing sweet enough to smell from ten yards away.

"Do you eat standing up all the time when I'm not here?"

I nodded. "There are fewer calories consumed if you eat over the sink. Didn't you know that?"

She smiled. "Not until just now. I'll have to try that myself."

My sister was notorious for putting out an entire formal place setting, even when she was dining alone. She got some great bargains buying discontinued patterns at china shops, since she rarely bought more than two of anything. It made her dinnerware an eclectic mix, but it suited Maddy's personality, so it worked for her.

As we ate, I said, "I figure we've got about an hour and a half before we get to the Slice. Where should we start?"

"I don't know about you, but I want to talk to Faith Baron," Maddy said. "There's nothing like a lover having the passion to kill to arouse my suspicions."

"Or the wronged husband," I said. "Steve could have done it, but I don't think Faith has it in her."

Maddy pointed the remnant of her cinnamon bun at me. "But then again, did you think there was the slightest chance she was having an affair with Richard Olsen before I found that letter?"

"No," I admitted. "I didn't see that coming. So, we talk to Faith and Steve Baron."

"But not at the same time," Maddy said.

"Of course not. Who else is on our list?"

She finished her bite, then said, "I'd love to know who he was blackmailing, and where all that money came from. You should have seen Sheila's face when she saw how much money was in Richard's checking account. I thought she was having a heart attack."

I thought about that a moment, then asked, "How sure are you that what you saw was sincere?"

"Pretty sure, why?"

"I'm just thinking, if she knew she was on that checking account, and how much was really in there, it would make a pretty nice motive for murder, don't you think?"

"She wasn't faking it," Maddy insisted. "I caught her when she passed out, remember? She was all dead weight."

I took a bite, then had another sip of coffee. "Okay, what if the size of the account was a surprise, but not the fact that she was included? Could that be why she fainted on you?"

"I suppose it's possible," Maddy allowed.

"As likely as Faith having an affair with Richard Olsen?"

She thought about it, then nodded. "I'd say they're about equal."

"So we add Sheila Olsen to our list. Who else makes the cut?"

"You mean besides the person being blackmailed? There's one thing we never considered."

"What's that?"

Maddy said, "What if Richard earned that money honestly? It's possible, isn't it?"

"Working for a company that shreds paper? I don't see how." Then another thought struck me. "Could he have been stealing from his employer?"

"I guess so," Maddy said. "Though that might be hard to find out. I don't even know who owns the business."

"Neither do I, but it could be an important thing to find out." I finished my bun, then a sudden thought struck home. "I wonder if Richard himself handled any of the documents that had to be shredded."

It didn't take Maddy two seconds to catch on.

"Do you think he was fishing in the documents for reasons to blackmail someone?"

"Or even more than one person," I said. "Who's to say he did it just once?"

Maddy shook her head. "The poor man's dead, and we're doing everything in our power to ruin his reputation before he's even in his grave."

"Come on, he wasn't exactly an angel. It appears that several people had their own reasons to wish him harm."

"And according to the police, even you."

"You don't need to bring that up," I said. "There's one person we've left out so far. We need to put Penny Olsen on the list of suspects."

Penny ran Penny's Antiques, a boutique that offered only the best-quality furniture and other heirlooms.

"That's it, blame it on the ex-wife," Maddy said. "Take the low road, why don't you."

"What, is there some kind of club you all belong to? If there is, are you the president?"

"There's no club," she said. "And just because I've been divorced a few times doesn't mean that I'd be in charge, even if there were one."

"We need to talk to her, Maddy," I repeated.

"Fine, have it your way. Penny's on the list, too." She frowned, then asked, "I wonder if you'll hear another word from Kevin about that block thrown through your car window?"

"That reminds me, I need to call Bob Pickering and have him take care of the Subaru before I forget." I reached for the phone and dialed the number on the list of emergency contacts on the side of my fridge.

Bob answered on the second ring. "Pickering Auto and Problem Solving," he said before he knew who was calling.

"That's good, because I've got a problem I need solved."

He chuckled, then said, "Sorry, Eleanor, I don't get involved in ongoing police investigations." There was a pause, and then he added, "Not usually."

"Don't worry, this isn't going to be bad. I need you to pick up my Subaru in back of the pizzeria and replace the driver's side window. You've still got that spare key, don't you?"

"I do. I can't imagine who would throw a cinder block through your window. What's gotten into people lately?"

"How did you hear about it?"

"I picked it up on my scanner last night. I leave it on when I go to bed. It's like white noise usually, but when your name was mentioned, it woke me right up."

"A block through my window didn't do much for me, either," I said. "Can you take care of it?"

"Consider it done," he said. "I'll have it ready for you in three days."

"Three days?" How could I get along without my car for three days? "Can you do any better than that, Bob?"

He hesitated, then said, "I might be able to squeeze you in today sometime, but it'll be late before I'm finished."

"Tell you what, if you get it done tonight, bring it back to the Slice and I'll make you your favorite pizza on the house as a bonus for prompt service. How does that sound?"

"Like I'm going to be eating dinner on you," he said.

After he hung up, Maddy said, "I don't even want to hear what that was about. I can't believe you're giving away food."

"Joe would have approved," I said. "He had a soft spot in his heart for Bob Pickering."

"Let's face it, your dear late husband liked an awful lot of unusual characters. He collected them like kids used to collect baseball cards."

"I know. That was one of the things I loved most about him. Now that that's taken care of, let me finish drying my hair and we can get started."

"Maybe by then we'll know who we're going to tackle first," Maddy said.

Maddy followed me upstairs, and as I finished my hair and put on my make-up, she sat on the edge of my bed.

My sister looked at me, and after a few seconds, she said, "I think we should tackle the Barons first."

I put down my eyelash curler, something Joe had said looked like a medieval torture device, and stared at her. "Both of them? Don't you think that might get a little dicey? What if Steve doesn't know his wife was having an affair? You know the man's temper. It might not be the best thing giving him a reason to explode."

"I didn't mean it that way. I've got another idea. You talk to Steve, and I'll handle Faith."

"No," I said with enough force to get her attention.

"Okay, settle down. There's no need to get your

shorts in a knot. You can have Faith, and I'll take Steve."

"That's not what I meant," I said. "We're not splitting up, do you understand? This is serious business. If we're right, we're going to be talking to a killer in the next few days, and I don't think it's something we should be doing by ourselves."

"Do you honestly think it will make much difference if there are two of us? It's not like we walk around town armed or anything."

I reached into my purse and pulled out my pepper spray. "I've got this."

Maddy laughed as she reached into her own bag and pulled out a sleek black handheld device. "I'm not unarmed, either."

"What's that?"

She said, "It's a stun gun. I got it at Molly Madison's party."

"As a favor?" I asked as I studied it in her hand.

"It wasn't that kind of party. It's like Tupperware or lingerie. Home-safety parties are popping up all over the place. I'm surprised you weren't invited."

"I probably was," I admitted. "I tend to throw away any mail I get from Molly. That woman could sell Christmas trees to Santa."

"Well, I thought it might be a good investment. Here, take a look at it."

I shied away from the offered device. "I don't think so."

"Come on, don't be such a baby. The safety's on." She stared at it a second, then said, "At least I think it is. Blast it, I need to get that manual out again."

"What's to keep you from stunning yourself every time you reach into your purse to get your car keys?"

"I haven't done it yet," Maddy said with a distinct air of superiority.

"I'm guessing it will just take one time," I said. "Would you put that thing away? You're making me nervous."

She studied it a second, flipped a small switch, then said, "I was right the first time. The safety's on now."

I felt immeasurably better once she put it back in her purse. I glanced in the mirror, saw that I was probably looking as good as I was going to get, and said, "Let's go tackle Faith."

"What do we do, walk up to her front door and ring the bell? How do we know her husband won't answer the door instead? Who knows, she might even still be asleep."

I glanced at my watch. "I doubt that. The woman runs by my house every morning about when I get my Charlotte paper. We wait for her outside, and I'm willing to bet she'll come to us."

"It beats chasing her all over town," Maddy agreed. "But I'm not exactly outfitted for a jog."

"We don't have to. I'm planning to do something to get her attention."

"What are you going to say?" Maddy asked.

"Not a word. I'm just going to hold this up." I picked up the lavender envelope Maddy had found in Richard's pocket and waved it in the air. I could still smell Obsession on it, or perhaps it was just my imagination.

"That should do the trick," my sister agreed.

"When she stops, are we going to accuse her of killing Richard, or do you have some other plan?"

"I'm not sure yet," I admitted. "A lot of what I say will depend on her reaction."

"In other words, we're playing it by ear."

I grinned. "That's what I do best."

"Then we'd better go down and stake out our places," she said.

Once we were outside, I began regretting wearing just a light jacket. It was somewhere around twenty degrees, and the sun was just starting to crest the hill in front of us. Maddy was wearing a toasty, thick coat and had donned gloves and a hat.

"I'm going back in and changing," I said.

"You can't," Maddy answered.

"Why not?"

"Because here comes Faith."

I rubbed my hands together, then got the letter out and prepared to wave it. Faith was on time, as usual. She had to be freezing, wearing a sleek black nylon running suit and a simple ear warmer. Her chestnut brown hair was pulled back into a ponytail, and it bobbed as she ran. I had to admit, she certainly looked fit in the outfit, and I wasn't sure I'd ever really noticed what a good physique she had, since it was normally hidden under layers of clothing.

"Hi, ladies," she said as she approached.

I put the envelope up in the air as I said, "Look what we found."

I swear, she nearly tripped when she saw the letter.

As Faith pulled up short, she asked, "Where did you get that?"

"From Richard Olsen," I said. Well, Maddy had plucked it out of his jacket, but Faith didn't have to know that.

She stood in front of us, and I wouldn't have believed it if I hadn't seen it for myself, but she actually tried to grab it out of my hands. I was so surprised, she might have made it if Maddy hadn't stepped in between us at the last second and blocked her.

"Behave, Faith. You wouldn't want us to show this to anyone else, would you?" I said.

She looked like a balloon suddenly deflating as she nearly crumpled onto the sidewalk. "I don't know what to do," she said as she started to cry.

It was Maddy's turn to look shocked, as I put an arm around Faith's shoulder and said, "Come on inside. I'll make you a cup of tea."

"That would be nice," Faith said.

As I led her back to the house, Maddy kept looking at me as if I'd suddenly sprouted horns, but I chose to ignore her.

Once I had Faith situated in the parlor, I told Maddy quietly, "Would you go make some tea? I might be able to get something out of her if I stay by her side. Unless you'd like to try it yourself."

"No thanks. I'll make the tea," she said.

I came back in and sat beside Faith. "I'm sorry; I didn't mean to blindside you like that." Though I honestly had meant to do exactly that, I wasn't about to admit that to her.

"I knew it would come out. I've been waiting for the police chief to knock on our front door ever since I heard about what happened to Richard." She stared at me for a second through reddened eyes. "I was so mad at you at first. I thought you did it, Eleanor."

"What changed your mind?"

"No offense, but I just don't think you have it in you."

"Why would I be offended by that?" I asked. "I appreciate the compliment."

"But you know what it's like to be accused of murder, don't you? You're going to give that letter to me, aren't you? It's the only right thing to do."

"You know I can't do that," I said. "It's evidence."

"Of what? That the jerk dumped me? I wrote some things I shouldn't have. You would have done the same thing yourself, and you know it. When I said I'd see him dead before he broke another woman's heart, I didn't actually mean it."

What was Faith talking about? There had to be another letter, one that we hadn't found on our impromptu search. I wasn't about to admit that to her, though. But that meant I had to warn Maddy.

"I'll be right back," I said as I started to stand.

She shot out a hand and grabbed my arm with more strength than I'd ever imagined she possessed. "Give me that letter, Eleanor."

I pulled my arm away, not without a significant effort on my part, and stood. "I said no."

"Then we're finished here," she said, just as Maddy came out with a pot of tea, three cups and saucers, and all the extras.

Faith nearly knocked the tray out of Maddy's hands as she left.

My sister looked harshly at me. "What did you say to her?"

"It's not so much what I told her, but what she divulged to me."

Maddy locked the door, put the tray down on the coffee table, then poured two cups. "So, don't hold back on me. I want to hear all of the details."

"It appears that Faith saw that letter and jumped to the wrong conclusion. Evidently she wrote another note to Richard, one not as cordial as the one you found."

"What did she say? Did she break up with him?"

"No, but you're not far off," I said as I took a sip of tea. "Apparently Richard broke up with her, and Faith wasn't very happy about it. She told me she wrote that she'd see him dead before he broke another woman's heart. You know what? I believe her. I'm starting to see a side of Faith I never knew existed." Then I added, "Both Barons are suspects."

"Should we go talk to our dear mayor and see if he denies knowing what was going on between his wife and the murder victim?"

"No, let's give Faith a little more time to stew. I've got a feeling she's not going to give up that easily." I picked up the envelope, then added, "In the meantime, what do we do with this?"

"I've got an idea," Maddy said as she plucked the letter out of my hand. There was a painting in the living room of a huge orchid by a Florida woman named Ruby Hall, which I'd taken a fancy to, and Maddy pulled it off the wall and slipped the letter into the back of the frame. "She'll never look for it there."

"Do you honestly think she'd break into my house to retrieve it?"

Maddy stared at me. "Wouldn't you? It sounds like it's pretty incriminating."

"If we actually had it," I said.

"She doesn't know that, though, does she?"

I grabbed my jacket. "Maybe we should go talk to Sheila. If there are more letters, Faith's going to start looking for them, and Sheila might get hurt in the process."

"Do you think it's that serious?"

I shrugged. "I don't know, but do you really want to take that chance with someone else's life? She deserves to know."

"I suppose you're right," Maddy said. "Who knows, maybe we can talk her into letting us help out again."

"I doubt it."

"At the very least," Maddy said as we walked out onto the covered porch and I locked the front door, "I can try to get that twenty she offered."

"Don't you dare," I said.

Maddy laughed. "Why would I do that? Then I wouldn't be able to hold it over your head anymore."

"There's always that," I said.

As we got into Maddy's car, I missed my Subaru. If I knew Bob, it would already be at his garage, waiting for a new window. If only repairing my reputation was as easy. It was going to take a lot of hard work and a little luck to get the stigma of the murder off me, but I was willing to do whatever it took, including turning the mayor's wife over to the police, if I ever got enough hard evidence that Kevin Hurley would believe.

Chapter 7

"Can we come in?" I asked Sheila as she answered the door to her brother's house.

"I've got a crew working here already," she said. "They're bonded, you know."

"Congratulations," Maddy said, obviously implying she'd dodged a bullet throwing out a couple of petty thieves like us. We'd seen three pristine white vans parked in front upon arriving, all sporting the Clean Team logo on their sides. Inside—at least from what we could see around Sheila—was a team of people outfitted in white jumpsuits methodically wiping out the last trace of Richard Olsen from his former home.

"Thank you," Sheila said, apparently missing the jab entirely. "I understand they're very good."

"And why wouldn't they be?" I asked. "Has a will turned up yet?"

Sheila frowned. "Not yet, but if it doesn't, I've been told that as Richard's closest living relative, I'll inherit everything he has—*had.*"

Was there a hint of avarice in her eyes as she said that?

"Oh," I said, "so you've already spoken with an attorney."

"It seemed the prudent thing to do, given the circumstances," she said.

"It's not Bob Lemon, is it?" Maddy asked.

"No, the woman's name is Armitage. She's from Charlotte, and from what I've heard, she's very good at this sort of thing."

I was about to say something when Maddy piped up, "Who exactly have you been talking to?"

"What do you mean?"

"Well," Maddy said, measuring her words out carefully, "you heard the cleaning crew you're using is good, and then you heard this Armitage woman is the one to call. I'm just wondering who's doing all the talking."

"A kind woman came by the house just after you two left," Sheila said. "She had a great deal of good advice for me, and from what I understand, her standing in the community is beyond reproach."

I had a sinking feeling that I knew exactly who she was talking about. "Faith Baron dropped in on you, didn't she?"

Sheila's eyes widened. "How on earth did you know that?"

"I don't know anything; I'm just guessing," I said.

Sheila took that in for a second, then shrugged as she replied, "I'd love to stand around and chat, but I'm so busy, I'm afraid I don't have the time. If you'll both excuse me, I've got a crew to oversee."

She didn't quite slam the door in our faces, but it was the next best thing.

As we walked back to Maddy's car, my sister said, "It didn't take Faith long to figure out that we know something. I wonder if she's got the cleaning crew and this attorney in her pocket."

"She wouldn't need the attorney, but I'm definitely skeptical about who the cleaners are really working for."

"What can we do about it?" Maddy asked.

"For now? Nothing. Faith's already outmaneuvered us."

Maddy looked back toward the house, then smiled. "Don't be so sure of that. Come on," she said as she started back toward the house.

"Where are we going? She's pretty much told us she's done talking to us."

"This time we're going to the back door."

"Have you completely lost your mind?"

"How could anyone tell," she said with a smile.

Maddy peeked inside one of the side windows, then tapped on the glass. A middle-aged woman with her hair tied up in a bandana noticed her, started to smile, then looked puzzled as my sister motioned her toward the back of the house.

"Do you mind telling me what's going on?" I asked as we walked back to meet her.

"It's just a thought I had," she said.

The woman came out to the back steps and said, "Maddy Spencer, you're going to get me fired. What do you want?"

"Hi, Celeste. It's good to see you, too."

She smiled slightly. "I'm supposed to be working here."

"That's what I want to talk to you about. What are you all doing with everything you find?"

Celeste looked behind her, then said, "We're searching for a will, or any paper that looks like it might be a legal document."

Maddy nodded. "And what about the personal stuff?"

Celeste frowned. "We're tossing it all. The clothes go to Goodwill, anything of value goes into the yard sale pile, and everything else gets bagged and dumped. By tonight, you won't know the poor man even lived here." It was pretty clear what Celeste thought of the speedy exorcism of Richard Olsen's presence.

"Then you won't be breaking any rules if you keep your eyes open for lavender envelopes, or anything else we might be able to use. We'll even feed you."

Celeste bit her lip, then looked hard at me. "That depends. Did you kill this man?"

It was a blunt question I hadn't expected. "No, ma'am, I did not."

Celeste pondered that a moment, then said, "Good enough."

"You believe me?" I asked, just a little incredulous.

"I can tell when people lie to me," she said with a shrug. "It's a knack I've had ever since I was a child."

"Then how can you stand being friends with my sister?" I asked.

"Hey, I'm right here," Maddy said.

Celeste laughed. "Your sister doesn't lie. She just likes to shade the truth to make her stories a little more interesting."

"What's the difference?" I asked, mainly in jest.

She didn't take it that way. "There's fibs, and

then there's deceit—two entirely different things, in my mind."

"Celeste," a voice called out from inside. "Where'd you go?"

"Right here," she called out. Then she said to us, "You two scoot. I'll catch up with you later."

"We'll be at A Slice of Delight," Maddy said.

I saw Sheila coming back toward the kitchen, and I practically had to pull Maddy off the back porch and into the bushes before she came out and caught us. I didn't want Celeste to get fired because of us, and more importantly, I wasn't all that keen about having Sheila discover that we were trying to recruit one of her new employees to our side.

After Sheila was gone, Maddy said, "Come on. Let's go."

"I never wanted to come back here in the first place."

"Eleanor, you've got to admit that it could help, having someone on the inside looking out for us."

"I'm not denying it," I said. As we neared her car, I asked, "How did you meet Celeste, and why didn't I hear about it?"

"You don't know everything about me," Maddy said.

"No? Gosh, and here I thought I did."

She shook her head, and I could see her suppressing a smile. "Celeste and I became friends a few years ago. We took a class together at the community center, and we still do things every now and then."

"What kind of class?"

Maddy started the car, then turned the radio up

to a deafening level. "I'm sorry," she shouted over the music, "I didn't hear the question!"

I reached over and turned the radio down to a more acceptable level, then repeated my question. "What was the class?"

"It was traffic school, okay?"

With my sister's lead foot, it didn't surprise me that she'd gotten a speeding ticket. But how had she kept the class from me? It had probably been a real effort, no matter how much it had been worth to keep me from teasing her about it.

Maddy frowned at me, then asked, "Any comments you'd care to make?"

"Not me," I said.

"Good," she replied as she took off toward the Slice. I saw her glance at the dashboard clock as she added, "Are you ready to make some pizza?"

"We still need to talk to Penny."

"She's not open for hours," Maddy said. "In the meantime, we'd better try to make some money."

"If we get any customers today, I'm ready to feed them," I said.

"Oh, they'll come, you can count on that."

"Why do you say that?"

Maddy grinned. "Because nobody in town has pizza anywhere near as good as yours. The national chains are consistent to the point of being bland. With you, no two pizzas are ever the same."

"Thanks. I think."

"It was a compliment, Eleanor."

"That's how I'm going to take it."

* * *

Thankfully, no one had attacked my pizza parlor
in the middle of the night, which was something
I'd been dreading most of the night. Somehow the
assault on the Subaru was less invasive than doing
something to A Slice of Delight. Maybe it was because so much of Joe was in the pizzeria.

As we walked in, I started flipping lights on, as
was my custom each morning when we arrived. It
let any passersby know that we were going to indeed be serving today, something that until the day
before had never really been in doubt. It felt good
to be back there, among all things cozy and familiar.

Maddy and I had a routine, and we went to
work. The pizza dough was my area of expertise,
and though my sister had been thoughtful enough
to make it the day before, I'd tried a slice last night
and it hadn't been up to my standards. I gathered
the yeast, water, salt, and bread flour together, then
added a few of the things that set my dough apart
from the rest. I had a shaker filled with my own
blend of herbs, and I also used a touch of olive oil
in my dough mix. As the yeast soaked in warm
water, I set about measuring the other ingredients,
almost working on autopilot, I'd done it so many
times before. I knew pizzerias that used frozen or
even partially baked crusts, but I liked the feel of
dough in my hands and was happy to give my customers something a touch different. The same
thing went for my pizza sauce, which was another
specialty of mine. I made it myself, with tomatoes,
onions, garlic, and a few spices I thought gave it a
distinctive taste.

While I worked on the basics, Maddy prepared our toppings and got ready for our sandwich orders. I refused to make the buns myself, but I couldn't see using store-bought either, so I had a deal with Paul, our baking neighbor, to supply the buns for the shop every day. He gave me a great price, and I took him some pizza every now and then. It was an arrangement that suited both of us.

After the yeast was ready, I began mixing the dough in the floor mixer until it was all thoroughly integrated. I kneaded the dough by hand, put it into a bowl, added a light layer of olive oil, then covered it and put it in under a proofing lamp. After I set the timer for sixty minutes to give the yeast a chance to work, I turned to Maddy.

"Do you need any help with your toppings?"

She ignored me. Then I noticed that her iPod earbuds were in.

"Maddy," I asked again, this time more forcefully.

She looked up at me. "Did you say something?"

I mouthed words but didn't utter a sound.

"I can't hear you," she said as she jerked the earpieces out. I could hear the music playing through the earpieces, though the sound was thankfully muted.

"That's because I wasn't saying it out loud. You're going to go deaf listening to that thing cranked up so high, you know that, don't you?"

"Sorry, 'Mom,' I'll try to do better. What did you want?"

"Do you need any help?"

She waved a knife in the air. "No, I've got it."

"I'm going to make up another batch of dough and freeze it. Then I'm going to go get our buns from Paul."

"Tell him I said hi," she said as she put the knife down long enough to re-place the earbuds.

I finished the backup batch of dough, locked up behind me, then walked down the brick promenade to Paul's Pastries. It felt good being out in the brisk morning. My arms could feel the effort I'd put into the dough, and I cherished the first break of my day.

At the bakery, I glanced in through the large windows under the dark green awning that jutted off the ancient brick facade. His shop's name was written in white letters on the awning front in a very friendly, welcoming font. Behind a huge array of display cases filled with the most delectable goodies, Paul was working at replenishing the shelves. Tall and thin, he was in his mid-twenties and sported a goatee as black as his hair. Paul had gone to law school after graduating college in two years, and after he passed the North Carolina state bar exam, he'd shelved his diploma and opened up his shop. He'd gotten his law degree for his father, but now he was doing something for himself. I couldn't say whether his education made him a better baker or not, but it was good having him around. The world had enough lawyers, in my opinion, and not enough bakers.

"Good morning," Paul greeted me as I walked in. "I was hoping I'd see you today."

"Sorry about yesterday. I'll pay for the bread I didn't get."

"Don't be silly, Eleanor. I'm just glad you're

opening again." He lowered his voice, though no one was in the bakery but the two of us. "If I can do anything—and I mean anything—to help you, I will. I'll even give you legal advice. All you have to do is ask."

I knew what a concession that was for him to make. "I appreciate it, Paul, but I've hired Bob Lemon to help."

"He's a good man," Paul said. With a twinkle in his eyes, he added, "No doubt Maddy had something to do with that."

"You can tell he's sweet on her, too?"

Paul laughed. "Everyone in Timber Ridge can tell. Hang on a second; I've got your buns in back."

Paul ducked through the swinging door and reappeared with a tray full of his wonderful hoagie rolls. "Here you go."

"Thanks. Would you like us to bring you some lunch today?"

"That would be great," Paul said. "After baking half the night, it's nice to have someone make me a meal."

His schedule was nearly opposite ours, since Paul started his day at one A.M. and finished up by two in the afternoon. It was a timetable that would have killed me. Then again, I was a good ten years older than he was.

"It must be tough finding someone to date with your hours," I said.

"Why, Eleanor, I didn't realize you felt that way about me."

That flustered me. "Paul, I didn't . . . I wasn't . . . I didn't mean me."

His laughter put me at ease. "Relax, I was just teasing you."

"I deserved it," I said. "It's none of my business."

"You should hear my mother. She doesn't care that I'm not practicing law, but she's absolutely determined that she have grandchildren while she's still young enough to enjoy them."

"Mothers can be that way, can't they?" I took the tray from him, butted the door open with my back, and waved to Paul by smiling and nodding my head as I walked back to the Slice.

I used one of our outdoor tables to set the tray of fresh bread on, then got out my keys and unlocked the door. The metal tables came in handy, one of the reasons I kept them outside year-round. Some folks surprised me by eating out there in all kinds of weather, but it was more for my convenience than theirs at this time of the year.

Maddy was just finishing up with her preparation station, though I still had time on the dough timer before I could punch it down and store it in the refrigerator. It was time to make the dough for our thin-crust pizzas, using a different set of ingredients and another procedure altogether. I put the yeast, high-gluten flour, and salt into the flour mixer, then added twenty cups of water to the mix. I set the timer for thirteen minutes, turned on the mixer, and forgot about it. It was a low-maintenance procedure, and there were days that I wished everyone would order thin-crust pizza. After the timer went off, I kneaded the dough, then shaped it into balls and stored it in the refrigerator. By the time I finished with that, the regular-crust dough was ready, so I punched it down, divided the dough into four pieces, rolled them into balls, then put them in the refrigerator as well.

The kitchen was nearly ready to open.

I just hoped at least one customer would come in.

Someone was pounding on the front door twenty minutes before we were due to open. I thought about ignoring the summons until noon, just like I I'd been doing with the telephone. With our skeleton staff of two, I wasn't about to take anything but walk-in orders until this mess was resolved, and that could be a very long time indeed.

Ultimately, though, I was afraid whoever wanted to get in so urgently was going to break down the front door.

I was surprised to see that it was Greg Hatcher, our delivery guy. Greg went to college three days a week and worked for me two more in the pizzeria, adding three nights of delivering as well. He looked more like a linebacker, with his thick build and his ever-short haircut, than the professional poet he aspired to be someday.

As I unlocked the door, I asked, "Greg, what are you doing here?"

"I came in to work my shift," he said. "Come on, Eleanor, it was only one day I missed. I really was sick, too. Yesterday was my day off, and I stayed in bed and slept. I'm much better. You're not going to fire me, are you?"

"Have you read a paper or watched the news?" I couldn't believe there was anyone in Timber Ridge who hadn't heard about Richard Olsen's murder.

"No, I watched a *Doctor Who* marathon on the SciFi Channel. Why, what did I miss? Did the world end or something?"

"It might have," I said. "Richard Olsen was murdered two nights ago."

"Richard who? I don't know the guy. Did he live in town?"

"He did," I said. "I found the body when I delivered his pizza, and the police think I had something to do with the murder."

Greg's shoulders slumped. "It's all my fault, then, isn't it?"

"You had no way of knowing," I said as I patted his shoulder. "It's okay, Greg."

"I don't see how," he said. "Eleanor, I really was sick. Katy wanted to come over, but I told her to stay home. I'm so sorry I got you into this mess."

"I'm not about to let you accept responsibility for something that wasn't your fault. We'll get through this. But until we do, we're not accepting any take-out orders, and I'm not answering the telephone. It's only walk-in orders for now."

"That's fine," Greg said. "I can wait on customers, sweep up, bus tables; whatever you want."

"Are you sure you don't mind working here, given how most of the community probably feels about me right now? Rita's already quit." I decided not to say anything about Josh just yet.

He smiled, and I could see what Katy Johnson saw in him. "Then you really do need me, and trust me, there's no place I'd rather be. Who's coming in later to help out?"

I'd glanced at the schedule, out of habit more

than anything else, and had seen Josh Hurley's name. "Sorry, it's just going to be you."

"Don't tell me," Greg said disgustedly. "Josh isn't coming in. It figures. He's been listening to his dad again."

"Josh wanted to work," I said in his defense, "but I told him he couldn't when he showed up here. His father and I had some words, and I really didn't have any choice."

Greg seemed to digest that, then said, "Okay, if he was willing to work, that's all that counts with me. I'll give him a call later to see how he's doing." Greg looked around the place and saw the chairs were still turned up and sitting on the tables. "In the meantime, I'll start getting the dining room ready."

"Thanks, Greg," I said, touched that he'd stay, given the circumstances.

"Don't thank me," he said with a smile. "Just make sure I get paid on time."

I must have looked at him oddly, because he added, "Hey, I was just kidding about my paycheck, you know that."

"I know. I just hope I can make payroll until this blows over."

Greg shrugged. "If you have to hold on to my pay if things get rocky, don't worry about it. I can get by."

I knew how much he depended on his income from working for me to put himself through school. "Don't start lying to me now," I said, trying to force a grin.

"Hey, if you feed me once a day, I can squeak by."

As Greg started setting up our dining area, I went back into the kitchen, where Maddy was listening to her iPod again and digging into the refrigerator. When she saw me, she took the earbuds out. "I'm hungry. Do you want something to eat before we open?" She must have heard Greg working out front. "Eleanor, somebody's here."

"Greg Hatcher's working the front today," I said.

"I didn't think anyone was coming in."

"He didn't hear what happened, and I didn't have the heart to turn him away."

"I'm glad you didn't," she said as she got out some dough and started forming a crust. We formed our pizzas by knuckling and stretching the dough to fit the pan. Some folks liked to see their crusts hand tossed, but Joe had been the one who'd mastered that technique, so it had died with him. Once the pizza was shaped and a ridge formed around the edge, Maddy poked holes in the bottom of it to let steam escape and handed it to me.

"You dress this one," she said.

I added a ladle of my homemade sauce, then used an elaborate variety of toppings. Whenever I couldn't decide what kind of pizza I wanted myself, I made one with just about everything on it. The menu called it a smorgasbord special, but Maddy and I called it a garbage pizza when we were alone.

I popped it onto the conveyor, then called out to Greg, "Pizza's in the fire."

"Great, I'm starving," he called back. "Should I unlock the front door, or would you like the honors?"

"Go ahead," I called out. "It's not like we're going to be swamped."

Maddy poked her head out through the kitchen door. "Eleanor, you should take a look at this."

"Why, is there something worth seeing?"

"Come on, just do it."

I wiped my hands on a dishrag and walked through the door.

To my surprise, there were at least a dozen people waiting outside in the cold to get into the Slice. "What's going on?"

Greg said, "They're hungry. I've got an idea. Why don't I unlock the door so they can come inside?"

"Sounds good," I said, a hint of laughter in my voice. Some residents of Timber Ridge might be staying away from my pizzeria, but clearly not all of them.

Maybe, just maybe, we'd be able to make it after all.

The three of us grabbed bites to eat when we could, and I made a bunch of pizzas and sandwiches over the next few hours, staying in back while Maddy and Greg handled the customers and the cash register. I probably should have at least showed my face every now and then, but I just couldn't deal with the stares, the well-meaning comments, or the open speculation of my fellow townsfolk.

Still, it wasn't fair to my coworkers for me to stay in back and make them take the heat of scrutiny, so at the first lull, I bit my lower lip, put on my best fake smile, and walked through the kitchen door to the dining area.

I wasn't sure what I'd been expecting, but the eight customers dining at the time barely even acknowledged my existence. Nancy Taylor, our postmistress, nodded in my direction, and Emily Haynes, a dental hygienist for Dr. Patrick, smiled at me, but that was it.

"Good to see you out front," Maddy said as she approached. "Why don't we trade off for a while? You can work out here, and I'll take over the kitchen duties."

She'd never offered to cook before, though she was perfectly capable of making just about everything I could. "Why the change of heart?" I asked.

"What are you talking about? I love to make pizza."

That got a chuckle that I couldn't repress in time. A few folks glanced over at us, but when everyone went back to their meals, I asked, "Since when?"

"I'm not going to dignify that with a response," she said as she handed her order pad to me. "Now, if you'll excuse me, I've got work to do."

I was beginning to regret my impulse to come out front as I stared at the customers. Greg was refilling drinks and busing tables, so I decided to stay at the register.

Nancy Taylor approached with her bill, and as I made change for her, she said, "I think you're so brave, Eleanor."

"I don't know that I'm particularly courageous," I said.

"Coming in here, knowing what some folks around town are saying about you? I'd say that's brave."

As she took her change, she lowered her voice and added, "Not that there aren't other folks around who shouldn't be dropping their heads in shame."

"What are you talking about, Nancy?"

"For one, Travis White was mad enough to kill Richard himself; you know that, don't you?"

Travis was a polite, white-haired man who worked for the gas company. He ate at the Slice at least twice a month, and I'd rarely heard an ill word from him. "Travis? Are you sure?"

"He lives beside Richard. The two of them have been arguing about their property line for years."

"That's not really a motive for murder, Nancy," I said. I'd heard them each grumbling about the other, but I couldn't imagine it evolving into homicide.

She frowned, then said, "Well then, did you know that Richard cut down Travis's favorite tree? He claimed it was on his side, but Travis knew that wasn't true. When Richard offered Travis twenty dollars for the firewood right in front of me last week, I thought Travis was going to kill him then and there."

"I didn't hear about that," I said. I knew how much some folks got attached to things they owned, but could sweet old Travis kill someone over a tree?

"No one else was in the post office when it happened, but I was there."

"Thanks, Nancy," I said loudly as Emily came up with her bill.

"Keep your chin up," Nancy said as she left.

Emily said, "That goes for me, too. I don't think you did it for one second."

"Thanks, I appreciate that."

"At least not with a knife." She pretended to ponder it for a moment, then added, "No, a poisoned mushroom would be more your speed. Or maybe arsenic in his sweet tea."

I looked at the book tucked into her purse and saw that it was an old favorite written by Charlotte MacLeod. "You have much too vivid an imagination," I said.

"There's no such thing," she said as she winked at me.

After the dining room cleared out, we had our normal afternoon lull, and Maddy and I did dishes and got ready for the next rush while Greg stayed out front, studying between times spent waiting on the occasional customer. I didn't mind him working on his school assignments while he was on my time. I figured his presence in front meant that I didn't have to waste half my day there, so it was well worth his minuscule salary.

As I dried the last dish, I said, "I'm going to go talk to Penny Olsen."

"Great idea," Maddy said as she drained the water in the sink. "Let's go."

"You need to stay here," I said.

"That's not going to happen, Eleanor. You're the one who instituted the buddy system, remember?"

"Somebody has to make the food if someone comes in," I explained.

"And who's better at that? You are, and we both

know it." She grabbed her purse, then said, "Don't worry, I'll tell you everything she says."

"You shouldn't go alone," I called after her as she headed for the kitchen door.

"Why not? You were going to."

"I give up," I said. "We'll close the pizzeria so we can both go."

"Eleanor, can we really afford to turn even one walk-in customer away at a time like this? We'll never talk to Penny if we wait until we can both go."

I didn't like it, but then again, I really didn't have much choice.

"Be careful," I said.

"I always am. Well, almost always," she said.

Ten minutes later, Maddy was back.

"That didn't take long. What happened? Did she refuse to talk to you?"

"She wasn't there," Maddy said. "There was a sign in her window saying she was on a buying trip and wouldn't be back for a few days."

I thought about that. "I wonder if the trip came up before Richard was murdered, or if she left town because of it."

"Are you just automatically assuming she had something to do with it?"

"No, but I don't think she's innocent just because she was married to the man at one time."

Maddy frowned. "I've never done a thing to any of my ex-husbands. In fact, I'd wager to say that the majority of them speak highly of me to this day."

"Would those be the ones not paying alimony anymore?"

She shook her head. "Only one of them is now, and it's so paltry it's barely worth cashing."

"Why don't you send the checks back, then?"

She laughed. "I'm going to assume you're kidding."

"That's okay by me," I said. "In the meantime, let's start prepping for dinner. After we're ready, I'll go back up front, and you can take the kitchen shift."

"We can always trade back," she said.

"Not just yet," I answered. "You were right. I need to get out there more and let people see I'm not cowering in a corner somewhere. Don't worry, though. It's not permanent. I promise."

"I'm holding you to that," she said as I walked out front to join Greg.

By the time our late-afternoon crowd began to trickle in, I was comfortable working the front again. Even though I knew how much Maddy preferred dealing with customers, I decided to give her a full shift in the kitchen so she could appreciate what I did at A Slice of Delight. That didn't mean I thought her job was easy, but it wasn't as tough as keeping up with half a dozen orders, and that didn't even include the pick-up and delivery services we usually ran.

In an hour, I realized that her job was no walk in the park, either. Along with Greg, I had made small talk with at least a dozen people, all the while keeping their orders straight, making sure their soda and sweet iced tea glasses were full, seating new customers, and busing a table or two thrown into the mix. Maybe we both needed a night of shared roles.

I was about ready to throw in the towel, promising myself I'd seat one more customer, when David Quinton came in. I was prepared to fend him off again when I noticed that he wasn't alone. There was a nice-looking redhead just behind him, and from the way she kept looking at him, it was clear they were there on a date. Well, good for him.

"Good evening," I said as I led them to one of our better tables.

"Thanks," David said. It was pretty clear he'd been expecting Maddy up front and had been surprised by my presence. That was too bad. You can't just walk into my pizza place and not expect to see me.

"Greg will be right with you to take your orders," I said as I started back toward the kitchen.

Greg intercepted me at the door. "I can't believe that."

"What, that one of our customers is here on a date? Take care of him, would you? I've got to talk to Maddy."

I found my sister in the kitchen, happily humming a tune. I expected to see her iPod in but saw it on the counter.

"Are you back here humming?"

She smiled. "I forgot how much fun this was," she said.

If she was bluffing, she was doing an excellent job.

"Sorry to steal your joy, but I need you to work the front."

"It's harder than it looks, isn't it?" There was a

gleam in her eyes as she asked the question, just waiting for me to lie.

"You know what? You're right. I think you and Greg both deserve a raise."

"What's going on, Eleanor?" she asked.

"What do you mean? I'm paying you a compliment."

Maddy took off her apron and threw it on the prep table. "That's what I mean. Something had to have happened. Otherwise you never would have let me get away with that crack about a raise."

I had decided to let her find out for herself, but I found the words tumbling out instead. "David Quinton's here, and he's not alone. He's on a date."

"No," Maddy said in obvious disbelief. "He wouldn't do that."

"He's right out front," I said. "I really can't blame him. I've turned him down enough times. Why shouldn't he find someone else to ask out? Didn't I tell him to do exactly that right here last night? He's just following my advice."

Maddy said, "Even so, did he have to do it in your restaurant? I've got to see this for myself."

"Don't," I said, making a grab for her.

But she was too elusive. Maddy ducked out for nine seconds, then came back in.

"That wasn't too suspicious," I said.

"Who cares? What's going on?"

"What do you mean?"

"He's not out there."

I peeked through the window in the door, but David and his date were gone. "Maybe Greg moved them."

As he came back to give me an order, I asked, "What happened to David and his date?"

"I have no idea," Greg said. "One second they were sitting there, and when I turned my back on them, they were gone."

"I can't imagine why," I said.

"Then why are your cheeks getting red?" Maddy asked.

"It's the heat back here," I said, dabbing at my dry forehead. Okay, seeing my would-be suitor out with someone else had stung a little more than I'd expected it to. It wasn't that I was being disloyal to my husband. Joe was gone, and he wasn't coming back. No one knew that better than I did.

So why?

I honestly had no idea.

"That frees up a table," I said. "Have you got any orders for me, Greg? I'm taking back my kitchen."

Greg looked at Maddy for a split second, and she nodded her approval, as if I needed that.

"Let me remind you two," I said, "I'm the one who writes the paychecks around here. That means I'm in charge. Now, both of you need to get back to work."

They left me alone in the kitchen, and as I filled the order Greg had just given me, I had to wonder if there was more to my feelings for David than I'd admitted.

I didn't have much time for worrying about that, though. Maddy came back ten minutes later and said, "Celeste is here, and she's got something for us."

Chapter 8

"What did you find out, Celeste?" Maddy asked as she led her way back into my kitchen.

"I thought you two promised me something to eat," she said as she looked around. "I'm so hungry, I could eat an entire pizza by myself right now."

"If you make it worth our while, I can make that happen," I said.

"But no food until we find out what you uncovered," Maddy said.

Celeste seemed to think about that, then said, "Why don't you make me one of your specialty pizzas, and while it's in the oven, I'll tell you what I found."

"It's a deal," I said. I prepared a medium crust, added the sauce, and started laying on the toppings and cheese.

After I was through, I put it on the conveyor and said, "All we do now is wait."

"Where's the big wood-fired oven?" she asked as she looked around.

"Not here," I said. "We use a conveyor oven.

Now, did you really come here to learn about pizza making, or do you have something for us?"

"I was just asking," she said.

After a second, she dug into her purse and pulled out a notice to appear in court. "How's this for a meal ticket?"

"Is it about the property line dispute?" I asked.

Maddy's eyebrows flew upward, since I'd neglected to tell her what Nancy Taylor had told me earlier.

"You know about that, do you?" Celeste asked.

She started to put the summons back into her purse, when Maddy said, "Since you brought it, I'll take a look at it." Maddy took the paper, then said, "Hey, this is just a copy. Where's the original?"

"Back at the house," Celeste said. "You didn't actually think I was going to steal anything, did you? I'm bonded, Maddy, and I can't afford a blemish on my record."

"This doesn't violate anything?" my sister asked as she waved the copy in the air.

"It's borderline, but I'll be all right as long as no one knows. That man had a copier in his office. Can you believe it?"

"I saw it," I said. "Did you find anything else?"

"Okay, how about this?" Celeste asked as she pulled out another sheet of paper.

"Another copy?" Maddy asked.

"A copy of a copy, I'm guessing." Celeste replied.

I took the paper and saw that it was an e-mail addressed to Richard Olsen. It appeared that there was going to be an internal audit of the sales reps' books for his company, and Richard was to report in two days.

He wasn't going to make it.

Within the e-mail, there was also a notification that because a grievance had been filed, security cameras had been installed in the master shredding facility and the tapes would be monitored every night to ensure customer privacy.

Below the body of the general e-mail, Carl Wilson, the company owner, had added that Richard needed to bring in everything that he had that was company property.

From the look of it, Richard had been about to get fired, and perhaps worse. Was he stealing from the company? I couldn't imagine them not noticing that a hundred thousand dollars was missing. And what about the grievance the owner had mentioned. Was it possible that my suspicions were right, that Richard had sorted through the papers to be shredded and had found something worth blackmailing for? The e-mail asked more questions than it answered, but it was certainly something that was worth looking into.

Celeste had been watching me, and as I handed the e-mail over to Maddy, I said, "You might have something there."

"Did you find any lavender envelopes?" I asked as Maddy scanned the document.

"There were a couple," Celeste admitted, "but before I could copy the letters inside, Ms. Olsen grabbed them out of my hand. I didn't even know she'd been watching me."

"So, Sheila knew what her brother was up to."

"She reacted pretty strongly when she saw those," Celeste replied.

"Is that it?" Maddy asked.

"There's one more thing. I found a bundle of empty envelopes, all with a P.O. box listed as the address. I brought one with me, in case it's important."

She handed me the envelope, and I saw it was the same box 10. So, it had been Richard's after all. That didn't make sense, though. I'd found plenty of envelopes in his files with his street address on them. Why have a post office box if you're already getting mail at home? I knew someone who would know, but there was no way Nancy Taylor, the postmistress, would tell me.

I hadn't found a key to the post office box among Richard's things, and I had to wonder if there was something in the box now, waiting for him to retrieve it. Should I ask Sheila if she had it? No, first I'd go to the post office in the morning and see if anything was inside it. The post office boxes had small see-through windows, making it easy enough to check.

"That's a lot of information. You did great," I said as her pizza came out of the other side of the conveyor. "Would you like this for here, or to go?"

"I'd like it in a box, if you don't mind," she said.

I cut it, then slid the pizza into one of our boxes. "Thanks, Celeste. Are you all finished cleaning the house?"

"It took a crew of eight, but we did it. There's not a trace of that man left there. I understand it's going on the market by the end of the week."

"How can that be?" I asked, the news surprising me.

"Didn't I tell you? We found the will, nearly straight away after you two left. The sister gets everything. No one else was even mentioned in the will. She didn't need it, though. It turns out her name was already on the deed, and she didn't even know it. Funny, the man left her all of his accounts, including the house, but she claims she never knew it."

"You're right; that is funny," I said.

After Celeste left, Maddy asked, "What are you thinking?"

"I can't stop playing with the idea that Sheila knew all along she was going to inherit," I said.

"I honestly didn't get that impression, but if you're right, what do we do about it?"

I thought about it, then said, "The only thing we can do is give her more rope, and see if she can fashion herself a noose."

"Don't forget, we have a handful of other suspects, too," Maddy said. "Faith Baron gets my vote at the moment. I can't believe her nerve."

"What about her husband? His temper's known pretty well all around town, and mayor or not, I'm sorry to say that I can see him stabbing the man who'd been cheating with his wife."

"Then again, there's still whoever Richard was blackmailing."

I nodded. "And we can't forget Travis or Richard's boss."

Maddy scratched her head. "I'm beginning to think we'd be better off figuring out who didn't have a motive to see the man dead."

We were still discussing the possibilities when Greg poked his head in through the kitchen door. "How about a hand out here, Maddy?"

"Sorry, I didn't mean to stay in the kitchen so long."

My sister grabbed her order pad as I asked, "Do you want me to take another shift out front? I don't mind, really."

She shook her head. "Thanks anyway, but if I do that, how am I going to earn any tips?"

"You actually get tips?" I asked.

"Don't worry; you'll get them too, someday. You're just out of practice waiting on customers. It probably wouldn't be a bad idea if we kept trading off, though. What if you're out sick? If I'm lousy at making pizzas, I'll drive off your customers. Greg can handle the front, and I can take the back. That way you can take your time and get better."

I didn't care to be so easily replaced, even in a hypothetical situation. "What if you're the one who's out?"

"How would you be able to tell?" she said with a smile. "I'm just here for decoration most days, anyway."

"I never said that, and if I even thought it, I was wrong. You work hard, too; I know that."

"So we're both wonderful. I'll go help Greg, and you keep the food coming."

I worked in silence, creating the orders as they were placed, but I was still left with enough downtime to ponder all we'd learned. Apparently Richard Olsen had been a busy man. Besides the pass he'd made at me, he'd been sleeping with—and breaking up with—the mayor's wife, been embroiled in a property line dispute with his hot-tempered neighbor, and possibly been stealing clients' secrets for blackmail and stealing cash from his boss. That didn't even touch the relationship he might have had with his ex-wife, who was still noticeably absent from town.

How did he find time to do anything else?

During the next lull, the kitchen door opened and Bob Pickering came through. "Maddy sent me back. Hope it's okay."

"That depends," I said as I wiped my hands on a towel. "Did you finish my car?"

"Come on, Eleanor, that's a big job, and you know it."

"So it's not ready?" I'd really been counting on getting my transportation back.

"I didn't say that," he said with a smile as he jangled my keys in front of me. "I just finished it up, even if I had to skip lunch to do it."

"Then I'll make up for it with your pizza," I said as I got more dough out of the refrigerator. It appeared that I was giving away entirely too many pizzas in the last few hours, but at least I was getting value for them. It was amazing how free food could entice people to do what I wanted. It didn't hurt that just about everybody loves pizza.

"What would you like on it?" I asked as I finished knuckling the dough around the pan and forming a ridge around it.

"You got it, I'll take it," he said.

"Are you sure? I'm not sure how everything we carry would do in one pie."

"Yeah, you're right," he said. After a moment's thought, he said, "I'll take one with cheese, then."

"Come on, I can do better than that," I said.

"No, cheese is what I want," Bob said.

I shrugged, then added as much cheese as I could fit on the pizza without having it spill out in the oven. If he wanted cheese, that was exactly what he was going to get.

Bob nodded his approval as he saw what I'd created for him, then leaned against the counter and watched as the pizza slowly disappeared into the oven. "That's a nice-looking rig you've got there. I could speed it up for you if you'd like."

I knew Bob was handy in a great many more areas than fixing cars, but just because he could do it didn't mean he should. "If you do that, the pizzas won't finish baking when they make it through the oven."

"I could crank that up for you, too. You could have pizzas in half the time."

"Thanks, Bob, but why don't we just leave things the way they are now. It won't be long. Can I get you something to drink while you're waiting?"

"Sure, that would be great."

I grabbed a cup from the cupboard, then asked, "What would you like?"

"A Coke would be great," he said as he reached for his wallet.

"It's on the house," I said.

"Eleanor, how do you expect to make a profit if you give your stuff away?"

"We could always barter," I said with a grin.

"No, thanks, I doubt I could eat that much pizza."

I went to the front and filled the cup with soda, put a lid on it, then carried it back into the kitchen. The pizza was done, but it looked too cheesy even for me. "Sorry, I think I overdid it," I said. "Do you have time to wait while I make you another one?"

"What are you talking about?" he asked as he looked over my shoulder. "That's perfect."

"Okay, if you're sure," I said as I cut it and slid it into a box.

He took the pizza, grabbed his drink, and I followed him out front and held the door open for him. "Thanks for getting to my window so fast, Bob," I said.

"You're welcome. I'll put the bill in the mail tomorrow."

"I'm counting on it," I said. I would gladly pay to have the use of my own car back. It was amazing how helpless I felt without my transportation. Now I wouldn't have to depend on Maddy to ferry me around town. While I was sure she didn't mind, I did. Since my widowhood, I'd become fiercely independent, almost too proud or stubborn to take help from anyone else.

Maybe David was right. There were walls I didn't need standing in my way, but I was afraid that by the time I made any progress in tearing them down, it would be too late.

It was twenty minutes till ten, and I had started cleaning up in back earlier so we could get out at a decent time. I had as many of the dishes finished as I could, so I decided to see what a mess the answering machine was. Since the murder, I hadn't kept up with checking the messages, so I knew I was going to have a bunch of them.

The number fifty flashed on my machine, which was the limit of messages it could hold. Who would have ever believed it would get that high? Grabbing a pen and some paper, I sat down at my cramped desk and hit REPLAY.

There were the expected comments of support, a few frustrated attempts to order pizza, and a couple of comments that were too rude to keep. Oddly enough, the last twenty calls were all hang-ups. How could that be? Wouldn't people get the message after a while and stop calling?

I had just hit the erase button when the phone rang. Though I had turned the ringer off the day before, I could still see the light flashing. Without even realizing I was doing it, I answered the phone, "A Slice of Delight."

There was a moment's hesitation, and then a low voice said, "I need a pizza delivered."

"I'm sorry, but we're getting ready to close, and our delivery service will be unavailable for the foreseeable future."

After another pause, the voice said, "I'll give you one hundred dollars for a pizza tonight."

"I'm sorry, but no." We got our share of nuts, but this one was quickly climbing to the top of the charts.

"Two hundred," the voice rasped out.

I suddenly realized that there was something going on here more than a pizza. I decided to play along. "Okay, I could probably make an exception for two hundred dollars. Who's calling, please?"

Another pause, then the voice said, "Shook."

That was an easy alias to come up with, since you couldn't swing a big stick in our part of the world without hitting someone named Shook.

"And where would you like this delivered?" I asked.

· No hesitation this time. "Eighty-two West End Avenue."

"Very good," I said as Maddy walked back into my office.

"Good-bye," the caller said. I shouted out, "Hang on a second! You didn't say what kind of pizza you wanted!"

After another hesitation, the voice said, "Plain," and then they hung up.

Maddy said, "I thought we weren't going to answer the telephone for a while, especially to take delivery orders."

I cradled the telephone back as I explained, "Something was very wrong with that call. They offered me two hundred dollars to deliver a pizza, but then they had to think about what kind they wanted. Does that sound like a pizza lover to you?"

"You're not going, are you?"

I thumbed the paper I'd written the address down on. "What choice do I have? This could lead me straight to the killer."

"Or get both of us killed," Maddy said. I was proud of my sister for including herself, as if it was just assumed that she'd be with me.

"We won't learn anything if we don't take a risk," I said.

"The same thing can be said if we're dead."

She reached for the phone, and I asked her, "Who are you calling?"

"Kevin Hurley," she said as she looked up Josh's home number on our employee list, posted by the telephone. "I'm not a big fan of the chief's, but this is actually something he needs to know."

I wanted to argue with her, but Maddy was right. It was one thing putting my own life in jeopardy, but I didn't have the right to risk hers, and I knew there was no way I was going to go without her. If there was one person in the world more stubborn than me, it had to be my sister.

"Chief, this is Maddy Spencer. We need you at the pizzeria."

She paused, then rolled her eyes as she said, "No, no one else is dead. But somebody's trying to lure us into a trap, and if you don't want our blood on your hands, you'll come over before we do something stupid."

She hung up, then smiled at me. "That should get him over here."

"Have you completely lost your mind?"

"What are you talking about?"

I shook my head. "It's one thing to antagonize him accidentally, but you jabbed him when you didn't have to."

"I didn't feel like explaining over the telephone," she said. "We can tell him what's going on when he gets here."

I pulled out the last of the day's dough and started forming it into the pan.

"What are you doing?" Maddy asked me.

"I'm making a pizza."

"Eleanor, they don't actually *want* a pizza; you know that, don't you?"

I shrugged. "I'm not going empty-handed. And if this all turns out to be a misunderstanding, I'm not missing the chance to make two hundred bucks." I added the sauce and cheese, then slid it onto the conveyor.

Kevin arrived in record time. One minute before ten, the police chief came bursting into the Slice, and I was more than a little relieved to see that his gun was still in its holster. No one else was in the restaurant, and I'd sent Greg home right after Maddy had made the call to the chief. There was no reason in the world to drag him into my mess any more than I already had.

"What's going on?" Kevin asked. "And let me warn you, it had better be good."

"Tell him about the call, Eleanor," Maddy said.

"I got a delivery call about ten minutes ago," I said.

"What a shock. Who would think someone would call in for a pizza and expect someone to bring it to them."

He had a right to make that crack, so I let it slide. "I was getting to that," I said. "The caller kept their voice low enough so that I couldn't say for sure if it was a man or a woman. When I told them I wasn't delivering, they offered me a hundred dollars."

That raised one of his eyebrows, so I continued before he could interject again. "When I turned them down, they made it two hundred dollars. I accepted, just to see what was going on. If that wasn't odd enough, after they gave me the address, they forgot to actually order a pizza. When I pressed them on it, they hesitated, then ordered a plain one, not a cheese pizza, but one that was plain. Would you pay two hundred dollars for that?"

"Where's the address?" he asked as he reached for his radio.

I looked at the slip. "Eighty-two West End Avenue."

He called up his dispatcher and asked for information on the address. Two minutes later, his radio beeped, and we all heard, "That's an empty lot, Chief. It's between two older buildings near the railroad tracks. What's going on?"

"I'm just heading over there," he said.

"Do you need backup?"

He paused, then said, "No, I can handle it. Chief out."

"Thanks," I said. "I'm the first to admit that I'm glad you're going with us."

"You're not going," he said flatly. Before Maddy could say anything, he added, "Neither one of you are."

"You can't do that," I said.

"Why can't I?"

I smiled. "The second they see your squad car, they'll know what's going on. We have to go in my Subaru, and we have to take a pizza with us." I pointed to the oven as the pizza came off the conveyor.

"Do you honestly think this is legitimate? If you do, you never should have called me in the first place."

"I couldn't be sure, could I? Now, are you coming with me, or not?"

He mulled it over, then said, "Fine, but I have some conditions."

"I'm listening," I said.

"The first one is a deal breaker. Maddy stays here," he said forcefully.

"I don't think so," she said.

"Then I'm leaving, and you two can do what you want. I won't jeopardize *two* civilians doing this. It's not negotiable."

"Please?" I asked Maddy. "This could be important."

"Fine," she said in a huff. "Since you two don't need me, I'll finish cleaning up the front. Come back here when you're done. I'll be waiting for you."

After she was gone, Kevin said, "I never thought she'd agree to that."

"Don't expect me to be so pliable," I said. "What are your other conditions?"

"We take your Subaru, but I drive."

"Done," I said.

"That was almost too easy."

"I'm not a huge fan of driving at night anyway, so I don't have a problem with you chauffeuring me around. What would the taxpayers think, though?"

"It doesn't matter. I'm on my own time here."

"But you're in uniform," I said.

"I hadn't gotten around to changing yet."

"Fair enough. Any other conditions?"

"If nobody shows up, I get the pizza," he said as he pointed to the pie.

"I can live with that," I said as I cut it and boxed it up.

"Are you ready?" he asked me.

"As I'll ever be."

As we walked through the front, Maddy scowled at Kevin and without saying a word nodded her encouragement to me.

I handed Kevin my keys, then slid into the passenger seat. As he started the car, he asked, "How'd you get that window replaced so quickly?"

"I have connections," I said.

"Like Bob Pickering," he replied. "I bet you bribed him with pizza, didn't you?"

"It's been known to happen in the past," I said. "He would have done it anyway. He's a friend, but it was my way of saying thank you."

"Hey, I think it's nice." As he drove to the edge of Timber Ridge, he said, "Listen, it's important that you do as I say when we get there. We'll wait in the car a few minutes; then if no one shows, I'll get out and look around."

"Are you sure you don't want anybody else backing you up?"

He shrugged. "You know what? It probably couldn't hurt. I'll see if Tanner's on duty." He got on his radio and called for one of his officers. "Lee, are you out there?"

"Right here, boss. I thought you went home."

"Something came up," he said as he glanced over at me. "What's your twenty?"

"I'm out on Viewmont Avenue," he said. "Everything's dead, though."

"Do me a favor. I'm going to West End, number eighty-two."

"You want me to meet you there?" It was clear that Lee Tanner was ready for some action, any action at all.

"No, I'm keeping this quiet." He explained the situation to his officer, then said, "I need you to come around to the alley behind West End. No lights or sirens, just keep an eye out in case someone comes through there."

"Got it. I'll be there in two minutes."

"Then you'll beat me. Hang back when you get close."

"Will do."

We drove the rest of the way in silence. The closer we got to the address, and the more run-down the neighborhood got, the happier I was that we'd called Kevin. I wasn't sure I would have had the nerve to make the delivery all by myself, after what I'd found the other night.

The street was empty as we approached the address.

I couldn't believe how black the night was. "It's really dark, isn't it?"

"Yeah, that might be because the streetlight's out."

My headlights caught a shattered reflection, and Kevin said, "Somebody must have just knocked it out."

His hand went to his side where he kept his firearm, and mine tightened on the pizza box in my lap. That dislodged my purse, and I leaned forward to retrieve it as we pulled up to the address. As I bent over, without any warning, the driver's side window shattered at the same instant I heard a boom.

I hadn't seen the flash from the gun, and before I could move, Kevin was out of the car. "Stay here," he barked.

I couldn't believe it. He ran toward where the shot must have come from, instead of running away from it.

I hated the idea that Kevin was out there in the dark chasing a madman, but I disliked the idea of sitting there waiting for the shooter to take another shot even more. At least I didn't have to give them a target. I slid the pizza onto the backseat and crouched so low in the car that I doubted anyone would even know I was there.

A torturous three minutes later, I heard footsteps approaching on the concrete, grinding a bit of the streetlight glass into the pavement as they neared.

I was vulnerable and exposed, but that didn't mean I was going down without a fight. I reached into my purse and grabbed my pepper spray, then opened the glove box and retrieved the window-breaking tool I kept there in case I had to get out in a hurry. Neither weapon would do me much good against a gun, but I still felt better having them.

"Ellie?" Kevin's voice called out. "Where are you?"

"I'm right here," I said as I straightened up in my seat. It was amazing how soft his voice had been when he'd called out my name. It was pretty clear that the chief, despite his protests to the contrary, still had a soft place in his heart for me. "Did you catch whoever took that shot at us?"

"No, he got away." Kevin got out his radio and said, "Lee, did you find anything?"

"No, sir. I'm not sure which way the shooter went, but he didn't come past me."

Just then, we heard a car pull out a block away, its tires screeching on the pavement. Slightly out of breath, Lee said, "I'm on it," and I had to wonder if he was running back to his car as he spoke.

Kevin looked at the shattered window, then asked, "You don't happen to have a broom or something like that, do you?"

"As a matter of fact, I do," I said. "Is it safe for me to get out and go around to the back?"

"I think so," Kevin said. "I'm guessing our shooter's long gone."

"I certainly hope so." I got out of the car, feeling an itching between my shoulder blades the entire time as I moved to the back cargo space.

I had a small whisk broom that I handed to Kevin. He shook his head, then took it anyway. "It should do."

He opened the driver's side door, then grabbed a trash bag I had in front and swept the glass into it. "That should do until we get you home."

"What about the glass on the street?" I asked.

"I'll have Lee take care of it."

Just then, his radio squawked, and Officer Tanner got on. "Sorry, he got away. The guy must have been flying to lose me. Should I keep looking?"

"No, why don't you come back here. We need a crime scene checked."

"Be there in two," he said, then signed off.

"Is that what my car is now, a crime scene?" I asked.

He pointed to the interior doorjamb near my head. "See that? It's where the bullet ended up." Kevin studied the trajectory, then said, "It's a good thing you ducked down to get your purse. That bullet was heading straight for you."

"Why, though? It doesn't make sense. I don't know anything, so why would the killer want to get rid of me?"

"It could have been random," he said.

"Or not," I replied.

After a moment, Kevin said, "I admit it's possible that whoever killed Richard might have taken that shot." There was a tacit implication that he finally believed I hadn't had anything to do with the murder. At least I hoped there was.

"I just don't know why," I said.

"There's something else. This could have been a robbery attempt that has nothing to do with Richard Olsen."

"Come on, do you honestly believe that?"

"As a matter of fact, I do," he said. "I read an article in the newspaper the other day that food delivery was one of the most dangerous jobs in the U.S. In big cities, they average a robbery a week."

"This isn't a big city," I said. "This was personal."

"Eleanor, you have no way of knowing that. The most likely explanation is that someone wanted to rob you."

"Then why shoot at me first?"

He shrugged. "If you're expecting me to explain why criminals do what they do, you're talking to the wrong guy. I don't try to analyze them. It's my job to catch them, lock them up, and let other people decide what to do with them."

"Kevin Hurley, are you honestly telling me that you believe this was a botched robbery attempt?"

"I admit it's not your run-of-the-mill holdup, but yeah, I think you got very lucky tonight."

"Well, I think you're wrong," I said curtly.

"Why should I have a hard time believing that?" he asked.

Officer Tanner showed up, and after nodding briefly to me, he asked, "What happened? Was it a robbery attempt?"

"Why does everyone keep saying that?" I snapped, sounding shrill even to myself. "That bullet was meant for me."

Neither man said a word, making it pretty obvious that they'd come to a conclusion and weren't about to budge from it unless they had real evidence to convince them otherwise.

"Can I leave now?" I asked. "I want to call Maddy to come and get me."

"Officer Tanner can take you home," Kevin said.

"I'm not going home. I promised my sister I'd meet her back at the Slice, and that's what I'm going to do."

Kevin said, "Listen, I understand this shook you up. You have every right to be upset, but don't read more into it than there is, okay?"

I ignored him as I grabbed my purse, then turned to Officer Tanner. "Are you taking me, or do I have to walk?"

"I'll be glad to take you, ma'am," he said. Was that a fleeting grin he managed to suppress, or was it my imagination? No doubt he was unaccustomed to hearing anyone speak to his boss like that, but at the moment, I didn't care. I just wanted to find someone who believed me, and I had a feeling it would be my sister.

There was no talking in the squad car as Officer Tanner drove me to the Slice, but I did break the silence to thank him for the ride once we arrived.

"All part of the service, ma'am," he said. He hesitated, then added, "Don't be too hard on the chief. He's got a tough job." The officer then tipped his hat to me and drove off.

Maddy must have seen the cruiser pull up, because she was outside on the sidewalk with me before I had a chance to even get to the front door.

"Are you all right? Where's your Subaru? Was

Kevin hurt?" She said all this while locking me in a bear hug.

"I'm fine," I said. "I can't say the same for the Subaru. Somebody shot out the driver's-side window. If I hadn't bent forward to grab my fallen purse, it could have easily hit me instead."

"How about Kevin?"

"He's okay," I said, "besides being utterly delusional. He thinks this was a random attempt to rob me, no matter how much I tried to convince him that it had something to do with Richard Olsen's murder."

Maddy bit her lip, and when she didn't say anything, I said, "Are you saying you think this is unrelated, too? Are you kidding me? You're my sister; you should at least take my side in this."

"Take it easy, Eleanor. We've talked about how lucky we've been not to be robbed," she said. "You know as well as I do that we're overdue, don't you think? All I'm saying is that we have to consider all the possibilities."

"I was the one who was just shot at," I said. "And I know it wasn't a robbery attempt."

"You're right. I'm so sorry. Let me get my purse and I'll take you home."

She ducked back inside the pizzeria, and I collapsed onto a bench while I waited. I knew it was possible that the gunshot hadn't been related to the murder, but I couldn't make myself believe that it was true. I'd uncovered something in my search for the killer so far, something that had made them uncomfortable about what I knew. I just wished I realized what that might be. I'd already talked to a couple of the people on my list, and if they had spread the word around town that Maddy and I were trying to solve the murder ourselves, it could have gotten back to the killer even if I hadn't confronted them directly. So where did that leave me? Was it in my best interests to act as though tonight was nothing more than a random act of violence, or should I treat it as a warning to stop meddling? As much as a part of me wanted to pull back and let Kevin figure out what had happened, that gunshot had just increased my determination to figure out who had killed Richard Olsen.

Whoever had taken that shot clearly hadn't counted on my cussed determination, or they never would have chambered the round.

Chapter 9

"We need to talk about this, Eleanor," Maddy said as we approached my house. "You should know that I believe you."

"You're just saying that."

"I am not. I've had some time to think about it," Maddy said. "If you say somebody tried to kill you tonight, then I believe you. You're right—I wasn't there. I can't even begin to imagine how violated you must feel. The question is, where do we go from here?"

I studied her under the passing streetlights. "Do you honestly mean that?"

She nodded. "I'm sorry I didn't take your side from the start. Besides, it's not productive thinking what happened tonight was random or a robbery attempt. If it was, the police will find who did it. But if it was tied to the killing, then we both need to be more careful."

"Odd, I was just thinking the opposite. Now that most of Timber Ridge knows we're trying to solve this murder, I say we pull out all the stops and start asking some really hard questions. It's time to make some people squirm."

"What's gotten into you?" Maddy asked as she pulled into my driveway. "I don't think I've ever seen you like this before."

"It could be because no one's taken a potshot at me until tonight," I said. "I'm more determined than ever to figure out what's going on."

"Would you like to work on it some more tonight? I'm not the least bit sleepy, and I can't imagine you shutting your eyes for hours, after what happened. So why don't we put the time to productive use and see if we can come up with a game plan?"

"If you're sure," I said. "I hate to drag you away from your personal life."

"Eleanor, we both know I haven't had a personal life in ages."

"It's not from a lack of opportunities," I said. "I happen to know a particular attorney who would love to spend more time with you."

As we got out of the car, she said, "Really? Do you truly want to start discussing each other's love life? Let's just forget all that and use our time a little more productively, shall we?"

"Sorry, I'll stay on task," I said as we approached my front porch. Joe had installed a motion-detecting light when we'd first started rehabbing the place. I'd argued with him about its appropriateness for our bungalow, but he'd insisted we needed it for safety purposes, and tonight, I was glad that was one argument I'd lost.

As the light came on, I dug out my key, and

Maddy and I went inside. It was time to see if we could regain control of a situation that had gotten suddenly out of hand.

Home was a haven for me, a place to get away from the world. With so many reminders of Joe everywhere I looked, I hated tainting my emotions about the place with talk of murder and motives, but I really had no choice. It had crept into my life, had placed a chokehold on my livelihood, and was becoming a real threat to me personally.

"How about something to drink before we get started?" Maddy asked.

"Let's see, I might have some red wine left." I had an unopened bottle of whiskey, but I was never going to break the wax seal. My late husband had been a huge fan of Maker's Mark whiskey, and I'd kept a bottle on hand, more out of sentimentality than anything else.

"I was thinking more along the lines of hot chocolate, but if you'd like something stronger, I'd be glad to run out to the liquor store for you."

"Hot chocolate would be great," I said. As I got out my own blend, personalized to my tastes with an equal portion of dark and milk chocolates, I said, "While I'm heating the milk, why don't you get a pad out of the kitchen desk and we can start a new list."

"I can do that," she said. "We've got quite a bit more information now, don't we?"

"With not much to back it up," I said.

"Come on, we'll figure this out."

"Yeah, there's nothing like the clarity a gunshot brings, is there?"

Maddy ignored the comment and drew a grid on the paper. "At least we have some names to go with our theories."

The milk began to heat through, and I took it off the stove and poured some into two mugs, already awaiting it with the chocolate in the bottom. As I stirred them, I asked, "Would you like marshmallows?"

"No, I'm a purist. You know that."

"Tastes change," I said as I put a dollop of whipped marshmallow on top of my steaming mug.

"Not that much," Maddy said. She took a sip, then smiled. "You've got a knack for hot chocolate, Eleanor."

"Maybe we should put it on the menu," I said, joking.

"It might not be a bad idea."

"I don't think it goes with pizza, do you?"

Maddy shrugged. "Well, I never thought pineapple would, either, but people order it all the time."

"Granted, but that's an aberration, in my mind."

She took another sip, then said, "But you don't mind selling them, do you?"

I smiled at her. "Taste is one thing; profit is another one entirely." I tapped the paper. "Let's see what you've got so far."

She spun the tablet around, and I saw four separate columns headed Name, Motive, Means, and Opportunity across the top. She'd started by listing our suspects' names, beginning with Faith Baron, followed by Steve Baron and Travis White.

"Who else should we add?" Maddy asked.

"Hand me your pen," I said.

I took it, then wrote down "Sheila Olsen." I looked up at the sound of Maddy's cough.

"Come on, do you really think she killed her own brother?"

"I think she had a hundred thousand reasons to," I said.

"She didn't know she was inheriting that kind of money," Maddy protested.

"We just have her word for that, though, don't we?"

Maddy frowned. "I don't know."

"This isn't a grand jury indictment. We're looking at possible suspects. No one's going to see this list but the two of us."

Maddy nodded, though I could tell it was rather reluctant.

I put Penny Olsen on the list, though I could tell my sister wasn't pleased with that addition, either.

"She deserves to be there, at least until we can eliminate her as a suspect."

"If that's the case, we should put your name on there, too. You're a likely culprit as well," Maddy said.

"You know, you're not always as funny as you think you are."

"Really? Because honestly, I think I'm hilarious."

"That makes one of us," I said, trying to hide my smile as I studied the list again. "Hey, what was Richard's boss's name? Do you remember?"

"It was Carl Wilson. Why, do you think he could have done it?"

"From the e-mail we've got, it looks like he had

every reason to be angry with Richard, and that's an important part of the three things we're looking for."

"But did he have the means and the opportunity?" Maddy asked.

"They all did, as far as I can tell. The knife was from Richard's kitchen, so that takes care of the means. We can ask them all for alibis, but I'm not sure we'll get any answers. There's no rational reason anybody on this list will tell us anything." I was suddenly feeling tired and defeated, my earlier anger gone.

Maddy put down her mug. "That shouldn't keep us from asking, though. What's gotten into you, Eleanor?"

"Honestly, it's just starting to sink in how close I came to dying. I'm tired, my nerves are shot, and I'm going through a jumble of emotions," I said. "It's a lot to deal with."

"We can go to bed and finish this in the morning," Maddy said softly.

"No, we need to focus on it right now. Is there anyone we're leaving off the list? Hang on a second." I wrote in "Mystery Blackmail Victim."

"That kind of leaves something to be desired, doesn't it? How in the world are we going to track them down?"

"I'm not sure," I said, just as I heard the front doorbell ring.

"Who could it be this time of night?" Maddy asked.

"I don't know." I grabbed Joe's shotgun from the cabinet, checked to make sure it was loaded, then said, "But I'm about to find out."

"Should you be pointing that thing at anybody?"

"My husband made sure I knew how to use it, Maddy. He tried to teach you, too, remember?"

She shuddered. "Guns make me nervous."

"Really? Getting shot at does it for me."

We approached the door together, but instead of opening it, I called out, "Who is it?"

"Police," a muffled voice said.

Maddy reached for the deadbolt, but I put my hand on hers to stop her. "Hang on a second," I whispered to her.

"What's your name and badge number?" I asked.

"Would you open the door? I want to talk to you." Almost as an afterthought, he said, "It's Kevin Hurley, and my badge number is double-oh six."

As I opened the door, Maddy asked him, "What's the matter, not good enough to be double-oh seven?"

"Truthfully, I wanted to avoid that kind of joke," he said as he eyed my shotgun, absently pointed in his direction. "Do you mind lowering that thing? The safety's off. Did you realize that?"

"How would I be able to defend myself and shoot somebody if it was on?" I asked as I did as he'd requested. "What brings you out here at this time of night?"

"Believe it or not, I wanted to see if you were okay. Do you need anything?"

I shrugged. "If you could catch Richard Olsen's murderer, I'd consider it a personal favor."

"The wheels are turning," he said as he nodded curtly.

"More like spinning in the mud," Maddy retorted.

Kevin shook his head. "Legal procedures and investigations take time."

"I'm not sure how much of that we've got," I said.

Kevin scowled at me. "You two aren't going to do anything stupid, are you?"

Maddy grinned. "You'll have to be more specific than that."

"I'm talking about digging into this case, and you know it."

I said, "We appreciate your concern, but we're both fine. Thanks for stopping in, Chief."

"So it's 'Chief' now and not Kevin. When did that happen?"

"When you stopped believing me," I said. "Good night."

He stared at me, obviously thinking about how to respond to that, but instead of commenting, he turned and left, leaving the front door wide open behind him.

"That went well," Maddy said.

I laughed, despite the dire situation.

As I put the shotgun back, Maddy asked, "If it had been a bad guy, could you really have shot him?"

"Without hesitation," I replied. "Joe always told me never to point it at someone unless I was willing to use it, and it's a lesson I learned well."

"I couldn't do it," Maddy said with a slight shudder.

"Let's just hope I never have to," I said. "Now, on to brighter topics. We've got our list. What do we do next?"

"We've talked to Faith. I think it's time we spoke with her husband."

"Maddy, we can't break up a marriage just because we're digging into this. It's just not right."

"Don't worry. I'm going to be subtle about it," she said. One glance at my expression made her add, "I can be as stealthy as the next woman. I can."

"I'll believe it when I see it," I said.

"Then you're in for a treat first thing tomorrow morning. While his not-so-devoted wife is out for her daily run, I think we should drop in and talk to Steve Baron."

"And Carl Wilson, too," I said. "We need to speak with him face-to-face, to see his reaction to our questions."

"I don't know. Do you think we'll be able to get it all done by nine? That's a tall order."

"We'll use the frozen crusts if we have to," I said. "That gives us until noon to snoop around."

"I thought you hated those things," Maddy said.

"I do, but I hate what's been happening around here far more. My customers will understand. Those crusts are pretty good, anyway."

"If they're that good, why don't you use them all the time?"

"I guess I like the feel of kneading the dough with my hands," I admitted. "But it's something I'm willing to forgo, at least for now."

"Wow, you really are serious about this," Maddy said.

"As serious as I can be," I said as I stifled a yawn. "I know it's just the shank of the evening for you, but it's past my bedtime. Feel free to stay up, make some popcorn, and watch a movie, but I'm going to bed."

"Ever the gracious hostess, Eleanor," she said.

"Come on, you know where the clean sheets and towels are, there's a new toothbrush I haven't gotten around to opening yet in the bathroom, and I'll leave a spare pair of pajamas on the bed. Good night."

"Night. And, Eleanor, I really do believe you about the shooter tonight. You should know that I've always got your back."

"Thanks, I've got yours, too."

When I woke up the next morning, Maddy was still asleep. I could afford to give her another twenty minutes while I made us both breakfast. It wasn't as fancy as the waffles she'd fed me recently, but my pancakes were still pretty good. As I waited for the griddle to heat up after mixing the batter, I dug into my purse and got out Bob Pickering's telephone number. He didn't officially open until eight, but I knew he was always there by seven, so I decided to schedule my car appointment early.

"Hey, Bob, it's Eleanor Swift."

"Hi yourself, Eleanor." He paused, then said, "There's nothing wrong with that window, is there? Sometimes those tracks are tricky. If it won't roll down, bring it by and I'll have another go at it."

"That's not it." I took a deep breath, then said, "I need a new one."

"Now just you hang on there a second, Eleanor. I said I could fix it, and I meant it. It won't take me ten minutes, and you don't even have to come by the shop. I'll swing by your place and have it done in a heartbeat."

"There's nothing to adjust," I said. "The window shattered into a thousand little pieces."

"It fell out? You're kidding me. I don't see how that could happen."

"That's because it didn't," I said as I saw the pre-heat light go off on the griddle. I cradled the telephone between my chin and my shoulder, then poured some batter rounds onto the matted black Teflon surface. "Somebody took a shot at me last night."

"Are you okay? What's gotten into this town?"

"I'm fine, and so is Chief Hurley."

"What's he got to do with this? You two weren't out dallying around, were you?"

I didn't even try to bite back my laughter. "When you hear pigs flying overhead and there's an ice hockey team in Hades, look for the two of us out on the town together. He was doing me a favor. I got a suspicious delivery call, and I wanted someone else there. We got to the address, and somebody shot out the window."

"Are both front windows gone?" he asked as I noticed that tiny bubbles were forming in the battered rounds. I slid my spatula under one, flipped it, then did its mates.

"No, just the driver's side. I hate to ask, but is there any way you can fix it today? I really need my car."

He paused, and I heard pages flipping. Finally, Bob said, "Eleanor, maybe we should make a standing appointment every day. I'm sure I can get you a better deal on windows if I buy them in bulk."

"I don't plan on making a habit of this," I said. "Can you help me out?"

"I can probably squeeze you in. Where's your car now?"

"I have no idea," I said as I removed the pancakes and dropped more batter onto the griddle. "You'll have to call the police station."

"Don't worry, I'll take care of it. It might not be a bad idea if you tried to keep a lower profile than you've been doing lately. Maybe then folks will stop coming after you."

"I'll keep that in mind," I said. As I hung up, Maddy came into the kitchen. My pajamas hung off her like flour sacks, but she still managed to look her usual cute self in them.

"Those smell great," she said as she grabbed a plate and loaded up. She looked around the counter, then asked, "Where's the syrup?"

"I forgot," I said as I dug into the small pantry and pulled out a bottle. "Give me a few minutes and I can heat some up on the stovetop."

"That's okay, I don't mind," she said as she drowned her hotcakes in it.

"Help yourself," I said, laughing despite the heavy mood in my heart. My sister had a way of cheering me up when the outlook for a smile was dismal.

"I did," she said after taking a bite. "Is that coffee I smell?"

It had been percolating on an automatic timer and was now ready. I poured her a cup, then got some for myself as well. It was time to flip the next batch of pancakes, and after I had them turned, I said, "Bob didn't believe me at first when I told him I needed a new car window."

"Can you blame him?" she said as she finished her small stack. "I'm sure he rarely gets back-to-back requests for something like that." She pointed to the pancakes on the griddle as she said, "Those look ready to me."

"Piggy. These are mine."

"You should make them bigger, then," she said.

"Okay, I'll split them with you."

She bit her lip, then said, "No, you're right. It's only fair. You go first."

"How can I, when you've already had some?" I put two of the small pancakes on my plate, then slid the other two onto Maddy's.

"You sure?"

"Just eat them before I change my mind."

She didn't need any more coaxing than that and quickly devoured the two on her plate.

"How do you eat like that and stay so slim?" I asked.

"Just lucky, I guess."

"You're telling me." I split the next batch, then finished off the batter.

"You don't want these, do you? Don't feel obligated. I just hate to throw good batter away."

Maddy held her plate out. "Then think about how much worse it would be to throw perfectly good pancakes away. I'll eat them while you're in the shower."

"Fine, be a glutton," I said with a grin as I put them on her plate. "Don't worry about the dishes. I'll get them later."

"Sounds good to me," she said.

After my shower, I came back out into the kitchen, my hair wrapped up in a towel and a cozy robe cinched tightly around my waist. Maddy was just finishing up the dishes, to my surprise.

"Hey, I thought we were going to leave them," I said.

"You know me, I hate to see a dirty dish. Why don't you finish rinsing these, and I'll get started on my shower." She frowned, then said, "On second thought, I'll do these. You get dressed. Then we can go to my place so I can get ready there."

"I don't mind if you use my shower," I said.

"Neither would I if I had anything clean to change into. Hurry up, though. We've got to brace the mayor while his wife's out jogging."

"I won't be long," I said. I dried my hair quickly, then assembled my make-up into a travel bag.

When I came back out, Maddy said, "I didn't mean you couldn't take the time to put your make-up on."

"I'll do it at your place while you're showering. You're right, we don't have a whole lot of time."

I hoped we wouldn't see anyone while driving to Maddy's, but if someone didn't like my "natural" look, that was too bad. Joe had always preferred me without much make-up, which had been a real relief to me. As girls, Maddy had been the one who stole Mom's lipstick, while I'd been more interested in Dad's cowboy boots.

After a quick shower and change back at her place, Maddy was presentable in record time.

"Let's go," I said.

"I thought you were going to put some make-up on," Maddy said.

"I did."

"Oh. It looks good."

"Liar."

She laughed. "You caught me. I wish you'd let me teach you the fine art of applying make-up. You could look really pretty, if you'd just try a little harder."

"Wow, that's a nice backhanded compliment. I especially like the way you spanked me there at the end."

"You know what I meant," she said.

"Why don't you stick to what you do best, and I'll do the same."

She shook her head. "Eleanor, if we're being honest about it, we're both out of our league right now."

I studied her carefully. "Does that mean you want to drop our investigation? We can, if it's making you uncomfortable."

"Uncomfortable, nothing. I'm scared to death. But that doesn't mean it doesn't need to be done," she said. "We didn't ask for this, but that doesn't mean we can turn our backs on it, either."

"You don't have to be involved," I said softly. "It's not your fight."

"It involves you, Eleanor. That makes it my fight."

There was no denying the strength of commitment in her voice. "Good. Then let's go find the mayor and see what he has to say for himself."

* * *

We found Steve Baron scraping the frost off his darkly tinted VW windshield when we pulled up in front of his house. He was bundled up against the cold, but so were we. Our part of North Carolina, though firmly in the South, still got its share of snow, frosts, and freezes. And while it wasn't as bad as Maine got every winter, it was enough to make folks in Florida shiver at the thought of the temperature drops we faced.

"Steve, can we talk to you?" I asked as we approached him. He was a large man with a ruddy complexion even without the cold weather we were experiencing, and I could see his closely cropped hair stand out on his neck. Steve Baron had prided himself on being the star quarterback on his high school football team, but that had been twenty years and thirty less pounds ago.

"What can I do for you ladies?" he asked. "I just love a brisk morning, don't you?"

"I like the Bahamas myself," Maddy said.

Steve chuckled. "Well, I wouldn't say no to a little hot sand under my feet, either, now that you mention it."

"The cold doesn't seem to bother your wife much," I said.

"Faith's got the constitution of a horse," he said, then realized how that must have sounded. "I didn't mean it that way," he added quickly.

"We know," Maddy said. "How are you two getting along these days?" Leave it to my sister to ask something like that.

I would have preferred we approach it a little more delicately, but that option was now gone.

Steve's gaze focused on each of us in turn. "Why? What have you heard?"

"That's an interesting way to respond to a question like that," I said.

The mayor shook his head. "It's a natural enough question. Being in the public eye like I am, folks tend to talk, even when there's nothing to say. I've heard the rumors about Faith, but that's all they are. She's a friendly woman, always has been. That leads to tongues wagging."

"Among other things," Maddy said.

"I'll thank you to tread carefully," Steve said, an angry edge in his voice.

"She didn't mean anything by it," I said, stepping in before Maddy could reply with something that would effectively end the conversation.

"The reason we came by was that we thought we saw you talking to Richard Olsen right before he died. That was you, wasn't it?"

Both he and Maddy gave me the same look of disbelief, but thankfully my sister's expression was out of his range of sight. I was taking a stab in the dark, but what else did we have at this point?

"I don't know what you're talking about," he said.

"If you weren't with Richard, where were you the night he was killed?" I asked. "The only reason I came to you before I talked to Kevin Hurley about it was that I wanted to give you a chance to explain it to me instead of the police."

The mayor looked at me, glanced over at Maddy, then returned his gaze to me. "I was with my wife."

"All evening?"

"Yes," he said after a moment's hesitation. "We were at Dusty's, in Clearmont, eating out. Is that all you wanted?" As he got into his car, he said, "If you ladies will excuse me, I've got important work to do at City Hall today."

I nodded, and after he was gone, we walked back to my sister's car.

Maddy said, "He was clearly lying, wasn't he?"

"I think so, too. The question is, which part was he lying about: the fact that they ate at Dusty's, or that they were together all evening?"

"There's only one way to find out. We need to talk to someone at the restaurant and see if anyone remembers seeing them there."

"That's not exactly information they'll be willing to give out, though, is it?"

Maddy said, "Normally I'd say no, but I've got a friend there who owes me a favor. What better time will there ever be to cash it in?"

"Do I want to know what the original favor was for?" I asked.

"I don't think so. Just accept it for what it's worth, and be glad that your sister isn't squeamish."

"Fine, you can call this afternoon. But what do we do in the meantime? There's no reason to talk to the mayor again until we have something a little more concrete than one of my bluffs."

"That was well done, by the way. That declaration of yours caught me completely off guard."

I smiled. "What can I say? I have my moments, too."

"I knew we had more in common than just our parents," she said.

"I guess there's only one other person we need

to talk with besides Travis. Let's go find Richard's boss and see if he'll talk to us."

We got into Maddy's car and went off searching for Carl Wilson. Hopefully, he'd be able to give us another piece of the puzzle of who had killed Richard Olsen.

We found Mr. Wilson at his desk in a cluster of small offices in what passed as Timber Ridge's industrial complex. Tucked in among copier repair shops, janitorial supply houses, and bulk office supplies firms was Shred It All.

Sitting at a desk with his nameplate prominently displayed, Carl Wilson was a pudgy man with no hair on his head, but instead, he sported a luxurious, thick black mustache. "Can I help you?"

"We need to speak with you about Richard Olsen," I said.

He didn't even wait for us to explain further. "There's more? I've had two formal complaints since the man died. All I can say is that we're very sorry about what happened, and we'll do everything in our power to make it right by you."

"It's pretty disturbing, isn't it?" Maddy asked rather glumly.

"You don't know the half of it. Who would have thought the man would sort through the documents before we shredded them? And then have the gall to try to blackmail our customers."

"It's criminal," I said, hoping he'd open up more.

"I'm fully aware of that. I've spoken with my attorneys, and we're offering compensation for those who were hurt by his actions." He grabbed a clipboard, then said, "If you'll give me your information, I'll see about adding your names to our list."

That was awkward, since we'd never been clients of the shredding service. Maddy took the clipboard and started to write, though, without any hesitation. When I glanced over at the form, I saw that she was carefully transcribing the lyrics to "Mary Had a Little Lamb." While she did that, I said, "I'd like to see the list of the others."

"Sorry, that's confidential," Wilson replied automatically.

I raised one eyebrow. "As confidential as your shredding service was supposed to be? It's a bit ironic that you're taking that position, don't you think?"

He looked as though he wanted to cry. "I had nothing to do with any of that. I'm just trying to clean up his mess." Wilson suddenly scowled. "If I had the power, I'd bring him back to life just to choke it out of him again."

The intense violence of the statement and his expression scared me more than I would have ever admitted. "You really hated him, didn't you?"

Wilson got control of his temper, then said quietly, "Not until he was dead. When he was alive, Richard was the nicest guy you'd ever want to meet. He exceeded every sales goal I ever gave him, and when we went out drinking after work, he was always good for a quick round of drinks. I wouldn't have thought so kindly of him if I'd known he was doing it with my money."

"Then he stole from you, too?" I asked.

Wilson nodded. "And I'm not just talking about my reputation. The man was a thief, pure and simple."

"Are we talking thousands, or more?" Maddy

asked, losing all interest in her pretense of filling out his form.

"Oh, I doubt it ever topped a grand, even if you added it all together. It's just the principle of it, you know? How's that form coming?"

"Just about done," Maddy said.

As she shifted her focus back to writing, I said, "Just between us, I'd really love to know who else your employee took advantage of."

"Sorry, I can't tell you. You know, I never caught what firm you two were with."

I was about to try to stall him when Maddy said, "I don't think I like your attitude." Her tone of voice was insulting, and I could see Wilson stare at her for a second before he reacted.

"I apologize if I was terse," he said, though there was no sympathy in his words or expression.

Maddy was having none of that, though. "Our lawyer told us it was a bad idea to come here, but we wanted to give you the benefit of the doubt. I see that he was right, and we were clearly wrong." She tore the form from the clipboard, wadded it up into a ball, then stuck it in her purse. "You'll be hearing from him by the end of business today."

Wilson dropped all pretense of trying to appease us. He growled, "Tell him to get in line."

"Good day, sir," I said quickly, and then Maddy and I stormed out of the office.

Once we were out of sight, Maddy said, "Wow, he wasn't a nice man at all, was he?"

I said, "Give him a break. We can't begin to understand the kind of pressure he must be under. I'm willing to bet he'll lose his business because of this."

"I'm not talking about Wilson. I mean Richard Olsen." As we got into her car, she asked, "I wonder who all he was blackmailing?"

"I don't know that we'll ever find out," I said.

Maddy frowned. "Don't give up so easily. I bet Bob Lemon could find out."

I couldn't believe she was even suggesting it. Bob had already done me a great favor by coming to the police station with me. I wasn't about to impose any more on him. "No, we can't do that."

"I'm sure Bob won't mind. All he has to do is posture a little, just enough to bully Wilson into giving us those names."

"Maddy, that's terrible. We shouldn't kick the man when he's down."

"When should we kick him, then? We need those names."

I thought about it as we drove toward the pizzeria, then said, "We don't really need them, you know."

"What are you talking about?"

I watched the traffic whiz by, then said, "Think about it, Maddy. The only people who'd be willing to report the blackmail attempts would be folks who didn't kill him. It would only bring scrutiny, something the killer couldn't afford. Nobody's that stupid."

"You think? I understand the criminal element isn't all that intelligent."

"That's because you get your opinions from watching *COPS* reruns. I can't see someone killing Richard Olsen because he was blackmailing them, then filing a complaint about it."

Maddy seemed to consider it, then nodded. "I suppose you're right."

"Think about it, though. If he was blackmailing two people who were willing to report it, he could have been blackmailing more that wouldn't dare."

"So, how do we find out?"

"It's got to be tied to that P.O. box," I said.

Maddy swung the car around, and I asked, "Where are we going?"

"I want to see this box, and if there's anything in it."

We drove to the post office, where the boxes were kept in a separate hallway nook. I had to admit, I was curious if there was anything in there myself.

Maddy and I walked in together, and as I pretended to search my purse for a key, we both glanced inside the clear glass window of number ten. There was a single letter in there, but we didn't need to open it to see who had sent it.

It was lavender, just like the ones Richard had received from Faith Baron.

But was it another love letter, or did this one contain something more?

Chapter 10

"It's another dead end," Maddy said as we walked back out to her car.

"What are you talking about?"

"It's obviously just another mash note," she said. "And I don't have any desire to read it, do you?"

"I'd still like to see what it says," I said. "Do you think there's a chance Sheila would show us?"

"I don't think she even realizes there's a P.O. box in her brother's name. From the speed that she cleared out those bank accounts, I doubt she'd leave any possible source of revenue untouched."

"That's true. She probably even cashed in the rolls of coins you two found."

"How'd you know?" Maddy asked. "She did it while we were at the bank together."

Then I remembered what had been nagging at the back of my mind. "You found something else in that box, didn't you?"

Maddy frowned, then said, "You know what? There was a scrap of paper in there, too. In the excitement of finding all of that money in the checking account, I forgot all about it."

"Did you happen to see what was written on the paper?"

Maddy nodded. "She handed it to me while we were in the vault." She frowned a second, then added, "I don't think I ever gave it back to her."

"You've had it the entire time and forgot it?"

My sister looked apologetic as she said, "Hey, things were a little crazy, what with her fainting and shattering my cell phone."

"Maddy, where's the piece of paper?"

She bit her lip, a sure sign my sister was concentrating, then said, "I have no idea, unless I stuffed it into my jacket pocket."

"Was this the jacket you were wearing?"

"No," Maddy said as she did another U-turn, slamming me against the passenger door.

"Would you please stop doing that?" I snapped.

"Sorry. We need to go to my apartment. That's where the jacket is now."

We got back to her place, and though we both searched high and low for it, the coat in question wasn't there.

"Somebody broke in and stole it," she said.

"The door was locked when we got here," I said. As I looked around, there were no signs that there'd been a burglary. I walked to the door and looked at the locks. No signs of forced entry, either. "You must have left it somewhere else."

"The only three places I've been are here, your place, and the pizzeria."

"I'm pretty sure it's not at my house," I said.

"Then let's go to the Slice."

I glanced at my watch. "If we hurry, we might be able to make fresh dough for today after all."

"Eleanor, we've got more important things to do than bake."

"My reputation is all I've got left, Maddy. If folks notice that something's a little off, they might not come back. And then where will we be?"

"Well, for starters, you won't be in jail for a crime you didn't commit."

"There's that," I said as I nodded. "But if the Slice goes under, we're both out of work. That's not inconsequential."

"No, I realize that. Tell you what. Let's go to the Slice, see what the note says, then decide after that."

"I can live with that," I said.

As we hurried toward the pizzeria, I wondered what might be on that scrap of paper. Could it be an important clue, or was it just some of the flotsam we all seem to accumulate in our lives? I hadn't been inside my own safety-deposit box since I'd retrieved Joe's will and life insurance policy. I didn't have any real idea what else was in there, since he'd taken almost exclusive care of it. One of these days I'd have to go in and clean it out, but I still couldn't bring myself to do it yet.

Maddy and I got to the Slice an hour past our usual time, but I could still make the regular- and thin-crust doughs we needed. I'd discovered a way to speed up the process, and though the quality might not be 100 percent, both would still be miles ahead of the frozen crusts we used in a pinch. Maddy searched for her jacket as I prepped the yeast and the other ingredients.

"It's not here," Maddy said a few minutes later.

"You must have left it somewhere else," I said as I kneaded the dough.

"I'm not talking about my jacket," she said as she held it up for me to see. "I'm saying that the note is gone."

"Are you sure you jammed it into your pocket?"

Maddy shrugged. "I'm never sure about anything anymore."

"Don't worry, it'll turn up sooner or later."

Maddy stared at me as she said, "You're taking this awfully casually. I thought we were going to spend the morning looking for clues."

"Funny, I thought we just had. We're not going to solve this overnight, Maddy. In the meantime, we've got work to do here."

My sister frowned. "I know you're right, but I feel so helpless. We can't leave it to Kevin Hurley. There's too much at stake."

"Hey, I'm not giving up," I said as I wiped a smudge of flour off my cheek with the back of one hand. "I'm just saying that we can't let the quality of our pizzas slip even a little. This is important, too."

"Okay, you're right," she said as she reached for her apron. "I'll get started on the toppings."

"That's the spirit. In the meantime, while we work we can still talk about what our next move should be."

After she washed up, Maddy began prepping the toppings trays, swinging her knife through the air periodically for special emphasis.

As I covered the dough with a washcloth to rise, I started making a fresh batch of our homemade sauce for the next day. After it cooked, it needed to be cooled, then strained, so it was always something I had to keep my eye on. I didn't mind, though. Making the sauce was one of my favorite jobs at the Slice.

As I sautéed the garlic and onion in butter on the stovetop, I said, "We've come up with a pretty strong list of suspects, don't you think?"

"Too many, if you ask me," she said. "I was kind of hoping we'd be able to eliminate some of them by now, but instead, it just keeps growing."

"I think we can cross Carl Wilson off our list," I said as I added the tomatoes, paste, salt, pepper, and my own blend of spices to the pot.

"Why do you say that?"

After I brought everything in the pot to a boil, I reduced the heat to a simmer and set the timer for two hours. All I had to do now was stir it occasionally, then mash the tomatoes from time to time while the heat did the hard work. "Did you see the look on his face? He felt betrayed. I don't think he had any idea what Richard had been up to."

"I don't know. I'm not ready to cross him off our list," Maddy said.

"Fine, we can keep digging, but I don't think he did it." As I started cleaning up my station, I asked, "Do you have anybody you're ready to cross off?"

"No, but that reminds me. I've got a call to make."

"You're not phoning Bob Lemon, are you? I thought we agreed not to do that."

"Take it easy. I'm calling my friend Cindy, at

Dusty's. I want to see if the Barons really were there most of the night."

"You don't believe anybody, do you?"

"Not when it comes to murder," Maddy said as she washed her hands.

"Even me?"

She pretended to look me over thoroughly. "Until I find something that makes me believe otherwise, I'm willing to give you the benefit of the doubt."

"Gee, thanks. I feel all warm and fuzzy inside."

Maddy laughed as she reached for the phone.

"I didn't think they opened till four," I said.

"I can't exactly call her at work, can I?" Maddy asked.

After she dialed the number, my sister said, "I'll take this into the dining room so it doesn't bother you."

"It won't bother me," I protested.

By the time I said it, she was gone. I wanted to hear at least her end of the conversation, but unless I walked out front, I wouldn't be able to. Maybe she'd have to reference the mysterious favor she'd done her friend and didn't want to do it within my hearing. If that was the case, I should be thanking her instead of scolding.

Four minutes later, she came back in smiling. "Well, that was interesting."

"What did she say?" I asked as I mashed the tomatoes again, then stirred the pot.

"She thinks they were there, but she could swear they left before nine."

I shrugged as I put down the wooden spoon I'd been using to stir. "That's not exactly something we can take to Kevin Hurley, is it?"

"I can do better than that," she said. "As soon as Cindy gets to work, she's going to check credit card receipts. It will have the exact time they paid on it, so that should be proof one way or the other, wouldn't you think?"

"Could we get a copy of it, or is that too risky?"

"I've already got it covered. Cindy was more than happy to promise to fax it here as soon as she gets it." We took faxed food orders, an idea of Joe's that hadn't worked out that well, but sometimes it was nice having a fax available for suppliers and such.

"Wow, that's some favor. I'd hate to think she's risking her job for us."

Maddy said, "Don't worry, she's not. I already told her if she couldn't get hold of the receipt not to sweat it, but knowing Cindy, she'll have it before four."

"In the meantime, we need to get ready for our lunch crowd, assuming there'll be one. Do you want to run the kitchen today, or the front?"

"Why don't we let Greg handle the front and we'll work together back here?"

I glanced at the schedule, though I knew it by heart. "Greg's not coming in today. He's got a psychology class at the college, and then he's doing his work-study at the library. It's Josh's shift today, but I'm pretty sure he won't be in, either."

"After getting shot at in your car, you'd think the chief of police would be smart enough to know that you didn't take a potshot at yourself."

"He still thinks what happened to us last night is unrelated to Richard Olsen's murder, so I'm pretty sure he still thinks I could have done it. And until somebody figures out who killed the man, we're going to be shorthanded."

"You could always hire someone else to take his place," Maddy said.

"I thought you liked Josh."

"I do," my sister protested, "but that doesn't mean we can ignore the fact that we'll be working alone today."

"Buck up," I said as I shoved her apron to her. "If today's anything like yesterday, I've got a feeling we're going to be able to handle it just fine."

"Just one thing, then," Maddy said.

"What's that?" I asked as I tied my own apron on.

"No more call-in orders, okay? I don't want to see my car window end up like yours."

"Nobody does, believe me," I said. "As far as I'm concerned, we can disconnect the blasted phone until this is over."

"We'd better not do that," Maddy said. "We might need it later."

"Fine, but the ringer stays off."

"Done," Maddy said. She glanced up at the clock, then added, "Two minutes till noon. I might as well open up."

"Come on, it'll be fun," I said.

"So you say."

After Maddy was gone, I leaned over and turned on the radio to get the local news and weather. It was a ritual, much like coming in and making dough fresh every morning, a series of tasks that let me know I still had a place in this world.

Three minutes later she came back into the kitchen.

I said, "That was quick. Do you have an order for me already?"

"Nobody's here," she said. "Usually we have at least four or five folks waiting by the door for us to open, but when I opened the door a minute ago, I could swear I saw a couple of tumbleweeds drifting past."

"There aren't any tumbleweeds in Timber Ridge," I said.

"I know, but if there were, they wouldn't have much competition for traveling space, at least not in front of our place."

I frowned. "Maybe everybody stayed in today. It's cold out, and the wind's picking up. I just heard on the radio that there's a chance of snow flurries later."

"If they come, we could use it as an excuse, but it's not keeping folks from shopping everywhere else. I glanced down the plaza, and Paul's Pastries is so busy he might have to turn some of them away."

"They'll come back to us," I said, with more hope in my voice than in my heart. "You need to be ready when they do."

"Fine, but I get the crossword puzzle," she said as she reached for the paper. We didn't take the Timber Ridge paper, since the owner/editor had such a grudge against our family, but that didn't mean we wanted to live without the news. Instead, we took the paper from Charlotte at the pizzeria. Much of the local news didn't matter to either one of us, but it kept us informed about national events and supplied a crossword puzzle every day; word jumbles; and Wuzzles, word puzzles that were fun to cipher out. Maddy and I usually alternated during lulls, but if this current respite kept up much longer, we'd have to subscribe to more newspapers just for their puzzles.

We ultimately got a few customers, but not enough to meet our basic expenses for the day, let alone the salaries Maddy and I drew. I was thinking about shutting the place down when I heard the fax beeping at me.

I walked back into the office and pulled the paper out of the tray. Cindy had faxed us the receipt, then added another sheet that said, "Here you go. I know this doesn't make us even, but I hope it knocks a little off my debt to you. Cindy."

I took the fax up front, prepared to pull Maddy aside to show her.

That wasn't going to be a problem, though, since we had the place to ourselves.

I handed her the paper, then said, "I'm going to make us a pizza. How does that sound?"

"I thought you'd never ask. I'll join you."

"What if someone comes in?"

Maddy said, "If it makes you feel any better, I'll prop the kitchen door open so I can hear the front door chime. Don't get your hopes up, though. This is usually a slow time for us anyway, and with the way things have been going today, I'd be surprised if someone came in asking for change."

"You've got a point," I said as I pulled out some dough and began knuckling it into a pan.

Maddy studied the document, then asked, "Did you see the time they left?"

"I don't know about that, but they paid at 7:02 P.M."

"Not exactly a late dinner, is it? They had plenty

of time to get back here and shove a knife into Richard Olsen by ten, when you found him."

"You think they did it together?" That possibility had never even occurred to me.

"No, it's a little too Hitchcock for my taste, but that doesn't mean one of them didn't slip away from home and do it alone."

"So their alibi isn't worth much, is it?"

"Certainly not the way Steve Baron made it sound."

"Then we keep digging," I said as I added sauce, then toppings and cheese.

"It's what we do lately, isn't it? It's frustrating not being able to eliminate anyone, isn't it?"

I nodded as I cleaned up the minuscule mess I'd just made. Joe and I had agreed from the first day of opening the Slice that our workstations would be as clean as we could make them. It hadn't been that hard for me to do, but Joe was a "clean-up-at-the-end-of-the-day" kind of guy, and it had taken months for him to acquire new habits. We'd made jokes about old dogs and new tricks, but I'd have given anything to clean up after him one last time. Funny how it was the little things I seemed to miss so much.

"Hey, are you okay?" Maddy asked, drawing me back to the present.

"I'm fine," I said as I wiped the prep counter down again.

"You were thinking of Joe, weren't you?" she asked, her voice softer than I'd heard it in several months.

"I was," I admitted. "How did you know?"

She seemed to think about it, then said, "You get this wistful look in your eyes that nearly breaks my heart. Eleanor, I don't want you to ever forget your husband, but is it really healthy to keep mourning him for the rest of your life?"

I wiped an errant tear that had somehow found its way to my cheek. "He was my one true love."

Maddy said, "I can't really say I've had that yet."

"With all the times you've been married?" I asked.

She smiled at me. "To be honest with you, after a while, they all kind of blur together. Let's see, how many times have I been married so far? Four? Or is it five? I keep losing track."

"I can't believe you just said 'so far.' Would you seriously ever get married again? I don't think you're exactly the poster child for marriage."

Maddy laughed. "Are you kidding me? If I didn't believe in the institution, do you think I'd keep practicing it? I'm a born romantic." She paused, then said, "I just haven't been as lucky as you were. I haven't found my 'happily ever after' yet, and you got yours on the first try."

"That's true, but my 'ever after' had an expiration date on it that nobody told me about beforehand."

She touched my shoulder lightly. "Better to have loved and lost and all of that, though, wouldn't you say?"

I nodded. "I would." The mood had grown entirely too somber, so I brightened up and added, "Don't worry, your Mr. Right is out there somewhere, as long as you keep looking."

Maddy smiled. "And if I don't find him right away, just think about how much fun I can have looking for him."

The pizza was ready, so I pulled it off the line, cut it into slices, and put it on a tray. "Shall we eat back here, or in the dining room?"

"I want to eat out front again," Maddy said. "If it starts to snow, I don't want to miss a flurry or a flake."

"I could use a little snow myself," I said, remembering how much fun we'd had with snow as kids. "Grab the drinks, then."

Maddy asked, "Do you want water again?"

I thought about it, then shook my head. "I'm going to be a real cowgirl today. I'll take a Coke."

"Good girl," Maddy said.

We'd barely taken our first bites when a light snow began to fall. They weren't the big, fat flakes that meant a large accumulation, just a wistful dusting of tiny crystals, barely enough to see on the brick pavers out front, but it was fun to watch, especially since we were inside with warm hands and full bellies.

There were a thousand worse places to be that I could think of right off the bat.

We were just getting started when Sheila Olsen walked in.

"Ladies," she said as she shook the snow off her jacket onto our freshly mopped floor. I knew that before the night was over, we'd have to clean it a dozen times.

"Hey, Sheila," I said as I started to stand. "What can I get for you?"

"That pizza looks absolutely divine," she said as she looked at the remaining slices of our lunch.

"Great, I'll make you one just like it," I said, determined not to feed her for free again, especially after knowing how much money she'd had dropped in her lap upon her brother's death.

"That would be lovely," she said. "While I'm waiting, a beer would be nice."

Maddy stood, then began collecting our dirty dishes and glasses as she said, "Nothing's changed since you used to live here, Sheila. The county's still dry." Though a few of the restaurants in town had tried to get a waiver for alcohol sales, it had been soundly defeated each time it had come to a vote. I myself had mixed feelings about the issue. I understood the appeal of a hot pizza and a cold beer, but then again, if I served alcohol to the public, I wouldn't be able to hire teenagers from the high school to work at the pizzeria. Not only were they a ready source of employees, but they were also willing to work for the minimum wage I could barely afford. And since no one else in town could serve beer either, it worked out fine for me. For those of my customers who insisted on having a beer with their meal, there was always takeout. Then I remembered I didn't offer that at the moment. That stand would have to change. I had to start answering my phone again. If folks got out of the habit of coming to me for their pizzas, I might never be able to get them back. No more deliveries until the murder was solved, though. If they wanted to eat at home, they were going to have to come by and pick up their pizzas themselves.

"Fine, I'll have a Coke then," she said. She studied me for a second, then added, "Cleaning house is dusty work, isn't it?"

"It can be," I said before Maddy could take a jab at her. I knew there had to be a reason she was coming by the Slice, and I doubted it was for my pizza, no matter how good I personally thought it was.

"When the pizza's ready, perhaps you two could join me." She looked around the empty dining hall, then added, "If time permits."

"We'll see what we can do," I said as I nodded a warning to Maddy not to snap at her. "We'll have that Coke right out."

Maddy got her drink, then came back into the kitchen fuming as I slid the pizza onto the conveyor.

"What's wrong?" I asked.

"The nerve of that woman," Maddy said. "She's out there acting like she owns Timber Ridge. It was all I could do not to dump that Coke on her head."

"I'm glad you resisted the impulse," I said as I wiped the counter down.

"Why, do you want to do it yourself? If you do, I want to at least watch."

I shook my head. "There'll be no Coke baths today," I said.

Maddy frowned. "You're just no fun anymore, are you?"

"I have my moments," I said. "Why do you suppose she wants us to join her?"

"I'm guessing she wants to brag about her new wealth," Maddy said. "Why else would she be here?"

"I've got a feeling it's not about bragging," I said.

When the pizza was nearly ready, I suggested, "Take her a pitcher, and add a pair of glasses for us. If Sheila wants to talk, I say we give her the opportunity."

"If she doesn't, can I dump the pitcher on her then?"

"We'll see," I said. "In the meantime, let's give her some rope and see where she goes with it. Follow my lead, all right?"

"Don't I always?"

I laughed. "I can't remember a time you have yet, but I'm still hopeful."

Maddy grinned. "I can't fault you for that, can I?"

After the pizza was ready, I cut it into eight pieces, then slid it onto a tray. Maddy did as I asked and got the pitcher, along with two glasses and three plates.

I said, "We already ate, remember?"

"I don't care. She ate our food before. I'm going to force myself to choke down at least one of her slices. How about you? Are you game?"

"I can always manage a slice," I said. "Much to my dismay."

Maddy patted my hip, then said, "Don't worry, a lot of men like curvy women."

"And for those who don't, there's always you," I said with a smile.

"Nice. We've got all our bases covered then, don't we? Are you ready to tackle Sheila?"

"As ready as I'm ever going to be," I said.

We took the food out to Sheila, who'd moved to a table in back, out of sight of passersby.

"I decided to move," she said as we joined her. "I hope you don't mind."

"As you pointed out, we're not exactly overflowing with customers at the moment, are we?" I asked.

"Don't worry, they'll come around. Just give them time."

A pep talk was the last thing I wanted from Sheila Olsen. She wanted something from us, though I didn't know exactly what that was yet.

I served her a slice while Maddy refilled her glass, all without being asked. I wanted her to be comfortable with us, relaxed enough to let something slip. To her credit, my sister was nicer than I'd ever seen her, playing her role to the fullest. I swear, I kept waiting for her to offer a pillow and a fan to our one customer, but if Sheila noticed the shift in attitude, she didn't show it outright.

After she took a bite, she said, "I don't know why you aren't more popular. Your pizzas are wonderful."

"Thanks," I said as Maddy leaned back and stuck her tongue out at Sheila, thankfully out of the woman's line of sight.

"I'm going to miss these," she said as she took another bite.

"Are you going somewhere?" I asked.

"I'm afraid there are too many memories of Richard here. I'm interviewing Realtors for the next two days. Then I'll be leaving Timber Ridge for good. It doesn't matter how long the house stays on the market. I don't have to be here to sell it."

"Did you find the will?" I asked, trying to keep my knowledge of the answer out of my voice.

"Yes, but it didn't matter. My sweet brother put my name on everything he owned. I had no idea he'd be so generous."

"How nice," I said, ignoring the faces my sister was making. Honestly, sometimes she could be so juvenile, not that I wasn't thinking dark thoughts myself. There hadn't even been a service yet, and she was already erasing her brother's presence from the world.

"I have a friend who might be able to help sell the house," Maddy said suddenly. If she knew someone personally in real estate in Timber Ridge, I wasn't aware of it. Then again, there were depths and levels to my sister that I fully realized I didn't know.

"I'd be glad to interview her," Sheila said. "Have her come by the house this afternoon or tomorrow."

"Actually, it's a man, and a rather handsome one at that," Maddy said. "I'll take care of it right now. I have to call him from the back, though. His number's in my purse."

After my sister darted off on her errand, I said, "It must be an awesome burden tying up the loose ends of someone else's life."

"More than I ever imagined," she said. "Have the police made any progress on discovering who killed him? Is there anyone they're looking at?"

Besides me? I wanted to ask but somehow managed to stifle. "Not that I've heard, but then again, the chief of police doesn't exactly confide in me."

"Nor me," she said. "In fact, I just came from his

office. He refused to give me any information at all. All he would say is that the case is still an open investigation. That doesn't sound very promising, does it?"

"No, it doesn't," I said. I suddenly remembered her promise to help us and realized it was a perfect opportunity to go fishing. "If you're still willing to help us investigate, Maddy and I would love to have you."

That certainly got her attention. "Who are your suspects so far?"

"That's the problem," I said. "We really don't have any." It was an outright lie, but I was looking for information at the moment, not dispensing it.

I wasn't sure she was buying it, though. "Honestly? Eleanor, you can tell me. He was my brother, after all."

"We haven't made any progress at all," I lied again. "I'm afraid my sister and I are much more suited to running a pizzeria than we are to solving crime."

"How disappointing," Sheila said. She looked down at the pizza, then said abruptly, "I'm afraid I'm full."

"Would you like me to box it up for you?"

"No, don't bother," she said as she stood.

"Let me get your bill," I said, hoping to stall her until Maddy came back.

It wasn't going to happen, though. Sheila threw a twenty on the table, then said, "Keep the change. Good-bye, Eleanor."

"Bye," I said as she disappeared back out into the snow, draping her jacket over her shoulders.

Maddy came back out, looked around, then said,

"Don't tell me you let her get away again. Honestly, Eleanor, you've got to start doing better."

"I couldn't lock her in," I said. "Did you get hold of your Realtor friend? Who is he, by the way?"

"Tom Frances," Maddy said.

"I didn't realize you and Tom were that close." I knew him enough to nod in his direction in public, but he wasn't a pizza kind of guy, at least not my kind of pizza. Tall and fit with gray creeping into his temples, he handled the high-end sales in our region, absolutely no homes like the place Richard Owens had lived in. "Isn't he a little too upscale for that neighborhood?"

She shrugged. "Be that as it may, he's going to go by this afternoon and talk to her. When he's finished, he's coming by to bring me up to date on what she said."

"Don't tell me; he owes you a favor, too."

She wouldn't answer, which was a response in and of itself. "Let's just say he was willing to do it for me and leave it at that."

"Who exactly *are* you?" I asked.

"What do you mean?"

"You're my sister, and I thought I knew everything there was to know about you, but you still manage to keep surprising me."

She just laughed. "Life's full of that, isn't it? Just accept my contributions for what they are. It's better for everyone if you don't ask for too many details."

"So I'm learning," I said as the front door chimed and we had a new customer.

It was a stranger to me, though I wouldn't have been surprised if Maddy had known her.

"Are you open for business?" the older woman asked as she looked around the empty dining room.

"Yes, ma'am," I said as I grabbed a menu. "Where would you like to sit?"

"By the window, if I could. I needed a place to come in from the cold, but I love watching it snow, don't you?"

"It's one of my favorite things in the world to do," I said.

She rubbed her hands together, then said, "Let's see. I'd like a cup of coffee to start with. Then I'll have a small cheese pizza."

"Very good," I said as I motioned Maddy to the back.

As she got the coffee, I said, "Sheila was pumping me about our investigation while you were calling your Realtor."

"He's not my Realtor," Maddy said. "So, what did you say?"

"I basically told her we were incompetent investigators with no clue about what happened to her brother."

"So you told her the truth," Maddy said as she laughed.

"Not exactly. We have a list of suspects, including her, but I didn't see any reason to tell her that."

"How did she react when you told her we had nothing?"

I scratched my lip as I said, "She said she was disappointed, but I could swear she looked relieved."

"But that could just have easily been your imagination," Maddy said as she left to deliver the coffee to our lone customer.

After I finished making the pizza and put it on the conveyor, I heard the door chime again and wondered if we'd lost our customer.

Instead, I saw a group of twenty people coming in, stamping their feet on the mat and hanging their coats up on the hooks along the wall.

In a few minutes, Maddy came back with their orders and explained, "Their bus broke down on its way to the mountains for a ski trip, so while they're waiting, they all decided to have some pizza."

"Let's hear it for mechanical malfunctions," I said as I started preparing the orders. Maybe, just maybe, we'd make enough today to break even after all. It would be a nice change of pace after the business lull we'd been experiencing.

At the very least, it would give Maddy and me something to do in the meantime.

Something we were both good at, at any rate.

Chapter 11

"**A**re you here on official police business, or is this a social call?" I asked Kevin Hurley as he walked back into my kitchen a little after eight.

"Eleanor, you know I don't make social calls in uniform," he said.

"Then what can I do for you, Chief?"

"You can still call me Kevin," he said, trying to smile, but not quite making it.

"As long as I'm on your list of suspects, I think it makes sense to be a little more formal, don't you? I *am* still on your list, aren't I?"

When he didn't deny it, I added, "Well, there you go."

"I'm here looking for Josh. Have you seen him?"

"Not since I threw him out for trying to work his shift," I said. "Why, is he missing?" Josh was a good kid, and I hoped nothing had happened to him.

"He's probably just hiding out to get back at me. He's your biggest fan. You know that, don't you?"

"I like him," I said. "He's got a good heart."

"Believe me, I know. I'm just afraid it's going to get him into real trouble one of these days."

"He'll turn up," I said. "He's not about to do anything stupid, like take off for long."

"I hope you're right." He started for the door, then stopped and turned back to me. "Listen, if he shows up, let me know, would you?"

"I will," I said. I'd get Josh's permission first, but Kevin had a point. He deserved to know where his son was.

"Thanks," he said. "That's all I'm asking."

After he was gone, Maddy came back. "What was that all about?"

"Josh is missing," I said.

Maddy didn't look the least troubled by the declaration.

I asked, "Aren't you concerned?"

"Not really. Come on, Eleanor, you know that Josh is just as headstrong as his father was at that age. He'll turn up."

"I hope you're right."

"Is that all he wanted?" Maddy asked.

"That was it. Now, don't you still have customers to wait on?"

"I'm going, I'm going. Who knew you'd turn out to be such a slave driver?"

I laughed. "If anybody in the world knows it, it should be you."

After she was gone, I started wondering where Josh might be. I hoped Maddy was right. I'd hate to think that he'd done something stupid on my account, like running away. There was nothing I could do about it at the moment, though, except wish that he'd turn up soon, and be all right.

My hands were buried in a sink of hot, sudsy water when Maddy came back. "I need you out front," she said.

"I'm kind of busy here," I said as I finished scrubbing the glass in my hand. We did our dishes in the sink, though Joe had promised to buy me a dishwasher as soon as we got on our feet. Six years later and I was still doing them by hand, but I didn't mind. It gave my thoughts a chance to wander as I scrubbed, rinsed, and dried. I'd read once that Agatha Christie said she came up with some of her best ideas while washing dishes, and I believed it.

"Dry your hands and come on out. Tom Frances is back from his meeting with Sheila, and I want you to hear what he has to say."

"You're his contact," I said. "You talk to him and let me know what's going on."

"Be that way," she said. "Maybe I won't tell you what he says."

I laughed. "I know you better than that. You won't be able to help yourself." As I wiped my nose with the back of my hand, I added, "Besides, I'm sure he'll talk freer if I'm not standing there looking over your shoulder."

Maddy shook her head. "Suit yourself. I just thought I'd offer."

The second she was gone, I had to fight the impulse to dry my hands and see what the Realtor had to say, but I still thought my instincts were dead-on. The only way I knew him was from the photograph on his FOR SALE signs all over town. Evidently he and Maddy were much closer. Besides, I had dishes to wash. Who else would do them? Maddy? I didn't think so. Greg wasn't working tonight, though he'd be in tomorrow. With Josh gone, we were severely shorthanded. Maybe I'd have to go by the high school and put up another HELP WANTED notice, but I hoped it wouldn't come to that. If it did, I wouldn't fire my new hire when and if Josh came back. It wasn't his fault that his dad had forbidden him to come to work for me, but I didn't have much choice about hiring someone else, either. I had a business to run, and if our level of customers ever approached where we'd been before Richard Olsen's murder, Maddy and I would never be able to do it with just Greg's part-time help. Rita's absence was leaving a real hole in our work schedule, but I wouldn't welcome her back. I rewarded loyalty, a quality she clearly didn't possess.

Maddy came back just as I finished the last pizza pan in my sink. I'd have to do the dishes again at least twice more before the night was over, but I'd gotten a jump on things, so at least we weren't falling behind.

As I wiped my hands on a dish towel, I asked, "What did he have to say?"

Maddy pretended to concentrate on something else. After a few seconds, she looked at me. "Sorry. Did you say something?"

"You know I did. What did your Realtor friend tell you about his meeting with Sheila?"

Maddy scrunched up her nose, then smiled. "I promised myself I was going to make you beg before I told you anything."

"You're in for a long wait, then," I said as I reached for a spare order pad. "While you're waiting, you can cook and I'll wait on customers." I added with a smile, "Hey, that way we're both waiting."

She grabbed my apron before I could get past her. "That's not fair."

"Do you really want to get into an argument with me about what's fair? Come on, Maddy, I don't think either one of us wants to stroll down that road, now do we?"

"Fine, give me the pad, and I'll tell you."

Since I'd had no intention of working the front, it was an easy point to concede. "Now tell me."

There was no more jousting for position now. Maddy said, "Tom told me that when he arrived Sheila started off by telling him that she wanted at least fifty percent above what the neighborhood comps were."

"Comps?"

"You know, comparable prices. Or is it compatible prices? How should I know? It means what other houses in the area are selling for."

"Comps. Got it," I said. "What was his response to that?"

"He told her she'd be sitting on the property for years if she meant what she said. Sheila told him that she didn't care, that she wasn't in any hurry to sell the house."

"That's the attitude I got from her earlier," I said. "How about you?"

"Absolutely. That's not the best part, though."

Maddy was smiling, and I knew I was going to have to drag it out of her, despite her initial acquiescence. Finally, I broke down and asked, "Go on and tell me. I know it's killing you. What's the best part?"

"She got a telephone call in the middle of their conversation and excused herself for not more than four minutes, from the way Tom told it. When she walked back into the room, she said she'd made a mistake earlier. She said she wanted fifty percent of the comps, not a hundred and fifty."

"That's odd. She must really want a quick sale."

"Tom said it was just as ridiculous to ask for too little as it had been trying to get too much. He said she's throwing money away, and he tried to tell her just that, but she wouldn't budge. Since Tom's commission would be slashed as well, he refused the contract. It's all pretty strange, isn't it?"

"But what does it mean?" I asked.

"I have no idea."

"Just another fact for the list," I said.

We were still discussing it when the kitchen door opened, and our First Couple of Timber Ridge walked in. I wasn't all that crazy about chatting with Faith and Steve Baron together, but from the set expressions on their faces, it didn't appear that I was going to have much choice.

At least Maddy was there with me. Two against two would have to do.

"You have some impatient customers out front," Steve said. "If they don't get some service soon, I doubt they'll stay."

"We can live without them," Maddy said.

"It's okay," I said. "You go ahead, Maddy. I can handle this."

"Are you sure?"

I just nodded, and Maddy left, but not before giving me a warning look to be careful. There was no need for it; I planned to keep a butcher knife close, just in case I had to defend myself. I also noticed that my sister kept the kitchen door propped open, so at least she'd be able to hear me if I had to call out for her.

"Can I help you two with something?" I said as I started chopping vegetables we didn't need. It gave me something to do with my hands and had the added bonus of allowing me to arm myself without raising their suspicions. "Maddy would be glad to wait on you, if you'll find a table out front. It won't be long."

"We're not here to eat," Faith said. "We need to talk to you."

"Let me do the talking, honey," Steve said.

"Then do it," Faith snapped at him. Was there trouble in paradise? I certainly hoped so, since I had my suspicions that at least one of them was a murderer, and possibly both were.

Steve said, "Eleanor, did you actually think that my wife and I didn't talk to each other? Faith and I trust each other completely, and we share everything."

"Even Richard Olsen?" I asked, clutching the knife a little tighter than I had to.

"That's ridiculous," Steve said. "I told you, there was nothing to that, just rumors and idle speculation."

I had a little more than that, but I wasn't sure I

was ready to show it to him. Before I could come back with something snappy, Faith said, "Steve, say what we came to say. I can't stand being here."

"Okay," the mayor said. He looked at me, his normally jovial countenance replaced with a hard stare. "Eleanor, stay out of our lives. If you meddle any further, it will be at your own peril."

A chill swept through me, and I was glad I had a knife in my hand. "What are you going to do if I don't? Are you going to stab me, too?"

"Don't say anything you might regret," he said.

"Trust me, there's no chance of that happening," I said.

The mayor shook his head. His voice was full of anger as he spoke. "I didn't stab him, and I'm not going to stab you. But what I can do is bring down a rain of fire on your head that will make the plagues of Egypt seem like child's play. All it would take is a word from me, and I can have so many health, fire, and building code inspectors in here that you'll be shut down before the ink is dry on the paperwork. Is that what you want to happen?"

"You wouldn't dare," I said. The man surely knew how to fight back. He was right, and we all knew it. No one can comply with every regulation and ordinance in the book, because some of them seemed to contradict each other. I didn't care how clean a restaurant was, if an inspector had a grudge against the owner, he could find a reason to shut the place down, whether it merited it or not.

"Try me," he said.

He turned to his wife, then asked, "Is there anything you'd like to add to that, dearest?"

"No, I think you covered everything beautifully,"

she said as she kissed his cheek. "Now let's go home so I can fix you a proper meal."

"Remember what I said," the mayor called out as he walked through the kitchen door back out into the dining room.

"There are a great many things I'll remember from this," I said softly to myself. If he was going to take the gloves off, then so was I. I still had that letter from Faith to Richard, and if I had to take a full page out in the paper and publish it there, I would. He'd made one major mistake coming to the Slice tonight.

He'd threatened the last real connection I had with my late husband.

And that was one thing I would not tolerate.

Maddy came back in, chatting without really looking at me. "What on earth was that all about? They trotted out of here like the kitchen was on fire. What did they say to you, anyway?" She looked at me then, and her voice hardened: "Eleanor, what happened? Did they threaten you?"

"Not physically," I said. "It was much worse than that."

"What could be worse than that?" she asked.

"They threatened the Slice," I explained.

After I told her everything they'd said, Maddy's face was as grim as I was sure mine was. "We're not going to take that, are we?"

"Do I look like I'm going to roll over and let them get away with it?" I asked.

"Good," she said after studying me. "We're finally going to take some action." There was a slight pause, and then she asked, "Do you happen to have any idea what that action might be?"

"Not yet," I said as my fist idly tapped my thigh. "When I come up with a plan, you'll be the first to know."

"I'm all for that," she said. "In the meantime, should I shoo our customers out, or do you want to finish the night?"

I glanced at the clock and saw that it was eight-thirty. "We have less than two hours. We might as well make a little money."

As Maddy nodded, I added, "Besides, that will give me time to think about tomorrow. I want to be ready to hit the ground running."

"I'll put my track shoes by the bed tonight," she said. As she gave me three orders to make, she said, "If you need me, just give me a holler and I'll be here."

"I know you will," I said. "In fact, I'm counting on it."

"Good," she said.

As I made the pizzas and sandwiches for the orders as they came in, I kept thinking about the mayor's threat. There was no doubt he could bring more scrutiny to my pizzeria than I wanted, but would he risk it? He was an elected official, accountable for his actions to the people of Timber Ridge. That meant he had to answer to them. Then again, before anyone realized what he was up to, I'd be out of business. If folks voted him out of office after I was shut down, it would be a hollow victory for me.

But now I had more incentive to solve the murder than I'd had yet. Was the mayor threatening me to hide his wife's secret affair, or was there something even darker he didn't want exposed?

Either way, I was more determined than ever to find out.

Maddy came in a few minutes before ten and said, "There's someone here to see you."

"Is it David Quinton?" I asked without really thinking the question through.

"No," Maddy said as she looked at me oddly. "Why, was he supposed to come by tonight?"

"Not that I know of," I said, trying to bury my question to her.

Of course, she wasn't about to let that go. "He really shook you up coming here with a date, didn't he?"

"No," I said a little louder than I should have. "He's free to see whoever he wants to. It's not like it's any of my business."

"If that's true, then why are you so worked up over it?"

"I'm not," I snapped, then took a few deep breaths before speaking again. In a calmer voice, I repeated, "I'm not. I was just asking. Who wants to see me?"

At that moment, the kitchen door opened and Bob Pickering came through, dangling a set of keys in front of him. "Did anyone here order a car with a brand new driver's-side window?"

"That's me," I said. "But you'd better keep your key. I might need you to bail me out again."

"No time soon, I hope. My supplier told me it would take him at least four days to get another window in stock. I won't even tell you the snide comments he made about my workmanship."

"It wasn't your fault," I said.

"I told him, but he didn't believe me."

"I'm sorry your reputation's taking a hit on my account," I said.

"Are you kidding? I have more customers than I can handle now. Maybe a little bad-news spread will get me home before ten o'clock at night."

"I owe you a pizza," I said as I dug into the refrigerator for the last of the dough I'd made that morning.

"Can I take a rain check?" he asked.

"Don't tell me you're tired of my pizzas after one night," I said, halfway joking with him.

"It's not that." He looked around, but Maddy had taken off the second we'd started talking, no doubt because she knew there wouldn't be anything discussed about the murder we were trying to solve. "It's just that I have a hard time eating cheese after nine o'clock. I must be getting old. I've got hair growing where it never did before, and I'm developing the digestive tract my grandmother had."

"My dad always used to say getting old wasn't for sissies," I said. "Not that I think you're old."

"It is amazing, isn't it? When I was your age, I used to think sixty was ancient. Now that I'm approaching it, though, I still feel like the pup I used to be." He smiled, then added, "Not that I haven't lost some of my bark."

"And bite as well, I'd wager," I said. "The next time you're in the mood for pizza, call me. If I haven't heard from you in a week, I'll make one and take it to your shop, so don't try to get out of it."

"No worries there." He frowned, then asked, "How are you, Eleanor?"

I shrugged. "Being accused of murder and shot at in the same week has made this a pretty tough week to take, but I've had worse ones."

He patted my shoulder, and I saw a tender side of him he normally never showed the world. "I know you have. I'm here if you need me, you understand that, don't you?"

"I do," I said, fighting the sudden urge to cry. It was amazing how being accused of murder could show me who my true friends really were, separating them from the ones who liked me only during the best of times.

"Then I'm off," he said. As he walked out the door, he waved good-bye. "As much as I enjoy these little chats, let's try to put the next one off for a while. At least over a car window. What do you say?"

"I'll do my best, but I can't make any promises."

He left laughing, and I suddenly felt better myself. Sometimes all it took was a kind word to pull me out of my funk, and at the moment, I could use every one of them I could get. It was late, and I was worn out, but at least I had my Subaru back, and that meant a modicum of independence. I loved my sister with all my heart, but being with her around the clock was starting to wear on me, and I knew it was getting to her, too. We enjoyed our time together, but we needed some apart as well.

After we finished cleaning up, Maddy and I locked up, then walked through the powdery snow to our cars. Less than an inch had fallen, and none of it had stuck to the roads. Still, it was pretty where it lay, and I enjoyed seeing the gray reflections of it on my drive home.

As I walked up the steps, I felt my breath quicken a little.

Someone was sitting on my front porch, and the person had either cut the power to my house or disabled the motion-detecting light.

Either way, it was all I could do not to scream.

"You should really get that light fixed," a voice said.

I felt my pulse start to slow when I realized that it was David Quinton.

"It was working last night," I said. "What are you doing here, David?"

"I need to talk to you," he said.

It was dark enough so that I could make out his basic shape, but I still wasn't able to see his face, or his expression. "Can't it wait until morning?"

"I doubt I'd get much sleep. Would you indulge me for one minute, if I promise to leave after I've had my say?"

I rubbed my hands together. "Fine. But at least come inside. I can make us some coffee so we can have a civilized conversation."

"I'd rather we didn't," he said.

"What, be civilized?"

"No, go inside. What I have to say is best said in the shadows."

I peered into the gloom, but though my eyesight had adjusted a little, it still wasn't as sharp as I hoped. "You're being awfully mysterious."

"I don't mean to be. What happened last night was a mistake. I never should have come to the Slice with a date."

"Is that what this is about? David, you're free to do whatever you like. You certainly don't owe me any explanations."

He stood and approached me, and I could smell his cologne. "I'd like to, though, don't you see? Eleanor, if you just gave me one chance, I could convince you, but you won't let me in."

"It's too soon," I said, taking a step back.

He reached out and took my arm. "Don't walk away from me. It's not fair."

I broke his grasp. "To who? You? I never gave you the slightest bit of encouragement, and you know it."

His slight laugh held no amusement in it. "Trust me, you don't have to convince me of that. I'm talking about you." He tried to lighten his tone as he added, "All I'm asking for is one dinner out. If you have a terrible time, I'll leave you alone. Think about it, Eleanor. Isn't it worth that, just to get me out of your hair once and for all?"

I thought about the offer for a few seconds, then said, "Let me get this straight. If I have dinner with you, you'll drop this pursuit for good. Are you willing to give me your word on that?"

"I am," he said.

"Okay, then. After this mess with Richard Olsen is over, I'll have dinner with you."

"I was thinking more along the lines of tomorrow night."

"Do you really think you should push your luck?"

His laugh this time was genuine. "If I hadn't, you never would have agreed to go out with me in the first place."

"It's one date, David. Make no mistake about it."

"Agreed. One date. Tomorrow night."

"Fine," I said as I brushed past him and started to put my key in the lock. The phone began to ring inside, and, of course, my haste made it twice as hard to fit my key into the lock. I finally got it open and turned to David. "You don't have to wait here, you know."

"I just want to make sure you get in safely."

I shook my head, darted inside, and flipped on the light. From the light of the hallway filtering out onto the porch, I could see his smile as I closed the door.

I got to the phone just as it died. That was okay with me. If they didn't want to leave a message, I felt no obligation to hit *69 and call them back.

The phone rang again as I hung it back up, and I snatched it from its cradle before it could ring again.

"Hello," I said, perhaps with a bit more impatience than I should have.

"Where have you been?" my sister asked over the line.

"I just got home," I said.

"You should have been inside five minutes ago."

Was she kidding me? "Sorry I missed curfew, 'Mom.' Does that mean I can't go to the spring dance?"

"Why were you late?"

So, for once, Maddy wasn't in the mood to play. "Someone was waiting for me on the porch when I walked up to the house."

"Are you all right?"

"Of course I am. It was David Quinton."

Maddy asked, "At this time of night? What did he want?"

"He asked me out on a date," I said.

"Poor guy, he must have skin as thick as a rhino's."

"I said yes."

There was a pause on the other end, then I could hear her gasp. Agreeing to go out with David was just about worth that reaction alone. "You said what?"

"We're having dinner together tomorrow night." I said it as matter-of-factly as I could manage.

"Just like that? He finally wore you down, did he?"

"It's not that at all," I said as I collected the day's mail that had been shoved through the slot in the door. Joe had installed a basket to catch it, a handy feature that wasn't in keeping with the house's history, not that I minded. Thinking of Joe made me wonder why I'd agreed to go out with someone else. "David promised me if I'd have dinner with him one time, he'd stop asking me out."

"You're going to give him a fair chance, aren't you?" Maddy asked guardedly.

"At what, winning my heart? Be serious. That part of my life is over. This was just the most expedient way to get him off my back."

"Well, as long as you're going into this with an open mind, it should be fine."

"It's too late for sarcasm," I said. "Now, unless there's something besides a bed check going on here, I'm saying good night."

"Night," Maddy said. "And, Eleanor?"

"Yes?"

"I'm proud of you. It's a big step."

"It's just dinner," I said.

"It's more than that, and you know it as well as I do, no matter how much you might protest otherwise."

"I'm hanging up now," I said, and then did exactly that.

Was Maddy right? Was I opening myself up to a new experience? No, I'd meant what I'd said. One dinner, and then David could move on to someone else.

That was all there was to it, and nothing more.

At least I thought so.

Well, maybe.

I guess I'd honestly just have to wait and see.

Without meaning to, I slept in the next morning. After tossing and turning most of the night, it ended up being one of those sleeps that I didn't enjoy so much as endure. When I looked out the window, I saw that the snow was nearly all gone, leaving a dark and gray day behind in its wake.

I had breakfast, then decided to take a long shower to wash some of the cobwebs out of my mind. It wouldn't do to be anything but 100 percent, especially since Maddy and I were going to redouble our efforts at solving the murder.

As I was drying off, I heard a large truck outside. When I peeked outside the bathroom window, I saw the recycling truck pulling away from in front of my house. Blast it all, not only had I forgotten to put my own trash and recycling out, but I still had those bundled newspapers from Richard Olsen's place cluttering up my garage. Now I'd have to dodge the stacks another week. Throwing them out wasn't an option, and we didn't have a drive-up recycling center in our county, so I was stuck with them, at least for seven more days.

If the morning so far was any indication, I was in for a long and frustrating day. Boy, oh boy, David would certainly be getting a real treat tonight if the trends so far continued. I should be in rare form by dinnertime.

Maddy was getting ready to ring my bell as I opened the door to get the paper.

I spotted her empty hands. "What, you didn't bring breakfast today?"

"There wasn't really time," she said. "Why didn't you call me earlier? I can't believe I overslept. Have you been waiting for me long?"

I shrugged. I wasn't about to admit that I hadn't been up all that long myself. "I didn't mind. It gave me a chance to do a few things around the house."

"Do you have any ideas where we should start?"

"I've got one," I said. "I think we should try Penny Olsen's place again."

Maddy scowled slightly. "I still think we're wasting our time. He was her ex-husband, Eleanor."

"That gives her more reason than most folks to want him dead then, doesn't it?"

Maddy shrugged. "We can try her shop, but I doubt she's back from her trip."

I grabbed my coat and locked the front door on our way out. "If she's ever coming back."

"What do you mean by that?"

"Think about it," I said. "It's a real possibility that she's gone for good."

"That would make her look guilty, don't you think?"

"I do," I said.

"Let's go see."

I headed for the garage when Maddy tapped my shoulder. "Why don't we leave your car here and take mine? It deserves a rest after the last few days it's been having."

"I suppose so," I said. "I was kind of looking forward to driving today, though."

She tossed me her keys. "Then you can chauffeur me around for a change."

I flipped the keys right back to her. "I don't think so."

"Then it's settled—I'll drive us in my car."

It wasn't an argument I cared about one way or the other, so I got in the passenger side and waited for my sister. She was probably right. The Subaru deserved a break, and maybe if I left it parked in my garage, the driver's-side window would make it twenty-four hours before anything else happened to it.

As we neared Penny's antique shop, Maddy said, "We need a backup plan in case she's not there."

"We can always talk to Sheila again."

"If she's still in town," Maddy said.

"Everyone seems to be leaving, don't they?"

"It looks like Timber Ridge isn't the haven folks once thought it was," Maddy said.

"It's the reality of the world we live in these days," I said. "No one's really safe, are they? Sometimes I think it's all just an illusion."

"My, that's a rather grim outlook. You'd better

lose that attitude before your big date tonight. Want to talk about it?"

"No," I said curtly, hoping to put that out of my mind until I had to deal with it later.

"Then how about some make-up tips?"

"Why don't we just enjoy the drive?" I said. "Talking just spoils it."

"Be that way," she said with a hint of laughter in her voice. After a few minutes, she added, "We're here." Maddy pointed to the window of Penny's antique shop and said, "See, I told you she was still gone. It's dark inside."

"But the sign's gone," I said. For an instant, I saw a brief flash of light inside the shop. "Did you see that?"

"What was it?" Maddy asked.

"I don't know, but I think we should find out."

As Maddy turned off the engine, she asked, "Is there any chance you want to call Kevin Hurley before we go barging in there?"

"Now, what fun would that be?" I asked. I got out of the car, but my sister didn't follow. "Aren't you coming?"

"I guess so, but I still think we should have some backup."

I pointed to her purse. "Still have your stun gun?"

"I don't go anywhere without it."

"Then we're armed."

"Really?" She looked at me a second. "What do you have?"

"Pepper spray and a bad attitude. That should be enough, don't you think?"

"It all depends on what we find in there."

"Then let's go look."

I couldn't see much through the darkened windows of the shop, and Maddy was getting ready to knock on the door when I grabbed her arm.

She said, "What's wrong? Did you change your mind about getting someone else over here?"

I shook my head. "No."

"Then what is it?"

Instead of answering, I put a hand on the door. "Let's try this first."

"It's got to be locked," Maddy said in a dismissive voice.

The phrase nearly died in her throat, though, as the door swung open, and I took my first step inside.

Chapter 12

"Who's there?" a voice called from the back of the shop the second I walked inside. "I'm warning you, I'm armed."

"It's Eleanor Swift," I called out quickly.

Penny Olsen stepped out of the shadows holding an old-fashioned rifle. I was taken aback by her appearance. The last time I'd seen her—just a month before—Penny had been a pretty, vibrant woman, but it was hard to reconcile that image with the woman standing before me. Her hair, normally so elegantly coifed, needed a good wash and comb, while her make-up was nonexistent.

"It's you," she said, obviously not that pleased to see me.

"Would you mind lowering that thing?" I asked as I gestured toward the gun.

"Oh, this? It's not even loaded."

Given her current state, I wondered how she could be sure. "I'd still appreciate it if you'd point it somewhere else."

"All right," she said as she reluctantly leaned it against the wall. "What do you want, Eleanor?"

"I need to talk to you," I said, motioning with one hand behind my back to keep Maddy outside. In the state Penny was in, I didn't want to push her any further than I had to, and I was afraid that my sister's style of shoving until someone felt no option but to shove back was going to be way over the top for the present situation.

"What are you doing with your hand?" Penny asked as she started to reach for the gun again.

"I had a cramp," I said. "Besides, you already told me it wasn't loaded."

"Yes, but was I telling the truth?"

She was acting decidedly erratic, even by my standards.

"It's understandable that you're upset, but I want you to know that I had nothing to do with what happened to your ex-husband."

"What are you talking about?"

There was an odd look in her eyes as she asked it, and I wondered if something inside her had snapped. Then it dawned on me all at once. "You really haven't heard, have you? I'm afraid I've got some bad news for you. It's about Richard."

"What about Richard? Nothing's wrong with him. I spoke with him just before I left town."

"When exactly was that?"

"Ten days ago," she said, putting herself well away before the murder.

"I'm sorry to have to be the one to tell you, but someone murdered him. I found the body, so I know he's dead."

I wasn't sure what I expected, but the look of relief I saw there wasn't even in the top ten choices.

"He's really dead?" Was that hope in her voice?

"I'm afraid so. I can't believe the police haven't talked to you yet."

She shrugged. "I just this moment got back into town. As a matter of fact, I haven't even been home. I came straight here to check on the shop." She made a clicking sound with her tongue, then said, "I can't believe it."

"Excuse me for saying so, but you don't seem all that distraught."

She laughed, another reaction just a little too odd for my taste. "There's a reason he was my ex-husband," she said.

"Still, you must have loved him at some point." Why I was defending the dead man's honor was beyond me, but I suppose it was because I believed that everyone deserved at least one mourner, even if I couldn't bring myself to fill that role for Richard Olsen.

"I suppose I must have, though it's difficult to recall now. He somehow managed to cheat me all the way to the end, didn't he?"

"What do you mean?" I kept my eyes on her, making sure she didn't retrieve that weapon. I had my doubts about it being unloaded, or Penny's compunction to use it.

"I had three more alimony payments coming from him, and then it was over. The courts decided that five years was enough, since I had my own business. Still, I would have loved to have had those last checks from him, just to spite him."

"You really hated him, didn't you?"

She shook her head. "I might have while we were married, but I got over it. Am I sorry he's dead? I don't even know how I feel yet, the news is so recent." She mulled it over a few seconds, then said, "I suppose that leach of a sister inherited everything, didn't she? Have they found the will yet?"

"Yes, but from what I understand, there was no need to. The house, the bank accounts, everything was in both their names. It all reverted to her the moment he died."

"That figures," Penny said. "He always did have a soft spot in his heart for her, though I never cared for the woman. I was never good enough for her precious brother, at least according to her. I can't believe he's actually gone."

Penny Olsen was obviously in the mood to talk about her ex-husband, and I might not have another chance to talk to her before Kevin Hurley did, and that was an opportunity I couldn't afford to pass up. "Do you know anybody who might have wanted to hurt him?" I asked.

"Do you have a pen and paper? We could make a list, but I'm afraid it would be easier going through the Timber Ridge phone book."

"Surely not everyone hated him," I said. "He had a way about him, especially with most women. I don't mean me, but I've heard some found him attractive."

"They certainly did when we were married. You know about him and the mayor's wife, don't you?"

I nodded. "She denies it, but I have my doubts."

"You should. I caught them together in the end. Why do you think I threw him out? He's been seeing Faith for a long time. They were sneaking around together even before she married our fair mayor. I'll wager you didn't know that." She paused, then added, "I wonder if one of them had the guts to kill him. I could see Steve doing it, but I'm not sure about Faith. Well, maybe if he broke it off with her."

I tried to keep my expression even, but she must have caught something in my glance. "He did, didn't he? The fool. I used words to go after him, but dear, sweet Faith would use a pistol. I warned him about her, but he wouldn't listen to me."

"I understand he was fighting with his neighbor about a property line," I said.

"That's nothing," she said as she waved a hand dismissively in the air. "He and Travis White disliked each other from the first time they met, and that line gave them something to argue about." She reached one hand down to a table and ran her fingers over a carved wooden elephant. "I wonder. . . ."

"What?"

"Oh, nothing."

"Go on, you can tell me," I said, hoping fervently that she wasn't through.

"Richard had a dirty little secret, one I didn't find out about until after the divorce."

I wasn't sure that it was something I wanted to hear, but if I was going to try to solve his murder, I needed to learn what I could about the man. "What was it?"

Penny's eyes lit up. "Why, Eleanor Swift, I believe you have a dark streak inside you I've never seen before."

"It's just human nature to be curious, wouldn't you say?"

She laughed. "Oh, I never doubted it in myself."

When it appeared she wasn't going to explain, I prodded her gently. "So, what was it? What was Richard hiding?"

She was about to tell me when the door opened. I turned to warn Maddy off, but instead, Kevin Hurley was there.

"Where have you been?" he asked as he walked up to us.

"I didn't realize I had to check in with you everywhere I went," I said.

"I'm talking to her," he said as he gestured to Penny. "Eleanor, I'll deal with you in a minute. Why don't you wait outside with your sister? I'll be with you both soon." Though it was phrased as a question, there was no denying that it was an order. I thought about defying him but then doubted that Penny would finish her story while he was standing there listening. If I was ever going to find out what she'd been about to tell me, it was going to have to wait.

As I walked outside, Maddy said, "I tried to warn you."

"Thanks. I can't believe he threw me out."

"You were certainly in there long enough. I couldn't believe it when you waved me off like that. I had half a mind to storm in, anyway."

"She was holding a gun on me when I walked in," I explained gently.

"Then again, maybe it was a good thing I stayed outside," Maddy said. "Someone had to keep watch, didn't they?"

"And a fine job you did," I said.

"Hey, it wasn't like I could blow my car horn or

something. He parked down the block and snuck up on me."

"I was just kidding," I said.

"Did you learn anything while you were inside?"

I nodded. "Unless Penny was lying to me, she didn't know about Richard's murder. She said she just got back into town, and from the look of her, I believed it. Her hair was a mess, and she didn't have any make-up on."

"Spare me the fashion report," Maddy said. "How did she react?"

"The instant I told her, I could swear she looked relieved by the news. After that, she got decidedly chatty. I'm not sure if it's true or not, but Penny said Richard was fooling around with Faith Baron even before she married Steve. Apparently it wasn't a fling. She must have really loved him, at least more than Penny ever did."

"So, when he dumped her, it could have been more than she could handle," Maddy said.

"Sounds like it," I said. "There's just one thing. I need to get back in there as soon as Kevin leaves. Penny was about to tell me something when Kevin came in. I'm not exactly certain what it was, but she called it Richard's dirty little secret."

"That could mean anything," Maddy said.

"I'm thinking she was talking about blackmail, but I didn't have a chance to let her tell me."

Kevin suddenly came back out, with Penny in tow.

"You're not arresting her, are you?" I asked.

"Not that it's any of your business, but we both decided we'd be more comfortable talking in my office."

"Is that true, Penny?" I asked.

She shrugged as Kevin said, "I'm still not sure how any of this is your business."

"Hey, you're the one who told me to wait outside for you."

He shook his head as he walked down the street with Penny right beside him. I followed a few paces back until he whirled around. "Eleanor, I'd advise you to just get into your car and drive away."

Maddy answered before I could. "Her car's still at home. She's riding with me today. Someone shot out her window, remember?"

That got Penny's attention. "Don't look at me. I was out of town. I couldn't have done it."

"No one accused you of anything," I said.

"I just wanted you to know."

Kevin walked her to his police cruiser without another word.

"Where should we go now?" Maddy asked as we got into her car.

"I'd like to talk to Carl Wilson again."

She turned to look at me. "Do you really think he had something to do with Olsen's murder?"

"No, but I'd love to strike a few names off the list before we go racing around town interviewing everyone in the telephone book. We never asked him for an alibi the last time, did we?"

"We didn't exactly leave on good terms, either. We lied to him about being clients to get information from him, so I doubt he's going to welcome us back with open arms."

"You're right about that," I said. "There's got to be some way to approach him, though."

"I have an idea," Maddy said.

"Well, don't hold out on me. Let's hear it."

"I've got to warn you, it's a little radical, something we haven't tried before."

"You've got my attention," I said.

"How about if we tell him the complete, total, and unvarnished truth? We're looking for the killer, and unless he did it, he might just cooperate."

"I think you've lost your mind," I said.

"Then you won't do it?"

"I never said that. What do we have to lose?"

"That's the spirit," Maddy said. "When we get there, let me do the talking."

"I can't make any promises," I said.

When we arrived at the shredding company, I put a hand on Maddy's arm before we went in. "Are you sure this is the best way to handle this?"

"No, but I wasn't able to come up with anything else on the drive over. Were you?"

"I'm drawing a blank," I admitted.

"The truth it is, then."

We walked in, and the smile Carl Wilson had plastered on his face quickly faded the moment he saw us.

"I thought you two weren't coming back until you had a lawyer."

Maddy said, "We lied to you, and we came here to apologize."

He looked more quizzical than angry. "Excuse me?"

"We came back to tell you we were sorry. We were never clients of your firm, so there was never any danger of us suing you for damages," Maddy explained.

He stood, and I could see the tension in his posture. "Then why did you both come here in the first place?"

"My sister," Maddy said as she put a hand on my shoulder, "has been accused by the police as the main murder suspect, and we're trying to clear her name."

He took a step forward, and it wasn't to offer his support. "How did you plan to do that, by pinning the murder on me?"

"Believe me, we realize we were wrong. There's one easy way to get rid of us, and then we'll both vanish from your life forever," Maddy said.

"I doubt that," he said, "but go ahead and tell me what it is you want."

"Do you have an alibi for the night of the murder?" Maddy asked gently.

"I've already gone over this with the police."

"Then it won't hurt to tell us, too," I said, ignoring the disapproving look in my sister's glance.

He looked at us a few seconds, then said, "What can it hurt? I was having dinner with a potential new business partner in Raleigh that night. It was too late to come back after a little wining and dining, so I stayed over until the next morning. Is that good enough for you?"

"Raleigh's not that far away," Maddy said. "I'm sorry, but you could have gone back and forth after the meal, and no one would be the wiser."

"It might even be why you made the appointment in the first place," I said. "It sounds good at first, doesn't it?"

Carl Wilson's face reddened slightly, and I thought for a second he was going to physically throw us out of his office. All of a sudden, though, he slumped down and leaned against his desk. "I told the police all of it, so I might as well tell you. After dinner, we went back to my room, and things got a little too close, if you know what I mean."

"We don't mean to pry," I said. "Whatever you do behind closed doors is your business, not ours."

"I never thought I'd do anything with Harriet Bambridge, I can tell you that," Wilson explained. "I can't hold my liquor—I never could—but that trip was a mistake in more ways than I can count. In the morning, she brusquely told me that we wouldn't be opening any branches in Raleigh, at least not with her money, and that I was to never contact her again. I'm sure the police will verify the story, since she called me right after she spoke with Chief Hurley and blessed me out six ways from Sunday. Is that good enough for you?"

"It is," I said. "I'm sorry we had to pry."

"I've just got one more thing to say to you both, and then I expect you to keep your word and leave me alone forever."

"What is it?" I asked.

He looked me dead in the eye and said, "If you did kill him, try not to feel bad about it. You did the world a favor, whether anyone realizes it or not. Now go."

Before I could protest my innocence, we were hustled out the door like a couple of vagrants looking for a handout.

Maddy glanced back at the door. "I don't know about you, but I believe him."

"I don't see how we can't," I said. "It would be too easy to check with Kevin to see if it's true."

"But we're not going to, are we?"

I grinned. "If you want to, feel free."

"No, thanks. So, we finally have someone we can cross off our list. Who does that leave?"

"We've still got the mayor and his wife, Olsen's sister, and his next-door neighbor."

Maddy added, "And don't forget whoever he was blackmailing."

"How can I? It's the biggest unknown in the equation."

We left the building, and as we got to Maddy's car, I saw that we should have been at the pizzeria half an hour before. If we could rush our investigation, I still might be able to speed up the dough-making process as I had the day before. But I had to put that out of my mind. If we had time, fine, but if not, we'd go with the frozen dough we had on hand.

This was too important, and I felt we were finally starting to make some real progress in the case.

At least more than the chief of police had been able to so far.

"I'm still waiting," Maddy said, bringing me out of my musings. "Where do we go next?"

"Start driving toward Richard Olsen's place," I said.

"Are we going to talk to Sheila again?" Maddy asked as she started the car.

"Not right off the bat. I'd like to have a conversation with Travis White."

"You really think he would kill Richard over a property line?"

"I hate to break it to you, but I'm sure it happens all the time," I said. "Travis White isn't going to like us butting into his business."

"We can try the honesty approach again," Maddy suggested.

"I'm not sure that's always the best policy, especially when we're dealing with a murderer."

"What could it hurt?" Maddy asked. "Honestly, I can't think of any other way of asking him for an alibi, can you?"

"We never asked Sheila for one either, did we? She just kind of showed up at the pizzeria the next day, and we never thought to ask where she'd been the night before."

Maddy frowned, then said, "You know what? You're right. How has she stayed under the radar the entire time, when she's the one who profits most from Richard's death? Have we had a blind spot about her?"

"Not entirely," I said. "She did make our list, remember?"

"But she hasn't been as high a priority as she should have been."

"Then we bump her up the list," I said. "But I still want to talk to Travis first."

When we got to the street in front of the two houses, Maddy stopped in front of the White place, parking just far enough away that Sheila wouldn't see us out the front window if she happened to be at her brother's place.

Travis White was out in the side yard between the two properties with some kind of tool in his hands and a pile of icy dirt at his feet.

As we got out of the car and cut across the dry, dead grass toward him, he called out, "Use the sidewalk, both of you."

"You're not," Maddy said, pointing at his shoes, planted firmly on the barren ground.

"Yeah, but it's my yard, isn't it?"

I grabbed Maddy's arm and pulled her over onto the sidewalk. We got as close as we could to the man, and I asked, "Could we talk to you a moment, Travis?"

He stopped working for a second, and I saw a posthole digger in his hands. "What are you planting?" I asked.

"Posts," he snapped.

"You're putting up a fence in January," Maddy said.

"You're a marvel at observation, aren't you?" Travis snapped. "Now what is it you want? I've got holes to dig, and this ground's as tough as concrete."

"It's an odd time of year to be digging them then, isn't it?" I asked.

I was expecting another outburst, but Travis merely nodded at my question. "It is, but I just got final revocation of rights from the dingbat next door, and as soon as I registered it at the courthouse, I started working on these holes. I'll have my fence up before the ink's dry on the deed."

"So, you bought the land in question?" I asked.

"Not all of it," he said, "just the strip that we were arguing over. Ten feet wide, and the length of our property. It's what was rightly mine in the first place until that crooked surveyor came to check the land, and Olsen sweet-talked him into moving the stake."

"You ended up paying for it twice?" I asked.

"I'd have done it four times if money was the only issue. Olsen knew I wanted it, so he wouldn't budge."

"But it's yours now," I said. "And it wouldn't have been if he was still alive."

He drove the digger deep into the cold, nearly frozen soil, and I could see the strength in the man, despite the white hair and wrinkles. There was no doubt in my mind he was perfectly capable of committing murder.

"Is there an accusation in there somewhere?" he asked, his gaze directed straight at me.

"Should there be? You had the motive, the means, and plenty of opportunity. The police have to have talked to you by now."

"They did," he said, "and I sent them on their way. I might have killed him; the man had a way of rubbing me the wrong way that was maddening, but I didn't, and I can prove it."

"How can you do that?" I asked.

He laughed, with a hollow echo of mirth within it. "I don't have to tell you that, now do I?" He reached for the diggers again, then said, "I'm no longer amused by this conversation, so I'll thank you both to get off my land." As he drove the diggers home again, he added with emphasis, *"Now."*

Maddy and I didn't tarry.

"We're going to have to ask Kevin what his alibi was, aren't we?" Maddy asked as we hurried back to the sidewalk.

"He's not going to tell us," I said. "For now, we're just going to have to believe that Travis is in the clear."

Maddy nodded. "We don't have much choice, do we?"

"No, but we can still ask Sheila for hers."

We walked up the steps to the Olsen house, but Maddy put a hand on my shoulder before we got to the door. "She's not here," she said.

I saw her point to the empty driveway. "Maybe her car's in the garage," I said.

"Knock then," she said.

I did, and when there was no response, I said, "We ask her later, then."

"What do we do in the meantime?"

I glanced at my watch. "We go to the Slice, speed up some dough, then open for business as usual."

Maddy clearly looked disappointed by my suggestion. "What's wrong? Don't you like working there anymore?" I asked her.

"That's not it. I'm happy being there," she said. "I was just hoping we'd make more progress than we have so far."

"We eliminated one and a half suspects," I said as we got into her car. "That's got to count for something."

"Where does the half come in?" she asked.

"We can't confirm his alibi, but Travis seemed pretty sure of himself. That should count for at least a half, shouldn't it?"

"I think we should crank it up to a whole," Maddy said. "After all, it wouldn't take much for the police to prove he was lying, and he's not locked up, so I'm guessing he's got a decent alibi, even if we don't know what it is."

"Then that's even better," I said. "Two suspects down, four to go."

"At least four," Maddy cautioned. "We still don't know how many people Richard was blackmailing."

"Are you trying to depress me?" I asked as we finally neared our parking spot in back of the building.

"I'm just trying to be pragmatic," she said.

"Well, do it another day, would you? For now, I'm going to focus on the four suspects we've got."

"I can live with that," she said.

We parked, then walked around to the front of the building. I half expected to find the front glass shattered or some other dire circumstance, but instead, the place looked exactly as we'd left it the night before.

As I unlocked the door, Maddy said, "I'm glad Greg's coming in today."

"He's always a good worker," I said.

Maddy looked at me oddly as she said, "It's more than that. Today he has the front, and I'm doing all the kitchen work."

I was about to ask her what she was talking about when it suddenly dawned on me that I wasn't going to be at the pizzeria tonight.

Against my better judgment, I was having dinner with David Quinton, going out on a date that I didn't want to be on. I didn't know how I'd get through it without feeling disloyal to Joe, but I had to somehow make it. After tonight, I'd never have to hear David ask me out again.

And I was pretty sure, though not entirely positive, that was what I wanted.

Our lunch crowd was a little stronger than it had been lately, and I found myself wondering if it was because folks were starting to realize that I wasn't a murderer, or if it was due to the fact that people loved our food and were willing to put little things like murder investigations aside for the sake of their growling stomachs.

Honestly, I wasn't sure I wanted to know.

The kitchen door opened a little before two, and I was surprised to find Penny Olsen come through instead of Greg or Maddy.

"Your sister told me it would be all right if I came straight back," she said. Her hair and make-up were back to their usual standards.

"You look nice," I said.

She self-consciously patted her hair. "Thank you, but compared to the last time you saw me, anything would be an improvement. I should have known better than to go anywhere looking like I did this morning."

"At least the police let you go home and change."

"That? That was nothing," she said, dismissing her earlier trip in a squad car as if it wasn't anything unusual for her. "I answered a few questions, and then Chief Hurley took me back to my shop so I could get my car. I had a quick nap and felt so much better." She frowned then as she added, "I need to get away. I see that now, but I thought I owed you an explanation before I took off."

"I thought you just got back from a long trip."

"You don't understand," Penny said. "I mean for good. I can't stay here in town, not now."

"Are you serious?" I couldn't believe she'd choose this moment to leave. "Why are you going?"

"The only reason I stayed was to be near Richard," she said, her words tumbling out like water out of a spilled cup. "I never stopped loving him, despite his errant ways. Now that he's gone, there's not much use in me sticking around."

I couldn't have been more surprised by the declaration than if she'd stated her readiness to assume the British throne. Then I looked into her eyes and saw that she was deadly serious. "Penny, I don't know what to say."

I wasn't sure how I'd meant it, but she took it oddly. "Eleanor, I know more than anyone else in the world that Richard had his faults, but I kept hoping he'd realize what a mistake he'd made throwing away our life together. I honestly thought he'd come back to me, but now that's never going to happen, so what's the use?"

"That's so sad," I said, at a loss for what else to say. "What are you going to do about your shop?"

She waved a hand in the air, dismissing the question. "My assistant, Jenny Hathaway, is buying me out. I'm giving her a wonderful deal, and she's taking it before I come to my senses. It's time for me to start over."

I knew what that felt like, so no matter how many things we had that separated us, there was evidently one thing we had in common: each of us had lost someone she loved. "I'm so sorry."

"I'll be all right," she said. "But I started to tell you something before the police chief showed up, and I think it's important you hear it before I leave town once and for all."

She looked toward the door, then lowered her voice as she said, "My ex-husband had a taste for blackmail that I never could stomach. He used to steal things from the piles he was supposed to shred, and he'd use them as leverage. He started hiding money in the oddest places around the house before he finally decided to put it in the bank. I never approved of his behavior, and I refused to take any of the money he made from it. When I told him I'd go to the police if he didn't stop, he just laughed at me. Eleanor, he told me that wasn't a problem, at least not as long as Kevin Hurley was the police chief."

"What did he mean by that? Was he blackmailing him, too?"

Penny just shrugged. "I never found out. As soon as Richard said it, he realized he'd admitted too much and he clammed up. All I know is, ever since I found out, I swear Hurley has been waiting for me to say something about it. I've never let on that I knew anything about his tie to my ex-husband, but with Richard dead, I'd still feel safer a long way from here. I'm going to California and start another shop." As she said it, she put one hand over her mouth. "Now I can't go there."

"Why not? I won't tell anyone."

"I can't risk it slipping out," she said. "No worries. I'll just have to find somewhere else." Penny sighed, then said, "I was looking forward to their climate, though. I've had enough snow to last me a lifetime." She glanced at my wall clock and asked, "Is that the time? I'm supposed to meet Jenny at the bank so we can finalize the takeover. I shouldn't have come by, but I needed you to know about the police chief. I know you two were close at one time, but you should be on guard. If anyone knows that a man can have more sides than we can see, it's me."

"Thanks for the information," I said.

"It's not just that," she said, looking concerned. "It's a warning. If he thinks for one second that I told you anything, you could be in danger, too."

I couldn't see Kevin hurting me, even with his buried temper, but Penny looked so earnest, it shook me a little.

"Is there a back way out of here?" she asked as she looked past my tiny office.

"Sure, we have a service door there, but we rarely use it."

"So much the better. Would it be too much trouble for you to let me out? I don't want anyone to see me coming out of here."

"I'd be glad to," I said as I led her to the back door, still barricaded. "You're not ashamed of being seen here, are you?"

"It's not that," Penny said. "I'm thinking more about your safety than my reputation. Be careful, Eleanor."

"You too," I said as I let her out.

After I slid the barrier back in place once she was gone, I had to wonder if she was being paranoid or perceptive. Was there a chance in the world Richard Olsen had something on Kevin Hurley and was using it to keep the police chief from coming after him? What could it be, though? Was there something dark in Kevin's past, or was it still in his present? I wanted to discount the theory, but somehow, I couldn't bring myself to do it. If I was being honest with myself, I had to admit that Kevin had a darker side than he let most people see.

I was still thinking about him when the kitchen door opened and the man himself came through. The bowl of mushrooms I'd just chopped fell out of my hands and scattered to the floor.

"You look like you've seen a ghost," he said.

"No, you just startled me. Can I help you with something?"

Without answering, he looked around the small space, even ducking into my office. "Where is she?"

"Maddy?" I asked as I swept up the ruined mushrooms. "She's supposed to be out front. Why do you want to talk to her?"

"I'm not talking about your sister," he said as he frowned at me. "You know full well I'm looking for Penny Olsen."

I had to steady myself before I spoke. "How did you know she was here? Have you been following her, or are you staking out my business? I'm not sure I'll like either answer, but I have a right to know."

"I'm not stalking anyone," he said. "I saw her come in, but she never left. I have a few more questions for her, that's it. Now, where did she go?"

I pointed toward the back door. "She left that way ten minutes ago."

"So, she was ducking me after all," he said.

"No, she decided to take a shortcut." I looked into his eyes, then asked softly, "Kevin, is everything all right?"

"Do you mean besides the fact that someone in town was murdered this week and my son's still missing? No, everything else is just fine; thanks for asking."

"You know what I mean," I said.

"As a matter of fact, I don't. Now, I need you to open this back door so I can get out." He looked at the bar and added, "That's a fire code violation. I'll have to write you up for it."

"Check the books. We've got a variance," I said.

"We'll see about that."

I knew the allowance was only for the hours when the pizzeria wasn't open for business, but there was nothing I could do about that. If I had to pay a few fines, it was still worth the sense of security that beam gave me. Instead of re-placing it, I leaned the beam against the back wall in case he came back with his ticket book.

After Kevin was gone, I'd just finished cutting up a fresh batch of mushrooms when the kitchen door opened again.

I'd steeled myself for the police chief's return, but this new visitor was even more unwelcome than he had been.

It was his wife, the former Marybeth Matheeny, and from the scowl on her face, she hadn't come by the Slice to compliment me on my pizza.

Chapter 13

"We need to talk," Marybeth said. There was a quiver in her voice, and from the look in her bloodshot eyes, she clearly hadn't been getting a lot of sleep lately. Marybeth had always been a curvy girl, even more than I'd been, but over the years she'd given in to it and now barely resembled the young woman who'd stolen my boyfriend once upon a time.

"I'm not so sure about that," I said, wondering if she'd just seen her husband leave my pizzeria. Could she still be unhappy with me after all these years? She'd gotten what she wanted, namely Kevin Hurley, but I'd heard grumblings around town that Marybeth had put her own spin on things, that Kevin had been hers, I'd taken him away, and then she'd stolen him back. Who knew? She'd said it so long, maybe she even believed it.

"I don't like you, and I know you don't care for me," she said.

"So why do we need to discuss it? I vote no."

"This isn't about us. No matter how we feel

about each other, there's one person we both care for."

This had gone too far. "Marybeth, I've been over Kevin since college. There's nothing there, trust me. I had the love of my life, and it was never your husband."

"I'm not talking about Kevin," she said, clearly shocked by my vehement denial.

Then I realized what I should have known the second she'd walked in. "You're talking about Josh, aren't you?"

"Of course I am," she said. "I never wanted him to work for you, and I never made a secret of it, but he loves it here. In the end, I just couldn't say no to him, and now you've driven him off."

"I've done nothing of the sort," I said. "I was as shocked that he ran away as anyone else was."

"You fired him," she said. "And don't try to deny it."

"Have you ever gotten anything right in your life?" I snapped at her. "Your husband asked me to keep Josh away from the pizzeria while there was a murder investigation going on, and I respected his wish. But I never fired your son. As soon as this mess is all straightened out, I'd love to have him back."

"Then help me find him," she pled, her voice cracking as she spoke. "My husband is the almighty chief of police, but he can't find his own son." She choked back a sob as she added, "I don't know what to do. I'm going crazy knowing that he's out there, scared and all alone."

She made it sound like Josh was twelve instead of nearly eighteen years old. He could most likely take care of himself, but then again, I wasn't his mother, so I couldn't begin to understand how Marybeth must have felt. And then suddenly I saw a piece of it. Her son's absence had driven her to come to me—the woman she hated most in the world—for help. No matter how I felt about her, I had to respect the power of emotion that must have taken.

"What can I do?" I asked.

"Has he been here since he ran away? Have you heard from him?"

"No, but I might know someone who has. Hang on, I'll be right back."

I ducked through the door and nearly knocked Maddy over. "Did you get all of that, or should I repeat any of it?"

"I missed the last bit, if you wouldn't mind."

"Seriously? You're eavesdropping on my conversations and not even bothering to deny it? Come on, Maddy."

"Give me some credit, Eleanor. It's not every day Marybeth Hurley comes storming in here. What did you do with Kevin? Did she find you two together?"

"You've lost your mind," I said.

"Slipped him out the back, did you? Smart thinking."

This was getting old fast. "Enough. Will you tell Greg I need to see him the first second he gets here? You cover his tables, too."

"If I do that, how am I supposed to listen in?"

"I'll catch you up later," I said. "Come on, this is important."

"Oh, all right," she said.

Ten seconds later, Greg met me by the drinks

station. I wanted a chance to chat with him before we both talked to Marybeth. "What's going on, boss?"

"I need to find Josh Hurley," I said.

"You and the rest of Timber Ridge," he said. "Why ask me?"

I put my hands on his shoulders and looked into his eyes. "Greg, his mother is going crazy in there. Where is he?"

"I don't know," Greg said, trying to shift his gaze from me.

"Greg," I repeated, not letting up one bit.

He pulled away, then said, "I mean it. I don't know where he is at this exact moment, and that's the literal truth."

I had to laugh. "You're mastering the fine art of lying, aren't you?"

"I don't know what you're talking about," he said.

"You know, for a true pro, it's when you tell the literal truth to disguise the intent of a lie. You don't know where he is right now, but I'm willing to bet you know where he spent last night, and where he'll be tonight."

Greg frowned. "He's going to kill me. I promised him I wouldn't say anything."

"If it makes you feel any better, tell him I threatened you with losing your job if you didn't tell me."

"Are you?" he asked, his face brighter than it should have been. "That would be great."

"So great that it's true," I said. "Where has he been staying?"

"On my couch. And he snores, too. I haven't

had a good night's sleep since he came to stay with me." He looked at me sadly, then asked, "Are you mad at me?"

"No, I won't blame you for trying to protect a friend," I said. "Let's not make a habit of lying to me, though, okay?"

"Sure," he said, the relief clear on his face. "You're too good at spotting lies anyway."

"Don't forget that, either. See if you can track Josh down later, but if you can't, send him home tonight, all right?"

"I'll try, but I can't make him go, and I wouldn't send his dad after him if I were you. If he doesn't come back on his own, he's just going to take off again."

"Understood. Thanks, Greg."

"Glad to help," he said as he returned to his station.

I walked back in to find Marybeth eating freely of the cut pepperoni rounds. "Sorry, I'm starving," she said.

"I'd be glad to make you something," I said, fully realizing that I couldn't serve any more of that particular topping until I could cut some fresh. I prided myself on cleanliness, and after Marybeth's hands had been in the toppings, I wasn't about to serve them to anyone else, even if the pepperoni rounds weren't cooked yet. There's watching the bottom line, which I did my best to keep low, but an overriding factor was that I put out the best food I possibly could, and I wasn't all that sure at the moment I could do that without chucking something out and starting over.

"No, I couldn't eat a thing," she said as she stuffed the pepperoni, still in her hand, into her mouth. "Did you find him?"

"Not yet, but I have high hopes he'll turn up soon."

Marybeth walked quickly toward me. "Who knows where he is? Tell me, and I'll have Kevin make him tell us where Josh is."

"I've got to make some telephone calls," I said. "The person I tried a second ago wasn't home." I wasn't about to give Greg Hatcher up as my source of information. Neither one of us wanted the Hurleys descending on him like a plague of locusts.

"Find him," Marybeth said as she took my hands in hers. I could feel the grease still on her fingers. "I'm begging you."

"I'll do what I can."

As she started for the kitchen door, she turned and said, "I'm sorry I had to come to you like this. I just didn't know where else to turn."

"If I can help, I will," I said.

Once she was gone, Maddy came through the door like a grizzly bear was chasing her.

I said, "Okay, okay, I give up. I'll tell you everything that just happened."

"There's no time for that now," Maddy said. "Your date just showed up."

I glanced at the clock and saw that it was indeed time.

"We're too busy," I said. "Would you mind telling him I have to postpone it until another time?"

"No way, Eleanor," she said. "It's slow, but even if every table was full, you'd still have to go. You can't break his heart like that. It's not fair."

"Fine," I said as I pulled off my apron. "I'm not going to have fun, though."

"That's the spirit," she said.

I was taking an inordinately long time washing my hands when Maddy finally asked, "How long are you going to keep him waiting?"

"Until he gets bored and wanders off," I said.

"You wish. But it's not going to happen. He looks awfully nice." She studied my attire, then asked, "You're wearing blue jeans? Seriously? You can do better than that, Eleanor, and you know it. Why didn't you bring something nicer to wear?"

"I never promised to get dressed up. If he doesn't like it, he'll just have to deal with it." Who knew? Maybe David would be the one who'd back out. "By the way, you need to cut more pepperoni."

She glanced at the nearly full container. "Why? Are we expecting a rush on it?"

I told her about finding rounds in Marybeth's hands, and she quickly nodded her agreement.

I took a deep breath, then walked out into the dining room. David was wearing a nice blue pin-striped suit, at least five levels above my casual attire.

"Sorry I didn't have time to dress up," I said.

"I think you look wonderful," David said as he undid his tie, then took his suit jacket off. "Are you ready?"

"I suppose," I said, unsure about his sudden and complete willingness to dress down. "Where are we going?"

"I'd thought about Raphael's," he said, which was the nicest restaurant in nine counties, "but on second thought, I'm suddenly more in the mood for a steak. How does the Wild Steer sound?"

His alternate choice was clearly more for my attire than his. "No, I'll go to Raphael's with you. Reservations are impossible to get there, and I'd hate for you to waste one."

"I can go there anytime," he said. "Wild Steer sounds good."

"Okay, if you're sure," I said.

"Just give me a second to change, and we can go."

"You brought more than one outfit for our dinner?" I'd barely caught myself in time not to say "date." Even if it was one, I wasn't about to name it as such.

"Hey, I used to be a Boy Scout, remember? 'Be prepared' is a credo I've taken to heart."

He went out and grabbed a bag from his car, came back, and vanished into the bathroom. Three minutes later he was in blue jeans, cowboy boots, and the dress shirt he'd already had on. "How's that?" he asked.

"Good," I reluctantly acknowledged. It appeared that no matter how I tried to sabotage the evening, David was ready for me. Maybe Maddy was right. Perhaps I should stop worrying about my baggage and try to have fun.

I wasn't making myself any promises, but I owed it to David to at least try.

As we drove to the Wild Steer, I asked David, "Did you bring clothes to change to suit mine, or did they just happen to be in your car?"

"That depends. Which answer gets me more points?"

"Nobody's keeping score, David. I'm just curious."

He shrugged. "I figured you might not have time to change, since you've been working all day. But if you did, I wanted to be ready for you." David smiled as he added, "I'm more comfortable in jeans anyway. How about you?"

"I wear them to work every day," I said. "It's one of my favorite parts of running the pizzeria."

"What other parts do you like?" he asked.

"Let's see. There's a lot to be said for being your own boss. On the other hand, I'm the hardest, most demanding employer I've ever had. The hours can be brutal, but I've got no one to complain to if they are."

He chuckled. "I asked you for pluses, Eleanor."

I took a deep breath, then said, "I love working with Maddy. And I really enjoy making pizza. There's something in me that enjoys satisfying people's basic needs. They come in hungry, and if I've done my job right, they leave happier than when they came in. The Slice is more than a pizzeria, though. Business deals are made there, and first dates, too."

"But not ours," he said.

"No, of course not. That's not what I meant. I was talking about teenagers. There aren't many places they can afford. I like to think I'm providing a public service to the community."

"You won't get any arguments from me," he said as he pulled into the parking lot of the steak house. It wasn't crowded yet, but there was a respectable number of cars there.

I started to open my door when David said, "Hang on one second."

"Don't tell me you're one of those men who insist on getting doors and holding out chairs," I said.

"As a matter of fact, I am, but that's not why I wanted you to wait." He turned in his seat and looked at me before speaking again. "I have no delusions about this date, no expectations. I can't begin to know how much you loved your husband, or how hard this is for you to do this. All I ask is that you try to relax and enjoy yourself. It's a chance to get away from the Slice for an hour or two, but don't read anything else into it. I believe we have enough in common to have a nice evening, no more and no less."

I bit my lip, then asked, "Do you always make long speeches before you feed your dates?"

"Not always," he said with a slight grin. "I just think those things needed to be said."

"Well, you've said them. Now, let's go see about getting me that steak you promised."

He nodded, and as he got out, I had my hand on the door before I remembered that David wanted to open it for me. I'd gone through stages in my life where I'd resented the courtesy, but thankfully I'd grown out of it. Why shouldn't I let him show me that he respected me, and wanted me to feel special? It wasn't exactly slapping me in the face with a wet fish, no matter what Maddy thought about the practice. She was a little too modern for my taste, and if a man wanted to open a door for me, or pick up a check, I wasn't about to discourage the practice.

"Thanks," I said as he opened the door.

"You're most welcome."

We walked across the parking lot, and he held the restaurant door open for me. There were two sets—an airlock of sorts—and just because I could, I held the second door open for him.

"Thank you," he said as he walked through. Whether he knew it or not, that was a test, and he'd just passed it. It took a strong man to open a door for me, but I felt it took an even stronger one to accept the gesture from me as well. Since I had no intention of reaching for the check, the door was the best opportunity to learn more about David.

While we were waiting for a hostess to appear, I looked around the restaurant. The owners had taken the country theme to extremes, with wagon wheels hanging from the ceilings and hardwood floors underneath. The tables looked like they would fit into any Wild West saloon, and country music flooded the place. I half expected to see bales of hay at some point, but so far, they'd resisted the temptation.

We were soon shown to a table by a buxom young blonde who seemed to take an inordinate amount of interest in my dinner date. After we were seated, she made sure to linger over him long enough to give him a broad smile and a not so subtle wink.

After she was gone, I said, "I think you've got yourself a fan."

"Sally's harmless," David said. "She flirts like that with everyone."

"Does she have the opportunity to flirt with you much?" I asked as I studied the menu.

"I eat here every now and then," he admitted, before perusing his own menu.

After seating a young man more her age nearby—without even a modicum of flirting, I noticed—she retrieved a basket of bread and sped to our table.

"I know how you like hot rolls," she said.

I honestly wasn't sure if she even knew I was there.

"Do you have any butter?" I asked, just to see if she'd make eye contact.

"Your waitress will take care of you," she replied without looking at me at all. Before she left, she put a hand on David's. "Now, if there's anything I can do to make your evening more pleasant, you be sure to let me know."

"Well, you could start with some butter," David said as he pulled his hand away.

"It would be my pleasure," she said.

I started laughing the second she was out of earshot. "My, my, my. Why do I feel like the third wheel here?"

"Like I said, Sally's harmless. Trust me."

"I'm not sure I can," I said.

"We could always go somewhere else if it bothers you," he offered.

"Don't be silly. I can remember a crush or two when I was that age."

He shook his head. "I hope you know that I've done nothing to encourage her," he said as a waiter approached, decked out in cowboy boots, blue jeans, and a pearl-buttoned shirt.

"Talking about Sally? It's true, she likes old . . . older men," our waiter said. "My name's Roscoe, and I'll be waiting on you tonight."

"Roscoe? Really?" I asked.

He leaned forward, mostly toward me. "Actually, it's Danny, but I like to try out different characters while working here. I'm a drama major at the college."

"How lovely," I said, then turned my attention back to the menu. "Roscoe," I told him with a smile, "I'd love a Coke and an ice water to start."

He nodded, then turned to David. "And you, sir?"

"The same," David said.

"Be right back," he said as he tipped a nonexistent hat to me.

"That's fun," I said. "I wonder what character Sally's playing?"

"I doubt they all do it," David said with a laugh.

"More's the pity," I replied.

After our drinks arrived and we ordered, I noticed Sally watching us. "She's really something, isn't she?"

He glanced over at her, then shook his head. "She's nine years old."

I looked at her again. "I'd say twice that, and perhaps add a year or two to it."

"I didn't notice," he said. "So tell me, have you always wanted to run a pizzeria?"

"No. Actually, it was Joe's idea, but like most of his plans, he had a way of infecting me with passion for it. There was something about him that made people want to please him, including me. Do you know what I mean?"

"I do," he said.

"I'm sorry. I shouldn't be talking about him during dinner."

"Nonsense," David said. "He was a big part of your life. Why wouldn't you talk about him?" He took a bite of bread, then said, "Your sister leaves quite a wake wherever she goes, doesn't she?"

There was no judgment in his voice as he said it, so I decided to take it in the good nature he clearly intended. "Maddy's a firm believer in the institution of marriage. She swears she's on the lookout for her next husband, and I honestly don't know if I believe her or not."

"There's nothing wrong with wanting someone else in your life," David said.

"Nor is there anything wrong with being by yourself."

"No, but it can get lonely sometimes," he said.

The tone of our conversation was getting much too serious for my taste. "You could always ask Sally out."

"I'm not that lonely," he said with a smile.

"Why, don't you think she's attractive? And don't lie to me."

"I never said she wasn't beautiful," he said.

"I said 'attractive,' but that's okay. So, are you telling me you haven't been tempted to ask her out?"

David looked surprised by the very idea of it. "I have no desire to look like an old fool chasing a young girl. No thanks."

A couple in the corner caught my eye, and when I looked at them, I saw them both look immediately away. "That's just great," I said.

"What's wrong?"

"Don't look now, but the people at that table were just talking about us."

To his credit, he didn't pivot and stare at them. Instead, he stretched and managed to sneak a peek that way.

"They aren't looking at us now. Why should they care if we're out having dinner together?"

"It's the murder that makes me interesting to them. I just know it."

"Come on, Eleanor, isn't there the least chance you're imagining it?"

"No," I said flatly. "Half the town probably thinks I killed Richard Olsen."

"Then that leaves half that doesn't," he said.

"I know that. Otherwise we wouldn't have any customers at the Slice. I still don't have to like it, though."

"Would you like me to say something to them?" he asked as he put his napkin on the table.

"Don't you dare," I said as I put a hand on his arm.

He shrugged, then repositioned the napkin. "Then let's just ignore them, okay?" He pointed over my shoulder and said, "Perfect timing."

I turned to see Roscoe, aka Danny, carrying two steaks on a tray, along with potatoes piled high with butter, sour cream, bacon bits, and chives and a platter of green beans.

After we got our food, Roscoe refilled our drinks, then faded into the background.

Eating took my mind off everything else, and if Chief Hurley himself had walked in at that moment, it couldn't have spoiled the mood.

After we were finished, I saw that Sally had gone off duty. I nudged David as I said, "She's probably out in the parking lot getting ready to follow us home."

"I guess it's just the price of being a handsome, desirable man," he said with a smile.

"My, don't we think the world of ourselves."

"So it's not just me? Good, I think you're attractive, too. What do you say? Are you up for a little dancing? How about a movie? I'm game for anything; all you have to do is ask."

"I'm sorry, but I really do have to get back to the pizzeria," I said.

He frowned in disappointment at my response for a split second, and if I hadn't been watching him closely, I'm sure I would have missed it. It was instantly replaced with a smile. "The Slice it is."

We chatted on the drive back to my restaurant, and when he came to the parking area out front, I said, "You don't need to walk me in. Thanks for a lovely evening. You know what? I had fun."

"So did I," he said. "Do you have any plans for tomorrow night? We could do it again, if you'd like."

"Maddy and I just take one night a week away from the restaurant," I said. While it was true we'd come to that agreement when she'd first come to work for me, it hadn't panned out. She hadn't found anyone worth dating, and it hadn't been an issue with me, either.

"Then I'll see you in seven days," he said. "Not that I won't come by in the meantime. That's still allowed, isn't it?"

"I never said I'd go out with you again," I said softly.

"No, but you didn't say you wouldn't, either."

He started to get out when I put a hand on his shoulder. "No need to get out. Thanks again."

"The pleasure was all mine," he said.

I walked back toward the restaurant, then turned around just as I walked in.

He was smiling at me, and I waved quickly before ducking inside.

"Tell me everything," Maddy said before I could get my coat off.

"You're supposed to be cooking," I said in a whisper.

"I am," she whispered back. "But Greg saw you drive up, so I came rushing out here. Come on, don't hold out on me."

"Let's talk about it in back," I said as I grabbed her arm and walked her toward the kitchen.

"Spoilsport," she said as I saw Greg grinning at me.

"What are you smiling at?" I asked.

"Me? Nothing. I'm not smiling at all," Greg replied.

"All evidence to the contrary," I said.

He shrugged. "What can I say? I'm an enigma."

Maddy and I walked into the kitchen, but before I could start to tell her about my evening, I saw something moving in my office.

"Call Kevin Hurley," I said as I reached for a cleaver. "We have company."

As Maddy's face paled and she reached for the telephone, a voice said, "There's no need to call him. I'm not ready to see him yet."

"Josh, how did you sneak in here?" I asked.

"I've got a key to the back," the young man said. "It's a good thing, too, because it's the only way I was going to come by."

"You must have forgotten to put the beam back up after you let Kevin out," Maddy said.

"Does it really matter?" Josh snapped. "Eleanor, I don't appreciate you having Greg kick me out of his place."

"Would you like a list of things I don't appreciate?" I asked. "It might start with being accused of murder, or maybe even having both your mother and father come into my kitchen and tell me what to do, all because of you."

"They did that?" he asked softly.

"Yes, what a shock. Your parents both love you, and they're worried about you." I reached up and smacked him not so gently on the side of the head.

He pulled back and rubbed the spot. "What was that for?"

"Don't be such a baby. I barely hit you. The next time you think about doing something stupid like running away, I suggest you remember that."

"I wasn't running away," Josh said.

"Funny, you surely gave your parents that impression." I told Maddy, "You need to cover the front." To my surprise, she didn't even complain as she left.

"That's because no one ever listens to me."

I finally took the time to notice Josh's appearance. His clothes were wrinkled, and his shirttail wasn't tucked into his khakis. Not only that, but his hair lacked its usual careful styling.

"I'm listening now," I said. "What's going on?"

"I tried to tell Dad what I saw, but he wouldn't believe me. He just kept saying that I was trying to cover for you. When I knew he wasn't going to do anything to protect me, I decided I had to do something on my own."

I pushed him down to a stool we kept in the kitchen. "You're not making any sense. Who's after you?"

"That's just it," he said. "I never got a good look at who was in the other car."

"What car, Josh?" It was like pulling weeds in July, extracting information from him.

"The car chasing Richard Olsen the night he was murdered."

That certainly got my attention. "Okay, take a deep breath, and start at the beginning. I want to hear everything."

He nodded, but then he started to get up.

"Where are you going?"

"I'm thirsty," he said. "I just want to get a drink."

"You stay right there," I said. "I'll get it for you."

I walked out to the dining room and filled up a glass with Coke. Maddy hurried over to me and hissed, "What did he say?"

"I don't know yet. He was thirsty, so I'm getting him a drink."

"Are you going to give him a neck rub, too? Come on, Eleanor."

"Leave it alone, Maddy. I know what I'm doing."

"If you're so smart, how do you know he's still back there? The door's unbolted, remember?"

"You've got a cynical view of the world, don't you?"

Maddy smiled, but there was no humor in it. "Funny how often I'm right, though, isn't it?"

I carried the Coke toward the back, not sure if Josh would still be there when I got into the kitchen again.

The stool where he'd been sitting was empty.

To make matters worse, Maddy had followed me back to the kitchen. "Don't you just hate it when I'm right?" she asked.

"Right about what?" Josh asked as he came out of my office.

Maddy actually looked disappointed that he was still there. "I thought you'd taken off," she admitted.

"Why in the world would I do that, when I took so much trouble coming here in the first place? That doesn't make much sense."

"Don't you have customers?" I asked Maddy as I smiled at her broadly.

"I do," she admitted, though she never moved a muscle to return to them.

"Go," I commanded, and to my surprise, she did just that.

"Sometimes I don't get you two," Josh said.

"Sometimes neither do I. Here's your drink," I said as I handed it to him.

He took a healthy gulp, then asked, "I don't suppose there's any leftover pizza lying around, is there?"

"No, but I can make you a fresh one, if you promise to talk to me."

"That's a deal," he said. "Not only is Greg's couch lumpy, but he's not much of a chef, you know what

I mean? If I have to look another peanut butter and jelly sandwich in the eye, I think I'll scream."

"Stop stalling, and start talking," I said as I knuckled some dough into a small pizza pan. "What did the car look like, and how did you happen to see it?"

"I was out jogging, and I remember the car because it almost came up onto the sidewalk and hit me. It was a black Volkswagen Beetle," he said. "I'd say it was pretty new, from the look of it."

The Barons drove that make and model, so why wasn't I surprised? "Are you sure you didn't see who was driving it?"

"Like I told you, it was pretty dark," Josh admitted.

"Was a man or a woman behind the wheel?" I asked, pressing him harder.

"I just told you, I have no idea."

"Then how can you even be sure about the car?"

He laughed. "Come on, it was pretty funny seeing that truck of his being chased by a VW Bug." He added, "But I don't think Mr. Olsen found it funny. I caught a glimpse of his face, and he didn't seem too amused about it. I could swear he looked scared half to death."

"Let me get this straight," I said. "You saw Richard Olsen's face enough to know that he was frightened, but you couldn't even tell if the driver of the car chasing him was a man or a woman?"

"That's what Dad said!" Josh yelled as he slammed the drink down onto the counter. "He didn't believe me, either."

"I never said that," I replied, careful to keep my voice calm and even. "I was just curious."

"The Bug's windows were tinted, okay? And I mean dark, too."

"That makes sense," I said, and he settled back onto the stool.

He nodded. "Of course it does, when you take the time to let me finish. Dad didn't believe me, and I didn't know who else to tell. The next night, I was out running again, and I spotted the VW. It was almost like it was out prowling around looking for me." He finished his Coke and offered me the glass. "Could I get some more?"

"When your pizza's done," I said. "Tell me more about what happened."

"I ran my usual route, but when I spotted the car, I got a little creeped out by it. When it got too close, I made a quick cut into Mrs. Abernathy's yard, and the funny thing was, I could swear it veered over to come after me."

"What did you do then?"

"I couldn't go home, could I? I ran to the first place I could think of, and that was Greg Hatcher's apartment. That's why I've been hiding, Eleanor. It had nothing to do with me acting childish, and I wish people would understand that."

"You've got to tell your father," I said, reaching for the telephone.

"He won't listen to me," Josh said. "I can't believe you want me to call him."

"He's not just your dad," I said. "He's the chief of police."

"Why should I tell him anything? He won't believe me."

I shook my head. "I'll stay right beside you when

you tell him," I said, knowing that I was getting myself into more grief with Kevin than I wanted, but not caring enough to stop myself. Josh had come to me for help, and I wasn't about to turn him away.

"You'd do that for me?" He seemed sincerely touched by my gesture.

"Hey, I back all my employees up," I said, trying to lighten the mood. Josh's dark temper was just below the surface, but he hadn't succeeded in burying it like his father had yet.

"That's just it," he said. "I'm not exactly an employee anymore, am I?"

"I never said that," I replied. "You were on leave; you weren't fired."

"Funny, it feels the same way to me."

"That's your problem," I said as I stared intently at him. "I can't do anything about that. Now call him."

He finally took the phone, but it was pretty clear he was reluctant to use it. "He's not going to believe me, I can tell you that now."

"Then it's on him, and not you. You still have to make the call."

Josh nodded reluctantly, then he took the portable phone into my office so he could have some privacy.

After twenty seconds, he came back in and said, "He's on his way."

"Did you tell him what happened?"

"Are you kidding? As soon as he found out I was here, he hung up on me. That's typical for my dad—patient with the world, but short-tempered with me."

"It's a family thing. Don't take it so personally," I said.

"It's kind of hard not to, you know?"

Josh's pizza came out of the oven, and I cut it and put it on a tray. "There you go. You might as well eat something while we're waiting. I'll get you a refill."

I'd waited to get him more Coke on purpose. I wanted a word with his father before he confronted Josh, and if he didn't like my parenting tips, it was just too bad.

I refilled Josh's glass as Maddy joined me.

"Having any luck with him?"

"He's eating now," I said, and before my sister could jump on me, I added, "He took off because of the Barons' black VW."

"Why? What did he see?"

"It's the car that was chasing Richard Olsen on the night he was murdered," I said.

Maddy frowned. "I didn't see anybody after him."

"They must have dropped the chase at some point," I said.

"Then why was Richard still speeding when I saw him?"

"Maddy, I believe Josh."

"And you don't believe me?"

"Of course I believe you," I said. "But there's no doubt in his mind that at least one of the Barons was in that car."

"But he couldn't see which one it was," Maddy said.

"No, he couldn't. How did you know that?"

"That's the car Steve Baron was scraping the windshield on when we talked to him. The windows were tinted to nearly black. Don't tell me you didn't notice."

"I was focusing on the mayor," I said, "not the car he was de-icing."

"They had a busy night, didn't they? Eating at Dusty's, then getting back in town in time to chase Richard Olsen around in their Beetle before stabbing him."

"It all makes sense, don't you think?"

My sister frowned instead of answering.

"Come on, Maddy," I said. "It's possible."

"I'm not denying it." She looked up and asked, "Did you know he was coming?"

I looked over my shoulder and saw Kevin Hurley heading toward us. "You might want to make yourself scarce," I said.

"Are you kidding me? I adore fireworks."

"Then you're going to absolutely love this."

Chapter 14

Kevin got within a foot of me before he snapped, "Where's my son?"

"We need to talk first," I said.

"I'm not in the mood, Eleanor," he said.

I put a hand on his chest. "Oh, do you think I'm playing around here? You're not going back there until I talk to you."

He paused then and studied me for a few long seconds. "Do you really think you can stop me?"

"If you have a tenth as much brains as you think you do, you'll do as I ask."

He didn't like it, but he didn't push my hand away, either.

"You've got thirty seconds," he said.

I started talking before he could begin his countdown.

"Your son doesn't think you believe him about the black VW."

"He told you that? The kid's got too much imagination."

"Or maybe he really saw one of the Barons chasing Richard Olsen. Did you even talk to the mayor and his wife, or have you been afraid to because of their pull around here?"

A glimpse of his temper came to the surface, and he didn't even bother fighting it back this time. "I know how to do my job, Eleanor. I checked their alibi. They were at Dusty's the night of the murder."

If he expected me to cower from that onslaught, he didn't know me at all. "They were there until just after seven. Check the credit card receipt. That gave them plenty of time to get back here and commit the murder."

"Are you poking your nose where it doesn't belong?"

"Somebody has to," I said. Though the dining room was sparsely populated, there wasn't a sound in the room as the chief and I argued. I couldn't do anything about that, though.

"You're interfering in official police business," he said as he glanced at his watch. "And your time's up."

He hurried through the kitchen door and was back out almost as quickly. "Where's my son?"

It was my turn to be surprised. "Do you mean he's not there?"

Kevin shook his head as he took off. "This isn't over," he said as he neared the front door.

After he was gone, I noticed that everyone was still looking at me. I looked at them all, then said, "Sorry about the interruption. To make it up to you all, we'll be delivering orders of cinnamon swirlies as soon as they're out of the oven, and they'll be on the house."

I hurried back into the kitchen and started pulling out dough from the fridge.

Maddy followed quickly behind me. "Have you lost your mind?"

"I wasn't about to let him steamroll his own child," I said as I rolled out pieces of dough and twisted them into braids.

"I'm talking about giving away food," she said.

"Can we really afford to lose the last few customers we have?" I asked.

"I guess not," Maddy said.

"Then melt some butter and get out the cinnamon sugar," I said. "We have some desserts to make."

After the dough was twisted, buttered, and dusted with cinnamon sugar, I started sending sheets through the oven.

"Why did he just take off like that?" Maddy asked.

"I thought you expected him to do just that."

She frowned. "I didn't think he'd leave you to deal with his own father. That's just not right."

"Take it easy on him, Maddy. I'm sure he was listening to every word we said. Would you have been able to stand there and take it yourself?"

"I guess you're right," she said. "I'm pretty proud of you."

"For giving away desserts?" I asked as I mixed the icing for the swirlies.

"Don't be a nit," she said. "You stood up to Kevin for Josh's sake."

"What can I say? I feel like the people who work here are family to me."

"I've always thought of you as a sister, myself," Maddy said as she put an arm around me.

We both laughed, and the tension was broken. I had no idea where Josh had headed, but I doubted it would be back to Greg Hatcher's place. Wherever he went, I hoped he was safe. He'd risked something coming to see me, and I was going to make sure it hadn't been in vain.

The next free second I had, I was going to pay a visit to the mayor and his wife, no matter how many wicked and evil threats he'd made.

After Maddy and I finished distributing the dessert confections, we were back in the kitchen washing up.

As she dried off a plate I handed her, she said, "Hey, I just realized you never finished telling me about your big date."

"I didn't know I'd even started," I said.

"Come on, give. I want details."

"Fine. We both had steak, baked potatoes, and green beans."

"Is that it?" Maddy asked.

"I was too full for dessert," I said as I tore off a bit of unclaimed dessert. After I ate it, I said, "That doesn't mean I've sworn off desserts forever, you know."

"I don't care about the menu," she said.

"Then why'd you ask?"

Maddy frowned at me. "Are you really this dense, or is it just an act?"

I shrugged. "I guess we'll never know."

"You're honestly not going to tell me what happened?"

I took my sister's hands in mine and said, "Nothing happened. We had a nice meal. Then he brought me back here. Sorry to disappoint you, but there were no sparks, no connection, and no good-night kiss."

She let out a big breath, then asked, "How am I supposed to live vicariously through you when you won't live?"

"Go out and find another husband," I said. "That should keep you busy for a year or two."

"Don't be so flip about it, or I just might," Maddy said. As she studied the pile of dishes waiting to be cleaned, she asked, "Do you want to switch off?"

"It's up to you. Surprise me," I said.

"That's us—two single gals who really know how to live."

We both laughed about it, but I wondered how much either one of us found it funny. Maddy was a natural at falling in love. She just hadn't mastered the art of staying married. I was a completely different case altogether. I'd been in love only once, but I'd thought it was going to be forever.

Yet here we were, with no one but each other.

At least we had that, though.

After we locked the doors and sent Greg on his way home, I turned to Maddy and said, "See you in the morning."

"What? No late-night sleuthing tonight?"

"That depends," I said as I looked around. "What did you have in mind?" The brick promenade was nearly deserted, and fog had moved in to replace the snow we'd had before. A few lampposts lit different areas of the expanse in front of the shops, leaving pockets of fuzzy light that barely extended into the gloom. It felt more like the English moors than our part of North Carolina.

"I think we should go talk to the Barons," she said.

"I don't know, Maddy. I'm not sure the mayor was bluffing about coming after my permits."

"We won't let him, Eleanor. If he tries it, he'll have the fight of his life on his hands. Just because he runs things around here doesn't give him the right to threaten our livelihood. If we let him keep us from investigating, he wins."

I thought about it a few moments, then said, "Okay, I'm game if you are. We might have more use for Bob Lemon after all. By the way, I haven't seen him over the past two days. Where's he been?"

"How should I know?" she asked a little too defensively.

"You do, don't you?"

"He called me before he left. He had to take a deposition out of town, but he'll be back tomorrow. The only reason Bob called was so you'd know how to get in touch with him if you needed him."

"If that's true," I said, "then why didn't he call me directly? He's got my phone number, too."

Maddy looked flustered by the line of questioning. "Who knows why any man does anything? Are we going to go talk to the Barons, or should I head home and leave you so you can fantasize another night about my love life?"

"Let's go see the mayor and his wife," I said.

"Excellent. I'll follow you to your house, and then you can ride with me."

"We could do it the other way around," I said as

we walked through the parklike alley toward our cars. At least there was a light there, though it stopped far short of illuminating the entire pathway. I could easily imagine someone stepping out of the fog and grabbing us, and without realizing it, I quickened my pace.

"I'll drive," she said. "I've had more experience in the fog."

"I don't see how," I said as I peered all around us. "This is really bad, isn't it?"

Maddy shrugged. "It's supposed to be worse tomorrow night."

"I can't imagine that."

"Just wait," she said. "I went camping with Jared once, or was it Kyle? Sometimes even I have trouble remembering what I did with which husband."

"Does it really matter who the spouse of the month was? What about your camping trip?"

"It had to be Kyle. Jared's idea of roughing it was going without room service." My loud sigh spurred her on. "Anyway, we were camping on the Skyline Drive, and the fog was so thick we nearly lost our way coming back from the shower house. I didn't think we'd ever make it home the next day."

"And it was as bad as this?"

"Worse," she said.

"Then I'm staying home tomorrow."

"You can't do that."

"Because of all our loyal customers?" I asked as we finally made it to our cars.

"Sure, if that works for you. See you soon. Don't drive too fast."

"Right back at you," I said.

I got into the Subaru, with Maddy following

right behind me, and we somehow managed to make it back to my house. By the time we got there, I was just as happy that my sister had insisted on driving. I was a bundle of nerves from our short trek to the house.

When I got in the passenger side, I said, "Let's go."

"It's time to poke the wasp nest with a stick," she said. Peering at the gloomy road ahead of us, Maddy said, "If you don't mind, I'd appreciate it if we didn't talk. I need to focus on the road, at least the parts of it I can see."

That was a request I had no trouble keeping. As we drove through the shrouded streets, I wondered about the sanity of the trip. Even if we made it to the Barons' house—which I was beginning to doubt was going to happen—how were we going to question them? We'd both been pretty blunt before, but tonight we were going to push it all of the way. It probably wouldn't be the smartest thing I'd ever done, and that encompassed quite a few boneheaded moves I'd made in the past.

I kept my thoughts to myself until Maddy neared the house. It had helped our travel that not many other folks were out in the fog.

I touched her arm lightly. "Pull over here, would you?"

She nodded as she did as I'd asked. "Are we going to sneak up on them?"

"We could do that if we parked in their driveway," I said. "I want to talk to you before we just go barging in there."

"You're not getting cold feet, are you?"

"I'm shivering everywhere, including my feet.

Maddy, what if we're right? What if one or both of the Barons killed Richard Olsen? Shouldn't we have some sort of way to defend ourselves?"

"I've still got my stun gun," she said, "and you've got your pepper spray."

"I'm talking about calling Kevin Hurley," I said.

"I'm sure the chief of police is going to trot right over to watch our backs, especially after the argument you two had this evening. Eleanor, I hate to break it to you, but I doubt if he'd cross the street to pour water on either one of us if we were on fire. We can handle this."

"You're delusional; you know that, don't you?"

She smiled at me. "I think it's one of my best features. Don't worry, we'll be safe enough."

I questioned the wisdom of the confrontation, but then I remembered how the couple had come into my kitchen and threatened me. That got my blood boiling again. I wasn't about to let them get away with it, and the murder investigation almost became secondary in my mind to standing up for myself.

"Let's go," I said.

"That's the spirit."

We got out of the car and walked the hundred yards to the Barons' house. They had a porch light on, which served as a glowing beacon for us.

I'd no sooner walked onto the porch when Faith Baron pulled the door open, dressed in a fancy party outfit.

"Come on in, Thompsons," she said. Then Faith saw that it was us.

"What are you two doing here?" she asked, the pleasant greeting dying on her lips as she spoke. "I thought my husband made it perfectly clear that we were finished talking to you."

I patted my empty jacket pocket. "We didn't come to talk. We've still got that letter you wrote Richard Olsen, and we wanted to see how you'd tap dance your way out of it when we show it to your husband."

Faith stepped out onto the porch, pulling the door behind her. "Give it to me."

"No," I said. "After we show Steve, I'm saving it for the police."

She looked surprised by that statement. "How could they possibly care that I was having an affair with Richard Olsen? Just because I slept with him once didn't mean I murdered him."

I heard a rustling in the bushes nearby, but when I turned to try to see what it was, I couldn't spot a thing.

Faith followed my gaze and commanded, "Buttons, get in here. It's no night for a cat to be out running around in the fog."

When there was no further movement, I turned back to her and said, "Go get your husband. We're not leaving until we talk to him."

"Don't do this," Faith said, the commanding tone in her voice becoming all at once compliant. "He doesn't know, not for sure, at any rate. That letter will kill my marriage."

"Like you killed Richard?" Maddy asked softly.

"Neither one of us killed him," she said curtly.

"But you chased him down the road in your car the night he died, didn't you?" I asked.

I was surprised to see a puzzled expression on her face. "That would have been impossible."

"How's that? We've got witnesses," I said.

"They didn't see us," she said. "Our car was in the shop that night. Call Bob Pickering and ask him if you don't believe me. We were supposed to pick it up, but our dinner reservations were too early, so we took my husband's car. By the time we got back into town, Pickering's was closed, so I didn't pick it up until the next morning."

"You're lying," Maddy said, but there wasn't a lot of belief in her words.

"Call Pickering and ask him yourself," Faith said. "Just don't show my husband that letter until you find out I'm telling the truth." The pleading in her voice died as she added, "If you show him tonight, by tomorrow morning I'll make sure he gets every inspector on the payroll checking out your pizza place. It's up to you."

I turned to Maddy. "This can wait until tomorrow."

"Okay," she said.

I looked at Faith and said, "If you're lying to us, we'll be back."

"Fine. Just go now, all right?"

"We're leaving."

Maddy and I were twenty yards away, safely buried in the fog, when we heard the front door open. We could both hear Steve Baron say, "What are you doing out here? I thought the Thompsons were here."

"It's the cat," Faith said. "She won't come in."

"Then leave her," her husband ordered. "Get back inside. You don't want to look like an idiot when our friends get here."

"Yes, dear," Faith said, and as she walked back

inside, I saw her look back over her shoulder toward us.

We made it back to Maddy's car, and I dug out my cell phone.

"Who are you calling?" she asked.

"Bob Pickering. I have to see if she's telling the truth."

"And if she's not, we're going back, aren't we?"

I nodded. "I'm tired of this mess. I just want it to be over."

"Dial away, then."

I had Bob's home number and dialed it, my hands shaking as I did. It wasn't just from the cold fog, though. I was getting close to finding the killer. I could feel it.

"Sorry to call you so late," I said when he picked up.

"I was just catching a movie," he said. "Don't tell me you lost another window, Eleanor. You still owe me the deductibles for your insurance on the last two."

"I'll come by in the morning and pay them," I said, "but I've got an odd question for you tonight about one of your customers."

"I don't exactly have privileged information on any of them," he said, "so I'll tell you what I can."

"It's pretty simple. Were you working on the Barons' VW the night Richard Olsen was murdered?"

"No, not that night," he said, and I felt my spirits soar. So, she'd been lying to me after all.

I was about to thank Bob and hang up when he added, "I'd fixed it that afternoon, but they didn't pick it up until the next morning. Something about an early dinner reservation, I believe. It came up all of a sudden, and they asked me to stay late so they could pick it up after dinner, but I told them in no uncertain terms that they weren't the only ones who'd be eating that night, and they could just as well wait until morning to pick it up, which is what they did. Why do you ask?"

"Where were the keys when it was in your garage?" I asked.

"On the peg board with all the rest of them," Bob admitted. "Believe it or not, I don't have duplicate keys to all of my customers' cars."

"Could anyone get to that board with the keys on it?"

"No, it would have to be one of my mechanics, since the board is back behind the desk." He thought about it a second, then admitted, "Though if a customer was there paying a bill, they'd be close enough to it to just reach over and snag a key. What's going on, Eleanor?"

"Nothing. I was just asking."

"There's more to this than you're saying."

"We can talk about it tomorrow," I said. "I'll be by before nine to pay you."

"That's fine. You don't have to rush."

"I hate owing anybody money, especially my friends."

After I hung up, I told Maddy what I'd learned, finishing up by saying, "So we have to take the Barons off our list."

"Not necessarily," Maddy said. "Have you ever considered the possibility that they left the car at Bob's on purpose so they'd have this alibi if anyone found out they'd been chasing Richard all over town?"

"I don't see how," I said. "They left the car there at the last minute, according to Bob. I can't see them going through all that work, then killing Richard Olsen in the heat of the moment."

"What makes you think the murder wasn't planned?"

"The knife, mostly," I said. "It was from his own kitchen. That sounds like it was spur of the moment to me."

"Or is that what they want you to think," Maddy said.

"We can go round and round like this all night, you know that, don't you?" I asked as a pair of headlights started toward us.

The car slowed near us, and for a second I had an irrational thought that the police chief had been following us and was going to arrest us both.

Then the sedan pulled into the Barons' driveway, and I realized it was most likely the long-awaited Thompsons.

"Let's get out of here," I said. "This fog is giving me the creeps."

"Okay, but I still say we bust in there and take care of this, once and for all."

"If I thought we had anything that even approached being solid, I'd agree with you. Maddy, whether we like it or not, this is just one more dead end."

"We're not just giving up, are we?"

"Maybe for tonight, but don't worry, we'll start poking around again tomorrow."

"That's my girl," she said as she started her car and drove me home.

I'd had such high hopes for the Barons as our main suspects, but suddenly I wasn't all that certain anymore.

Maddy was right about one thing, though. One or both of the Barons might have been clever enough to set the whole thing up.

But if they were that smart, were we good enough to catch them?

By the next morning, the fog had lifted, and the world looked bright and fresh. I had coffee in the dining room as I admired the way the sunlight reflected off the oak that Joe and I had so painstakingly restored. Maddy had tried to convince me to move out soon after my husband's death, but I couldn't do it. My life was in a shambles, but I had a home, a haven that protected me from the world and, more importantly, kept a strong link to Joe that would never end.

And one dinner out with David wasn't going to change that. I'd have to call him sometime soon to let him know that our one chance was over. I might be able to open my heart again sometime, but it wasn't now, at least not with him. The closeness and easiness we'd experienced almost felt like a betrayal to my husband's memory, though I knew it was a ridiculous way to look at it.

But feelings weren't always logical, and mine at the moment were swirling in a thousand different directions.

I got dressed and left the house early. Maddy

and I hadn't made any specific plans for today, but I had a stop to make before I went to the Slice. I owed Bob money, and I was going to take care of that as soon as I could.

 I found Bob talking on the phone, his face already frosted with grease.

"I'm sorry, but I don't know what to tell you," he said into the receiver. "Your car was running fine when you left here."

He shrugged an apology, but I just smiled as I got my checkbook out. I knew my deductible, so I could write the check. I probably should have just dropped it off in the mail, but I wanted a chance to thank Bob again personally for taking such good care of me.

"I'll look at it again, but I'll tell you right now, I couldn't find anything wrong with it the first time." He paused, then added, "Then take it to a Mercedes dealership if you think they're any better than I am."

He slammed the phone down with a flourish.

"Let me guess—another happily satisfied customer," I said as I handed him the check I'd just written.

"Some people shouldn't own automobiles. I had it in my shop two days, but none of the guys could find anything wrong with it. I didn't charge her a penny, but did that satisfy her? It did not."

He shook his head vigorously, then added, "Let's talk about more pleasant things." He looked at the check, then said, "Exactly right. You didn't have to bring it by, though. I trust you."

"How else could I do this?" I asked as I hugged him.

He pulled away quickly. "Hey, you're going to get yourself dirty."

"I don't care. Thanks, Bob. You're a lifesaver."

"Anytime," he said. As I walked back to my car, he added, "Just not in the next three days. I should be able to get more windows in by then."

"Hopefully that trend is over," I said.

I'd come to ask him about the Barons' VW as well, but as I started to speak, the telephone rang again.

He said, "Pickering's, hang on a second," then looked at me. "Was that all?"

"I hate to bother you, but do you have a list of cars that were here the night Richard Olsen was murdered?"

"No, but I could probably scare one up for you. Why, is it important?"

"I don't know, but it might be."

He nodded. "I'll have it for you sometime after lunch. Is that soon enough? We're really buried right now."

"That's fine. Thanks again," I said, but he was already talking on the telephone again. I would have loved to go through his receipts and appointments right then, but I'd already pushed my luck with him, and if there was one man in Timber Ridge I didn't want mad at me, it was my mechanic.

I walked in the door three minutes before nine and found Maddy pacing around the dining room of the pizzeria.

"Why isn't your cell phone on?" she snapped at me.

"It is," I said.

"Oh, really?" She pulled her own cell phone out and punched in a number. The phone rang and rang until Maddy said, "If it's ringing, you're not answering."

I pulled the phone out of my purse and flipped it open. The screen was blank.

"I must have forgotten to turn it off yesterday. Can I borrow your charger?"

"It won't fit your telephone," she said as she stowed hers back into her purse.

"What's so urgent that it couldn't wait until now?" I asked.

"This," she said as she waved a piece of paper in front of me.

"Am I supposed to know what that is?" I asked.

"You should. It's the paper I pulled out of Richard Olsen's safety-deposit box."

"Where'd you find it?" I asked as I held out my hand.

"It was in my jeans. I don't know how I missed it the first time I checked."

I tried to smooth the paper out, but it was wrinkled beyond belief. "What happened to it?"

"I washed it, okay?" she said with a snap to her voice.

"It's not going to do much good then, is it?"

"There's one thing you can still read. The paper must have been folded just right, but it's still there."

I studied the paper but couldn't make anything out. "I'm sorry, I don't see it."

She snatched the paper from me, then frowned as she looked at it. "It was right there," Maddy said as she pointed to a spot. "Hang on a second."

She turned on one of the lights and held the paper up to it. "Come here. You can still see it."

I leaned forward and tried to see what she was talking about. At first I missed it, but then she shifted it just right, and for a moment, I caught a glimpse of something.

It was a series of letters and numbers: SN3 769.

"What does it mean, though?" I asked Maddy.

"You don't bank at Third Southern National, do you?" she asked.

"You know I don't," I said.

"One of my husbands used to," she said. "I've been staring at that number for an hour waiting for you to answer your phone or show up. I'm not positive, but I think Richard Olsen had another safety-deposit box that we didn't know about."

"Even if that's what this is—which I'm not saying at all—we still can't get in. We need Sheila for that."

"Then let's go see if we can find her," Maddy said. "We've got time before you have to rush your crust."

"I don't know," I said. "She's not exactly our biggest fan at the moment, is she?"

"All the better to ask her before she leaves town," Maddy said.

"How do you even know where she's staying? There's no furniture left at the house, and I don't see Sheila curling up on the floor, do you?"

"I'll have Tom Frances call her and have her meet us."

I couldn't think of any more reasons to say no. "Call him, but if he refuses to do it, I'm making dough."

"He won't say no," Maddy said.

She called him, and within one minute, he agreed to make the call.

"Remind me never to get on your bad side," I said.

"You've got it."

Her phone rang, and after a brief conversation, she hung up. "Funny thing is, Sheila's at her brother's house after all. Tom wasn't too pleased with me, but he said he'd come by in half an hour. Come on, what are we waiting for, a golden invitation?"

Reluctantly, I followed my sister out to her car. "We're running out of time, you know that, don't you?"

"All the more reason to jump on this while we can. Just take it easy, we'll be there in a flash."

"That's what I'm afraid of. You drive too fast, you know that, don't you?"

"At least it's not foggy anymore."

"Not until tonight," I said.

There were still no cars in sight when we arrived at the house, and I wanted to peek inside the garage, but Maddy pulled me away. "What are you doing?" I asked.

"We don't have the time to skulk around," she said. "And besides, this time we've got an invitation."

"We don't. Your Realtor friend does."

"Same thing," Maddy said.

I saw some movement around the side of the house, and before my sister could restrain me, I hurried toward it. She followed, fussing at me all the way, but someone had been back there, and I was going to see who it was.

I was startled to see Faith Baron running away from us down the alley.

I had a feeling in the pit of my stomach that we were too late. Maddy and I hadn't acted quickly enough, and the murderer had returned to the scene of her crime, only to strike again.

Chapter 15

"Was that who I think it was?" Maddy asked me as she stopped beside me.

"It was Faith Baron," I said, starting to visibly shake. "I don't want to go in there. I found the last one."

Maddy looked at me, then glanced over at the house. "Do you think Sheila's really dead?"

"Don't you?" I asked.

"I haven't given it much thought," Maddy admitted.

"Call Kevin Hurley," I said as I headed toward the house.

"Hang on a second," she said. "If there's another body in there, let him be the one who finds it."

"How are we going to explain even being here, let alone calling in the homicide? He'll lock us both up."

"Then let's get out of here before anyone sees us," Maddy said as Travis White called out, "What are you two doing lurking in the alley behind my house?"

"We weren't here to see you," I said.

Travis nodded. "If you came to see Sheila, you'd better dart in right now. The last I heard, she's leaving town forever this evening."

"We don't want to bother her," I said, trying to get us out of there.

"Nonsense. Don't be so timid."

Travis headed for the Olsen back door, and we had no option but to follow.

As he approached the window, he muttered, "That's odd."

"What is?" I asked.

When he didn't answer, I moved around and looked for myself. That was one of my problems. My curiosity often got the better of me, mostly at the worst possible time.

But when I looked inside, I saw that Sheila was still alive, leaning over the fireplace burning the contents of a small box!

"Thank goodness she's all right," I said without realizing I'd spoken aloud.

Travis turned to look at me oddly. "Isn't that an odd thing to say."

Maddy came to my rescue. "She's still traumatized about finding Richard's body. It's really affected her."

That got a note of sympathy from him. "As well it might."

He tapped on the door, and Sheila looked at us quickly before dumping the last bit of contents into the fire. What on earth was she burning? All I knew was that it wasn't firewood.

She came to the back door, and after she opened

it, Sheila said, "It's customary for visitors to come to the front door."

Travis said, "Don't get yourself in a snit. We came to say good-bye."

"Good-bye," Sheila said as she started to close the door on us.

"Hang on a second. We'd like to talk to you," I said, maneuvering my foot into the doorway before she could close it all the way.

"All three of you?" Sheila asked.

"No, just them," Travis said with a snort of disgust. "Me, I'm done with you."

He stomped off, and after he was gone, Maddy couldn't help herself and started laughing. I joined in, and a few seconds later, I actually saw Sheila smile. "I'll miss that odd old bird," she said, "as hard as that might be to believe."

"I understand completely," I said.

"What can I do for you two?" she asked.

"It's about the safety-deposit box," Maddy said.

Sheila's eyes narrowed for just a split second before she managed to compose herself. "We cleared it out together, remember?"

Maddy said, "We forgot all about this, though. Remember? We found this paper, too." She held the slip of paper up, but carefully disguised the fact that the printing on it was nearly gone.

"I'd forgotten you had that," Sheila said. "I'll have it back now, please. After all, it belonged to my brother."

Maddy still held it back. "It's got another number on it, a safety-deposit box from Third Southern National."

The hint of triumph in her voice was nearly thick enough to see.

It vanished instantly as Sheila said, "So you found it, too. You might as well come inside."

Warning bells were going off in my head, and I found myself wishing we'd called Kevin Hurley after all. "That's fine. We don't really need to stay."

Maddy looked at me as though I were crazy. "Don't listen to her, Sheila. We'd be delighted to come in."

At that point, I really didn't have any other option but to follow my crazy sister inside.

We all walked into the living room, and I glanced down at the fireplace.

"Having one last blaze?" I asked.

"You might say that," Sheila said. "Those are the things I found in that second safety-deposit box you were telling me about. It appears my dear, sweet brother had a penchant for blackmail. Dirty business, that."

"So you just burned everything you found?" I asked.

Sheila nodded. "Not without a few tears, either. I wasn't sure what I'd found at first, but it didn't take long to put it all together. After that, I stopped reading it." She took a poker and nudged the last bits of paper into the dying flames.

"I didn't know what else to do," she said.

"You could have turned it all over to the police," I suggested.

"What, and have these people live through the trauma of being exposed after all? I don't think so."

Maddy asked, "Is it any worse than waiting for someone else to call asking for money? It has to be torture waiting for a stranger's tap on your shoulder."

"I never thought of it that way," Sheila said softly as she stared into the flames. "It's too late now. It's all gone."

"Are you sure?" I asked.

"I found his post office box key near the one to the safety-deposit box," she said. "There was one last letter at the post office box, and I canceled the box after I retrieved it. From now on, the letters will go back to their senders. It's all done now."

"Not quite," I said. "We saw one of our suspects running away from your house a few minutes ago. That's what we were doing in back."

"I didn't think you had any suspects," she said. "Who was it?"

Maddy started to answer but I cut her off. "We aren't completely sure, so it's not right to say."

"She has a right to know," Maddy said. "Her life could be in danger."

"Tell me," Sheila said. "It's only fair."

They both had a point. If I didn't tell Sheila, and something happened to her, I'd never be able to forgive myself. "It was Faith Baron."

Sheila's expression hardened. "The tramp that was having an affair with my brother. Why would she want to hurt me?"

"Did you burn any letters in lavender envelopes?" I asked.

"There was a stack of them," Sheila admitted.

"There's your answer. Faith wrote them to your

brother, and he must have been using them against her." I looked at the last of the embers. "You didn't happen to read any of them, did you?"

"No, I figured it was none of my business."

I looked at Maddy. "But will Faith believe that? Did she see Sheila with the letters?"

"More importantly, did she see me burn them?" Sheila asked.

"You'd better call the police," I said.

Sheila was taken aback by the suggestion. "How can I possibly do that? My brother wasn't a saint, but I'm not about to expose his last dirty little secret to the police."

"Aren't you afraid of what might happen?" I asked.

"I'm leaving tonight. In the meantime, I'll keep an eye open."

"Why delay it," Maddy said. "It doesn't make any sense taking a chance."

"I found a buyer for the house. They want to meet me here later to sign the papers."

Suddenly I felt guilty for my part in setting the meeting up. "Tom Frances was calling you for us," I confessed.

"He doesn't represent the buyer," Sheila said. "But honestly, why did you two think you needed subterfuge to meet me? I would have gladly come by the pizzeria before I left. I've been a little on edge these past few days, but you have to understand, my system's gone through more shocks than I thought I could take." She smiled as she added, "Though it did seem to cure me of my tendency to faint. That's the only silver lining in this entire mess. Except for my brother's generosity, that is." Sheila sifted the ashes, put them in the black bucket by the fireplace, then started to carry them outside. Maddy and I followed her to the ash pit in the backyard, where the secrets Richard had exploited were finally gone.

"It's a bad business, but at least it's over," she said.

"I hope so," I said.

"What do you mean by that?" Sheila asked me.

I wasn't about to tell her about Penny's belief that Richard had been blackmailing our chief of police. "We know the leverage your brother kept is gone, but the folks he was blackmailing don't."

"What did you expect me to do, send them all letters telling them they were off the hook? How could I have possibly done that?"

"I don't have the slightest idea," I said. "I'm just saying you need to be careful."

"You don't have to keep repeating it. I'm not a child." She glanced at her watch, then said, "Now, if you two will excuse me, I've got some errands to run before my meeting this afternoon. Thanks for coming by."

"Glad to," I said.

After Sheila went back inside, Maddy and I started walking back to her car.

As we did, my sister said, "I believe her."

I nodded. "I do, too. Burning it all might not have been my first reaction, but I think it's a good one. That information is better off destroyed."

"I still think she should have called the police about what she found. She's taking a real chance by not doing that."

"How's that?"

Maddy said, "Think about it. We know she destroyed that stuff, but how would anyone else? It just follows that anyone being blackmailed by Richard would assume that his sister had the information now."

"How would they know Richard was the one blackmailing them?" I asked. "He had a post office box, so you have to think he was at least a little careful."

"Somebody must have known," Maddy said. "Unless Faith or her husband killed him. Why was Faith here? Did we really stop something bad from happening just by showing up?"

"I wish I knew," I said. "I feel so helpless right now. We can't go to the police—Kevin would probably lock us both up if he knew what we've been up to—and we can't confront Faith, at least not without more evidence than we've seen so far."

"Don't forget, we still have that letter from her to Richard," Maddy suggested.

"That confirms they were having an affair. In my mind, that's a long way from proving she killed him."

"Then what do we do?" Maddy asked.

"I'm not sure there's anything we can do," I said. I pointed to my watch. "I need some time to think about it, and I can do that at the Slice just as easily as I can driving around town with you. Let's go make some dough, and in the meantime, we can try to figure out what's going on."

"We might as well," Maddy said as we got into her car.

"That's what I like, enthusiasm in the people I work with," I said.

"Eleanor, even you have to admit that making pizza isn't nearly as exciting as tracking a killer."

"Who said excitement was all that great?" I asked. "Give me the predictability of yeast, flour, and salt any day."

I couldn't stop thinking about Faith Baron, and her presence behind Richard Olsen's house. Was it a part of her regular jogging route, or was there something more ominous about her being there? Even if Sheila wasn't taking the threat seriously, Maddy and I were. But what could either one of us do? If I called Kevin Hurley, I was opening myself up to a great deal of aggravation, and what could I tell him, honestly? The only thing I had proof of was that Faith and Richard had an affair.

Did I owe it to Sheila to show him that much, even though she'd destroyed a bundle of letters herself? And for that matter, if Faith saw Sheila destroy those documents, she might think I was the only one with proof tying her with the murder victim.

Suddenly, I didn't feel so safe myself. No matter what, I had to get that letter in the chief of police's hands. If he wanted to lock me up for withholding it, then so be it. I wasn't going to hand it over in my kitchen, though. I had to get that letter from home, then take it to the station. It would be much harder for him to dismiss me if we were in his office. At least I hoped so.

We opened to a small stream of customers, and by two, our lunch crowd had ended, with a few folks occasionally coming by for a quick soda or sandwich. I often thought of closing between two and three o'clock just to give us all a break. The income I'd miss would barely show on my cash register report at the end of the day, and the hour of free time would be most welcome.

Now was as good a time as any to implement the new policy, I decided.

I walked out front and found Maddy and Greg sitting at a table talking. Greg had the decency to stand when his boss came out, but Maddy barely looked up.

"We're closing," I said.

"Come on, business isn't that bad," Maddy said.

Greg grabbed a dishrag. "I'll clean the tables again."

"It's no reflection on the business or your job performances," I said, "and it's not permanent. I was just thinking we'd shut down for an hour in the afternoon, at least for a week or two, to see how it goes."

"That's a brilliant idea," Maddy said.

I turned to Greg. "How about you?"

"Isn't there anything I could do while we're closed? To be honest with you, I need the hours."

I thought about it, then said, "The storage room needs to be cleaned and organized. You can work on that while we're closed, if you really want to."

"That would be great," Greg said. "I'll jump right on it."

Maddy looked at me after he was gone and asked, "What are you going to do on our break? I can't see you going home and taking a nap."

"What makes you think I'm going anywhere?

How do you know I'm not planning to help Greg with the storage room?"

"Because you'd already be back there working instead of being out here talking to me. Don't try to duck the question. You've got an idea, don't you?"

"Not anything I want to drag you into," I said.

"Good luck with that. We're together on this, no matter what."

"Okay, but don't ever say I didn't warn you. I'm going to get that letter of Faith Baron's we found and I'm giving it to Kevin Hurley."

I waited for a storm, but my sister just smiled. "I think that's an excellent idea. I would have suggested it myself, but given your history with the police chief, I wasn't about to make you do something you weren't comfortable with."

"You don't trust Faith, either?"

"Certainly not with any of my husbands," she said, "but I don't know if she's a murderer. Do you?"

"Can we really take the chance that she's not? Whether she killed Richard or not, Kevin still deserves to know what was going on between them."

"And what if Richard was blackmailing Kevin as well? Wasn't that what you were told?"

"Then we can put his mind at ease and tell him what Sheila did with the evidence. It's only right."

Maddy shook her head. "Then you don't mind having a police chief with something so bad in his past he was being blackmailed for it?"

"Kevin's not a bad man, or a bad law enforcement officer," I said.

"Wow, I didn't realize you'd become such a fan."

"Maddy, are you coming with me, or not?" I'd grown tired of the cat-and-mouse edge to our conversation.

"Just try to stop me," she said.

I called out, "Bye, Greg, we're locking the door behind us."

"Bye," he called back, his voice muffled through the closed door.

"I'll drive, if you don't mind," Maddy said. "That way if anybody wants to take a shot at you, they won't know you're with me."

"Who else rides around town with you?" I asked as I got into her car.

"That's not the point. That Subaru of yours must have a target on it or something."

"I resent that," I said as she headed toward my house.

"But you don't deny it," she said.

Four minutes later we were at the house.

I turned to Maddy and said, "Wait right here. I'll be back in a second."

She shut off the engine as she said, "I don't think so. For the foreseeable future, I go where you go."

"Nobody's lurking in the shadows of my own home waiting to grab me," I said.

"Then we won't have to use this," Maddy said, pulling the stun gun out of her purse. "But if we do, I want to be ready."

I unlocked the door, and we slipped inside. Maddy actually went to the trouble of dead bolting the lock as I reached behind the orchid painting and collected the lavender letter. I'd half expected it to be gone, and was relieved to find it still there.

"Check inside to make sure she didn't just leave the envelope," Maddy said over my shoulder.

I did as instructed and found the letter still inside.

"It's here."

"Then let's go find Chief Hurley," she said.

"You'll have to wait over there," Helen Murphy, the police dispatcher and receptionist, said after we'd asked to see Kevin and she'd called him on the internal phone line. "The chief's tied up right now."

I leaned forward and said softly, "Is he really busy, or is he just blowing us off?"

Helen said sternly, "I'm sure the chief would never do that. He's in a meeting, but it shouldn't be long now." Losing the frown, Helen said, "Sorry, I just do as I'm told."

"I understand," I said. "By the way, how's Amy? I haven't heard from her in years."

"She just had her first baby. Would you like to see a picture? She's the most beautiful little girl in the world. I just love being a great-aunt."

"I'm hoping someday to be a pretty good one," I said, "if my sister ever has any kids of her own."

Helen laughed. "How about you? Any prospects? I heard you had dinner with an eligible young man last night."

"So, we'll be waiting right over there," I said, completely ignoring the question. "Let us know when the chief can see us."

Maddy was leafing through an old issue of *Field*

and Stream when I joined her. "Thinking about taking up fly-fishing, are you?" I asked.

"It was either this or *Trucks, Trucks, Trucks.*" She put down the magazine. "What was Helen laughing about?"

"Her niece Amy just had a baby."

"And I'm willing to bet the conversation quickly shifted to your date with David last night."

"How could you possibly know that? Were you eavesdropping?"

"I didn't have to," she said. "In a small town, what other question could she ask? Speaking of which, you never told me when you were seeing him again."

"I'm not," I said, trying to make the statement flat and not open for discussion. It was futile, and I knew it, but at least I made the gesture.

"Don't be so thickheaded," she said. "You don't exactly have your choice of men panting after you, do you?"

"Said the kettle to the pot," I answered. "One is too many for me. He's a nice man, but he's not Joe."

I hadn't meant to say the last bit, but it wasn't like it wasn't the truth.

Maddy said, much too loudly, "For heaven's sake, Eleanor, it's time to move on."

Everyone in the room was suddenly looking at us.

"Would you like to repeat that a little louder? I'm not sure Greg heard you all the way back at the Slice."

"You're hopeless, you know that, don't you?"

"I keep forgetting, are we talking about me or you?"

She was about to reply when Helen interrupted. "He'll see you both now."

I stood. "You can wait here if you'd like."

"No, thanks," she said.

We went back to Kevin's office. Sometimes we reverted to childhood arguments without any warning, and boys had been a part of that dialogue for as long as we'd first noticed the difference.

Kevin was sitting behind his desk, still on the phone with someone. His office was austere, with few photos and memorabilia. One thing he did have was a picture of him and his son, Josh, fishing somewhere in a mountain stream.

I pointed to it and said to Maddy, "Look, someone else who likes to fish."

For some reason she found that amusing and started laughing so loud that it earned a dirty look from Kevin.

He whispered something into the phone, hung up, then asked Maddy, "What's so funny?"

"Sometimes the world just strikes me that way. How about you?"

"My son's still missing, I have an unsolved homicide on my hands, and you two are suddenly in my office. I don't find anything all that funny at the moment."

"I'm really sorry about Josh," I said. "I can't imagine where he might be."

"Should you even be in here without your attorney?"

I'd forgotten all about Bob Lemon. He was going to scold me for sure, and I should have invited him to this party, if only I'd thought of it. "Probably," I said. "But this couldn't wait."

Maddy asked, "Let's get back to Josh. Eleanor, do you honestly think he'd tell you where he was? You ratted him out the last time he told you, remember?"

"That's not fair," I snapped. "It wasn't my fault."

Kevin asked, "Do I really need to be here for this? If you two are just going to argue, why don't you do it out in the hallway? I've got some telephone calls I need to return."

"Sorry," I said as I pulled out the letter and slid it across the desk to him. "We thought you should see it."

He looked at the envelope without touching it, then deftly flipped it open and extracted the letter with two pens, never touching any of it. After opening the letter and reading it, he shoved it back toward us. "What is that supposed to prove?"

"Faith and Richard were having an affair," I said. "That's a motive for murder."

"Lots of people sleep around," Kevin said. "There's got to be more than that."

"They broke up recently," Maddy snapped. "Faith told us herself when we asked her about this letter."

Kevin's face clouded up. "So what I've been hearing around town is true. You two have been butting into police business, haven't you?"

"Think of it as fact-finding," I said. "It worked, didn't it? I bet you didn't know about the affair."

"You'd lose your money if you did," he said. "I've spoken with her twice, and I'm satisfied at this point that she didn't kill Richard Olsen."

"How is that possible?" I asked, my voice growing shrill. "You're not still hung up on the restaurant alibi, are you?"

"I'm not under any obligation to tell you anything I don't want you to know," he said. "But just so you know that I'm not totally incompetent at my job, I know that their VW was in the shop the night of the murder. Anyone could have taken those keys and chased Olsen across town." He added, "You could have done it yourself."

"For the thousandth time, I didn't kill him," I said.

Maddy stood and gestured for me to join her. "Come on, Eleanor. I told you he wouldn't listen to us."

I stood and said, "You were right, but I had to try." I turned back to Kevin and said, "If something happens to Sheila Olsen, it's going to be on your head, and not mine."

"What about Sheila?" Kevin asked, suddenly interested in the conversation again.

"Nothing," Maddy said. "She didn't mean anything by it."

"Hang on, that's not fair," I said. "I told you I'd tell him, and I haven't changed my mind."

"You don't owe him anything," Maddy said.

"For the love of Pete, would one of you tell me what's going on?" Kevin bellowed.

"Richard Olsen was blackmailing some folks in town," I said, searching his face for a reaction.

"Go on, I'm listening."

"Sheila found the safety-deposit box where the leverage was all stashed, so she destroyed it," I added quickly.

The look of relief on his face was evident, though he tried to hide it from us. "It's all gone, then?"

"Every last shred of it," I said.

"She should have turned it over to me," Kevin said.

"Probably, but this way is best, don't you think?" I said.

Kevin shrugged. "There might have been a motive for murder buried somewhere in there."

"True, but if there was, it's gone now," I said.

He reached for the phone, then told an officer on the other end, "Find Faith Baron. I'd like to talk to her." Then he added, almost as a second thought, "And keep an eye out for Sheila Olsen. No, it's not urgent. I'd just like to have a word with both of them."

After he hung up, he turned to us and said, "Thanks for coming by." As he glanced at his watch, he asked, "Don't you have a restaurant to run?"

"We're going there right now," I said.

Maddy waited until we were in the car on our way back to the Slice to say, "That rumor was right. The police chief was definitely relieved when you told him that evidence was destroyed."

"We don't know that for sure," I said, for some odd reason defending Kevin.

"You're kidding, right? He should have been furious when you told him everything had been burned, but he hardly seemed upset by the news at all."

"Hey, he's going to talk to Faith and keep an eye out for Sheila. That's a win in my book."

"And we go back to making pizza," Maddy said.

"For now, it's all we can do."

We were near the pizzeria when I said, "I'm still glad we told him the truth."

"Let's just hope he does something about it," Maddy said.

I was relieved to turn over what we'd learned to Kevin. Maybe now I could get back to my business, and my life.

But not yet.

David Quinton was standing in front of the Slice, and worse yet, he had a bouquet of flowers in his hand.

Chapter 16

"Good, you're back," David said, as he handed me the flowers. "Do you have a second?"

"Honestly, it's not a great time for me," I said.

Maddy got out her keys. "Go on, I can get things started inside."

I rolled my eyes at her, but there was really nothing I could do. "Come on in, then. I'll get you a soda."

"If you don't mind, I'd really like to talk to you out here. It's not as intimidating if we're away from the Slice. That's clearly your domain."

"That's a good thing," I said.

"For you, maybe."

"Okay then, let's take a walk."

I gave my sister the flowers as Maddy flipped the sign out front to OPEN as David and I started walking down the promenade. Paul was sweeping the pavers in front of his shop, and he waved to me as we walked by.

"I want to talk to you about last night," he said.

"Funny, I need to talk to you about it, too," I replied.

"Let me go first."

I wanted to stop him before he said anything he'd be embarrassed about later, since I was ending this here and now. "I really should have my say."

"Eleanor, can I have my way just once?"

"If it's that important to you," I said as we went by Little Tykes, a clothing store for only the wealthiest families in Timber Ridge. Annie Farrar was in the window dressing a little-girl mannequin in an outfit I couldn't afford on my best day, and she nodded toward me and smiled.

"It is," he said. "Maybe this was a mistake."

I was about to agree out of relief when he added, "It's like you're the mayor of the square, you know? I need your full attention."

I pointed to a bench that was away from the shops. "We can sit over there."

It was still cold, but at least the fog was gone, though it was forecast again for this evening. I bundled my jacket closer as we sat down.

"Go ahead," I said, "You've got my full, undivided attention."

"Don't say no," he said.

"What are you talking about? I just said I would listen."

"I mean don't cancel our next date. I know you've had time to think about it, and your first reaction is to back away from me, but I'm asking you for a real chance."

"I never promised you more than one dinner," I said, uncomfortable with his intensity.

"Do you really think that's enough time to decide if you'd like to see more of me?" I started to say something when he interrupted. "Okay, if our date last night was horrible, I can understand you wanting to end things, but we had fun. Both of us did, so don't try to deny it."

"I wasn't about to," I said. "But it's still too soon."

"How long does it take?" David asked. "It's been two years since Joe died."

"The way I feel right now, it could be ten or twenty more," I said, not wanting to hurt him with my blunt honesty, but not really having any other choice.

"Or it could be our next date. My point is, how are you going to know if you don't give yourself a chance?"

"David, I like you, I really do."

"But," he said. "Why does there always have to be a 'but.' "

"Not always, just this time," I said.

"Before you say something we'll both regret, let's try this another way. Have dinner with me next week, and once a week after that until you're tired of my company. For my part, I won't pressure you anymore about dating me."

"I'd be doing just that, though, wouldn't I?"

He laughed. "We can set some ground rules. We'll take turns driving, picking the restaurant, and even paying, if it would make you more comfortable getting the check once in a while. All I'm asking for is your company. I've got to warn you, though. I won't try to kiss you good night, so if you change your mind about me, you're going to have to be the one who makes the first move."

I laughed in spite of the serious nature of the conversation. "I can't believe I'm negotiating this with you."

"Why not? We make each other laugh; you can't deny that. Is there any better reason to spend time together?"

"I guess not," I said.

"Then it's settled," David said as he leapt to his feet. "Next week it's your turn, so be thinking about it."

He was gone before I had a chance to protest any further. I walked back to the Slice and practically dumped my sister to the ground when I opened the front door.

"He left pretty suddenly," she said.

"Why shouldn't he? He won."

A look of joy spread across her face. "You're going to start dating him?"

"No. We're having dinner one night a week, and we're taking turns driving, picking the restaurant, and paying."

Maddy looked confused. "And how is that not dating?"

"There won't be any romantic angle," I said.

Maddy shook her head. "I don't know, it sounds like you're dating."

"Well, I'm not," I snapped at her. "Now, are we getting ready for the evening crowd or not?"

"We're on it," she said, adding a salute behind my back. I saw the reflection of it in the window, but I decided to let it pass.

* * *

Greg came back with an order, and I could tell there was something he wanted to say to me.

"Go on, spit it out," I said as I prepared the toppings on the pizza he'd requested. The layer of cheese was on the sauce and I started dealing pepperoni slices like they were playing cards.

"What are you talking about?"

"You're not mesmerized by the way I make pizzas, since you've seen me do it a thousand times. There's something on your mind, and I don't have the energy to drag it out of you."

"I'm worried about Josh," he said.

"So am I," I answered. "Did he say something to you last night?"

"That's just it. He never came by the apartment, and he's stayed with me since he left his folks' house. So where is he?"

"Does he have any other friends in town he trusts?" I asked as I slid the completed pizza onto the conveyor.

"Sure, but I don't think there's anyone else he could be staying with. It's a lot to ask of someone, you know?"

"But you never seemed to mind," I said as I cleaned up the workstation.

Greg shrugged. "He'd do the same for me. I figured why not."

I thought about it a minute, then said, "Maybe he went back home last night."

"Not after what he heard his dad say in here. I doubt he'll ever go back."

"He's got to, sooner or later. This will blow over between him and his dad."

Greg started playing with the sauce ladle. "That's

not the only thing keeping him away. He's concerned about that VW trying to run him down."

"I wish I knew who was driving it," I said, "but it looks like it was in the shop waiting to be picked up. Anybody could have swiped the keys."

"But not just anybody would be coldhearted enough to run somebody over," he said as Maddy came in.

"You've got a new table," she said, and Greg left to wait on them.

"What are you two chatting about?" Maddy said as she stole a pepperoni slice and ate it.

I'd asked her not to do that a thousand times, but I wasn't in the mood for a fight tonight, so I let it slide. "Greg's worried about Josh," I said.

"The whole world is. From what I've heard around town, Kevin's spending every free second he's got looking for him. No matter what other flaws he has—and trust me, I'm anything but the police chief's biggest fan—he loves that kid."

"I know, but nobody can make Josh show up until he's ready, or at least until he feels it's safe to come home again."

"That's right; he thinks somebody's trying to kill him."

"The mysterious black VW rears its head again," I said as I grabbed the phone.

"Who are you calling?"

"I want to see if Bob Pickering has been able to come up with a list for me yet."

I dialed his number, but it went straight to the answering machine, with a message that the shop was closed, and I could try back tomorrow.

"He's not there," I said. "He must have forgotten about me."

"I doubt that," Maddy said. "You're his favorite customer."

I shrugged. "He told me he might not be able to get to it this evening. I'm sure he'll have something for me in the morning."

"Nothing's going to happen tonight anyway," Maddy said.

Greg came back with another order, and as he handed it to me, he asked, "Have either one of you looked outside lately?"

"There aren't any windows back here, remember?" Since the building abutted the neighbors on each side, the only other place for a window was in back. Even if we had one, all it would show would be the alley where Maddy and I parked every day.

"You might want to come up front, then," Greg said.

I made the subs and put them on the conveyor, then followed the two of them out front. After nodding my greetings to our customers, I looked outside. The fog had doubled its intensity from the night before. As I looked out across the promenade, I couldn't even see the parking spaces our customers used. The closest lampposts were just blobs of light hovering in the air, while the others were completely obscured by the dense mist.

I was amazed anyone had braved the weather just to eat my food.

"Maybe we should close early," I said as I glanced at the clock. We only had another ninety minutes, but it could get worse in the meantime.

Greg said, "We can if you want, but I don't think it's going to get any thicker. I say we risk it."

Maddy said, "I'm with him. We already shut down for an hour this afternoon. Let's stay open and see what happens."

"Okay, but just remember, I offered."

I went back to the kitchen, and to my surprise, a few more orders made their way to me.

I personally thought everyone out in that kind of weather was insane.

We got two calls asking if we were still open, and when I told the callers we were, they sounded pleased. I'd grown accustomed to turning down the delivery requests, but many of my loyal customers had been relieved that I was taking call-in orders again. It added an extra hassle to my days, but if it meant mollifying my regulars, I was more than willing to do it.

It was ten minutes until closing, and I hadn't had an order in twenty minutes. When I walked out front, I was surprised to see that the place was deserted. Greg and Maddy were cleaning up, so I walked to the front, flipped the OPEN sign to CLOSED, and said, "As soon as you take care of the front, you two can go home."

"We don't mind staying," Greg said as Maddy nodded her agreement.

"I know you don't, but I don't mind, really. Go on."

Greg said, "If you're sure." He started flipping chairs onto tables at a record pace, and in a few minutes, he was finished.

"See you tomorrow afternoon," he said.

I unlocked the door and let him out into a world of whiteness. "Are you sure you can get home all right?"

"I've walked this way a thousand times," he said. "I'll be fine."

Before I looked back at him, he was gone, vanished in the mist.

Maddy said, "What a mess."

"You need to be really careful driving home," I said.

"Why don't I follow you, just to make sure you get there okay?"

"Maddy, I don't need an escort, or a chaperone. I'll be fine."

She frowned. "I don't like leaving you alone like this."

"For goodness' sake, I've buried a husband; I can deal with a little fog." As much as I loved my sister, we had been spending a great deal of time together lately, and I could use a break.

"Fine, be that way," she said as she grabbed her coat.

"I didn't mean anything by it," I said, trying to apologize.

"Of course you didn't," she said. "Good night."

She started to disappear into the fog when I called out, "Call me when you get home."

"Your cell phone's dead, remember?"

I'd forgotten all about that. "Then I'll wait here until you make it there. You can call me at the Slice."

"Now who's the one who's independent?" she asked. Maddy reached into her purse, then swore under her breath.

"What's wrong?" I asked.

"I can't believe I left my cell phone at home. I know exactly where it is, too—sitting right on the kitchen counter." She thought a few seconds, then said, "Tell you what. We'll each give the other one thirty minutes to get home. Then I'll call you if I haven't heard from you by then, okay?"

"It's a deal. See you in the morning," I said, but she was already gone.

I walked back into the Slice. I had just finished cleaning up the kitchen when the telephone rang.

It was Sheila Olsen, and from the sound of her voice, she was terrified. "Help me," she whispered.

It took me a second to realize she was the one calling. "Sheila? Is that you? I can barely hear you."

"Faith Baron's here at Richard's house," she said with a gasp. "She's talking crazy and waving a knife around. I ran into the bathroom, but she's hammering at the door."

I could hear pounding in the background.

"Hold on. I'll call the police," I said as I started to hang up.

"Don't!" she shouted. "Hurley's in on it, too. Richard was blackmailing him when he found out Faith was sleeping with the police chief, too."

"Kevin and Faith? Really?"

"I've got the photos to prove it. I didn't burn everything, and now they want them back. He's on his way over here. You've got to help me."

"What can I do?" I asked.

"Come get me. The window's been nearly painted shut, but I can get it open if I have enough time. Drive to the house and you can pick me up. Please, I'm begging you."

"I'm on my way," I said.

I might not be able to call the police, but at least I could call Maddy. Then I remembered that she didn't have her cell phone with her, so there was no way I could get in touch with her in time. I left a message on her answering machine and hoped she'd get it in time.

It looked like I was going to have to do this all alone.

As I crept slowly through the fog toward Richard Olsen's house, I thought of a thousand things I should have done instead of rushing off to save her. If what she told me about Kevin was true, I still could have called Helen Murphy, or even the state police. What was I doing risking my life like this? I had half a mind to turn around and go back to the pizzeria, but there was a small chance I could save Sheila's life if I acted boldly. What choice did I have?

By some miracle I made it to the right street. Instead of pulling up in front of the Olsen house, I parked near Travis White's place and got out of the Subaru.

I could see there were blobs of light where the house should be, but it was still too foggy to make anything else out except the general illumination. I took out my pepper spray, and wished I had Maddy's stun gun as well.

As I started toward the house, I kept thinking about all the clues my sister and I had uncovered. How was it possible that we'd missed the fact that

Kevin was having an affair with Faith Baron? It just didn't make sense. I knew Kevin, and no matter what he might have done in his life after he betrayed my trust by the lake, I honestly believed that he'd never do it again. His faithfulness to his wife was well known around town, and I'd heard rumors that a few women had tried to get him to break it, all without success.

That's when I knew that Sheila had been lying to me on the phone. And there was only one reason she'd do that.

She was setting a trap for me.

After all, she'd been the one who'd stood the most to gain from her brother's death. Sheila might not have known how much she was going to inherit, but I had to wonder if she'd known her name was on all of his accounts, including the deed to his house. She would have had to sign papers for access cards to his accounts, and I didn't buy her story that she hadn't paid attention to what she'd been signing.

And now she was wrapping up another loose end. The only problem was, that loose end was me.

I had to get out of there!

My fingers tightened on the pepper spray as I started back toward my car in the fog. I knew I was in over my head. I just hoped I could make it out in time.

But I was hopelessly lost in the fog.

I had to be getting close to the Subaru, but just as I thought I was getting near it, an arm reached out of the fog and knocked the pepper spray out of my hands.

Sheila had found me.

And through the swirling mist, I saw a butcher knife clutched in her hand.

"Where's that nosy sister of yours?" she asked as she peered around in the fog.

"She's right behind me," I said, hoping the bluff would work.

Sheila just laughed. "Good, I hope she's close enough to watch me slit your throat."

"Right here?" I asked, not believing that I'd been so easily duped. I'd solved the case, but not until it was too late to bring in the police.

She paused, then said, "No, I don't want anyone finding you that easily, and who knows how long I can count on this fog. Go on; head toward the house."

I was about to protest when I saw her jab the knife blade in my direction. I didn't need any more incentive than that.

"How can you be sure where it is?" I asked.

"My sense of direction is impeccable," she answered.

"Faith never was here, was she?"

"Oh, she's here all right," Sheila said. "Not only is she as nosy as you are, but she is going to pay for sleeping with my brother. I know he had his faults, but messing around with a married woman wasn't one of them until she came along."

"Then she's still alive?"

Sheila cackled softly. "For now. I wanted someone to witness her last breath, and you'll do nicely. If we're lucky, your sister will show up to see yours."

I had to get away from her while I still could. I took my first step away from her into the mist when I felt the knife slash my arm. It wasn't a deep cut, but it sent blazes of pain through me, and it stopped me in my tracks.

Sheila said, "Go ahead and run. I'll find you, and then I'll make it ten times worse for you."

She'd clearly lost her mind.

"Why me?" I asked, hoping she'd at least satisfy my curiosity before she killed me. I pressed my hand against the cut to slow the blood seeping out of me, and the touch shot another jolt of pain through me.

"You know too much about my brother, and I finally realized that you'd never let his murder go. I can't afford to leave you or your sister alive."

"It was all me. Maddy doesn't know anything about what I've been up to," I said in a hopeless attempt to at least spare her my fate.

"Don't lie to me, Eleanor. I know the two of you have been all over town trying to solve my brother's murder, like a pair of Nancy Drews."

"I just don't get it. How could you kill your own flesh and blood?" I asked. I was doing more than buying time. I honestly wanted to know what could possess someone to do such an unspeakable thing. Maddy and I certainly had our differences at times, but I would die to protect her, and I knew she would do the same for me.

She actually looked sad in the dim light filtering through the fog. "I didn't mean to kill him." After a moment's hesitation, Sheila added softly, "I got into some trouble, and I had to have money to get out of it. I knew Richard always had more than he needed, and I was his sister. If he'd just given me some when I asked for it the first time, he'd still be alive. What happened was more his fault than mine, when you think about it."

This woman was seriously crazy, but if I was going to know what really happened to Richard Olsen, I'd never have a better chance to find out. "You were chasing him through town in the Barons' VW, weren't you? Did you plan that all along, too?"

"This is getting tedious," Sheila said. "Keep moving."

I wasn't going to go anywhere, at least until she threatened me with that knife again. "Don't you want to tell someone what happened? They say confession is good for the soul. What could it hurt? It's not like I'm going to be around to tell anyone."

"Maybe you're right," she said. "I'll keep talking as long as you keep walking."

"I don't know which way to go," I said, telling the truth.

She gestured straight ahead with her knife. "I'll tell you when to turn."

After a few steps, I said, "So, you were going to tell me about the chase."

Sheila almost sounded gleeful as she replied, "We need to go back to that afternoon if you're going to understand. My car broke down on my way here, and after I put it in the shop, I walked to Richard's house to ask him for a loan. He turned me down cold. No matter how much I begged, he wouldn't budge." Her voice took on a harder edge as she continued, "I knew there had to be money hidden somewhere in his house, though. He's been squirreling cash away in odd places since he was a kid. I used to borrow from him back then, until he got too crafty for me." She hesitated, then added, "But I had to get him out of the way first. When I left his house, I remembered the key display at the mechanic's, so I pretended to check on the status of my car and grabbed a set of keys from the board that were marked 'finished' when no one was looking. After that, I wandered around for a while, then came back and got the car after dark."

"What were you planning to do?" I asked, stopping without even realizing it.

She poked me in the back, thankfully with the blunt end of the knife, instead of its sharp point. "Keep walking, Eleanor."

"Sorry." Why was I apologizing? My southern manners were bred too deeply within me, I suppose.

After I started moving again, Sheila said, "I put on a mask and started hunting for him around town. I figured if I could force him into a telephone pole, he'd be in the hospital at least overnight, and I'd have time to search his place in peace. He was too good a driver, though. Every time I went for him, he somehow managed to get away. I ditched the car a few blocks away, then went back to his house, thinking maybe I could sneak inside. He caught me, though."

"And that's when you killed him?"

Her voice sounded as though she were lecturing a small child on table manners. "I never would have done anything to him if he hadn't laughed at me. He called me weak. I lost my temper and admitted that I'd been driving the black Volkswagen, and that's when he lost his temper."

"Are you saying you killed him in self-defense?"

She chuckled softly. "If anyone ever catches me, I might say just that, but just between us girls, that's not what happened. He screamed at me, called me crazy, and grabbed his phone to call the police. He should have grabbed the knife instead. It was sitting on the counter, no doubt waiting for that pizza you were bringing him, only I didn't know that yet. I told him to put the phone down, and if he'd listened to me, I wouldn't have had to stab him. Richard had no one to blame but himself. I was starting to search the house with a flashlight I found there, and then you showed up. I waited for you to step inside so I could take care of you, too, but you wouldn't do it!" She was actually scolding me for not cooperating with her plan to kill me.

How close had I come to dying that night? I didn't even want to think about it.

She continued, a little petulantly, "When you went back to your car, I slipped out of the house. The next day, I had to know if you saw me hiding in the shadows, so there was only one thing I could do. I walked into the pizza shop, ready to get rid of you if you recognized me. When you clearly didn't, I knew I was home free. Then you and your sister helped make me richer than I ever could have imagined, and I was ready to leave this place forever, but you wouldn't let it go, would you? Now I'm going to finish this once and for all so I can start over somewhere else."

"My sister's never going to let up. She'll hunt you down when she finds out you killed me."

After a moment, Sheila said, "Then I'll just have to take care of her as well before I leave."

What had I done? By trying to save myself, I may just have condemned my sister. "Leave her alone."

"We'll see," she said.

As we walked on, I realized we had to be getting close to the house unless Sheila's self-proclaimed sense of direction was way off. I didn't have much more time to act. Maybe if I got her angry enough, she'd make a mistake and I could get away to warn Maddy. "I can't believe how petty you are. You killed your own brother for a fistful of cash."

"He wasn't living that great a life, was he? Between his adultery and blackmailing, I might have actually done him a favor. As far as we know, he's in a better place now."

"Maybe you should join him as soon as you can," I said, not caring anymore that I was provoking her.

"No doubt I will, but not anytime soon," Sheila said. "I can't say the same thing for you, though."

My arm seemed to throb harder at the sound of her words, as if my spirit were draining away from me with my blood.

There was a momentary break in the fog, and we were close enough that I could see the house. How had she done it? I never could have found it in the thick mist.

What I spotted inside chilled me more than the cold fog embracing me.

Faith Baron was on the floor, trussed with plastic restraints and muted by duct tape over her mouth. The look of panic in her eyes told me all I needed to know. She knew just as well as I did that most likely neither one of us was going to live to see another dawn.

I had one last chance before I ended up like Faith. Sheila took her eyes off me for one second as her free hand touched the doorknob to open it, and I threw myself away from her, stumbling into the swirling fog.

She was right on my heels, and I could feel the knife blade cutting the air less than an inch from the back of my neck. I ran blindly on, knowing that my one chance lay in getting away, and getting help. I ran through the fog, and I could always seem to hear her just behind me. With the worst luck I'd ever experienced in my life, the mist seemed to be dissipating, at least where we were. It wasn't enough to give me any kind of real visibility, but Sheila wasn't having much trouble following me.

As I ran, I stumbled over something and fell to the ground. There was an outline of two poles on the ground beside me, and I recognized the post-hole digger Travis White had been using to construct his fence. They were long and awkward, so as a weapon, I'd never be able to swing the tool with enough force to stop Sheila. I was about to give up hope when I spotted a shiny metal post lying beside the digger.

It was a weapon I could use.

Sheila was standing right over me as she said, "Get up, Eleanor. I'm tired of playing games. Why aren't you cooperating?" It was as if she were scolding a small child.

I grabbed the metal post and swung it upward at

her. I missed the knife, but I caught her shoulder and heard her grunt in pain.

I hoped something was broken.

I stood and faced her, holding on to the post like it was a fencing foil.

"That hurt," she snapped at me. The indignation in her voice was hard to believe.

"I'm just sorry I didn't crack your skull," I said.

She looked at me a few seconds, then said, "If you try that again, I'll run this knife straight into your heart."

I feinted one way, then shifted the post the other and moved in to hit her again.

She was quicker than she looked, though, and she took a step back at the precise time my post was heading for her head. Almost as an afterthought, she shot the knife out at me, and I felt it bite the skin of my already injured arm. The pain from the strike was so intense that I nearly dropped my weapon, but I knew if I did that, I wouldn't live another ten seconds. This woman was clearly insane, but that didn't slow her down in the least.

It was going to take an all-out attack if I was going to have any hope of surviving at all. Not only was I in pain, but my grip was getting weaker by the second from the loss of blood. I could feel it running down my arm and onto the post, already slick with condensation.

I had to move fast while I still could.

There was no attempt at trickery this time. Without warning, I lunged toward her, not swinging this time, but driving the post straight toward her chest. The blow hit home, and I saw her body fall back into the returning fog. I had to disarm her, but I wasn't sure I had it in me to crush her skull with the post even though she'd just tried to kill me.

"Drop the knife," I said.

"I lost it when you hit me," she answered weakly. "I give up. You're too strong for me."

I breathed a sigh of relief as I watched her struggle to her feet.

It took me a second to realize that I should have hit her again after all as I felt my feet come out from under me. She'd managed to pick up the posthole digger and whip the tool at my ankles, and now I was the one going down.

I hit the ground and felt the post slip out of my hands. Scrambling for it, I found it just as Sheila launched herself at me again. The knife blade gleamed as it cut through the fog toward my heart, and I barely blocked its path with the post before it could strike home. Although the knife missed, the impact of Sheila's body on mine nearly drove the breath out of me. I had to get away from her before she could stab me again. Forgetting the post for a second, I took advantage of her proximity and drove the heel of my good hand into her nose. I felt a satisfying snap as it hit, and I could feel her blood on my hand.

Her scream of pain was like music to me.

Sheila rolled off me, and I found my feet again, the post back in my grasp.

But the woman must have been possessed. She made it to her feet before I did, despite the pain she had to be experiencing, and before I could do anything to save myself, the knife was at my throat.

"Drop the post," she snarled.

I didn't really have much choice. I did as she ordered.

I'd put up a good fight, but in the end, it appeared that it was too little, too late.

I kept waiting for the knife to move, but something stayed her arm.

"What are you waiting for?" I wailed. "Go ahead and get it over with."

"Not until we get into the house," she whispered in my ear. "You're going to pay for your insolence," she added.

"How's that nose feeling?" I asked. "It made a great sound when it broke, didn't it?" If I was going to die, at least I was going to do it on my own terms.

We walked back to the house, both of us bloody and still bleeding, and I felt like it had been hours since I'd arrived at the Olsen house.

We were near the house again when I felt the last of my energy start to fade. "I don't care what you do, I'm not going to make it any easier for you to hide my murder. You're going to have to kill me right here and drag my body the rest of the way."

The knife started to prick at my neck, and I could feel the blood start to flow from the wound. "You're not as brave as you think you are."

I was stunned to hear someone laughing, then realized it was coming from me. "I'm not brave at all. I'm just tired of being shoved around." The laughter was hysterical as it echoed through the fog.

"I knew you were weak," she said. "That's how I got you to come here."

"I came to help you," I answered.

"That's what I was counting on," she said.

Before I could answer her, I heard footsteps racing toward us, and Sheila and I both turned toward them.

"You never counted on me, though, did you?" Josh Hurley shouted as he flew out of the fog, hurling himself at Sheila. She turned in surprise, and I watched in horror as her knife sunk into his side.

"Run!" he screamed at me. "Save yourself!"

"No!" I shouted back as I threw myself onto Sheila. She tried to pull the blade out of Josh, but he held on to her hands with his.

I wrapped my hands around her throat. I had to get her off Josh, and that's what drove me on, despite having one dead arm and almost no strength left in me.

I managed to drive her to the ground, and I had a forearm over her throat when I heard someone shouting out my name.

It was Maddy, and I nearly cried when I heard her voice.

"Over here!" I shouted. "Hurry! We need help!"

"Who else is with you?!" I heard Kevin Hurley call out.

"It's Josh! Sheila Olsen just stabbed him in the side!" I shouted, my voice filling with tears.

To Kevin's eternal credit, he must have fought every paternal instinct he had as he came to Sheila first instead of his son. Taking time to slap handcuffs on her, he didn't go to Josh until he was sure she wasn't going anywhere.

Only then did he kneel beside his son, taking his head onto his lap. I heard him speak soothingly to him for a second. Then he called for an ambulance on his radio.

Maddy came to me, and I collapsed against her as I tried to stand.

"You're bleeding," she said in horror.

"It's just a couple of scratches," I said, trying to keep my hysteria at bay. "I've never been so happy to see you in my life," I said. "What took you so long?"

She looked as though she wanted to cry. "Bob Pickering was waiting at my apartment when he couldn't find you at your house," she said. "He had the list you asked for, and you'll never guess whose name was on it."

"Sheila's," I said.

"Then you knew?"

"Not until just a few minutes ago," I answered.

"She brought her car to the shop the day of the murder, so not only was she in town earlier than she admitted to us, but she had every opportunity to steal the VW car keys."

"It makes sense once you know everything. Faith Baron is inside," I said.

Maddy's face paled. "Is she dead?"

"No, but I'm guessing she's going to be traumatized by what happened." I started to feel faint and slumped back down to the ground, despite Maddy's efforts to hold me up.

And that's the last thing I remembered for a while.

"Good, you're awake," Kevin Hurley said as my eyes fluttered open. I was in a sterile white hospital room, and the bed beside me was empty. I wondered how I rated that, but I wasn't about to complain.

"How's your son doing?"

Kevin frowned. "He got out of surgery an hour ago. They think he'll be fine. Somehow the knife managed to miss anything vital."

"That's wonderful," I said. "He saved my life, you know. You should be proud of your son. He's a hero."

"That's what he said about you before he passed out," Kevin said. "If you hadn't jumped on Sheila instead of running away like he told you to, he'd most likely be dead." His voice choked at that possibility.

"Maybe we saved each other. How did he find me?"

Kevin shook his head. "My crazy son was shadowing you. He was afraid you were in danger, so he decided it was his job to protect you. Can you believe that?"

"I can," I said. "He's a fine young man."

"I know." There was an awkward silence, and then he said, "You're going to be okay. Neither cut hit muscle. You're pretty lucky, you know that, don't you?"

I shifted and felt the pain again, though it was muted now. "Funny, I don't feel all that lucky," I said. "I thought she was going to kill me."

"She wanted to," Kevin said. "Who would have believed Sheila Olsen could snap like that." He paused, then looked down at me. "Besides you. How did you know she killed her brother? I can't believe I missed that."

I thought about taking credit for figuring it out, but I couldn't bring myself to lie to him, not after what I'd gone through. "Sorry to disappoint you, but I didn't know until just before the very end. Sheila called me and told me Faith was trying to kill her, and like an idiot, I rushed right over there to save her. It wasn't until I realized that she was lying about you having an affair with Faith that everything fell into place, and then it was too late to do anything about it."

"So, that's why you didn't call me," he said softly.

I couldn't meet his gaze as I explained, "She told me that you were having an affair with Faith, and that Richard was blackmailing you about it."

Kevin shook his head sadly. "And you believed her."

"In the end, I knew you'd never make the same mistake again after what happened to us. But I knew Richard had *something* on you," I said, still keeping my head down. "Don't try to deny it."

"My wife had a problem a while back with prescription drugs," he finally said. "She had back surgery and got hooked on her meds."

"You don't have to tell me this," I said.

"I think I owe you at least that. She got cleaned up, but we didn't want anyone to know, especially Josh. We got the first demand for money, and she paid it without telling me. It wasn't too tough to track the P.O. box drop to Richard, but when I threatened to arrest him, he said he'd tell all of Timber Ridge that the police chief's wife was on drugs. I should have taken him down anyway, but I couldn't do that to my family." His facade started to crack as he said, "If I'd done my job, Richard

Olsen would have been in jail, his sister wouldn't have had the chance to kill him, and my son wouldn't be lying in the recovery room."

"You protected your family," I said. "It's easy to understand."

He let out a deep sigh. "It's all over now. I'm resigning in the morning."

"Don't do that," I said, surprised to hear the tenderness in my voice.

"Why not? You of all people have a reason to be angry with me."

"You can't control the crazies of the world," I said. "You made a mistake, and you paid for it. That's no reason to throw the rest of your life away."

"It's all going to come out," Kevin said.

"Not if you keep your mouth shut," I said. "Sheila destroyed the evidence without looking at most of it. She said blackmail was beneath her. Funny, I didn't think murderers ever tried to take the high moral ground. Chances are that nobody knows but you, your wife, and me, and I'm not going to say anything."

"You really wouldn't?"

I shook my head. "I won't even tell Maddy, and I tell her everything. Your secret's safe with me. Don't do anything you'll regret later."

"I do love being the chief," he said.

"Then don't throw that away."

"Maybe I won't," he said, and I could see a glimmer of hope in his eyes.

I was about to say something when my door flew open and Maddy came in, carrying a vase full of roses.

"You shouldn't have," I said as I smiled at her.

"I didn't. They're from David Quinton."

I shook my head. "That man doesn't know when to give up, does he?"

Kevin said, "I like him."

Maddy grinned. "Another ringing endorsement."

Kevin started to leave, then reached down and patted my good hand. "Thank you. For everything."

"Tell Josh I said thanks myself," I said.

"I will."

After he was gone, Maddy asked, "What was that all about?"

"I wouldn't even know where to start," I said. "If those are from David, what did you get me?"

"Are you saying my mere presence isn't enough?" she asked as she laughed.

"It's exactly what I need," I said as my voice cracked. "Could I get some water, maybe?"

She checked the pitcher beside my bed. "Your ice is all melted. I'll be right back."

As she left to get the water, I marveled at what had transpired over the last week. It was hard to believe that in a town as small as Timber Ridge, so much could happen.

A few days later, I was back home and going out of my mind with boredom. Maddy and Greg were running the Slice in my absence, but I was getting antsy to return to work. I just about had all my strength back, and the idleness was driving me crazy.

I wheeled my trash can to the curb, then decided to get rid of those newspapers still cluttering my garage. The bundles were heavy, though, and as I tried to lift the first one, it slipped out of my hands and tumbled to the floor.

As the newspapers spilled, a handful of hundred-dollar bills scattered onto the floor as well.

It appeared that Richard Olsen hadn't entirely stopped hiding money in his home.

For an instant I considered how much I could use the money, but it was only for an instant.

Before I could change my mind, I called Kevin Hurley to tell him what I'd found.

Let him worry about it.

I had a pizzeria to run, whether my employees were ready for me to come back to work or not.

My Basic Pizza Dough Recipe

It's taken me years to come up with what I consider to be the perfect pizza dough recipe, and I'd like to share it with you. Pizzas are so fun to make, it's not fair to leave it up to the chains.

This recipe yields one thick crust for one medium 14-inch pizza or two 7-inch small pizzas, the perfect place to start:

¾ cup warm water
1 tablespoon white sugar
½ ounce active dry yeast (2 packets at ¼ ounce each)
1 teaspoon extra virgin olive oil
¼ teaspoon salt
¼ teaspoon ground oregano (optional)
2 cups bread flour

In a large mixing bowl, combine the warm water, sugar, yeast, olive oil, salt, and ground oregano (if desired) until the yeast dissolves. Wait 3 minutes. Then add the flour to the bowl, mixing as you go. Mix on slow speed for 3–4 minutes, using a dough hook on your mixer if you have one. After the dough is thoroughly mixed, knead it on a floured counter for another 3–4 minutes, or until the dough is elastic to the touch. The dough will be a little sticky, but it shouldn't cling to your hands. Form into a ball. Spray a clean bowl with PAM, put the dough in it, turning the ball once to lightly coat the top. Cover the bowl with a towel. Then put the dough in a warm place and let it rise for about 1 hour. After it has risen, punch it down, and it's ready to use immediately, or you can refrigerate it until you're ready to use it later that day.

On a counter dusted lightly with cornmeal, shape the dough with your hands until you have a round approximately the size you need. Using your knuckles, spread out the dough the rest of the way, forming a ridge along the outside edges. Then add your sauce, any toppings you like, and a blend of cheese. I like to use 3 parts mozzarella to 1 part provolone, but it's your pizza, so top it however you like. I use about a cup of cheese on each of my small pizzas, but again, it's all a matter of taste.

I typically make two 7-inch pizzas instead of one 14-inch, since the smaller size fits best in my portable brick pizza oven, but you can use your regular oven with a pizza stone and get nearly the same results. Bake the 7-inch rounds at 425°F for about 8 minutes, or until the crust starts to turn a dark gold and the cheese is bronzed on the top. The cornmeal will prevent it from sticking to the stone, but I like to turn the pizza a time or two as it bakes, just in case. You can use a pizza peel (a flat, round wooden tool with a long handle), or for the smaller pizzas, an ovenproof pancake flipper works great. After that, cut and enjoy!

My Basic Quick Pizza Sauce Recipe

There are several perfectly fine pizza sauces on the grocery store shelves these days, but this sauce recipe is easy to make, and I figure if I'm going to the trouble to make my own pizza dough, why not make the sauce as well? This is a recipe I like to use when I don't have the time to simmer a sauce, so feel free to change the amount of spices you use if it's not exactly to your own taste. After all, it's your pizza!

8-ounce can tomato sauce (one with added garlic and oregano is fine, but plain does nicely too)
1 tablespoon extra virgin olive oil
1 tablespoon tomato paste
¼ teaspoon ground oregano
¼ teaspoon fine dried basil leaves
1 teaspoon white granulated sugar
¼ teaspoon garlic powder
1 dash salt
1 dash pepper

The best thing this sauce has going for it is that it couldn't be simpler to make, because it doesn't need to be heated. Mix the ingredients together in a bowl. Then add the sauce to your pizza crust just as it is. I like to add the sauce using a spoon and spread it around until I get it just right. For my family, who likes light sauce, I use 3–4 tablespoons, but use all you want! Whatever sauce is left over we store in the fridge for a few days, but usually it doesn't last that long around my house.

Your pizza is now ready for toppings and cheese!

For once, it seems, no one is trying to pin a murder on Eleanor Swift, owner of the scrumptious pizzeria A Slice of Delight in the quiet little town of Timber Ridge, North Carolina. But someone has to answer for that body in her kitchen . . . and it looks like the final stop for Greg Hatcher, her deliveryman, may be the state penitentiary . . .

Eleanor *knows* Greg would never have lethally bashed his own brother in the head with a pizza-rolling pin. Sure, Wade was greedily claiming far more than his fair share of their family inheritance. And Greg did catch his ex-girlfriend Katy smooching on the couch with Wade. It's no wonder that Timber Ridge's police chief—and Eleanor's ex-sweetheart—has his sights set on finding and arresting poor Greg.

But as Eleanor and her saucy sister Maddy dig a little deeper into the mystery, they find Wade's enemies begin to outnumber the slices on a large pie. This is one mystery that's made to order, and if Eleanor and Maddy don't find out who killed Wade, Greg's delivery days are over. But while finding the killer is one thing, escaping alive to dish the goods to the police is quite another . . .

Please turn the page for an exciting sneak peek of PEPPERONI PIZZA CAN BE MURDER coming next month!

Chapter 1

My name is Eleanor Swift, and for once, nobody was trying to pin a murder on me, even though it happened in my pizzeria, A Slice of Delight. A dead body in the kitchen—with a large thin-crust pepperoni pizza and a bloody rolling pin on either side of it—could have easily put me in the crosshairs of the police investigation.

But I wasn't completely off the hook, even though I had a perfect alibi.

My deliveryman was being accused of the homicide, so I could hardly stay out of it, could I?

At least that's what I kept trying to tell Kevin Hurley, the chief of police for Timber Ridge, North Carolina. And he might have believed me—or even listened to my argument—if I hadn't dumped him back in high school nearly twenty years ago. It was a long time for someone to hold a grudge, but he clutched it like a starving man grabbing for the last donut in the box.

* * *

Two days before the murder, my sister, Maddy, came into the pizzeria fifteen minutes late from her allotted hour afternoon break. It was a little after three, and things were generally slow then, but I wasn't about to start any precedents with my one full-time employee, even if she was my only family left. Maddy had been divorced several times, but that never stopped her from looking for her next future ex-husband. When my husband, Joe, had died, she'd come to work for me after her last divorce. I should say *latest divorce,* because with Maddy, it was hard to say what might happen down the road.

"You're late," I said as I handed her my order pad.

"Sorry," she answered, smiling brightly at me as her body language clearly denied the sincerity of her apology. My sister and I were studies in contrast, and not just because of her record number of weddings and my widowhood after being married to the same man for more than ten years. Maddy was tall and thin, and her hair had been blond so long, I doubted her roots even remembered what color they should be. I was shorter and quite a bit curvier, while my hair was the original chestnut brown it had always been.

"Why don't I believe you?" I asked as I started back to the kitchen. Sometimes I worked the front, but the back was where I was most comfortable, the place that I belonged.

"I just ran into David Quinton," she said with a wicked smile.

That merited a bump on my adrenaline scale, though I wasn't about to admit it to anyone else, not even Maddy. David had been pursuing me for some time, and I'd finally decided to let him catch me. Well, sort of. We had a standing dinner date once a week for the past several months, alternating restaurants and who picked up the tab. It was nearly May, and I couldn't believe the weekly meal had so quickly become a habit for me, something I looked forward to when times were slow at the pizzeria.

"I saw that smile," Maddy added. "Don't bother denying it." When I shook my head, she added in a more serious tone, "Eleanor, you're not being disloyal to Joe if you admit that you like spending time with David."

"Please. I get that same line from him every week, don't you start on me." I bit my lip, and then against my better judgment, I asked, "What did he have to say?"

"He wanted to know how I was doing," Maddy said with that smug expression of hers.

"That's it?" Maybe my part-time beau was getting tired of our chaste dinners and had decided to go after my sister, instead.

She grinned. "No, he asked about you, too. Why don't you call him?"

I shook my head. "We're having dinner in three days. I can wait that long to get together, if he can."

Maddy shook her head. "You're more stubborn than I am, and there aren't many people I can say that about."

"I'll take that as a compliment."

"You can take it however you'd like, but we both know that's not what I meant." We were back by the soda fountain, and for the first time, Maddy looked around the dining room. It was nearly deserted, but I knew what—or, more appropriately, who—was missing.

She frowned. "Where's Greg? He didn't take off on you, did he?"

Greg Hatcher was my main deliveryman, and since we'd just recently started taking telephone orders again after a really unpleasant time, I needed him at the pizzeria more than ever. Maddy knew how much pressure his absences placed on me, and while my sister might take more than her fair number of shots at me, she was always the first one to defend me if she thought I needed it.

"Don't worry so much. I let him go."

"You fired him? Eleanor, we need someone to deliver the pizza, and he needs the paycheck so he can stay in college. How could you do that?"

"Take it easy. I didn't get rid of him. He had an errand to run."

Maddy wasn't mollified. "That's not like Greg to leave you here by yourself. What was so important that it couldn't wait until I got back?" She shook her head, and then added, "He didn't duck out on you to see Katy Johnson, did he?"

Katy went to college nearby with Greg, and they'd been dating off and on since he'd first come to work for me two years ago.

"No. As a matter of fact, they broke up."

"Again? If they're so unhappy with each other, why do they keep getting back together?"

I looked at her and fought the laughter I was feeling. "You're giving relationship advice? Seriously?"

"Hey, several of my ex-husbands would gladly write

me references," she said. "Just because we split up
doesn't mean we aren't all still friends. Well, mostly,"
she added uncertainly, no doubt ticking names off
her internal matrimonial roster and putting them
in columns likely labeled FOR and AGAINST.

"Fine, you're the relationship guru," I said, "but
Greg didn't run off on me, I gave him my blessing
to take off. He had a meeting with Bob Lemon."

Bob was a local attorney who, despite appearing
to be quite sane in most respects, was lobbying to
be Maddy's next ex-husband. To his chagrin, he
was failing at it miserably, too.

"What's Bob got to do with him? Greg's not
being sued, is he?"

"No," I said as I donned my kitchen apron. We'd
slowly migrated to the back where my pizza oven
and supplies were kept, but Maddy kept the door
that separated the two spaces open with the edge
of her left shoe. "It's about his inheritance."

"It's finally happening? I thought Wade was still
holding everything up. Don't tell me he finally
broke down and signed the blasted agreement."

"Not yet, but Bob and Greg have high hopes."
Greg's older brother, Wade, was keeping their grandparents' estate open long past any semblance of
sanity. Greg had told us his brother's request was
simple and nonnegotiable. He wanted three-
quarters of everything, despite how the will read,
what their own parents said, or what the letter from
their grandparents themselves outlined. Greg's
grandparents had died the year before when a gas
leak and subsequent explosion in their home had
taken them both. They'd forgone their grown children in their joint wills, instead leaving an estate

approaching two hundred thousand dollars to their two grandchildren, to be divided equally between them.

Apparently, it was the last part that Wade had trouble with.

"I honestly didn't think he'd ever budge," Maddy said. "I've heard of people who never back down."

"It happens." When our parents had died, there had been just enough money to pay their bills, a perfect arrangement in my mind. They'd enjoyed themselves up to the very end, and while I'd hated to see them go, they'd left this world as close to breaking even as I would have thought possible. In a way, they left us the greatest gift of all, precious memories instead of stocks and bonds. I wouldn't have traded a million dollars for the memories I had of them, and I knew my sister wouldn't, either.

"Trust me, I'm not naïve enough to think it doesn't," she said, "but more than that, it's not uncommon for the eldest son to expect more than his siblings. Some folks believe it's the right way to handle things. They're like royalty. Once there's a successor to the throne, the rest of the boys are just spares. It's got to be tough on Greg dealing with that, on top of losing his grandparents."

"He's handling it better than either one of us would," I said.

To her credit, my sister didn't protest the assertion.

She stood there a second, and then asked, "I wonder what made Wade change his mind?"

I smiled. "Greg thinks he knows. His brother's been counting on getting his hands on some of that money, and from the sound of it, he's taken out some loans that weren't issued by any bank, if you know what I mean. Evidently, the collecting agents are getting antsy and applying a whole new kind of pressure to Wade."

"How stupid is he?" Maddy asked. "That's just begging for trouble."

"Hey, it's probably the only thing that's motivating him to come to the bargaining table. Apparently, Wade doesn't make that much working as a bookkeeper for Roger Henderson. Bob's brokering the deal, so we should know something when Greg comes back." I gave my sister a stern look as I added, "Don't interrogate him about it, though. It's his life, and if he wants to tell us, he will. Otherwise, it's none of our business."

Maddy just laughed. "You don't think there's a chance on earth I'm going to agree to that, do you?"

"No, but I can hope, can't I?"

"Whatever gets you through the afternoon," Maddy said.

Greg walked into the pizzeria kitchen two minutes later, a thunderstorm dancing in his eyes.

"Do I even need to ask how it went?" I asked as I handed him his apron.

"What do you think? It's the same old Wade. No matter how much my parents protest the fact that their darling little Wade has finally changed, they just don't realize that the only way he's changed is that he's gotten better at lying to them." As Greg threw his apron on over his head, he added, "He's not fooling me, though."

"Does he honestly want more than half?" Maddy asked.

I would have chided her about the intrusion,

but I kept my mouth shut. I wanted to know the answer to that one myself.

"Oh, yes," Greg said. "Only he's not going to get it. I could use the money, but I'm not as desperate as he is. I stormed out of the meeting. You should have heard the garbage I had to listen to from him. I told him I'd rather see the money go to the lawyers than give in to him. He might not have believed me before, but I've got a hunch he finally got the message. You know what? I meant every word of it. If he's going to be this stubborn about it, I'll finish school, pay off my loans when I can, and just let him hang in the wind. We've got three more years before the courts intervene."

"He could sue you, couldn't he?"

"Bob says that Wade would have to agree to a contingency fee if he did that, so at least my brother knows that he'll make even less if he takes me to court. He might be a greedy jerk, but he's generally not that stupid." Greg looked at us both for a moment, then said, "I don't get it."

"Get what?" I asked.

"How do you two get along so well? You're two sisters who work together. If I'm in the same room with my brother for more than three minutes, a fight breaks out."

"We fight," Maddy said.

"Trust me, we do," I added.

"But you genuinely care for each other," Greg said, shaking his head sadly. "I wish I had that, more than I could ever tell you." After a moment of silence, he said softly, "I had a sister. Did I ever tell you that?"

I'd known Greg and his family practically all of

his life, but I hadn't known that. "What happened to her?"

"She died three days after she was born," Greg said. "She would have been the oldest, and Wade would have been put in his place. My parents were so happy when my brother survived, they gave him a double dose of love, and I got stuck with the scraps."

Greg wasn't being the least bit melodramatic. Though Wade had been in and out of trouble all of his life, Greg had been the faithful, true, obedient son, for all the good it did him in his parents' eyes. Wade was the favorite, Greg was the spare. No wonder Wade felt so entitled, considering the way he'd been raised. It didn't make it right, but it did make sense, in his skewed family dynamic.

I couldn't take the weight of Greg's sadness. "You know, Maddy and I think of you as family," I said.

My sister didn't say a word. She just reached out and patted his shoulder.

Greg nodded briefly, then wiped at his eyes with the back of his arm. "These allergies are killing me. I'd better get to work."

Greg hurried out into the dining room, but Maddy stayed behind. "That boy got a rotten deal in life, didn't he?"

I nodded. "He hasn't let it spoil him, though. He's tough."

"He's not that tough," Maddy said.

"Then he's coping. Greg's a survivor. He'll deal with his brother, and if he needs us, all we can do is be here for him."

"We can, and we will," Maddy said. She peeked out the door, and then added, "We've got some customers, so I'd better get out there and give him a hand."

"Maddy, don't say anything else to him about what happened at Bob's office this afternoon, okay?"

"I wouldn't dream of it," she said. She started to leave, hesitated, then turned around and wrapped me in her arms. "I love you, Sis."

"I love you, too," I said, startled by her declaration. Maddy wasn't the kind of woman ordinarily to show affection, unless it was toward her latest marriage target.

After she was gone, I got out the broom and started to make another circuit of the kitchen floor before I began cooking. The place could never be too clean for me, and the health inspector had given us a string of nearly perfect scores since we'd opened the pizzeria.

Maddy came rushing into the back as I was finishing up, and she startled me so much that I dropped my broom.

I hoped and prayed nothing had gone wrong. "What is it? Did something happen?"

She leaned down to pick up my broom, then handed it to me as she said, "Relax, Eleanor. A big group just came in, and I wanted to give you a heads-up so you could get started on crusts."

"How many people are we talking about?" I asked.

Maddy smiled. "I was going to call you after you got things started, but I can't wait that long. Look out the door."

I wasn't sure what to expect, and I thought I was ready for just about anything, but I was still surprised to find twenty-five Elvis Presley impersonators milling about the restaurant when I peeked out through the door. The Elvis imitators were white, black, Asian, Hispanic, men, women, and one kid who couldn't even be in his teens yet. "What on earth is going on?"

"They're headed to Graceland in Memphis," Maddy said.

"And they're driving through Timber Ridge?" I asked as I openly stared at them.

"They started in D.C. and they're headed down to I-40 West," she explained. "It's a pilgrimage. Can you believe it?"

"On days like today, I can believe just about anything."

Greg joined us, and I could see him smiling despite his earlier bad mood. "This is so cool." He looked at his order pad, and then asked me, "Can you make fried peanut-butter-and-banana sandwiches?"

"I could, but I'm not going to," I said. "They can order off the menu like everyone else."

"That's what I told them. They said they'd settle for five large specials if you wouldn't do these."

"That I can do," I said as I headed back to the kitchen. As I knuckled my freshly made dough into pans, I started an assembly line putting the pizzas together. I'd have to chop and slice more toppings before the dinner crowd showed up, but I didn't mind. Maybe tonight we'd make up for some of the slow days we had at the Slice every now and then. There was nothing like a stuffed cash register to make me smile. Money wasn't the source of happiness for me, nor was it the root of all evil. It was simply a way to keep A Slice of Delight up and running. Honestly, without the pizzeria, I didn't know what I'd do with myself.

As the pizzas went onto the conveyor heading into the oven, I kept loading the line until each one was waiting its turn. As they cooked, I started restocking our toppings bins for our evening shift.

When Maddy rejoined me, she spotted the first pizza coming out of the oven and grabbed a pair of tongs. "Mind if I give you a hand? The natives are getting restless."

"Be my guest," I said. "Did you leave Greg out there all alone?"

"Are you kidding me? He's having the time of his life. Who knew he was such an Elvis fan?"

"It appears there's a great deal we don't know about him," I said.

Maddy transferred the first pizza to a serving platter and cut it into eight slices. "Keep them coming," she called out to me as she disappeared back into the dining room.

I stopped chopping peppers and took her place at the far end of the conveyor. By the time I delivered the pizzas, I had three new orders for dessert pizzas from the traveling impersonators, so I started on those so they'd be ready in time. It was a different kind of pizza altogether, featuring cookie dough crust with melted chocolate on top and drizzled with icing to finish it off. I also made an apple cinnamon dessert pizza some days, but I was fresh out of ingredients for that one.

As I delivered the desserts, my efforts were met with an appreciative audience. A few of my regulars had wandered in, and I was afraid they'd be put off by the dining Elvis group. Instead, they seemed to act as though I was providing them with entertainment along with their meal. My husband and I had talked about putting a jukebox in as soon as we could afford one, but the dream had died with Joe. As it was, I couldn't see how the investment would pay for itself, and I had to keep a close eye on the bottom line, or I wouldn't be able to afford luxuries like electricity and water.

I moved to the cash register, and nearly without exception, as they paid for their meals, every member of the Elvis entourage said, "Thank you, thank you very much."

By the time they were gone, I needed a break, and from the expression on the charter bus driver's face, so did he.

Neither one of us was going to get one, though.

I helped Maddy and Greg clean up; then I returned to the kitchen to finish prepping more toppings.

We had a brisk business for the rest of the day, and I kept busy making orders as they came in. We could handle the crowds most of the time with just two or three of us, but there were times when I could have used an extra set of hands. Josh Hurley, the chief of police's son, had supplied that help at one time, but the chief wasn't all that eager to have his only son return to work for me.

I decided that particular foolishness had gone on long enough.

I called the police station, and wasn't surprised when Helen Murphy answered. She was the receptionist and dispatcher for our local law enforcement, and I didn't think I'd ever called there when she didn't answer the telephone herself.

"Helen, it's Eleanor Swift," I said.

"Hello, Eleanor. What can I do for you?"

"I was wondering if I could talk to the chief."

She hesitated, then asked softly, "Do you mean he's not there yet?"

"No, why would he come here?"

Helen was about to tell me when the kitchen door opened, and the chief himself stepped in. "Never mind, he just walked through the door."

"Were you looking for me?" he asked. Kevin Hurley was tall and lanky, and I could see a smattering of gray creeping into his temples, which didn't make me feel any younger, since I was a year older.

"That can wait. What brings you to my pizzeria?"

He frowned at me as he admitted, "It's Josh. He's been hounding me for months to talk to you, and I hate to say it, but my son has finally worn me down. He wants to know if he can come back to work."

"That's always been your decision, not mine," I said. Kevin had forbidden his son to work for me during a recent bad time, and I was beginning to believe that the ban had become permanent.

"Well, he's driving me nuts, and I don't care what his mother says, I think you should hire him back. He's only got a month left until he leaves for his summer college classes, but it would be great if he could spend some of that time working here for you."

"I don't want to cause trouble at home for you," I said. Kevin's wife, Marybeth, wasn't a big fan of mine, and if I was being honest about it, the feeling was pretty much mutual.

"Don't worry about that, I can handle it." He stared at his hands as he asked, "So, what do you say? Can he come back to work?"

"Are you sure you're okay with it?" I asked softly.

"I'm tired of his attitude," Kevin said. "I'd consider it a personal favor."

"Then it's done. Tell him he can start this evening."

"How about tomorrow?" Kevin asked. "He's got a big test tomorrow he needs to study for."

"Why don't you have him call me and we'll work a schedule out."

"He'll call you within the hour." Kevin moved toward the door; then he paused for a second. "What was it that you wanted to talk to me about?"

I wasn't about to admit that it was the same topic of his son's employment. The way things had worked out, the chief of police was going to feel obligated to me, and it might be leverage I would need sooner or later. "I was just wondering if you'd heard anything about the rezoned parking in back. Are they really going to get rid of it to widen the alley?"

"It's not up to me," he said, "but I honestly doubt it. The town council has it on the agenda once a year, but it never passes. If you're worried about it, you could always talk to the mayor."

"I have been, but he's not exactly my biggest fan. I thought you might know something. Thanks, anyway. Now if you'll excuse me, I've got work to do."

"Thanks again, Ellie," he said, and before I could

voice my displeasure at the ancient pet name, he was gone. Only a handful of people had ever called me "Ellie," and just two men ever got away with it. I loved the way my name sounded when my husband, Joe, had said it, but Kevin's intonation just brought back the hurt he had caused me in school. Maybe he wasn't the only one holding a grudge about what had happened all those years ago. I'd caught him with the woman he eventually married. The only problem had been that he'd been dating me at the time, too.

"Get over it, Eleanor," I scolded myself aloud. "That was a lifetime ago."

Maddy came into the kitchen and looked around. "Who were you just talking to?"

"I was giving myself a little pep talk," I admitted.

Her eyes widened for a second, and then she said, "All right, that's good to know. When you're finished cheering yourself on, I've got another order for you. Come on, Eleanor, you can do it. Make that pizza. Make that pizza. Rah, rah, rah."

"I love it when you're funny," I said as I took the order from her. "I don't mean now. I mean when you're actually amusing."

I started working the crust into the pan when I realized she was still lingering by the kitchen door.

"Was there something else?"

"Aren't you going to tell me what he said?" Maddy asked.

"Who are we talking about?" I responded, playing as dumb as I dared and fighting to keep a straight face as I did it.

"Don't give me that. What did the police chief want? And don't tell me he was ordering a pizza. I saw the look on his face when he came into the Slice."

I thought about stringing her along, but I had work to do, and so did she. "He wanted to know if Josh could come back to work."

"It's about time," she said.

"Better late than never."

"Is he coming tonight?" Maddy asked as she looked around at the disarray my kitchen had become.

"No such luck. Maybe tomorrow, though. Do you think we can handle things until then?"

"Are you kidding? Greg and I are acting like a well-oiled machine out there."

"Then I suggest you get back to it," I said as I added the layer of cheese that went down on top of the sauce, and just before the pepperoni.

"Slave driver," my sister said as she darted through the door before I could respond.

All I could do was laugh. It would be good getting my best staff back together, though it was about to change again soon. Josh would be going away before long, and I'd have to hire his replacement. Greg had been lobbying for a friend of his from college, but I wanted another high-school kid. I liked the way it kept the Slice tied in with the local school, and besides, an eager teenager properly motivated was a blessing to my business. I'd hired a few duds over the years, but they'd quickly quit once they saw how hard the work was. When I found someone I could count on, a hard worker who didn't complain and generally showed up on time, I always figured out a way to bump their pay to keep them happy.

Now I'd have to start interviewing again, a job I dearly dreaded.

But not today.

At the moment, I had a full dining room, two hard workers serving out front, and a plentiful supply of dough and toppings.

It was all I could ask for.

A little later, there was a knock at the pizzeria's back door, but I ignored it. We used it to take in supplies during regular business hours, and sometimes we even got our cars that way, but mostly having a door there was more of a nuisance than anything else.

The knocking became a pounding, and I got a little aggravated.

"Come around to the front," I yelled through the door.

"Eleanor, it's Paul."

I recognized my favorite baker's voice instantly. I glanced at the clock and saw that it was almost nine o'clock. For a baker, that was like three A.M. for anyone else.

"Paul, aren't you out a little past your bedtime?"

"Tell me about it," he said as I let him in. He was a tall and handsome young man in his late twenties, with a black goatee and big brown eyes. "I'd normally be asleep by now, but I was on a date."

"I don't need to know any more. From the look on your face, it didn't turn out too well, did it?"

He nodded. "Since I'm up, anyway, could you make me a small cheese pizza? I can't deal with people out front right now."

As I got out some dough and started kneading it into the pan, I said, "Pull up a stool. Tell you what,

I won't even charge you for this, if you keep me company and tell me what was so bad with this woman."

He did as I asked, and as I added sauce and cheese, Paul said, "She's a night owl. In fact, she said she doesn't start coming alive until ten at night. Not exactly a perfect match, is she? Why do I let my mom fix me up with these girls? I'm never going to learn."

"Come on, there's no harm in being a hopeless romantic," I said.

"Well, I've got the first part down pat, I'm hopeless, all right. I need to find a girl who works the same hours I do, but how am I going to do that?"

"It can be a cold world out there, but you can't give up."

He looked sadder than I'd ever seen him. Then he mumbled something so softly, I couldn't quite make it out.

"What did you say?"

"Nothing," Paul said, just a little louder.

"I know better than that. Now tell me, or I'll eat your pizza myself."

"I was out of line, Eleanor. I'll pay for the pizza, if I can get it to go. I'm not fit to be around anyone tonight."

I stood in front of him. "That wasn't our deal. I want to know what you said."

He looked at me steadily, silently pleading for me to drop it, but I couldn't do it. I'd just figured out what he'd said.

"I'm not going to tell you."

"Then I'll tell you. You said that I've given up on romance."

He hung his head even lower. "So you heard me after all."

"It took a minute to figure it out." I took his hands in mine. "Paul, look at me."

He was reluctant to at first, but finally, he lifted his head.

When he did, I said, "I found my one true love with Joe. That's what's different about my situation."

He held my stare. "Eleanor, do you really believe we just get one love in our lives?"

"If we're lucky," I said, releasing his hands. I glanced at the conveyor and saw that his pizza was ready. After I sliced it and boxed it up, I handed it to him.

"I still think I should pay for this," he said as he took it.

"Tell you what. Next time I want to indulge in one of your éclairs, you can look the other way when it comes time to pay."

That brought out a smile. "That's what I love, the barter system. Still, one éclair isn't worth as much as one of your pizzas."

"That's a matter of opinion," I said. "But if you insist, I'm sure Maddy wouldn't say no to one, too."

"It's a deal." He took the box, and then as I let him back out through the rear door, he said, "I'm sorry if I ruined your evening. I shouldn't have bothered you on a night when I feel so sad."

"Nonsense. Friends are for rainy days, and sunny ones, too. Anytime you need to talk, you know where I am."

"Thanks."

I let him out, and then locked the door behind him. Paul was a good man with a strong and caring heart, and I hoped that one day he'd find his own true love.

I'd meant what I'd said about mine. For me, it had been Joe, and would always be Joe.

I had a great life, and for the most part, I enjoyed every minute of it.

It was good being me.

At least it was until later that night when someone stuck a gun in my face.